west country

h d munro

West Country

Copyright@2019, H.D. Munro

All rights reserved.

No part of this book may be reproduced or transmitted in any form by any means electrical or mechanical, including photocopy, without permission in writing from the author.

This book is a work of fiction. Names, characters, businesses, organisations, places and events are either imagined or, if real, are used fictitiously. Any resemblance to actual persons, living or dead is entirely coincidental.

ISBN: 9781690819448

-1. He pushed his greasy black hair back from his eyes and put on a baseball cap backwards. He walked down into the valley and into a dense copse which comprised a strange mix of oak and holly. Under his arm he carried a .410 shotgun. The .410 is the smallest calibre shotgun available. They are used for killing rats and rabbits and, in the U.S., as 'self-defence' weapons. This particular version of the .410 was especially small. The double barrel had been sawn off to a length of little over 10 inches, and the wooden butt had been whittled down to less than half its intended size. The weapon looked more like a vintage pistol than a shotgun. But it was easy to transport, and conceal.

He positioned himself on the low bough of a big oak and waited. Before long a rabbit emerged from the undergrowth. It was only about ten yards from the country boy and the crack of the gun was muffled by the trees as the animal sprung four feet into the air, already dead with half its head missing. He was not impressed. The rabbit had been too easy and he suspected that something was wrong. He jumped down from the tree, rested his weapon against it and examined his prey. Shit. Just as he thought. Myxomatosis. The disease came and went periodically; just now it seemed to be rife. There was nothing to actually say that you couldn't eat a 'mixxy' rabbit. It was just that nobody did. They were the walking dead. Half blind and stupefied they stumbled about until they dropped, their innards eaten away by the sickness.

0. Four months later.

She probably did not hear the gun; such was the shocking impact of the explosion and the lead pellets as they ripped upwards through her neck and jaw. Her final view of the world was the sight of her remaining eye, staring in the rear view mirror at what was left of her face. One and a half seconds later she died.

1. Four years earlier.

Heather Boyle's bottom lip quivered. She stood to attention on the parade ground of the Metropolitan Police Training School. There were forty of them in all. Fresh young coppers right at the end of the production line. It had been a hard slog, those three months. Learning about criminal process and political correctness. About the rank system and ethnic diversity. About forensic science and diverging religious beliefs. But she had made it. Now she just wanted her dad to be there. He had died before she had joined up and probably really would not have approved very enthusiastically. But he still would have been proud. Awe dad, why did you have to go and die. But her mum was there. In tears as usual. She had been joined for the day by Don Pryce, a lawyer and family friend. He was also a widower and Heather kind of suspected he was working on a little plan which featured him getting her mum into bed – no problem – and then marrying her and sharing in the family money – big problem. Heather worried about her mum and two younger brothers Rob and Sam. The death of their father had affected them both badly, particularly Sam, the youngest, who had been only 15 at the time. The boys were staying with their grandmother for the day so that Heather's mum and her friend could see the graduation. Heather wished that they had come too. Her lip quivered more and the tears started to roll. But soon the sadness gave way to a budding anger as the Commandant spoke.

'Ladies and gentleman,' he announced to the audience of parents, siblings, partners and mates just there for a laugh,

'It is my regular honour to present this parade and I do so every three months with undiminished pride. What you see before you are the products of the finest police training establishment in the world. These young men and women have embraced the opportunities given them by the Metropolitan Police and will now embark on highly successful and immensely enjoyable careers....'

2. Heather would never forget those words. Those stupid, self-congratulatory words of an arrogant man. That had been four years ago.

She had not stayed with the Met, choosing for a number of reasons, one in particular, to transfer under Regulation 43 to the Dorset Constabulary. London had turned bad for her and when her mother Julie married Don Pryce and moved to Dorchester to start a small legal practice she decided to go with them. She was 25 now and was still determined to stop Don from getting his hands on the family dosh.

So Heather Boyle was now a resident of Dorchester, the county town of Dorset. She quite liked it. It certainly beat the west London suburban sprawl they had left behind. The transfer from the Met to Dorset went smoothly enough and she appeared before Deputy Chief Constable Sprake in her new uniform quite unfazed. The four years in the Met she was sure had prepared her for just about anything. She had disarmed knifemen, dragged rotting bodies from the Thames, passed an advanced driving course, achieved a brown belt in judo, stayed up all night drinking and had had a number of sexual relationships, all bar one of which had been enjoyable. So now she was up for new challenges.

But she worried that there would not be enough for her to do in Dorset, particularly as she was keen to get into the CID. She had done her junior course at detective training school in the Met and had been engaged on plain clothes jobs whilst she waited to become a confirmed CID officer. But now she was back in uniform and would have to join the queue again.

'Welcome to Dorset Heather,' said Sprake. 'I'm sure you'll be very happy here. We have what I call a family Force; we look after each other and work as a fairly happy family, we....'

'How long will it be before my application for the CID is processed sir?' interrupted Heather.

The Dep stared at her for a second, reassessing this pushy young woman, before going on,

'We consider one another in this big family, and we don't jump queues. There's a queue to get into specialist departments Heather, and the CID is one of those departments. Officers can wait ten years to achieve detective status in Dorset; were you not told this during the recruitment process? Someone should have told you....'

'Oh, I'm sure they did sir, it's just, you know, I want to pick up where I left off in the Met or I'll lose my skills, do you know what I mean sir?'

'Yes of course Heather, I understand. But you've also got to understand that we are not here for your benefit. It's actually the other way round. You are here because we think that you can be of use to us. You are here to serve the people of Dorset. That comes first and your career comes second. Understand?' He grinned as he said this.

'Yes sir.'

'Off you go then'.

3. The middle of five boys, Darren Pyke never had much in the way of attention. Kids like that either grow up not expecting much from life and just get on with mediocre existences or get angry and frustrated and overcompensate. Darren had never shown any indication that he was going to fall into the former category. As a toddler he competed against his brothers, both elder and junior, and usually won. He had a comprehensive toolbox containing useful implements such as deception, violence, threats of the same, arson, forgery, charm and good looks. A criminal.

The Pyke local authority house was a three up, two down affair, quite large in comparison to most of the others on the estate. Ginny Pyke the mother, worn out at the age of fifty, cleaned farmer's houses with red hands and bent back sixty hours a week. Old Gordon Pyke, an unemployed carpet weaver, drank. And the boys ran riot. Stockard didn't have its own police station and the cops used to have to come from Bridport or Lyme Regis when the Pyke boys were at it. Young Gordon, the eldest, was rarely at home having achieved a measure of success designing, building and maintaining fairground equipment. His work took him far and wide and he was therefore never involved in local shenanigans. However Josh, Darren, Wayne and Joe always featured when it kicked off in Stockard. And often when it kicked off elsewhere in the county. They particularly liked to travel to Lyme Regis a few miles south on the coast. A fashionable and cosmopolitan resort in the summer, Lyme had late night pubs, posh birds and soft, bored teenagers who thought they were hard if they bought some gear from the Pyke Bros. Gear? Yes, gear - drugs. By the time he was 23 Josh Pyke was doing a nice trade in cannabis and cocaine which he travelled to Bristol for and concealed impressively in and around various parts of his anatomy.

4. Darren was Josh's minder and enforcer, with Wayne, 18, looking after young Joe who at only 16 just tagged along. On Darren's 22nd birthday the boys had a day trip to Lyme. It was a Friday. Darren had picked up some cash in hand wages for cleaning a silage pit for a local farmer. Josh had a sock full of herbal and six grams of which Charlie stuck up his arse in a modified .303 rifle shell he'd picked up from one of the ranges. He figured that the cannabis was not much of a problem these days and the only law enforcement punters that would poke your arse and require you to shit were the customs lot at Heathrow. That was a long way away.

When the four of them walked into the Ship Pub on the seafront the landlord, Billy Skimmer, a Londoner, knew he was in danger of losing his license. He had been warned by the Dorset Police in no uncertain terms about his pub being used for drugs deals and the local magistrates took a dim view of it also. So he picked up the phone and made a quick call to Bridport Police Station, the only one in the area to be manned at that time in the evening. Then he put the receiver back into its cradle and stepped forward to intercept the boys' request for service.

'You're not welcome here lads, sorry,' he said as he put his hand gently on the barmaid's arm as she was about to serve them.

'What d'you mean?' piped up young Joe, keen to get his ore in, 'I'm eighteen.'

'That's not the reason,' replied Skimmer, needlessly. The other three were glaring at him, particularly Darren. They knew the reason. They had a rep for drugs and trouble and it followed them wherever they went in the county. Which was good for business in one sense, but not so good when you just wanted a pint. Josh shuffled a bit and looked around him. He knew that Skimmer would have already called the police and that they would attend if they didn't have anything better to do. He knew he would get turned over; pockets, socks but not a strip search. They wouldn't have time to take him back to Bridport for that. He didn't want to lose his herbal before making even one deal. So he decided that they should politely leave.

'C'mon lads. He's frightened of us; we make him a bit nervous. Thought you were all hard cunts from London.' The last sentence to Skimmer.

'Just leave. The police are on their way.'

The four of them filed out, Darren took up the rear and issued Skimmer with a lingering, murderous stare before he too turned to walk out of the door. None of them had seen Katie Pentreath and her parents sitting in the corner. They had been in the pub for about ten minutes before the Pykes had arrived and were just having a quick drink before going on to the local theatre. Sally Pentreath, Katie's mother, was a keen amateur dramatist who regularly dragged her husband Bert and daughter Katie to the Mermaid Theatre in Lyme. Bert and Katie didn't even know what play was on and weren't really interested. Mum was hopefully recovering from breast cancer and keeping her happy was not too much to ask. It had been the last day of the spring term and she had arrived home from Sussex Uni in Brighton at teatime.

5. Bert Pentreath was a native of Cornwall but had moved to Dorset for the opportunity to farm good, arable soil and not just breed sheep and pigs he couldn't sell. A lease on 250 acres had come up when only child Katie was a toddler and he and Sally had decided to go for it. It had been fairly successful and the family had gone on to buy a second leasehold

and move into a big, draughty farmhouse about four miles south of Crewkerne, in the Triangle. The Triangle is the bit carved out if you draw a line from Bridport to Lyme, then from Lyme to Crewkerne and then from Crewkerne back to Bridport. The nearer to the centre of the triangle you get the easier it is to get lost and the stranger the people seem to be. Many of the isolated properties have no running water and rely on the plumbing in of natural springs. Not in itself a problem but the use of copper piping combined with the very high acidity of the water means that those with fair or grey hair who bathe in it develop green hair. Those who don't bathe in it stink. So, in the Triangle you either stink or, if you're blond or grey, you have green hair.

The Pentreath's farm was called Upper Brooklands and had about four hundred acres of good arable land and another 100 or so not so good but okay for a few sheep – and horses. Katie was mad on horses and she had two. The reason she had chosen Sussex University, at which she was a student of veterinary surgery, was that it was close enough to home and to her two horses, Rosie and Gabriella. She could at least get home every weekend. She doted on them and term time Monday mornings would see her struggling back to college still smelling of the stables.

6. 'They seemed a rough lot,' remarked Bert, after the Pykes had made their slow, surly exit. 'Obviously looking for trouble'. As he said this he looked at his daughter. He couldn't help feeling slightly troubled by the expression she wore.

'Come along you two, or we'll miss the start, we can't do that because this is the last night of the production before it moves to London. Come on.'

Sally gathered her bag and led her husband and daughter out of the pub, not before Bert had nearly choked trying to gulp down his pint too fast.

Out on the street Bert was relieved to find that the boys were nowhere to be seen. Well, he wasn't actually correct. As the family made their way over the road toward the theatre something made Katie turn around. He was standing alone in a shop doorway. The last one to have left the pub.

Darren Pyke regarded the family with contempt. He heard the mother and father chatting in their nice accents, her nagging shrill in the summer air, cooling it. He watched as the girl turned to regard him, and then turned away again, hurriedly, to catch up with her parents. He didn't like the way in which she had looked him up and down. Snooty fucking cow. His three brothers having gone on to the pubs near the harbour, Darren had deliberately tarried to see which police came. Sometimes the cops would drop off a plain clothes monkey with a hidden radio to go on a recce. If that was going to be the case tonight Darren wanted a look at him – or her. But the police never turned up. Skimmer must have called them off. Darren turned and followed his brothers who were by now a couple of hundred metres ahead. They made their way along the front to the harbour where the lack of residential population meant that the three pubs there stayed open late and loud. Josh was keen to do business and Darren needed to be by his side.

7. The four of them walked into the Yacht Hotel and Josh ordered the drinks. Four pints of Stella. Darren stood to one side and surveyed the population. Everyone avoided eye contact with him. One of the barmaids recognised them and made a point of being sweet. If things got ugly she wouldn't want to be on the wrong side of this lot. Josh paid, distributed the pints and they filed outside and walked into a relatively dark section of the patio area which led out onto the beach. Then Darren took up position away from the other four in a place from which he could see who was approaching from the busy part of town. He looked across at the other three as he heard Josh's mobile go. A distinctive rap tone. A short conversation followed after which Josh said something to Joe and the youngster made his way across the patio to where Darren was standing.

'Talbot's coming down from Chard, should be here in ten. Says he'll be on his own,' said Joe to Darren with an air of being the important messenger. He was not yet old enough to realise there was no such thing.

'Yeah, I bet he fucking will be,' came the experienced reply.

8. After leaving the Dep's office Heather walked down to the canteen at Dorset Police HQ and bought herself a coffee and a KitKat. She sat in the corner; it was the middle of the afternoon and very quiet. Had she done the right thing coming here? Her mum was pleased and she knew she was needed at home but, shit, what sort of a Force was this? Five to ten year wait to get into the CID. And the shifts; one weekend off a month – if you're lucky. She had also just learned that getting leave approved in the summer months was hard as well, what with the tourist trade on the coast being obviously seasonal. She would just have to keep her head down and gob shut. Oh, and there was that other little matter that probably wouldn't go down too well in parochial Dorset... mmm, yes. Keep that well under wraps for the foreseeable future. Definitely.

She finished her snack, stuck her civilian parka on over her uniform and left the building. It was Friday and her shifts did not commence until the following Tuesday. She looked forward to the weekend. A mate and ex-colleague Alex Miller was coming from London for a couple of days. She had joined the Met with Alex and they had always been close. Although quite athletic, he had bad skin, greasy hair and smoked. Heather's mum could not see what her daughter saw in him.

She walked around a few of the twee Dorchester streets for a while, enjoying the warm air. She could not take her parka off because she would end up getting involved in something, so she sweated a little. When she saw a white van parked half on the road and half on the pavement and right on a corner her annoyance was aroused further. Can't get into the CID for a while but I'll have some fun with prats who do that.

'Sorry love, won't do it when you're on duty'

She looked up to see the tall black haired youth standing by the van. She had not seen him at first. She did not like the way he was looking at her. Not one bit. His voice was jovial, almost respectful. But his look, his expression, was feral, loathsome. Like there was something hiding in there. She turned and hurried away, a shiver down her spine.

Darren Pyke lit a cigarette and got into his van. He had an idea he would see more of that copper. He made a mental note to make sure it would be on his terms, not hers.

When she got back to her mother's house Alex was already there. He was standing in the courtyard having a cigarette. His car, a Jeep, was parked up awkwardly and was filthy dirty. Alex was a compact, athletic 28 year old who usually dressed in army surplus camouflage trousers with pockets on the legs, along with tee-shirts or hoodies, depending on the weather. And he was very untidy; everything he did, every move he made, was a mess or left a mess. Heather was close to him though and always made allowances. She admired and was mildly excited by his cavalier attitude. Always prepared to roll the dice, take risks, was our Alex. In Heather's eyes this made him a good copper. Just one of those who had the Midas touch. He would walk round a corner and bump into a laden burglar. Every car he pulled had drugs in it or a disqual driver behind the wheel. Every time he spun a drum on a warrant he would come up trumps. A nose for it, as they said.

Actually, the trick was just to work harder than anyone else but not to show it. That was a hard thing to do in a merit based, or ostensibly merit based society; work hard whilst making people think you were not working hard. A lot of people tended to do the opposite.

'Take you long?' She asked, casually, as if she didn't care, which she didn't.

'Cuppla hours.'

'You were speeding then bruv.'

'Yeah. Got any beer?'

'Yeah, put the fag out and come inside.'

And that was how they spoke, like a couple of teenagers trying to be cool. Once inside the conversation became even more desultory. Alex located the TV control and found Sky Sports News on the plasma. Heather, having cracked a bottle of Kronenbourg for each of them, sat down and flicked through a copy of the Evening Standard that Alex had had in one of his trouser side pockets.

'When d'you start then, county mounty?'

'Tuesday, 2 pm, a week of lates.'

'At least they didn't start you on nights.'

'Would've preferred it, could have got to know the roads better.'

'How, it gets dark here dunnit? No lit sign or street lights, eh?'

'Point, yeah but… look Alex, are you just going to take the piss out of me? If so fuck off back to London, it's hard enough as it is mate.'

'Ooooooowwwuh! Touchy, touchy,'

He leaned forward and grabbed her hand.

'Listen Heather, remember what I told you less than two months ago, just before you left, remember what I said….'

'Yeah, yeah okay, but still, back off a bit, I'm feeling insecure just now, well shaky…' she trailed off and gazed out of the window, keen to sever eye contact so he would not see the tears welling up. But he saw her face redden and decided to change the subject.

'Where are you taking me tonight then, honey pie?'

She lightened up. 'Anywhere you like, my sweet, anywhere you like. I'm starving and I need a drink. Call a cab, I don't want to drive.'

9. 'Look Simon, I've got a lot of work to do. Just because it's the

summer doesn't mean I'm free all the time. The horses need a lot of attention and I can't just drop everything and come to Brighton for the weekend....'

Katie Pentreath was talking to her boyfriend of two years, Simon Murdoch. He was a fellow veterinary student but did not take his studies so seriously. A good bit brighter than Katie he did not have to work as hard. There was a lot of partying going on in Brighton and he wanted her there, not tucked away on her parent's farm in the middle of nowhere.

'Okay, okay, I'll come to you then. I could be there inside two hours, we'll....'

'No Simon. I need some space. Fucking hell I've only been away from you less than 24 hours. Can't you go out with your mates or something? I need to spend some time with my parents and my horses and my bloody books. You know I'm struggling with the biochemistry, and next year it's the finals.'

Simon hung up on her. She replaced the receiver gently, leaned heavily against the phone and sighed. She supposed she was lucky, really, he was handsome, wealthy and had a good future. But God did he stifle her, so possessive. She supposed that he might go out and get smashed now and pick up some bird in front of everybody to prove a point. To try to make her jealous. But she would not be jealous, she would be relieved. She had recently decided that she did not really like Simon Murdoch, as much as he obviously loved her. But at least everything was so predictable with him. The tally ho cheerfulness, the rugby shirts, the Pimms parties and blazers. True, she was a farmer's kid, as was he. But her dad had worked his farm, made it grow, sweated blood. Simon's family had money whether they worked for it or not. It was just there, to be taken for granted. Bad harvest? So what, sell a corner plot to a builder, sell one of the cars, re-lease some of the machinery. Bottomless. Whereas Bert Pentreath had to sweat and worry about the weather and the cost of animal feed and the cost of repairs to his Land Rover which was always falling apart. There were farmers and there were landed gentry who called themselves farmers.

10. Darren gunned that white van across the A35 and onto the Crewkerne Road and north toward Stockard. Josh sat beside him and the two younguns bounced around in the back, complaining.

'Steady on Daz, there ain't cushions back here,' protested Joe.

'Shut the fuck up!' And then to his elder brother, 'How much did you sell?'

'Good bit, made about a oner, one twenty.'

'Aw fuck off Daz, that's not a good bit, that's only 25 quid each at best. Jesus, for fucks sake, it's not worth the fuckin' risk bruv….'

'Yeah, yeah, I know, I know, we need to do better.'

'We've got petrol to put in and tax to pay on the van. We've got mum's birthday soon, it's never fuckin' ending.'

'Leave it with me. I've got something coming up in my mind. Should make a real difference.' Josh had obviously been thinking. He did not bullshit Darren and he did, to be fair, occasionally come up with some good ideas. Darren decided to leave it there and wait and see. About a mile before they entered Stockard they passed an old cottage that actually backed onto the road and faced away from it towards a valley called Rockham Ditch. This was real Triangle country. The cottage was called, rather grandly, Everett House, and was occupied by a family of that name. The effect of copper pipes and spring water was particularly pronounced in this little cohabiting group of relatives. They had, amongst other things, the customary green hair. The back of Everett House was continued on either side along the road by a fairly high stone wall. This made it hard for anyone to see the Everett's business from the road. One really had to stop, apply for entry at the gate via an anachronistic electric intercom, and then pay a visit. Not that they were an unwelcoming bunch. On the contrary, once you had gained access it was difficult to refuse the flowing hospitality. Flowing being the operative word. The Everetts were renowned for their unlicensed activities, one of which being the production of all manner of alcoholic beverages. They never actually sold it though so they never got prosecuted. It was widely rumored however that they did, on an organized basis, make a lot of money out of other unlicensed practices. But then the whole Triangle buzzed with rumour. So much so that no law enforcement agency would waste its time there. There were never any complaints and if there were they were invariably from competing unlicensed practitioners, so to speak. The Rockham Ditch is not as bad as it sounds and the Everetts owned quite a few acres therein of lush grassland on which they bred fine ponies. They always had about a dozen or so, it seemed, but the numbers would fluctuate as sales were made and foals were born. Their stables were antiquated but adequate and the two horseboxes that, together with a powerful Land Rover, comprised their fleet were remarkably compliant with vehicular regulations. Not their only source of income though, ponies, only one of a few.

'Pull over,' said Josh. Darren complied. Josh got out and walked back to the gate in the wall with the intercom. He pressed a button, lit a cigarette and was barely on his third drag when the gate was opened by Mrs. Everett, all smiles and a huge tangle of grey-green hair. She nearly pulled Josh in through the opening and then slammed the gate shut.

'Is he givin' her one?' mused Darren, half to his younger brothers in the back and half to himself.

'He better not be long or I'm fucking leaving him here.'

Josh wasn't long and within about five minutes he came back out of the gate and someone shut it behind him. He had a little smile on his face as he got back into the van. Darren regarded him suspiciously for a second or two then gunned the van down the lane, toward Stockard and home to the Pyke residence.

11. Heather and Alex got out of the cab in Lyme Regis, Alex paid the fare and they went into the Goat pub. The Goat was in a back street, not on the seafront, and was generally populated by local characters. Alex

had been there before when on holiday with his parents as a lad and he wanted to revisit. Heather took one look around and didn't like it. The pub was a mish-mash of second hand furniture, mismatched carpets, tacky ornaments, a filthy fish tank and a barmaid with dirty fingernails. And she could smell the loos. She liked a place with character, but this place was just a mess. A bloke that looked old but probably wasn't sat at the bar and regarded them blankly before going back to hand rolling cigarettes which were accumulating in an untidy pile before him. At some point he was going to have to go outside and smoke one. In the meantime rolling them seemed to be taking his mind off the smoking ban.

Alex and Heather sat down at a table near the fish tank. Alex was happy and had already downed half of his pint. Heather sipped a glass of red wine with a wrinkled nose. Alex ignored this and launched into conversation. If he didn't talk he would want to smoke and once he started going outside for a fag it would be every five minutes. He found if he could get through the first couple of pints without a puff he would be okay until about the eighth pint by which time it wouldn't really matter because he would be talking bollocks anyway.

'D'you have to re-join the Federation?' Every cop in England and Wales below the rank of Superintendent is a member of the Police Federation. It's their union. They have to be a member but they do not have to pay into a voluntary fund. If they don't pay however they don't get help when they drop in the shit, which working cops regularly do.

'Course not, I never left the job, remember, just transferred to Dorset. No break in service.' She was still looking around the place, trying to decide where she would start on a refurb and thinking how she was definitely not cut out to dwell indoors.

'I'm a Fed rep now,' announced Alex, just before he took a long pull at his pint. She blinked as she took this in and turned slowly round to face him.

'Really, what brought that on?'

'Somebody just suggested that I do it. I have a way with guvnors, they seem to listen to me. I'm not a canteen cowboy, ranting and raving about management being a bunch of prats like some of them do, I go with a reasoned argument and get results.'

'Good for you mate. Hope it doesn't interfere with your thief-taking though.'

'It won't, I promise.'

'My God, a working class hero, eh?' she mused as she turned away again to torture herself with the jarring juxtaposition of the furniture and fittings. Then she looked around at Alex again. She was being rude to him, off-hand - and she suddenly felt guilty.

'I'm sorry I'm not being much company Al, I'm just pissed off that I'm going to have to wait so long to get into the position I was in, on the brink of making CID. I'm beginning to think I've made a mistake coming here. I was summoned to see the Dep today and the condescending shit he gave me was both at the same time sickening and threatening.'

'Yeah, I told you, you'll have to watch your step. These shit-kicking Forces don't like us Mets coming down here and telling them what to do....'

'I've no intention of telling anybody what to do Alex; I just want a career....'

'You had one of those in London, remember, and a bunch of good mates, and a social life, and a decent gaff. It was your choice to be with your mum, live the quiet life. None of us can understand it though. Why you left to come here – the land of fossils and wet weekends....'

She knew he was lying. They understood alright, just didn't talk about it much.

'Yeah, okay, okay. Don't make me feel worse than I already do. Thought you'd come to cheer me up?'

He put his arm around her and she instinctively stiffened a little. She hated it when he did that. It was like he was never going to give up. Even though she had told him.

The door of the pub swung open and in walked a short stocky lad with longish blond hair. Well, not exactly blond. Yes, you guessed it, sort of greenish.

'Pint o' Sark please Dianne.' Dianne Hammond had been the landlady of the Goat for three and half years, before that she had run it with her husband Robin who had died in a road accident. She was a cheerful lady, but with an eye for trouble makers and a quick tongue.

'Of course Emmett, and how are you today my sweet?'

'Fine, why d'you ask?' said Emmett Everett, defensively.

'Just wondered. You look ever so smart.' This made things worse because Emmet did not, and never did, look smart. He invariably dressed like some sort of West Country cowboy; pointed boots, checked shirt, leather waistcoat, wide brown belt keeping up drainpipe jeans.

'You takin' the piss outta me Dianne?'

'No my sweet, course not,' as she said this she winked at Heather and Alex who were listening with grins.

'What a yokel. He'll be one of your snouts in a few weeks Heather. Tell you all about stolen tractors and criminal damage to lobster pots.'

'Fuck off,' she responded, with a laugh.

12. Gabriella and Rosie started at a trot from the bottom of the field when they saw Katie at the gate. She had been there for a few minutes, watching them graze peacefully and they hadn't noticed her at first. But

as soon as they did the competition started. By the time they got to her they were both galloping. She jumped over the gate and hugged them both at the same time, one huge head in each arm. Within a second she was covered in saliva and giggling with joy. She had her pockets full of carrots and small apples which she shared evenly between the two horses, and then they settled down and behaved a little less excitedly, each quite satisfied that Katie loved her more than the other. The greeting and fuss lasted about twenty minutes before Katie backed away from the gate and turned to walk the quarter of a mile or so back to the farmhouse to have tea with her parents. She would see them again in the morning; take them for a hack. She walked slowly, rolling a cigarette. She figured she could roll and smoke a thin one before reaching the house and so would not be caught. Her parents didn't know and would not approve. She licked the Rizla and twisted and folded. Seemed okay. She took out a book of matches and began striking. She had stopped walking by now and the slight summer breeze was making the job difficult. So intense was her concentration on the job in hand she did not see the white van approach and stop. Two big arms came out of the driver's window. The hand at the end of one of them held a Zippo lighter; the hand at the end of the other sheltered the burning wick from the breeze. She looked up and gazed at the dancing flame. After a second she stuck her fag in her mouth and leaned forward for contact and a light. Pulling on the smoke she stepped back and thanked white van man. He had floppy black hair and a wide grin. The lighter flame and smoke had blurred her vision so she didn't quite catch his eyes.

'Thank you very much,' she said with a polite smile.

'No problem,' said Darren Pyke, before snapping the lighter shut and tossing it to her. She caught it. ''Ere, keep it, those matches are no good.'

'I couldn't possibly...' but he was gone. As the van moved off she caught sight of his eyes for a split second as he looked at her in the rear view wing mirror of the van, and she had him. One of the boys in the pub that night. One of the bad boys. She put the lighter in the front pocket of her jeans. It was warm against her thigh.

13. Heather and Alex were eating down in one of the harbour restaurants. Lyme had once been a fairly dull, family resort. But it never became a home for the elderly simply because there were too many hills. It seem like everywhere you walked was either one in ten up or one in ten down. You were never on the flat. Not good for bath chairs, so they stayed 100 mile east along the coast in Bournemouth. Not dull these days though, Lyme. Pretty trendy actually. A good town council made sure there was always something going on in the summer – jazz festivals, Lifeboat week, the regatta, always something. The pubs had live bands at the weekends and the food for some reason had got good. The pair of them – cannot call them a couple – had fish from Lyme bay and fresh veg from a local organic farm – or so said the menu. It was delicious, they agreed. That was about the only thing they agreed on mind. The rest of the time they bickered, mostly about Heather's reasons for moving to Dorset. She had been so good in the Met. So promising. All that shit about her wanting to be with her mother, he did not believe it for one second. There was more to this shit than met the eye, and he had a good idea what it was. But he knew better than to ask her straight. 'How's your mum?'

'You already asked me that twice today.'

'Well, just making conversation.'

'No you're not.'

'Yes I am. How's the gold digger then?'

'That's better, get to the point. He's fine. Looking after her if I'm honest.'

Time to give her a poke in the ribs, he decided.

'Caroline sends her regards.'

That stopped her dead. Her fork was on its way to her mouth and it didn't make it, dropping back down to her plate. She looked him in the eye.

'You don't hardly know Caroline. How did she know you were coming here?'

'Word gets around the nick. She didn't like it. I could tell by the way she spoke to me, like she was jealous or something.'

Heather was on the back foot. 'Why would she be jealous of you? She knows there's nothing between us.'

Alex crammed his mouth full of sea bass, took a pull on his beer and changed the subject.

'Look at that poster on the wall over there, there's a band on at a pub called the Flag tonight, 'Free Range Rude' they call themselves. That was a line out of a Hannibal Lecter film.'

Silence.

'Want to go?'

'Yeah okay,' she answered softly, looking up at the poster and then at him. For just a second, perhaps not even that, he thought maybe she'd softened, just maybe.

She had not softened one bit. She had merely reflected for a moment on the past. Caroline Sherry was a thing of the past. And the wound had healed.

14. Old man Pyke was in his usual drunken state. Sat at the newspaper covered kitchen table pouring scrumpy out of a half- gallon plastic canister into a big china pint pot. He got a mate of his to bring the stuff up from Newton Abbot after the horse racing. He drank about a gallon a day which at about 8% alcohol was a lot of booze. He belched as Darren walked through the door. He acknowledged his father briefly and went to the fridge and extracted bacon and eggs which he loaded onto a big frying pan the bottom of which was an inch thick in solidified lard. On went the gas. On went the pan and its contents were soon sizzling, half

submerged.

'Make some for me, son,' said the old man.

'Okay dad,' said Darren. In a normal household the young would have little time for dysfunctional parents. But the Pyke family were fiercely loyal to each other. There was no point in falling out with your own blood when everybody else hated you. The Pykes stuck together and faced the world. They certainly had no friends in Stockard. It was like they should really have a couple of acres nearer the center of the triangle, sort of around where the Everetts were stationed. But they were stuck in this fucking council house next door to complainers and across the street from narcs.

Smelling the food, young Wayne and Joe came thundering down the carpetless stairs from their room. Darren shook his head and took out another frying pan, lit another ring, scooped some more lard and doubled his efforts. Soon all four of them were tucking in to a cholesterol feast. Old Gordon shared his scrumpy out and by the time Ginny got back from cleaning everything was washed up and spick and span. She would fend for herself; get fish and chips or something. The boys asked for little from her in the way of housework, she had suffered enough over the years and good times didn't look like they were around the corner.

15. Katie kicked off her boots and padded across the cool stone tiles of the big farmhouse kitchen. Her parents Bert and Sally had gone over to the neighbouring farm to socialise and swap stories about the price of feed and the agreed location of their respective silage pits, so Katie had the house to herself. She planned to have the full next day with Rosie and Gabriella, totally spoil them, and then get down to some serious study the following day. It was about 7pm so she had a snack and ran a big steamy bath. As she pulled her jeans off the Zippo lighter fell out of her pocket. She picked it up and something made her examine it. She had seen plenty of these cheap things around the campus at uni, but there was something different about this one. Not the cannabis leaf emblazoned on one side,

that was pretty standard, but the letters roughly scratched on the other – a D and a P. The initials DP. D.P.

As she sank into the bath she thought of that young man in the pub with his brothers, and how he then reappeared the next day in a battered old white van to give her a light and then toss her the lighter with his initials on it. She wondered what would happen next. What the next development would be. The fact that she was so sure that there would be one sent a shiver down her spine, in spite of the piping hot water in which she now lay. What was it about this part of the world?

16. The weekend passed by for Heather and Alex without any real incident, just the crackle of tension between them. It sort of held them together and kept them apart; a stasis rendering the relationship redundant in terms of any future between them, but anything but, they both sensed, in terms of their separate futures. People often instinctively know when to invest in each other; they have a precognitive understanding of the future without having the faintest idea of what actually might happen. It was like this with Heather Boyle and Alex Miller. He guessed he would never get his wicked way with her, but felt that one day he would be very pleased to have her by his side. This feature of the feeling was reciprocated. She needed that connection with her past, with the chaotic but civilised life of being a copper in the Metropolis. So for both of them the relationship was one of treading water; keeping it ticking over.

The Free Range Rude gig at the Flag had been okay, as it happened. They had needed each other there as the crowd packed together. Alex's presence kept away any potential suitors from his female companion, and his female companion was, after all, a female companion. He didn't love Heather, but he found her attractive and a boost to his ego to be with. What a waste. After the gig they'd waited ages for a taxi back to Dorchester and it had cost a fortune. When they got back Alex was not surprised to see that Heather's mum had made up his bed on the big leather sofa. He decided that he would drive back to London the next morning. Enough country air and celibacy was enough country air and celibacy. Yet he did not for one minute regret making the journey and putting up with Heather's studied off-handedness. Something was going to happen, he felt, and it would not be long.

17. On a Tuesday afternoon, towards the end of May, PC Heather Boyle turned up at Bridport Police Station to report for duty. She began at the stores and asked to be allocated a locker. Wally, the store man – powerful figure – cheerfully showed her where the female locker room was situated and gave her a key. She stowed her parka and the front panel of her car radio. Removing these was standard practice in London. There was probably no need for it here, but old habits die hard. She had parked her Renault Clio out in the street, free of charge. Unbelievable.

She turned the key in her locker, removed it and slipped it into the pocket of her skirt. As she left she caught sight of herself in a full length mirror situated beside the door. Above was a laminated sign –'Will the public like what they see?' she decided that the public could fuck themselves if they didn't. The fact was that she did. A bit on the heavy side but not fat. About 5'8", flat stomach and small arse. She rolled her shoulders and felt her trapezius muscles stretch and watched her neck thicken. She wasn't butch at all, just looked like she shouldn't be messed with.

When she got into the parade room the rest of the team were already there. They stopped chatting and looked around at her.

'Hi, I'm Heather. I've joined you from the Met and I'm going to teach you all how to be coppers!' then she grinned at them. This broke the ice and they all grinned in appreciation. Pre-emptive.

'Oh, are you now? Well, to be honest some of us could do with being told. What made you come down to these parts Heather?' This was from a thirty something PC called Gary Webster. She was quite taken aback by the fact that he spoke with a strong Yorkshire accent.

'Wanted to move to England,' she replied, and they all liked this. There were seven of them in all, two of them women who were predictably cool towards her. Sharon Cozens was one of them.

'Sick of all them black men were you?' Then, more confidentially, but loud enough for them all to hear, 'Is it true what they say?'

Heather was just a little taken aback by this, but recovered with, 'Why d'you want to know, things not too good down here on that front?'

'She wouldn't know,' Gary got in, 'always talking about it, aren't you Shaz, and we all know what that means.' Sharon went red and Heather felt sorry for her. She'd only been trying to be one of the lads.

Carl Bentner, an older PC who had been faffing with his utility belt during this bit of banter and seemingly not paying much attention, piped up, 'Anyway Heather, welcome to the Triangle, one of the most dangerous parts of the world to police. Things happen here that'll turn your hair, I promise you.'

Heather let out what she thought was an appreciative laugh, and then stifled it when nobody joined. They all just looked at her as they readied themselves for inspection. Not nastily at all, just, well, looked at her as if they all thought the same thing at the same time. They didn't even look at each other, just at her for a few seconds, curiously.

Then in came Sergeant Tomlinson, a big, bluff man in his late forties. He had a broad smile, a twinkle in his eye and smelled of beer. He carried a number of computer printouts. As he entered those who had been sitting stood up. It all went quiet. They obviously respected him.

'You must be Heather Boyle, then,' he said and held out a huge hand which she shook as firmly as she could.

'Yes sergeant, pleased to meet you.'

'Welcome on board. They making you feel at home?'

'Yes, sergeant.'

'Watch them mind, sex mad, every last one of them. All they talk about.'

Heather just smiled and lowered her eyes.

The parade was not unlike those in the Met; the sergeant read out the crimes reported during the previous shift, any operational orders from the Chief Super and any intelligence reports from surrounding forces, especially concerning vehicles that need to be looked out for. One such report concerned rather strangely a horse box that had been seen being towed on the M3 towards London on the previous day. It had borne the tie on trade plates of an unregistered vehicle that had later been involved in a drugs related incident in Brixton, London. All the West Country forces had been asked to keep a look out for it and a description was circulated. Brown wooden horsebox with white fiberglass roof. Heather didn't know anything about horses or horseboxes but found this bulletin quite astonishing. A horsebox in Brixton? Drugs related incident? What she found even more intriguing was that her new colleagues jotted down the details in their pocket books without showing the slightest surprise. In that instant Heather Boyle's attitude shifted. Just a bit.

18. Darren Pyke parked the white van up at the end of the Cobb in Lyme Regis, pointing away from the busy part of the area and towards the A35. He guessed that he may not in a short while, have a lot of time to turn the vehicle around before heading for the Triangle and home to Stockard. Josh had got a lift from Stockard to Axminster and had travelled from there to Lyme by bus. The boys figured it best not to be seen together unnecessarily. Darren didn't lock the van and walked along Ozone Road and stood in a darkened shop doorway. It was nearly ten o'clock at night and was as dark as it was going to get. The street lighting was dim and the illumination afforded by the three pubs was warm and cosy, especially when accompanied by the laughter of early season holiday makers and local teenagers home from college for the summer.

Darren did not acknowledge Josh as the older brother, wearing a long billed baseball cap, he sauntered into the Flag. He was deliberately 20 minutes early; the meeting wasn't until 10.15. Darren rolled a fag and searched for his lighter. Fuck; why had he given it to that bird? Why? He had asked himself that question a number of times over the preceding two days and had not come up with an answer. Not an honest one anyway. There had just been something about her. You see Darren, unlike his brothers it had to be said, was not thick. In fact he was a deep thinking introvert. He covered this by being unafraid of violence or any other sort of confrontation. In fact he was so keen to cover his inner depth that he frequently over compensated by behaving like a lunatic. There were occasions however when he was forced to confront his inner self and contemplate the distinct possibility that he might actually be a bit of a romantic. It wasn't that, no. He wasn't in love with a girl he had only set eyes on twice. Not that love at first sight shit. It was just that he felt a need to reach out. Make a connection with someone. Someone from the other side who just happened to be a good looking girl. Lovely looking, really. Gorgeous. And now he didn't have a light.

The couple came out of the Seagull Inn which is actually next door to the Flag. A young man and woman in their twenties. The first thing the young man did upon getting out of the pub door was to light a cigarette. Darren walked across the narrow street and approached him,

'Can I have a light please mate?'

'Sure' said Alex Miller before handing Darren his plastic Bic.

Darren wasted no time in firing up his roll-up, the gas flame uplighting his face. Heather watched and froze. Half blinded by the lighter and a bit giddy from the first drag of unfiltered tobacco smoke, Darren handed back the Bic and receded into the shadows without a word.

Alex, thoroughly enjoying his own first nicotine hit in about two hours, sensed a slight change in the demeanour of his companion as they walked away. She was actually holding onto his arm. Stoically refusing to allow himself the notion that his luck was on the up, he turned to her, saying,

'You okay? What's the matter, you're shivering....'

'I'm fine... I think somebody just walked over my grave, weird feeling that....'

She tailed off and released his arm to walk simply alongside him, about a yard apart.

'Yeah,' he replied, empathetically, 'Makes you shudder, like.'

Alex was on his second visit inside a month. He had been surprised to say the least when Heather had called to ask him to make the journey to Dorset. He knew she was probably just bored. But hope sprang eternal.

19. Darren watched the couple disappear along the seafront. He had not recognised the female police officer to whom he had spoken, about a fortnight previously.

The Flag was quite busy but not packed. Josh had leant on the bar for ten minutes and had downed half his pint of cider before retiring to the gents. In the cubicle he had firstly half-filled the pan with toilet paper before dropping his pants, sitting down and squeezing out his bullet. A small amount of shit accompanied it but the operation was not as messy as it occasionally could be. He retrieved the bullet from its loo paper nest without touching the turd, wiped it off, waited until he was sure nobody was using the urinal and then left the cubicle to wash his hands and the little brass cylinder. He worked quickly; unscrewing the rounded lid and tapping out the white powder into equally shared amounts between four very small clear plastic sachets with airtight press-seals. He put these into his pocket, together with the now empty bullet which he rinsed out under the tap before screwing the lid back on. Now he was in danger and had to do the deal ASAP. Talbot was due any minute so he walked through the pub and out onto the poorly lit beach. It was low tide and there was plenty of space. Talbot had entered the pub whilst he was in the loo and followed him, after a decent interval, onto the sand.

'You alright mate?' asked Talbot when he was sure he was within earshot of Josh. Josh turned around casually and replied, 'Yeah, you?'

'Fine, got the dodgy gear then?'

'Nothin' dodgy about my gear Talbot. You got the dosh?'

'Yep.'

'Let's do it then,' and the quick exchange took place. Josh walked around the side of the pub with two hundred quid in his back pocket and headed for the street, leaving Talbot to walk away along the beach. He felt somehow that it wasn't over though, and hoped that Darren had waited. Talbot's money would be good, they'd checked him out and a few nights previously they had discussed the business relationship in principle. But Talbot was heavy and had some heavy mates from the Somerset town of Chard. As Josh walked through an alley between the Flag pub and an old building that separated it from the Seagull Inn he heard movement behind, tried to turn but did not stand a chance. His face hit the ancient paving stones and was forced to stay there whilst his brief ownership of two hundred quid was briskly terminated. He lay still as his attackers trampled over him and headed for the street end of the alleyway. He knew what was about to happen. The scream was ear-splitting as Darren's asp smashed the chard boy's shoulder. The other one tried to run back but Josh had got to his feet and was running headlong at the escapee. He delivered a kick to the crotch with such force that it actually knocked the kid out cold. Christ only knew the damage it had done to his testicles. The first Chardian was rolled in a ball sobbing with pain, clutching his broken shoulder. The money was retrieved from him in exchange for a quick couple of heel stamps to the face from Josh. The Pyke brothers walked quickly out of the alley and to the van and made a quick and unseen exit from Lyme Regis. Talbot, having heard the scream, backtracked along the beach to investigate. Discovering what had happened he just walked calmly away to his car and drove home to Chard. Those two wankers could die for all he cared. They'd fucked up a simple job. Couldn't even roll a Triangle hillbilly. Tossers. They'd get picked up when the pubs kicked out. Anyway, at least he had a dozen grams of Charlie to show for the night's work. It could have been so much better, but at least he was in front; would make a tidy profit in Chard, and have a good night for himself and his bird to boot.

20. When Darren and Josh pulled up in the white van outside their house in Stockard there was a police car there.

'Keep calm Joshy boy, we're clean remember, and two hundred quid ain't a lot of money. Darren tossed his asp into the back of the vehicle and it clattered about before coming to rest amongst some gardening tools and old lawnmower parts. They got out of the van and walked up the garden path. There was no gate to open, that'd been ripped off years ago and the front lawn, if you could call it that, had two old Mini Coopers parked on it. Another one of the old man's abandoned projects. The Pyke garden spoiled the street really as many of the residents had bought their abodes and were trying their best to make the area look nice. But there's always one family is there not? The only Pyke who was a bit embarrassed was old Ginny. She had not long returned home from her fourth cleaning job of her long day to find the old man had thrown a scrumpy-fuelled wobbler and had smashed the place up. Ginny had had enough of this and had called the police. She had done this before and the appearance of the patrol car parked outside the house whilst some poor cop had to dispense marriage guidance advice served to enhance the Pyke reputation. Darren was a bit embarrassed too, but kept to himself, instead feigning hostility to the officer who stood in the kitchen warning the old man about his behaviour and citing Force domestic violence policy.

'You got fuck all better to do Tom?'

Special Constable Tom Ballard had been working as an unpaid volunteer cop in the Triangle since Darren had nicked his first bike. They knew each other well.

'Obviously not Darren, otherwise I'd be doing it.' Darren stood alongside the officer and they surveyed the scene in silence for a few seconds. This was a particularly bad one. Every plate in the kitchen was lying in bits, Ginny was sitting in bits, head in hands, and the old man was slumped in a wooden armchair with a very distant look on his face, like he was having some sort of out of body experience. A couple of scrumpy canisters lay on the floor, empty needless to say and for the first time in his life Darren came to the conclusion that his father was mentally ill. He wouldn't even remember this in the morning. By that time Ginny and the boys would have cleaned up the mess and Ginny would be off again on a fifteen hour day to replace the broken crockery and put food on the table. Darren would split the two hundred quid and give her half. He and Josh would share the rest and Wayne and Joe could fuck themselves. They had refused to go on the Lyme job, saying they were busy in nearby Charmouth playing skittles. What a load of bollocks. Darren knew exactly where Wayne and Joe had been and it had been nowhere near Charmouth. They had been with the green hair gang – the Everetts – drinking moonshine. They would stay with the Everetts that night; uncharacteristically sensible because of the heat in the area about drink driving. The cops were obsessed with it, a fact which for obvious reasons suited Josh and Darren.

21. Heather's first couple of shifts went without much incident. She had missed out on the assaults on the Chard boys in the alley between the two pubs in Lyme; that incident had taken place when she was off duty having finished a 2 to 10. She was out on patrol now with old Reg Bull, or Red Bull as they called him after the drink. A rather melancholy bloke in his fifties, coming up to retirement. He knew just about every soul in the county worth knowing, especially all the publicans.

'You know Heather,' he said, breaking off from his usual tour operator's monologue about the streets, the farms, the characters and the history, 'whenever someone transfers here from the Met it's always for a reason.'

How profound, though Heather. You're hardly likely to do it for no reason.

'You think so, Reg?'

'Yeah. Take our present Chief Constable for example. She was just a Chief Super in the Met. She'll stay here for a couple of years, open a few fetes, make few speeches, rename one or two incentives and call them her own, and then bugger off back to London as an Assistant Commissioner or something. Just you wait. They just come here to practice. Easy, you see. No ethnic minorities, terrorists, riots or nothing. Just a bunch of carrot crunchers moaning about traffic restrictions and noisy pubs during the summer season.'

'Well, I'm here to stay, and if I did go back to London it wouldn't be as Assistant Commissioner. I dropped a rank to get here.'

'What do you mean? Were you a sergeant?'

'No, but I was nearly a CID officer, and now I'm nowhere near being one.'

'Oh, so you consider being a DC better than being a PC, do you?'

Heather knew she'd made a mistake.

'Well, no, not really, but….'

'Yes you do, tell the truth. Most of the CID are like that. Consider themselves better than us wooden tops, as they call us. Let me tell you something, they're a lazy bunch of bastards in this county. Always in the pubs, on the mump. Couldn't give a shit about doing any work.'

'Yeah, well, I wasn't like that Reg; I liked nicking people, and then getting convictions at court.'

'You can do that in uniform you know. The secret is to just wait, be patient, and study the intelligence. The younguns aren't interested. All they want to do is knock people off for drink drive. They think that's police work. Not that it isn't, it's just that it's easy. I have to do it myself sometimes, and you will, especially when there's an accident. But when you do, always search the motor. Always look in the glove compartment. There's a big drugs problem in these parts. The top brass'll deny it – so called victimless crime you see, never reported as a statistic - but it's there, and it's damaging. A mate of mine, he's a Special in Chard, he has a daughter who he's convinced is doing cocaine. She won't admit it but he's convinced. He reckons it comes down from Bristol and London and he's chipping away at it. Nobody believes him or takes any notice but knowing him he'll get a result. Tom Ballard's his name. When we do nights next week I'll take you to meet him. He'll like you.

'Thanks,' said Heather. Hells' bells, so meeting a Special was going to be a highlight of her night shift the following week. She felt really low at that point. Aside from PCSOs, Specials were in her books the lowest form of police life. In the Met, Specials were just part-time volunteers who turn out and work for nothing and pinch your overtime.

'Reg,' Heather was trying her best to appear interested. There had been a ten minute silence during which Reg had appeared to have given up trying instill some interest in his young charge and she didn't want to hurt his feelings.

'Yes, love,' he replied eagerly as he pulled the car out of a B road and onto the A35 to head back to Bridport for a meal break.

'Those two lads who got a beating on the Cobb the other night, pretty serious it seemed.'

'Yeah, especially that shoulder injury. Use of a weapon that, nasty.'

'Drugs related?'

'Course it was Heather! Now you think properly. Those two are from Chard it turned out. They had to go the Exeter hospital you know, bad beatings. The Devon Bobbies asked them a load of questions for us but couldn't get any real answers they knew who had duffed them up but couldn't say. Got to be a drug deal gone wrong. I reckon they parted with the gear to someone in the Flag or the Seagull and instead of cash they got a trip to hospital. They reckon one of them will have to have surgery on his shoulder. The other one, well, he won't be much good to his girlfriend for a while if you know what I mean. Nasty.'

'You got any ideas.'

'Yep.'

'Who then?'

'Wait till we speak to Tom next week. Softly softly catchy monkey.'

'What's that supposed to mean? If you've got suspicions we should steam in now. Rattle a few cages.'

'What the hell for? The Chard boys won't make statements, there'll be no forensics and they didn't have any money or drugs on them. But Tom'll have ideas, I bet. Just be patient Heather. This ain't London.'

Didn't she know it.

22. Katie Pentreath had to force herself to get her books out and arrange them on her desk in her room so it at least looked like she was doing some work. It was always the same at the beginning of a holiday period. Got to get down to it. She had no excuses. She didn't have to work like some of her friends at uni who had poor parents and had to earn their keep when they were at home in the summer. Bert and Sally had made it clear to her that all she had to do was look after the horses and help around the house a bit, cook a few meals perhaps. Not work behind bars in Lyme or in Tesco's in Axminster. She was lucky, but dreaded failing her exams. Finals next year, then on to postgraduate studies. She wondered if she would ever make it but soldiered on. One term at a time. No missing lectures like Simon Murdoch, her so-called boyfriend. As she shuffled a few notes and opened a biochemistry book she thought about Simon. He would be enjoying a lie in with an expensive hangover. It didn't matter to him, really. Nothing really mattered to Simon and she suspected that included her – except when he needed a shag of course.

All of a sudden she stopped what she was doing and froze, just staring into space. She realised in that very instant that she did not want to see

Simon Murdoch again. She did not like him, love him, respect him or anything that he stood for. He was genetically bright and would probably do well, the prick, but so what. Fucking wanker. He was like a Harry Enfield character – 'Tim Nice-But-Dim'. She sniggered at this and wondered why it had taken this long to work it out. But then something strange seemed to have happened within the past few days and she was working a lot of things out, without even trying. Her dad was spraying crops in their biggest field, her mum was in Axminster shopping at an organic food market – they didn't even see the irony – and she, their precious vet-to-be daughter, was working things out and having rather worrying ideas about life and people and stuff in general.

23. The Senior Management Team at Dorchester Police HQ were having what they called 'morning prayers.' The Chief Constable, Joanne Bache, a woman with considerable good looks and French blood, sat at the head of the table and looked bored. The Dep, James Sprake, was in full swing and he loved the sound of his own voice. He had briefed the team – three Chief Supers, two DCIs, the Force HR manager Samantha Warner and the Force Solicitor Craig Sutherland – on anything he thought important. This invariably included anything to do with internal politics, financial management and the antics of the Federation, which both he and Sutherland hated. Chief Constable Bache wanted to know about crime and, once Sprake appeared to have run out of steam she rather rudely turned to DCI Rob Sherrell who headed the southern region CID which covered Bridport and Lyme. 'What happened the other night in Lyme Rob? Nasty double assault I hear.'

'Yes Ma'am, two Chard boys aged 21 and 23, one of them seems to have taken an iron bar on the shoulder, the other got so badly kicked in the, er, testicles that he needed surgery. Well, they both did....'

'What, both testicles?'

'No, ma'am, just one of them, the other had....'

'Yes, I know, only joking....'

There followed a few sycophantic guffaws from the around the table.

'Yes, yes, Rob, I know. Look, was that incident drugs related?'

Sherrell pondered this.

'We're not sure. The two lads are refusing to cooperate. The Avon and Somerset police in Chard are being sluggish to get statements from them and Devon and Cornwall were useless at Exeter hospital. I think it would be too early to say that the assaults were drug related. Kids come down to Lyme from Chard all the time looking for a bit of action, they probably just went too far chatting up someone else's girlfriends, that's all. Neither had any money or any drugs on them. Their local records in Chard just have them as a couple of local lads up for a laugh now and again.'

'How did they get to Lyme the other night?' probed the Chief Constable.

'Like I say ma'am we know very little, our Avon and Somerset colleagues are....'

'Yes, I know them all too well. What happens on our coast is bottom of their priorities. Okay let's move on. Derrick, the parking problem around Bridport swimming pool....'

And with that the meeting left behind forever the small matter of a serious assault arising from the trafficking of Class 'A' drugs on England's picturesque Dorset coastline.

24. Horses do not really communicate that much when all is well in their lives. Gabriella and Rosie had no worries. Their meadow was luxuriant in all sorts of grasses and flowers, it was big enough and had in its shaded corner; a dry, draught-proof stable with plenty of straw and water. So the two horses grazed away the days happily, each having her own space but both taking comfort in the other's presence. It was only

when someone arrived to visit that competition set in. And when that someone was Katie Pentreath the jealousy was like that of two human infants. Katie could only take one horse at a time for a hack. If she attempted to ride one whilst leading the other, the unladen animal would niggle and bitch the whole way, even biting the ridden horse when it thought Katie wasn't looking. So it was one at a time ladies because you just cannot be trusted to behave! It was Gabriella's turn on the day in question and Rosie knew it because it had been her hack the day before. She tried to stop the bigger horse getting to the gate and what could be described as a fight broke out. Katie lost it a bit and gave Rosie a smack across the backside with her crop. The smaller horse gave the human a baleful look, turned away and walked off in a serious sulk, leaving the smug Gabrielle to be saddled up and mounted.

Katie loved both her horses and the beginning of any hack was dominated by worry about the horse she'd left behind in the field. She wished she had a co-rider but knew no-one who was interested. Simon hated horses and she was actually glad of that because if he was a rider she would be persuaded by Rosie and Gabriella to invite him to stay so that both animals could be ridden together. Anyway, she was on Gabbie now and as the image of the chastened and crestfallen Rosie receded she decided to go for a long one. She headed on a walk along a narrow metalled road for a about half a mile before turning onto a bridle path which took them up onto Brooklands Ridge. From the top of the ridge on a clear day you could see almost all of the Dorset coast from Golden Cap to Torbay. Katie loved that view. The horses were probably sick of it.

25. Darren Pyke walked into the public bar of the Golden Hind in Natters Combe and looked disdainfully around at the dozen or so locals who went quiet and avoided his eye. He ordered a pint of Stella and gave the barmaid a twenty pound note.

'Sorry, but have you got anything smaller?'

'No, but I got something a lot bigger if you want to see that,' he sneered.

The lass turned scarlet and took the note out the back to get change from her dad, Billy Nodwell, the publican. Silence for thirty seconds.

'He said what!' came the roar and with that Nodwell charged from the living quarters into the bar and in one movement reached over the bar with his huge arms and grabbed Darren by the lapels, pulling him hard onto the wooden counter and nearly impaling him on a real ale pump handle.

Darren had not expected this. He knew Nodwell from old and figured him just to be a farmhand made good; all brawn and no brain. It didn't take a genius to run the Golden Hind, serving warm beer to the same bunch of yokels every night. But Darren, perceptive as he usually was, had underestimated Billy Nodwell.

'Right, you little piece of inbred shit, take your fucking ill-got twenty pound note and fuck right off!'

With that Nodwell shoved Darren backwards off of the bar with such force that the 22 year-old lost his balance and landed flat on his backside at the feet of a big guy with bushy sideboards who nonchalantly stamped on Darren's hand that was outstretched backwards on the floor to break his fall. The motley population of the bar laughed and Darren got to his feet, humiliated. It did not help that his asp was still in the back of the van - or perhaps it did; God knows what sort of damage he would have inflicted if the trusty stolen police issue weapon had been in its usual place in the back pocket of his jeans. He regained a semblance of composure, made a show of dusting himself down and walked slowly out of the pub with a smile on his face. A smile that said 'I'll be back.'

He got into the van and headed for Stockard and home. His anger at what had just occurred put another ten miles an hour on his usual excessive speed and he had to brake very hard indeed when he saw the horse rider coming over the brow of a hill. The road, like most in rural Dorset, was very narrow and was bordered by very high, thick hedges. Driving around these roads is like negotiating a maze of curved corridors. There are skid marks everywhere as drivers have to stop suddenly and either impose themselves on oncoming traffic or reverse hundreds of yards to find a gateway into which to reverse to let someone pass. Darren was in no mood to accord precedence to a horse, but something made him do so. In fact he pulled over and stopped. It was the rider he was looking at. It was her. Her that had his lighter. He got out of the van and fished frantically for the stub of a roll up he'd extinguished before entering the Golden Hind. He put it in his mouth and walked to meet the horse, slowly so as not to spook it. Darren was good with horses and as he took the bridle he asked the rider,

'May I have a light please?'

She had already recognised him and had not objected to his obstruction. Rather she welcomed it. This guy had never really left her thoughts in a tangential sort of way. Previous contact with him had stirred disquiet within her and now it was stirring again. She had to half stand in the stirrups to get her hand into her pocket. Her jeans were tucked into her riding boots and Darren watched, as her thighs flexed to support the weight of her torso, for the two seconds it took to retrieve the lighter. She managed to keep her decorum and remain silent, lofty both in position and demeanour.

'Thanks,' said Darren, nonchalantly as he spun the wheel of the Zippo with a flick of his thumb and fired up his dog end. It was as if there was nothing unusual about getting a light from a woman on horseback. He tossed the lighter back up to her and she caught it without taking her eye off of his; thank God for that she thought, I'm staying cool as a cucumber.

Darren turned his attention back to Gabriella who had snorted her disapproval of the puff of smoke that had just gone much too near her large nostrils.

'Sorry, my love, we smokers are so inconsiderate. Wait for a second.'

Darren turned and walked briskly to his van, leant in and brought out something in his hand. Katie was becoming nervous; must be going, she felt like saying, and would have under normal circumstances, but something told her that these circumstances were not normal, anything but. She was scared, a bit, but also mesmerised. Darren returned with an apple, a small Granny Smith which he gave to Gabby.

'There you are my pet, a token of apology and appreciation.'

The horse crunched once, the apple disappeared and Darren had a friend for life.

'Well Gabriella that was nice wasn't it?' Katie was surprised how well the words came out, considering that her esophagus felt very constricted. They were, after all, the first she had spoken to a human that day.

'Gabriella, perhaps you'd like to introduce me to the person sitting on your back, eh?' The horse eyed him for a second as if giving consideration to the request and then good naturedly biffed him the face with her wet nose. Darren dodged back failing to keep out of the way, laughing. Katie laughed too.

'Katie. Katie Pentreath. And what does D.P. stand for?'

Darren Pyke had to think for a split second before he realised where this came from, but ignored the question, simply replying,

'Darren. Darren Pyke.' He reached up his hand and they shook, quite formally.

'I'll let you go now.' He turned away, got into his van and was gone. Rather too abruptly she thought. No small talk. Not an inkling of depth, nothing to say 'there is more of me and I may see you around.' It was as if a portcullis had come down and the encounter had been terminated. A one-off occurrence with a beginning and an end, now wrapped up. Finished. That's what it was - 'as if' – but she knew without a doubt that reality was going to be very different. She finished her hack with Gabby and took the horse back to the field where they found Rosie sulking badly. The white horse (Gabby was chestnut) would not come to greet them at the gate and turned to face the hedge at the other end of the paddock. She couldn't see them so they couldn't see her. Katie laughed and Gabriella snorted haughtily, not having the wit to understand that it would be her turn to sulk tomorrow.

26. Heather sat opposite Reg Bull in the canteen at Bridport Police Station. It was just after 6pm and they had been driving around aimlessly for the best part of four hours. Their meal orders had gone in and the little tickets on the table in front of them had numbers on them which would be called out when the food was ready to be collected from the hatch. They had both ordered chicken curry and rice and they both knew it would be crap. Reg was railing his pupil with a war story about how he single handily wrested a BMW steering wheel from a would be salvager at the scene of some serious public order problems when a container ship got wrecked in Lyme Bay a few years previously. Heather laughed; she remembered seeing news coverage of this: 'Lyme Bay to eBay'. Then they were joined as a grey suited man sat down at the table and made it clear with his body language that he had important conversation to make. The grey suit was complimented by a pale cream shirt with cutaway collars, a dark green tie and silver cufflinks. The wearer was clean shaven with neat dark hair parted on the side. He sat at the end of the small table and leaned forward so that he was almost between Heather and Reg. He stared at Heather. She ignored this and kept looking at Reg, her head tilted a little in the direction of the interloper to prompt an introduction. Reg turned to the new man in Heather's life.

'Hello Tom.' He said cheerfully.

'Hello Reg', said the new man, without taking his eyes off Heather.

'This is Heather Boyle Tom, she's just....'

'Yes I know.' Still staring at her.

'Heather,' continued Reg, 'this is Detective Sergeant Tom Decker.'

Heather turned to Decker and held out her hand.

'Pleased to meet you Sergeant.' He looked at her outstretched palm for a second before taking it briefly. His eyes then returned to hers. His look was one of assessment; not very pleasant.

'Yes. And you. Gather you were nearly a detective in the Met,' this was flat but loaded.

'Well, I suppose so, but it's different there. Quicker pace of life.' She was not at all sure that she was getting this right. Reg was looking at her, interested as to how she was going to cope with this. Now then girl, let's see what you're like when things get a bit less pink and fluffy, he thought, slightly cruelly.

'Really?' asked Decker, one eyebrow rising. 'So you're finding it a bit slow here are you?'

'I knew you were going to say that. What I meant was that... er....'

'Why have you come here?' this was in a quieter tone, slightly menacing.

'Fancied a change,' a hardness tinged in Heather's tone and she held Decker's stare.

'What sort of change are you after? An easy life?'

'No, I want to get into the CID and deal with crime and criminals.'

'What, so you can't do that in uniform? You saying that Reg here doesn't knock villains off?'

'No. I'm not saying that at all. And Reg knows it,' she look at Reg who was nodding in supportive agreement and frowning at Decker.

'When I said I fancied a change I didn't mean work, I meant lifestyle. I was sick of living in shared accommodation in London, bedsits in Shepherds bush, hostels in Ealing. Here I can live with me Mum and have me cooking done for me, not to mention me washing.'

She was trying to take the edge off of the conversation by being chatty and Cockney and dependent on her mother. But Decker didn't soften. If anything his gaze hardened and didn't leave her as he rose. He closed his eyes briefly as he turned and walked away. He had not ordered any food or tea or coffee. He had simply popped in for some confrontation.

'What's his problem?' Heather shrugged her shoulders and showed her palms as she asked Reg this question. Reg's eyes were following Decker out of the canteen.

'I don't know Heather. That was bad, even for him, all I can say is he's got a lot on his plate. The DI here is fu… excuse me, bloody useless and Tom has to do the work. Almost all of the serious stuff gets shoved his way and the strain shows sometimes. No excuse for that though.'

'Oh, don't worry Reg. I expect suspicion. I'm a townie come down to the sticks to jump the queue.'

'Are you?'

'Yes Reg, I need to get into the CID. I was gutted the other day when the Deputy Chief Constable told me about the four year waiting list. That was the opposite of what I was told when I first applied to transfer to Dorset. "Oh yes, your career will pick up where it left off, don't worry, we acknowledge and recognise Met training courses etc. etc. etc.'

'Sounds like you were had over my girl.'

'Yeah, well, I'm not having it Reg….'

'Heather,' Reg leaned forward over the table, 'You've been here less than a week. Slow down. You are being talked about and people think you're pushy. You are going about things wrong. You need to speak to a friend of mine. He'll put you right. He's on the Joint Branch Board and he can give good advice.'

'What's the Joint Branch Board?'

'The Federation. The Police Federation of England and Wales. The Dorset Joint Branch Board is like the Dorset Force's branch of it. Don't tell me you never had any dealings with the Federation when you were in the Met.'

'I didn't. I knew they were sort of there, like, but, well, they were just a couple of old PCs with cushy jobs that they were given so they could do Federation stuff. Nobody took much notice of them.'

'Was there never any trouble at your nick? Nobody getting done for discipline offences?'

'Not really Reg. When anyone dropped in the shit there it was usually heavy criminal stuff and they usually went down at the Old Bailey. Not much point in disciplining a copper doing five years, he's automatically sacked.'

'Yeah, but there must be the ordinary stuff, assaults on detainees, Lady Muck not happy with her parking ticket saying that you'd been rude to her, just people complaining, you know... .'

'Yeah, you get all that sort of stuff but it never goes anywhere. Except for the card players, they're a pain.' She said this with a laugh.

'Card players? What do you mean?'

'Race card, pink card, sex card, green card, D card – that's disability, a new one. Cor, when they come in to complain the Inspector has his work cut out. D'you get that here?'

Reg was regarding Heather thoughtfully and listening to how she said things, rather than what she said. She had a way of categorising events, situations, people and groups. This was new to Reg. There really were not enough similar-fact occurrences or situations in Dorset to enable this sort of systematic thinking. Everything here was one off, unusual. Everything that happened, that was. Which wasn't much. This place is getting stranger by the day, thought Heather.

27. It was quarter past two in the morning when Darren Pyke coasted his

van down a country hill toward the Golden Hind. He let the vehicle roll to a stop as the road flattened out. He got out and closed the door ever so quietly. He had passed the pub silently and was about two hundred yards further down the road, actually towards Stockard. He was almost casual as he felt around at the roadside for a suitably sized rock. There was only a quarter moon and therefore very little light to work by. The pub was in complete darkness as he hurled a rock about the size of his own fist at the stained glass of the front window. It impacted with a crunch, not very loud but causing great damage to both the coloured panes and the lead retaining latticework. He waited for some reaction. Nothing, nobody had woken. Let's have another one then. One for the road, so to speak. The second rock hit the larger pane in the door and this time there was a lot of noise. A dog at a local farm started to bark and the lights upstairs in the pub came on. Darren sprinted to the van, started it up (holding his breath) – sometimes it didn't fire the first time - and was gone as Billy Nodwell ran barefoot out into the road trying to get sight of the number plate between the receding taillights. He didn't succeed but managed to establish that the lights belonged to a van.

About seven minutes later Darren was in Stockard. He was not stupid and did not take the van home, parking it up instead three streets away from the Pyke house. From there the remainder of his journey took him through a back alley and along a service road to a gap in the fence at the bottom of their trash filled garden. Then it was up on the utility room roof and in through his bedroom window. He had never even been out that night.

28. Katie got home from the horses and sat down with her books. Her parents were still out and she had the house to herself. Apart from Musbury the cat who began wrapping himself around her legs, purring loudly. She did not have much time for Musbury and put him into the farm yard. Stupid animal, catch some mice, work for your keep. Back inside she turned a few pages and managed to settle into some anatomy. She had a number of assignments to accomplish over the holidays and

one involved a comparative study of the reproductive systems of primates as compared to the bovine species. Within a few minutes she was well into it, surprising herself by the ease with which she overcame her initial reluctance to get started. Primates v Bovines. Humans v Horses. Reproductive systems. Organs. Fucking. Not thoughts, these, more like hormonal undertones. Movements. She read and made notes on her laptop. Or tried to; it was playing up and she needed a new one. They were coming in at about £400 at the time and she didn't have the money. It was a bit of a problem as she knew that, as always with small farmers, her parents were struggling. So she pecked away at the keyboard, backing up onto a data stick every few sentences, ever fearful of a crash and loss.

She heard the front door go and a cheerful 'Helloo' from her mum. 'Helloo' she echoed and rushed at another sentence before going downstairs.

Sally Pentreath was unloading organic food into the larder, which was already quite full.

'Mum, anybody would think we lived in the middle of London and that there was going to be a nuclear attack tomorrow.'

'Taking advantage of cut price stuff dear. It's called financial planning.'

Katie detected an edge to her mother's voice and didn't like it. What the fuck had she done wrong now?

'Everything okay, mum?' Cheerfully, hopefully.

'Yes.' Tersely.

'Good.' Sarcastically. 'Glad to hear it.'

Katie went back to her room. She really couldn't be arsed with her mother's moods just now. She had a shed-load of work to do, finals in less than a year, an arsehole for a boyfriend, two demanding horses. And yes, this other bit of nonsense that she did not want to think about.

29. The Chief Constable started the day as she always did. 6.40 and she was at her desk. The cleaners had just left and she didn't expect her first staff to be in for another hour or so. Time to get on with some work. In the top of her tray was a fax from the Home Office. She dreaded these and there was only one theme – cut back on spending. Her PA had deliberately scheduled her sight of this so that it would be on top of the pile first thing in the morning, when no-one else was in the building. The Chief Constable read it quickly and then had to read it again. It was worse than ever. An 18% reduction in overtime expenditure was necessary to keep financial targets in sight for the next three months. They must be fucking joking, she thought, this is Dorset, not fucking Derbyshire. Half the country tips down here during August and these are family people, the backbone of the country, taxpayers who can't afford to go abroad, they're entitled to their holidays and they're entitled to a police service whilst they're having them.

Joanne Bache had risen pretty rapidly up through the ranks. Unusually, she had begun her police life in the north on Merseyside, before moving for the almost mandatory period in the Met where she reached the rank of Commander. She was one of the first woman Chiefs to have taken a Force without having had a Deputy Chief's job elsewhere and this was an achievement. Something else was unusual, very unusual, about her; she had not always been a woman. Joanne Bache, since her early promotion to sergeant and thereafter, had always been the highest ranking transgender police officer in the country. Probably, she occasionally reflected, in the world. The subject was widely known but never discussed. She was single and lived alone. She did nothing but work and drank nothing but water. She was rarely seen socially other than at formal functions where her presence was mandatory and where she wore uniform. In fact, few could remember ever having seen her out of uniform. But anyway, all this did not solve the more serious problem of how she was going to police one of the busiest coastlines in the country with a handful of cops and no overtime budget to speak of. Already some parts of the county relied on Specials, unpaid reservists, to uphold the law. She wanted them to stay in the rural areas to deal with the hillbillies. Police Community Support Officers were a pain in the arse and she refused to deploy them in Lyme or Bridport. They were there to walk around shopping centres in pairs with their thumbs up their arses pretending to be coppers. Most of them were PCSOs because they were too thick to be coppers or Specials, the latter being properly trained with full powers, and some of them were in the job so they could get up to mischief, the Chief was sure of that. So it would be down to stretching the already over-stretched Bridport and Lyme Divisions even further, and have them keep an eye on the Triangle.

Dorset, she had understood for a long time, was a strange place – just like the rest of rural England. All very picturesque on the surface with chirruping hedgerows, wheeling buzzards, cheerful farmers with Tweed jackets and rosy cheeks. Yes, all very twee. But beneath this – a horrible, horrible underbelly. Agricultural life did not pay and was highly competitive and the farmers hated each other. Locals who had lived in the region for generations couldn't buy their own houses because of the Incomers – people moving to the county from London and buying up the cottages and converting the barns, forcing prices skywards. They were hated but they were growing in number. About 50% of west Dorset is populated by Incomers. Then there are the Overspillers. They are incomers also but of a different kind. Cheap land around the small town had been purchased by local authorities who sold on at a big profit to the metropolitan authorities – Bristol, Cardiff, London, Manchester even, and some of the dregs of their troublesome populations had been moved into Dorset. Thanks a bunch. The Southlands estate in Stockard was one of those developments, but at least the Pyke family were 'proper Dorset people,' even if their behaviour was anything but proper.

This underbelly fascinated the Chief. She could identify with it, she being proof in human living form that all was not necessarily how it seemed. This insight helped the Chief.

30. Emmett Everett returned from his hunting trip thoroughly disgruntled and empty handed. He had put three more mixxy rabbits out of their misery and had left the corpses for the flies and crows. Even the foxes

could have a feast. The disease only attacked rabbits. As Emmett walked up the hill to the house he saw the white van at the road side and knew that Darren Pyke would be waiting at the other side of the high gate. He was right and the two greeted one another with simultaneous alright's. Emmett knew that Darren was after something, otherwise he would not be there. So the green haired lad let in the black haired young man and they both went into the steaming Everett kitchen where the huge Aga stove belted out an unbearable heat and the smell of drying laundry mixed with the steam of boiling vegetables. Mrs. Everett was busy with her chores, the old man was nowhere to be seen, tending the horses probably, and Emmett's rarely seen and probably unregistered siblings would be up to various rural unpleasantries, such as snaring rabbits or poaching fish.

The two young men sat down and faced each other. Darren had bullied Emmett at school, a fact that created an unbreakable barrier between them and Darren knew that he would never be forgiven. On the other hand Emmet got on well with Wayne and Joe, Darren's two younger brothers, and was civil for their sakes if nothing else. And there would in any case be something else. This meeting was to be about business. No doubt. And Darren would be seeking some sort of service for which payment would be made. Probably late, but made all the same.

'I need to pick up a horse from Bristol Emmett, any chance of the use of a box?'

'When?'

'Next week. Josh has a pony to deliver to an Incomer girl down on the coast. He did the deal yesterday, got half of the money and her dad wants to see something on four legs in their little posh paddock. I'll only be gone three or four hours.'

Emmett was not stupid. What the Pyke brothers knew about horses you could put in a frog's ear.

'No problem Darren. Are you going to tow it?'

'Yeah, course, and tie-on plates.'

'Didn't know you were into horses Daz.'

'There you go then Emmett, have to diversify to progress, don't you.'

'Eh?'

'Don't matter. I'll give you a bell when I decide when we're going, okay.'

'Okay Daz, whatever.'

31. Detective Inspector Kevin Packington had 29 years in the job, all of it in Dorset. He had seen a lot of changes and most of them he did not like. In fact all of them he did not like. If he had been under any compulsion to be honest with himself he would have conceded that actually the only real change that had taken place was that he had got old – and nobody really likes that one. His kids had long since flown the nest and he lived with his wife in a nice part of Dorchester. They argued about what they were going to do when he retired the following year. She wanted to move down to the coast; he wanted to go and live in Spain or France or somewhere away from fucking Dorset and its holiday makers and rain and all the people who would always regard him as a copper, retired on not.

As he set off from the main County CID office at Force HQ he contemplated the day ahead of him. His basic rule was to don his Coke-bottle shoulders and dodge everything that came his way. Bridport would be the first stop, then a pint or two in Charmouth, then to Lyme where he sort of half looked forward to meeting a new WPC, the transfer from the Met who he had been told was quite tasty. She had been making noises apparently about getting into the CID and the Dep was keen that her 'expectations should be managed'. Meeting her, he anticipated, would be the highlight of his day, the rest would be shit as usual. Having done a flying visit to the small CID office in Bridport, showing face in the right places, he drove to Charmouth for a beer in the Skittle, a recently refurbished nightmare trying to attract holiday makers from the more fashionable Lyme a mile along the coast. He introduced himself to the young couple in charge, noting that the pub was empty and that they had probably mortgaged everything they owned to realise their dream of being in charge of what was promised by the company to be an overnight gold mine. Poor sods, he thought. They would be skint after one summer and next year the place would be gobbling up the equity of another pair of suckers. He wished them luck, gave them his business card and headed for Lyme and the Goat. He was pleased to get there. Having parked up out of sight he went in and ordered a pint and steak and chips. Debbie did good grub and he would have some peace to think about the flea he had had in his ear at HQ that morning. It had been Sherrell, the Force Detective Chief Inspector, harping on about the Chief and her obsession with finance. Packington did not like Sherrell who he considered an ambitious arselicker. The twat never missed a Chief's meeting. What proper CID officer likes going to Chief's meetings? Anyway, the word was that they had to cut back on overtime over the summer.

That was all very well for the woodentops, as Packington called the uniformed branch. They could just swear in more Specials or cancel leave applications and bus a few extra helmets down from Crewkerne to the coast on a weekend. And anyway, if the uniform couldn't deal with things the crime rate went up and who was left to mop up the mess? Yes, that's right, the CID. The lazy drunken CID who never did fuck all and dressed how they liked and got Christmas hampers and bribes and had loads of time to shoot and play golf and shag.... Packington's thoughts became venomous and he pulled himself up before he 'went into one', as he called his frequent descent into black moods.

Then he had an idea. He was fairly chummy with this new bird's 'parent PC', Reg 'Red' Bull. He took out his phone, dialled Lyme and asked to be patched through to Red.

'Red? Kevin Packington.'

'Hello Guv, how are you?'

'Fine Red. You got this new kid with you?'

'Yeah, she's here alright, keeping me on my toes.'

Reg and Heather were walking along the seafront and had been talking about the burgeoning drugs and punch-up problem on the coastline.

'Bring her up to the Goat, will you. I'll buy the pair of you a drink. I need to talk to her.'

Reg's heart sank. He did not need this. He was trying to knock the booze on the head for a month or two and knew where this would lead.

'Okay Guv, be there in ten.'

'Fine, Red, see you.' The DI hung up and ordered another pint.

'We're going drinking on duty now Heather. Do much of that in the Met?'

'No, I did not. Where are we going and who's this 'guv'?'

'We're going for a quick one with Detective Inspector Packington. There is a CID office in Lyme but he has his own annexe to it. It's called the Goat. Been there?'

'Yes, once, bit of a shit-hole isn't it?'

'Yeah, but it's out of the way. Here.' He handed her a tightly rolled up plastic shopping bag. 'Put your epaulettes and hat in this just before we go in.'

They approached the pub from the back and through the carpark. Reg noted that Packington had driven and wondered if he would continue to get away with motoring around the county pissed until he retired. He had seen many a cop get the automatic bullet for drink driving when they were on the point of picking up their pension. That way they lost 50% of it, for the sake of a few beers.

'Hello Guv, this is Heather Boyle, joined the County a couple of weeks ago.'

Packington was immediately unimpressed and didn't get up. He eyed Heather up and down and extended his hand, which she took, briefly. Yeah, she was good enough looking he supposed, but there was something about her; hostile.

And she knew that was the impression she had given. She regretted this but could not help it. She had always exuded her feelings, had Heather, always. Out of the pores of her skin. And at that point in time she felt that she had made a great mistake, coming to this shit-kicking county. Meeting the DI in the pub. What a joke. They had done that stuff in the Met in the 70s, she thought.

Packington gave Reg some money and sent him to the bar for the drinks. Heather had an orange juice and her mentor had a pint of bitter. The DI had a double scotch. They all sat around the small table.

'So Heather, you want to get into the Department I'm told.'

She was taken aback slightly; word had travelled fast, she must have made an impression with the Dep, and probably not a very good one.

'Yes sir, that's right. As soon as possible.'

The 'sir' was not obsequious, just formal.

'I expect you've been told there's a bit of a queue.'

'Yeah, about four years long.'

'Yes, that would be one way of looking at it, four years to make substantive detective constable, but there are other investigative jobs on the go where you don't have to dress like a muppet and eat out of Tupperware in closed-up canteens.'

Reg had to get his oar in. 'Mr. Packington thinks we're just a bunch of uniform carriers; forget about all the time we spend grafting whilst

Dorset's finest detectives are on the piss.'

Packington ignored this, not taking his eyes off Heather, trying to gauge her, work out why he was not enjoying this experience.

'What jobs are those, sir?'

'The main one is domestic violence. We have a unit up in Crewkerne with big problems. I need someone there with investigative experience. I've seen your record. You just may fit the bill.'

She was hooked and her guard nearly fell.

'That's bri...' then, checking herself, 'that sounds interesting sir.'

Reg stared at the carpet. He wouldn't have minded a go at that. But he was a bloke and too old, just serving his time. Reg just occasionally allowed himself a bit of bitterness; well, quite often really.

Packington continued, 'I've got to be honest with you, you won't get much help and, er, there's no overtime,' as he said this he looked at Reg whose attention had been refocused all of a sudden.

'That's right Reg, applies to everyone now, overtime is just for emergencies this summer. I'll be putting a memo out on it later.'

Reg stared at Packington. Bloody typical, wasn't it. He who did fuck all was telling the workers of the county that they were going to be short of money. Cops lived for their overtime. It made a poor pay reasonable. Every police force in the country had trouble with its overtime budget because officers were always trying to work longer hours to secure a better wage. It was very difficult to stop. A Bobby may be coming to the end of an eight hour shift when, hey, he remembers that guy in so-and-so street that needs to be spoken to about a suspected theft of a car radio; well, whadaya know, there he is in his garden. Come to the nick for tea and chat my son, don't worry, we'll bail you out later pending further enquiries but in the meantime I got meself two hours at time-and-a-third.

'When do I start?' Reg heard Heather ask. All of a sudden it felt like he wasn't there, so he got up and went to the bar and bought a round that included a pint and a large scotch for himself - which he quickly sank before carrying his pint and another large scotch for the DI and Heather's drink back to the table. He would leave the car in the nick car park and get a bus tonight. He'd worked hard. He deserved it. Anyway, the world wasn't about the likes of him anymore. So what the hell.

'As soon as I can get you off of shift work and into the office. You did enough investigative work in London so you won't have to be mentored. The problem is that because of the overtime famine you may have to wear two hats. Like a few hours down here with old Reg in his panda car and then up to Crewkerne to look at a bit of wife beating or child abuse.'

'Your joking,' intervened Reg, 'you can't expect her to do domestic violence part-time.'

'Who asked you Reg? You try running this division on jack shit money.'

Reg held his tongue. He was actually a little surprised and quite pleased with himself that he'd had a pop at the DI.

Packington and Heather talked about crime in the county and the differences from London. Reg sulked and formed the intention to get drunk. Packington saw that the old man had no intention of leaving the pub so he took Heather to Lyme police station in his private car. She continued to carry her detachable epaulettes and hat in the plastic bag. As Packington pulled into the back of Lyme police station and parked alongside Reg's old Ford Focus she thought of the kind, middle aged man who had showed her round the county for that last two weeks. She felt guilty that she'd just dumped him in the pub but, well, it seemed that it was meant to happen like this. She was with the DI for God's sake, and she would get help from him, a leg up on the ladder if she managed the situation carefully. She just hoped he didn't have plans to do anything with his leg - that was all.

As the pair walked in through the back door Tom Decker was walking down the stairs.

'Afternoon Tom,' said Packington, over-cheerfully. A bit sarcastically, it struck Heather.

'Guvnor.' Mumbled Decker, without even looking up. Packington snorted. The smell of roasting martyr, he thought. There's the guy with the world on his shoulders, the guy who has to do everything, who works for no extra payment at the weekends, the bleeding heart. Wanker, thought Packington. Let him get on with it. Heather noted how Decker had not met the DI's eyes. A bit unlike the bullying stare he'd dished out to her the other day. The DI parted company from her and went upstairs to the administrative offices. He told her he'd ring her. He'd get her number from her personnel file. Heather betted he would.

It was a shade before 3pm and the early shift for the uniformed branch was coming to an end. The troops were drifting in to return their radios and CS gas and book off. Heather got a couple of old fashioned looks from her shift colleagues who'd seen her come back with the DI, minus Reg.

'Where's PC Bull?' asked Wally Driscoll the station sergeant, a normally relaxed and informal West Country man in his forties.

Heather did not know what to say, but she met the supervisor's eye and arched her eyebrows as if to say, 'Don't put me on the spot sarge, he's got a mobile phone.'

Driscoll nodded at these unspoken words and turned away, smiling slightly. Heather changed into her civvies and headed home to Dorchester. Reg propped up the bar in the Goat. The early evening bar flies had begun to gather and he found himself sadly enjoying their undemanding company as he deteriorated into drunkenness. He would catch the bus back home to Axminster later. Tell his wife an old mate had died, or something.

32. It was Rosie's turn to hack and Gabby's turn to be consumed with jealousy. Katie rode the little grey horse along the bank of the river Lyme

and up towards the viaduct at Uplyme. From there she would get across the A35 – always a nerve racking exercise on horseback – and head towards Brucklands Ridge. She'd just managed to get the wide-eyed Rosie over the main road when she saw the white van with the horsebox in tow. It was heading towards her and she momentarily considered flight. So, that was how it felt, she thought, fight or flight. How exciting. Darren pulled up with his tattooed elbow out of the window and a knowing smile on his face.

'Don't worry, I'm not going to say it.'

'Say what,' she asked, reasonably.

'Say, "We've got to stop meeting like this",' he said.

'Okay. I won't say it either then.'

'What, "We've got to stop meeting like this"?'

'No, you just did.'

'Eh?'

'Doesn't matter.'

He looked confused and the smile had gone. His expression was now not altogether a pleasant one and a little eel in her stomach shot under its rock. Fear. He had frightened her and this she found exciting.

'Have you got a horse in there?' she nodded at the box.

'Not at the minute.' He started to roll a cigarette.

'Oh. Right. Fine.'

'Why? You want me to put one of yours on board. I could get a good price.'

'No thanks.' She stood in the stirrups and fumbled for the lighter. He looked at her thighs. She tossed him the lighter.

He lit his roll-up, snapped the lighter shut and tossed it back to her. She caught it. Expertly, now.

He gunned the engine of the big van and disappeared flashing a very friendly smile, smoke pouring out of his nostrils. The horsebox bounced along in tow, obviously empty.

Was she being stalked by this man who warmed her bowels, made her nervous? She knew there was something there but couldn't define it. She was a heterosexual woman with a short but healthy sexual CV. She was also a bright young woman who valued above all else her independence and success in a world where the female of the species was taking an increasingly leading role in the professions. She did not like that a cross between a country yokel and white van man was scaring her with his smiles. She took Rosie for the remainder of the hack before reuniting her with the sulking Gabriella. Then she went home and hurled herself at her books. Biochemistry. Anatomy. Virology. That was her favourite, virology. She was fascinated by the fact that no-one had ever really worked out what a virus was. They still argued whether it was animal, vegetable or mineral. She was fascinated how something that could be so devastating was so small. She read once that putting a virus on a single skin cell was like putting a pea on a football pitch. Beyond comprehension. There was so much in the everyday world that was simply beyond comprehension. Her father had once told Katie that, although a committed Christian, he actually had a measure of sympathy for Buddhism. This was because, he said, Buddhists did not try to pigeon-hole their God, give him sons or human wives or attribute miraculous events to his hand. Buddha said, according to her father, that God could not be understood so there was no point in trying. That had helped Katie get through her adolescence. Don't beat yourself up if you don't understand something because some things happen for reasons that have no obligation to make themselves known. Perhaps not even for a thousand years.

33. Decker was wary of Packington. The drunken old DI had, after all,

been round the block a couple of times and knew everyone in Dorset worth knowing. Decker had a paranoia about Freemasons and firmly believed that Packington was a member of the Brotherhood. As it happens, he wasn't, but he knew Decker suspected him of it and this caused him amusement. Stupid man. Good copper – not great, they didn't have to work so hard – but good. But a stupid man all the same. Packington was amused by the fact that Decker thought that by taking the world (Dorset) on his shoulders and signing for all the enquiries and being seen at Dorchester Crown Court every other week, and clearing up a lot of the burglaries and assaults - he was going to get promoted. Bollocks. True, he had passed the inspectors exam over two years previously, but, like everything else in county-mounty land, there was a queue. Decker had already been pipped at the post by office-bound tossers for a number of DI postings and was getting bitterer and bitterer.

Disappointingly, he tended to take it out on his underlings. Not that there were many of them. He had two DCs at Bridport and three at Lyme over the summer. And these staffing levels dropped during the closed season. One of his Lyme DCs was a young man called Stuart Townsend. He had been a uniform PC for the statutory two years before being posted to the crime squad in Bournemouth. Now that was a busy place in the summer, and all year round really. The city of Bournemouth, with its rich middle class, university, thriving commercial area and the highest aging population in the country, provided rich pickings for all forms of criminal life. From fraudsmen to muggers; from deluded bogus doctors to sex attackers who were turned on by wrinkles. A myriad of sociopaths operated in the lovely city of Bournemouth. Townsend had trained well there and had learned a lot. A happy sort of guy he was not bored in Lyme though and his imagination kept him going as he pondered the mysteries of the Triangle. An avid reader of intelligence material, he was fascinated by second, third and fourth grade (the latter often bordering on the realms of fantasy) reports that there was some very serious goings-on in the deepest sticks. And now there was a new bird on the block. Heather Boyle. Transfer from the Met. He couldn't wait to meet her. Maybe she had some ideas and contacts that could be of use. He'd heard she'd been on a crime squad and was hungry for CID work. Good news.

Not just another fucking traffic cop then. Good news.

Decker walked into the Lyme CID office as Townsend was printing off some crime reports from the computer database.

'Much in overnight Stu?'

'Yep, usual shit, all crap, all urgent. I'll take four attempted thefts from motor vehicles, two burglaries in Stockard and a domestic in Charmouth.'

'Domestic?'

'Yeah, the Lashley family. Old man's come in pissed and given one of the girls a good walloping. Fucking inbred shit they are. I'll get it….'

'Give it to the new girl. Packington's putting her on the DVU at Crewkerne, so she needs the practice. She's on earlies, old Reg Bull can drop her over there.'

'Fine by me.' Stuart was pleased in that it was one less job for him, one less tedious job into the bargain. But then, thinking about it, he would have quite liked to have escorted the budding detective to her first investigation in the county.

'Yeah, fine…' Pause. 'Just a suggestion sarge, but would it not be easier for me to drop her there. Leave Reg to his mooching around the harbour at this time in the morning. The traders'll moan if they don't have uniform presence at delivery time.'

Decker regarded Stuart Townsend suspiciously. 'Yeah okay then, but I don't want you giving her one.'

'If I do it'll be your fault sarge, putting ideas into my young impressionable head. And you a supervisor an' all.'

Decker grunted and walked out. He could not help but like Stuart Townsend. Actually envied his cheeriness. Also he was the only DC he could trust to do the work properly. He let him have a reasonable share of it; the rest he did himself. He had already taken most of the overnight stuff from a terminal in the intelligence office and had a busy day ahead of him. Bournemouth had been on the phone first thing. A team of Scousers was taking the place apart and the word was that they were on their way west to Torquay on the Devon coast but that they were going to stop off for a couple of nights at a campsite between Charmouth and Lyme. Decker hated Scousers, they were the bain of the south coast. Clever and ruthless thieves, this lot would send the crime figures skywards in 24 hours before moving on. He pocketed his printouts, got into his car and headed for the named campsite.

34. Sally Pentreath got home at lunchtime to find her daughter immersed in her studies. Books were spread out all over the big farmhouse kitchen table and the smell of fresh coffee and toast – the staple diet of the English undergraduate – was very welcoming.

'Wow, coffee 'n' toast. Can I have some?'

'Course.'

'I'll get my own then.' This followed a brief pause as Sally experienced a tinge of disappointment that her daughter had not got up and offered help. Either with carrying in the shopping her mother had just lugged from the Land Rover, or to actually put a fresh pot on and fresh slices in.

'Sorry. Mum, just getting to a good bit.' This was true, to be honest. Third year virology is not a subject you can study whilst multitasking in the kitchen.

'Katie.' Uh-oh, there was something coming up here, Katie could tell by the tone.

'Mum?'

'You're not thinking of selling one of the horses are you?'

'What?!' She was incensed, 'No! Why?'

Sally backed off, showing her palms, hands up. 'Okay, okay, just asking. He must have been winding me up.'

'Who must have been winding you up?'

'Lad in a white van with a horsebox on the back of it. He was stopped at the paddock just now, looking at the horse. I pulled over to ask him if I could help, you know, and he just smiled, said that Rosie and Gabby were worth a lot of money and would we be interested. He was pleasant enough, charming really, so I just said no and he doffed his cap, and left. Just wondered if you'd said anything. D'you know this boy?'

Katie had started to shake a little.

'Yes, I know him. His name is Darren and I keep bumping into him.'

'What's the matter, are you okay? Is he giving you any bother?' her mother had started to walk towards her, seeing that something was not quite right.

'Everything's fine mum, He's okay, must live locally, I just keep seeing him on the roads, that's all.'

'He's doesn't live locally Katie, otherwise I would know him. He'll come from Stockard or Chard I bet. White van and horsebox, I ask you. You make sure you chain that gate on the paddock before he has Rosie an' Gabby off whether you like it or not.' With that her mother was gone, coffee and toast forgotten. She had sensed something she didn't like. Mums are like that.

That was virology out the window then. Katie Pentreath slumped down in the chair and realised that, in fact, virology had really been struggling to survive all morning with 50% of her mind churning away on the much more challenging subject of Darren Pyke, or DP as she had named him in her imagination. She decided that she was going to go out for a drink that evening, by herself, clear her mind, hopefully bump into… a few old… friends… and stop thinking about….

35. Darren was in the Nags Head in Stockard drinking Stella Artois and playing pool.

'Harry fucking Redknapp? Back at the Saints? You must be fucking joking mate! He's a traitorous bastard, that's what he is. A total cunt. We wouldn't 'ave him back, he'll slip us again, we'd go down, an' you fuckin' know it mate….'

Darren was trying to concentrate on a difficult cushion shot and this loudmouth football bore was distracting him. Every time he pulled to que back to strike the voice would let out a loud 'fuck' or 'cunt', often one after the other. Darren straightened up and let the cue fall from his hand. It made a loud clatter as it hit the wooden floorboards. He turned slowly to face the cause of his annoyance. The cause, a big man called Eddie Tooks, stopped talking, but held Darren's gaze, cocking his head to one side as if to say: "Yes? Problem?"

'Yes? Problem?' said Tooks.

'There will be, if you don't shut the fuck up while I take my shot.'

There was a bit of nervous laughter from the assembled afternoon pond life, but not from Tooks.

'Oh, is that right now Darren? Is that right?'

'Yes it fucking is Tooksie.'

'Well, best we take a little walk outside Pykey me boy.' Silence in the bar as Tooks slid off his barstool and theatrically beckoned Darren to the door before opening it to step out. He made the mistake of turning his back for a full second.

Eddie Tooks's head hit the door frame and was held there by Darren's forearm with such force that he roared and vomited simultaneously. Blood spurted from Tooks's eyebrow as it opened against the hard wooden edge and mixed with the spew that now ran viscously down the yellow painted woodwork. And Darren held him there. And the silent pub watched as he turned his head to challenge anyone to intervene. No movement for another three full seconds. Darren pulled Tooks off the door frame and swung him round into the bar as hard as he could. As he let go he put his foot out and the big man went flying headlong across the floor, clutching his eye and whimpering like a puppy.

Darren picked up his queue and quickly took the long awaited shot. Not only did he miss but also managed to put the black ball into the centre pocket, thereby losing the game. All he did was look down and blush and say 'Shit'. One of Tooks's mates helped him up and towards the door which was now being held open by someone else. As he left he turned and spoke, slurring and unfocused, in Darren's direction.

'I'm reporting this Pykey. I'm 'aving you nicked you scum.'

Darren looked up from his embarrassment, as if somehow surprised by this return to a settled matter.

'Fine.' He said, quietly and offhandedly as he turned back to the table, shaking his head in dismay at the blundered shot that had cost him the game.

'Want another one Daz?' asked his opponent, Barry Palmer, himself keen to get the afternoon back on track, put this unpleasant event behind them.

'Yeah,' said Darren, politely, 'unless there's anyone else who wants a game, in which case you stay on the table Barry.'

They looked around. Silence. Everyone was looking at Darren, everyone was thinking how the fuck he did that: one second a psychopath, the next a sweet honey pie. Then the barmaid put a record on the jukebox, a freebee from behind the counter. The rumble of barroom conversation stuttered with a few false starts before regaining its rhythm. Darren and Barry played another frame which Darren won before saying a quick cheerio to anyone and everyone and making a low key exit to let them talk about him freely.

He left the van in the Nag's Head car park and walked the half mile or so home. Too many Stellas to drive and the Old Bill were probably taking a statement from that fucker Tooks by now and would no doubt be round looking for him before the day was out. More shit. More shit in a shitty, horrible, pointless fucking life. He supposed he could pop in and see Maxine for a while, give her one. But then her mother would be pissed by now and wanting a portion as well. He kept quiet about that little relationship, did our Darren. Other blokes in Stockard would brag about that, shagging a bird and her mother at the same time. But Darren was different. He kept quiet about it, sensed there was perhaps a moral issue lurking there, sensed that it perhaps wasn't quite the full ticket. He was quite proud of that; knowing that it was wrong, knowing that he should be setting his sights a bit higher. He reckoned that his shame put him above the other people in his life. Anyway, he just went home, made himself a fry-up and waited for the police.

36. 'Get your uniform off.'

'I beg your pardon.'

'You heard, get your uniform off.'

PC Heather Boyle regarded this detective with immediate interest. She had just been told to go to the CID office and see DC Townsend about an enquiry. She had been pleased to oblige and had experienced a tingle of excitement as she'd climbed the stairs to the first floor.

'DC Townsend, I presume.'

'If you take your uniform off you can call me Stuart.'

'In that case I'll stick to DC Townsend.' She was used to this sort of banter. Loved it.

'Okay, you got me. They want you to do a little job in Charmouth, a domestic violence case. I'm going to Bridport so I'll drop you over. You need to change into civvies though, you might have to sit in a shit-hole taking a long statement for a while.'

'Sure, fine, but I've only got jeans and a tee-shirt.'

'Could be a problem - you'll be overdressed where you're going.'

'I can't wait. Tell me more.'

Stuart got up and put his jacket on, fishing amongst the chaos on his desk for the keys to the CID car.

'The Lashley family, housebound diddycoys, old man's always duffing up his wife and daughters. He's in Bridport cells just now, the night duty nicked him. What you got to do is take a statement from the old woman and one of the daughters.'

'Fine. That's great.' She didn't really mean this; she'd never done DV before and thought it was always just a uniform matter, not detective work. She didn't know the first thing about it other than in the Met it was high profile, politically correct, and attracted a lot of funds and overtime. She wanted to make an impression though, so acted keen and tenacious and diligent and all the things that it said on her transfer CV.

37. 'I've given that new girl at Lyme something to do Guv, Domestic Violence Unit.'

It was ten o'clock the following morning and Kevin Packington was at HQ speaking to the Force Detective Chief Inspector Robin Sherrell. Sherrell looked up from his mountainous desk – he doubled up as the Chief Constable's Staff Officer – and frowned.

'But that's in Crewkerne is it not? How's she going to get from Lyme to Crewkerne every day?'

'She won't have to Guv, she can do it from the Lyme terminal, just pop up to Crewkerne twice a week or so to check the paperwork. There's a couple of uniforms up there all the time anyway, dealing with the Stockard pond life. Most of it's routine, our bright little transferee from the Met can take care of the interesting stuff.'

Sherrell seemed pleased and nodded his approval.

'Good. Should keep her quiet.'

He'd heard about what Met transferees could do in the sticks. He had a mate who was Superintendent in the Avon and Somerset force next door. He'd had a Met transfer go through them like a dose of salts. He had been a male of mixed race and had taken the force to the Employment Tribunal on grounds of racial discrimination when he didn't get his own way. And he'd won, causing all sorts of shit to hit the fan.

Packington was shuffling out of the door when Sherrell's head came up from the paperwork again and, without turning, said,

'I'm sitting with the Chief on a discipline board this afternoon, can you watch my desk for couple of hours Kevin?' It wasn't really a question.

Packington's heart sank. What the fuck were all those tossers at Bournemouth doing, why was it always the west of the county that got the shit jobs and the low funds. Always. Cross, Packington decided to have a pop.

'Guvnor, with all due respect,' at this Sherrell turned round to face him, Packington continued, 'I'm running round like a blue arsed fly to keep the west policed, I've got a team of scousers just descended on Lyme, I need to be there. Can't you get somebody from Poole or Bournemouth? I need to get back to my manor.'

Sherrell looked at the older man and considered this.

'No Kevin. And do you know why? Because it's one of your stupid helmets that's causing the discipline hearing in the first place. Your bloody PC Norman Hogg, Federation bloody agitator, he's the one insisting that this full hearing takes place. Insisting on a PC pleading not guilty to an honesty and integrity charge after being caught fucking shoplifting!'

'That's not my fault! I know Hoggy and he wouldn't be doing this for fun. I've heard about it and the Federation case is that the PC, what's his name, Cozens, has got mental issues, so he's entitled to contest it, maybe he needs help, not the sack....'

'Yes, yes, alright Kev, I know, but these hearings are such a waste of time and put the Chief in a right mood, and I've got to work with her.'

Packington calmed down. 'Old Norman Hogg loves it, doesn't he? Getting the Chief riled up. He does it for sport. Okay, I'll be back this afternoon to sit in your hot seat. Don't leave me any shit to deal with though Guv.'

They both laughed and Packington left for breakfast in the HQ canteen.

38. Heather was having breakfast in the tiny canteen at Lyme police station. Not that they got anything cooked there, they had to bring their own food in. She had bought a pasty from the shop around the corner and was sitting nibbling away as she wrote up some notes of her encounter with the Lashley girls the previous day. They, that's mum and daughter, had both given lengthy statements about how the old man had come in pissed and given them a slapping and how they wanted to be re-housed and given police protection. They want to move out of Charmouth and into Lyme. But then most people who lived in Charmouth wanted to move to Lyme. Heather had made a meal of it and had looked up all sorts of things on the Force intranet about how domestic violence victims had to be treated and how she had to involve the social services etc., etc. She didn't really like herself for behaving like this, conjuring up a little empire, making a nothing job into something more than what it was, but she had her career to think about.

There were two other officers in the room, at the far side, talking in low voices. One she had never seen before, he looked dreadful, thin and pale.

The other she had seen around the station but had not been introduced. She got the impression he was somebody of some influence though. Then Stuart Townsend walked in; he acknowledged the older PC with obvious and genuine pleasure,

'Hey, Groundhog, mornin' to you! What are you up...?'

At then he stopped, Norman Hogg looked up from his deep conversation and shook his head at Stuart, as if to say: "Not now, mate".

'Oh, sorry mate, I'll catch you later.' He was pleased to shrink into a chair opposite Heather.

'How'd it go then? Charged the old man yet? Attempted murder?'

'Don't take the piss Stu, it's a serious matter, domestic violence. Got to be done properly.' She half smiled as she said this, letting him know that she was not all that serious. He smiled back, knowingly.

'I've had the good sergeant Decker at me this morning. Some nastiness up Stockard way. We'll have a look-see and I can take you to Crewkerne after that, introduce you to your DV colleagues.

Heather had already seen the collator's resume, noting that the name Darren Pyke seemed to be synonymous with a mini crime wave over the last couple of days. Smashed window of the Golden Hind and a bashed bumpkin in the Nags Head. Was this guy expecting a visit?

Stuart went on. 'There's a family in Stockard – I'm sure you've heard of them by now – well into everything. Had SOCA down here asking questions about them a couple of months ago – that's the Serious and Organised Crime....'

'Yeah Stuart, I know what SOCA is.'

'Yeah, well, they don't come here often, and we're sort of proud of the family in question....'

'The Pykes,'

'That's them, we're... well, they're a pain in the arse, especially Darren but, hey, they're ours. Good old Dorset boys. Put us on the map a bit.'

'Sounds like you're mates with them.'

'Not really but, you know, takes a thief to catch a thief and they know everything that goes down in west Dorset Heather, everything.'

This interested Heather. This sort of talk reminded her of the darker side of the Met CID. She was impressed.

'You got any of them registered, as informants like?'

'Wouldn't tell you if I had. Come on. Let's go and meet them. You can tell me what you think.'

39. Katie had taken the Land Rover down to Lyme the previous evening. She'd parked at the top of the town and walked down the steep hill to the harbour, or the Cobb as it's called. She'd remembered the film The French Lieutenant's Woman starring Meryl Streep and had seen the stone steps on the breakwater that had featured in a scene in the old movie. Lyme milked that a bit and was often referenced to it in the various tacky little guide books published about the town. She had walked into the Flag and had got herself a glass of red wine. Swearing to herself about the prices catching up with London and Brighton, she had walked through the bar with her drink and onto the raised patio area that overlooked the beach. It was early evening and the families still ruled the day. Screaming kids, stressed out parents and the monotonous hum of the bouncy castle engine. Fucking noise pollution, she'd thought, even here - and had then chided herself for being mean. She'd sat down at a table and perused an abandoned local rag.

MAN SERIOUSLY ASSAULTED IN LYME ALLEY read a headline, the following article went on to describe what was obviously the alleyway between the Flag and the Seagull pubs and how it had been the scene a few evenings previously of a serious assault. The details were scanty, police enquiries were continuing. This was nasty for Lyme, she'd thought. The victim had been hit with a weapon and had been taken to Exeter Hospital for surgery on his shoulder. Nasty, for Lyme. She had rolled a cigarette and flipped over the pages to the 'Horses' column in the free ads.

She was half way through her wine and had flipped open the lid of the Zippo to light her fag when another one appeared. It was placed gently on the table by a silhouette standing between her and the low evening sun. Obviously the silhouette had to be that of Darren Pyke. That went without saying, but she would have liked to have been able to see him at that particular point in time.

40. Now it was the next morning and she was lying in bed, trying to piece together the evening. The Land Rover was still in Lyme – she had had to get a cab home. Her dad was not impressed. She smiled though; this was exciting. Darren Pyke had got her drunk and had behaved like a real gentleman. He had even called the cab on his mobile phone. 'You don't want to be seen in a white van with the likes of me now, do you Katie,' he had said, reading her mind like it was the newspaper on the table, causing her to turn the colour of an electric fire. The conversation had flowed well, and she guessed that it would have even without the booze. He had been drinking Stella, like most working class boys – bitter was for yuppies, he had said, before apologising. She had already by that time told him about Simon Murdoch back in Brighton and how he was nice but a bit posh. She had found herself being keen to distance herself from the middle class farmer's daughter image she feared she presented. There had been no need. Darren was very perceptive anyway but knew of her father's farm and the fairly low income profile that had resulted from his little casing exercise a year or so previously when the Pyke brothers were going through their farm-breaking phase. Two bob, he'd decided, before moving on to richer pickings further east.

She remembered talking to him about horses, about how the prices shot up if you could get them up to Hampshire and Oxfordshire, she remembered agreeing to look in her horse owners' magazines for selling opportunities, of being reminded that he had the use of a horsebox. She remembered him telling her that people didn't really like him and his brothers and she remembered not being surprised. And then she remembered agreeing to see him again. She wondered if he was thinking about her.

41. Darren Pyke was indeed thinking about Katie Pentreath, but not quite so lucidly, and he was not in bed. He was driving to Bristol with an empty horsebox bouncing along behind and an extremely nervous older brother by his side.

'We need to be in St Paul's by ten,' said Josh.

'I'm going as fast as I fucking can with this thing on the back,' answered Darren irritably. 'Why we have to use a fucking horsebox when there's fuck all in the back of the van I'll never know.'

But this was a lie and Josh didn't even bother to answer. Darren knew his brother and knew the elaborate care he applied to the serious objective of avoiding arrest. In the same way that no copper looked up peoples' arses in these parts for brass bullet cases full of cocaine, no copper was imaginative enough to think that the floor of a horsebox would be used for transporting three kilos of cannabis in plastic bags underneath six inches of shit. Sniffer dogs didn't stand a chance, poor things.

So, Darren was actually rather taken by his elder brother's innovative methods, even if they were a bit over the top. Darren reckoned privately that Josh took after their mother: creative, self-possessed. Darren was not quite sure who he himself took after. Not his father really, apart from the mental illness his dad suffered from which was mostly he reckoned down to cider, he was quite a gentle person. He never lost his temper whilst sober. This was in comparison to Darren whose violent temper was never far away, drunk or sober. Just in case. Daz didn't watch much television, but knew about people with split personalities; Jekyll and Hyde. He knew as well that some said that he was like that. They didn't say it to his face, mind. Oh no.

They wound their way northwards through Chard and towards Taunton. There they hit the M5 motorway and headed at increased speed to Bristol, arriving just on 10am. The St Paul's area had been revamped some over the previous ten years and wasn't quite the no-go area it had been. Still a lot of black faces though and this made the boys nervous. Whilst Josh was quite cosmopolitan in his views and able to communicate with pretty much everyone who came along Darren felt like a fish out of water as soon as he was north of Chard. He knew that this was wrong and envied his brother's adaptability. He was getting better though, he consoled himself. Katie-girl was an example. A couple of years ago he would not have had the confidence to speak to her, never mind sit with her for two hours. He found that Katie was making this otherwise nerve-racking trip easier for him. He kept thinking about her kind patience with him. He had never been shown such patience, and that was why, he reckoned, that he was confident with her; he sort of knew that she was not going to rebuff him without warning, get up and walk away, turn a corner when she saw him coming, ignore him when they bumped into each other. He sensed this and was infatuated. He pulled up at the meeting point by the canal as directed by Josh, his mind barely on the job. The spades were waiting.

42. So when Heather and Stuart pulled up at the Pyke residence they were not about to see Darren and Josh. Young Joe answered the door in his vest and shorts. He thought that it was more bother about their dad's smashing little time a few evenings ago and let them in.

'Mornin' Gordon,' said Stuart cheerfully to the old man who looked up from his newspaper.

'Oh, Christ, what is it now?'

'Nothing, nothing, just popped by to see how you are. Wondered if Darren was about?'

'No, they've gone out.'

'Who's 'they', Darren and Josh?'

'Yeah, look, what's the matter mate, why're you lot always picking on my boys?'

'We're not picking on anybody Gordon. Other people are telling us that your boys are a pain the neck and we can't ignore that sort of information. Where've they gone?'

'I dunno, got a bit of work I suppose. They tell me fuck all mate, you should know that... sorry, didn't mean to swear in front of the lady officer.'

Heather was standing behind and to the side of Stuart.

'Don't mind me Mr. Pyke.'

'Oh, 'Mr. Pyke' Eh? You're posh.'

'This is Heather, Gordon, she's new on the manor. Going to be helping out with the domestic violence stuff for a while. She comes from London, don't you Heather?' With that Stuart moved slightly, turning around so that he was facing her with most of his back towards the old man, like he was regarding her from a local point of view, sharing old Gordon's perspective. At that second she felt exposed and vulnerable, an outsider, Stuart was one of them and she wasn't.

'Yes,' she said, quietly to Stuart as if old Gordon wasn't even there, 'I come from London.' She said it like it was a confession.

A few minutes later they were back in the car. Having left old Gordon Pyke to wonder why he had just been introduced to the new domestic violence copper. A little warning perhaps? Or was it a favour – know thy enemy Gordon, for the next time you smash your house up. Any closeness and trust that Heather had been starting to feel towards Stuart had evaporated. He had taken the piss out of her in front of one of the county's low life. He had sided against her and she would not forget that.

As she sat in the passenger seat she chanced a glance at his face and saw the unmistakable trace of a smirk. Not a word was said for the next quarter of an hour, the time it took them to get from Stockard to Crewkerne.

43. Police Constable 192 Cozens stood before the Board in full uniform. His trousers were pressed and his shoes shone. Police discipline hearings follow basically the same format as criminal proceedings. The prosecution is comprised of a member of the Force's Professional Standards Department who was usually represented by the Force Solicitor. The defendant is obviously the accused officer and he or she is either represented by a representative of the Police Federation or in more serious cases can have a solicitor or barrister, paid for by the Federation. This particular case was serious enough but PC Cozens had decided, on the advice of his 'Fed rep' PC Hogg, not to have legal representation as it was known to antagonise the Chief.

Chief Constable Joanne Bache asked the Force solicitor, Mr. Craig Sutherland, to read out the charge and this was promptly done. PC Cozens was asked if he pleaded guilty or not guilty and he pleaded guilty. It was now down to Norman Hogg to save his job by way of mitigation.

'Ma'am,' began the old campaigner, 'this officer is unwell. He has pleaded guilty to the alleged transgression but asks with the most profound respect that you take into account some medical facts....'

'PC Hogg, you are not going to tell me that you intend to introduce medical evidence in mitigation are you?' The Chief feigned irritability.

'I'm afraid so Ma'am, the....'

'Mr. Sutherland, do you have any observations to make?'

'Er, yes Ma'am, we have been given no warning of this, it should surely have been the responsibility of the defence to disclose the medical evidence so that we would have had a chance to consult our own medical experts.'

'Quite. Why is this PC Hogg? Why the ambush?'

The Groundhog was in his element.

'Ma'am, it has not been easy to obtain this evidence. The Federation has gone to considerable expense to finance the examination and subsequent report. The medical investigation had to be carried out over a period of several weeks and it was not until yesterday that it became available to us in its present form. Ma'am, if it would assist you I am quite prepared to agree to an adjournment so that Mr. Sutherland has time to assimilate the mitigating facts and indeed perhaps make a decision as to whether it remains in the public interest to proceed with this case or to have this officer treated for his illness and rehabilitated back into the police service from which, as you know, he is currently suspended.'

The Chief could barely keep a straight face. She had known Norman Hogg since he attended her office to introduce himself on the first day of her appointment. On occasions he had been a priceless source of information, particularly in respect of the behaviour of some of her superintendents; there had also been occasions, like the current situation, when he would be the bane of her life. She had written off the afternoon to hear this case and now she was going to have to re-diarise her time. The funny part was Sutherland's face. She couldn't stand him and it gave her pleasure to see him look stupid.

'Mr. Sutherland?'

'Er, yes, Ma'am, I think that would probably be best. Perhaps we should put this case back to give us more time to consider the medical evidence. However I have little doubt that it will not make much difference….'

'How do you work that out when you haven't seen it yet – it might change the whole thing?'

Ma'am, quite. But if I can put it another way, neither this officer nor Mr.

Hogg has made any intimation to myself or the PSD that he is ill or has at any time been ill....'

Norman came in, 'If you had not have suspended him he'd have gone off sick.'

Sutherland was stuck for words and remained silent. The Chief took over.

'Okay PC Cozens, this matter will be put over for the reason already aired. Additionally I want you to see the Force medical examiner as soon as possible. Mr. Hogg will make the necessary arrangements.' With a little smile playing on her face she stood, nodded to Norman Hogg and walked out of the room, followed by Rob Sherrell and a nameless superintendent from Bournemouth.

A few minutes later Sherrell was back in his office and a relieved Kevin Packington departed for an early afternoon pint, or three.

44. A van pulling a horsebox in the St Paul's area of Bristol was a very unusual sight. The country boy occupants of the white van then talking to two yardies who had just pulled up in a BMW 8 Series was something you just couldn't make up. So by necessity, matters progressed quickly as pre-arranged. Josh slid out of the van and walked quickly to the BMW and sat in the passenger seat, the former occupant of which took his place in the van beside Darren. The BMW moved off. The van stayed put. Darren did not take his eyes off of his new companion, a wiry, dreadlocked youth who was as nervous as he was. Darren thought about Emmet's loaded .410 in easy reach behind his seat, all he had to do was reach back over his shoulder and pull it out. He had practised the move many times, as he had the story about a shotgun licence – his brother Gordon's, but that was mere detail - being in the post, which was actually the truth. In his right hand side pocket Darren had five hundred pounds. When the BMW returned and Josh stepped out of it he would be carrying a Tesco bag laden with shopping that would include a sealed parcel that was not bought from the supermarket. Once out of the BMW with the shopping he would start walking towards the van and, if all was

well, would signal to his brother with three nods of his head. It was then that Darren would hand over the money to his passenger who would then get out of the van and change places with Josh. The vehicles could be then driven their separate ways. A few streets away Darren would pull over and Josh, unable to relax until this was done, would get out and bury the sealed parcel under the manure in the horsebox. With that they would make for the M5. And that was how it happened, all according to plan, smooth as clockwork. A meeting of two cultures, a business transaction arranged over mobile telephones between parties who had never been introduced, could barely understand each other's accents and could not possibly trust each other. No lawyers, no written agreements, no accountants, no pleasantries or games of golf, no offices or conference rooms. Just drugs and money.

45. 'Oh, come on Katie, make an effort. You could be here in not more than an hour and a half, it'll be the last time you can see Jackson before he offs to America, it'll be a laugh, we can chuck him in the sea or something.'

Simon Murdoch was trying to persuade Katie to attend a party in Brighton to honour the departure to the U.S. of someone she considered the U.S. deserved. She could not stand the sight of Jackson Friend, the son of a High Court Judge who had somehow secured a place for one year at Yale University. He was a drinking mate of Simon and was to Katie the epitome of everything she hated about Simon's circles. Money, privilege and offensive behaviour.

'Simon, you really must be joking. I'm not coming, but I tell you what, I'll celebrate Jackson's departure from this country. I'll think about him this Friday evening and raise a glass to the ocean, how's that?'

'Okay, fine. Suppose I didn't really expect anything else from you. Can I come and visit you soon?'

'Yeah, sure, soon.'

'When though?'

'Soon, I'll let you know.'

'Have you met someone else down there?' This was not really a question, just a bit of desperate banter by Simon, for the want of something to say. But Katie felt herself blush all the same.

'No, course not you idiot. I'm having a complete break from people, full stop. Just me and my horses and my mum and dad. It's bliss so stay away for now, let me get my shit together and do some studying, then I just might let you come down for a day or two.'

'Book me in at the Alexandria, okay…?'

'When the time comes you can book yourself in.'

'Yesssss!' He was on a promise.

'Now go and have a cold shower. Bye.' She hung up and poured herself a large glass of red wine, taking it over to the table and her books. All the time she was thinking about Darren Pyke.

46. The white van with the horsebox disappeared into the Everett's valley just after 1pm. Darren and Josh had argued on the way back from Bristol. Had Josh checked the contents of the sealed black plastic package? No. Why not? How did he know it was the right stuff and not just more horseshit to go with the rest of what was in the box? Didn't have time to check it, and the plastic was really thick, couldn't break through just like that, not without a knife. Why hadn't he taken a knife for that purpose? Didn't know. And so it went on. A bit unfair really. Darren the security guy, the enforcer, giving the dealer retrospective advice. Should really just stick to his remit. Thus it was that as soon as they were safe on Everett land out came the package and in went the knife. It was the right stuff and Josh breathed a big sigh of relief. Darren's mood lifted and he took the bungee roped plates off the back of

the box and paid Emmet a nice little £50 for its use. A sizable wedge of cannabis was removed from the package before it was resealed and hidden in the Everett silage pit at the bottom of their valley. Again, no chance for sniffer dogs.

Oddly, the .410 shotgun was completely forgotten about and remained in position behind the driver's seat of the van.

Now they had to sell the stuff. Darren had about twenty quid left. This was the low point in the proceedings, when all the cash had been converted and the dope now had to be sold. The boys got into the van. It was about 2pm and they were hungry. They headed for Crewkerne where they would get some lunch and offload some dope.

All through that morning, in spite of the somewhat stressful assignment he'd been on, Darren's mind had been elsewhere. Yes, he had been thinking, he was taken by this bird Katie. What was more he thought he might actually be in with a chance. Not just to fuck her, he wanted for once to put that to one side. There was something more here, he sensed. It wasn't just that she was good looking, or that she was bright and posh and a farmer's daughter. It was that she was actually giving him time. He could not help keep thinking about how she had listened. Had let him buy her four glasses of wine and had sat and listened to him. She had not been bored and, above all, she had not been frightened; it was part of his trade to recognise when someone was frightened of him. No, he actually thought that she just might be interested. Careful Daz, he thought to himself, careful of high hopes. It's a long way to fall.

47. Stuart Townsend pulled the CID car up in the backyard of Crewkerne Police Station as Heather's mobile phone rang.

'Hello,' she answered, flatly.

'Hello Heather, how're you doing?'

'Who's that?' Genuinely bewildered.

'What do you mean "Who's that?" it's Alex you dopey cow, how are ya?'

'Oh, sorry, yeah fine mate, fine. I'm with a colleague at the minute, can I ring you back?'

'Hang on, just a quickie, this is work, don't worry, I might have something for you, listening?'

'Yeah, go on then.'

'There's team of scousers on their way down to you....'

'They're here already, I'm ahead of you....'

'Yeah, clever cow, but do you know their names yet?'

'Probably not, go on.' She got a pen out and pulled a memo pad from the glove compartment.

'Not so fast, not so fast,' Alex Miller could hear just the faintest knock of opportunity, 'What's in it for me?'

'A shag?' She turned her head and winked at the startled Stuart Townsend.

'Done,' I'll be fucking lucky, thought Alex, 'Your main man is a skinny little twat called Garrigan, Danny Garrigan, got that?'

'Yep, go on.'

'His minders are the Kelly brothers, Paul and Barry, they look like twins but they're a year apart. The others chop and change a bit but they are the main three. They know all the rest and they always have first pickings. The others aren't allowed into a town before those three have been through it. The word is that if any of the hangers on cross them, their families get a pasting back in Liverpool.'

'Alex, will all this not come down on daily circulations?'

'Yeah, in a couple of days, it's my info, so it's up to me when I chuck it in the pot to be shared out. At this point in time the only cop outside Shepherds Bush to have this starting price is my beautiful friend Heather Boyle, okay?'

'Sweet. Alex, I'll get back to you.'

'Yeah. When do I get paid?'

'I'll get back to you,' she giggled, and terminated the call.

'Friend of yours?' came the obvious question from Townsend.

'Could say that.' Heather was grinning and getting out of the car as she answered. She tucked the memo pad into her pocket. She had made sure that Townsend had not seen what she had written.

48. The Chief used her private bathroom to the rear of her office suite. She had an unforeseen hour to spare so had taken a shower and was brushing her hair as she heard her phone buzzing. She had forgotten to have her calls held so she wrapped a towel around herself and walked through to her desk.

'Yes? Chief Constable.'

'Ma'am, it's Derrick at Bournemouth. We've been hit by our little Liverpudlian crime-wave. Over twenty thefts from motor vehicles over the past 12 hours and they've only just got here. We've got officers at all the car parks but it's not enough. Any chance I can raise some help from Hampshire?'

The Bournemouth Chief Super was a bit of a flapper, a panic-button merchant at the best of times. Give him a bit of a problem and Joanne Bache wondered how he had ever made it to where he was. Help from Hampshire, her arse.

'No Derrick, manage it yourself. Get the town council to put temporary

CCTV up on the lamp posts, there's a firm in town does it, they're forever mailshotting me about how they can rig up a network within two hours. Ring my secretary; she's got the number, South Coast Security or something like that.'

'Okay, Ma'am, thanks for that.'

Fucking hell, she thought, and went back into her bathroom.

49. The Plug and Pie was Crewkerne's attempt at 21st century drinking. Devoid of carpets or soft furnishings it had had its heart ripped out when it ceased to be called the Somerset Arms over a year previously, a name it had enjoyed for a century or more. Now it was just a yapping hell with plasma screens and drunken kids from every village within a ten mile radius.

Darren and Josh walked in at about 2pm. It was fairly quiet with just a few bored students home from uni watching Sky Sports News.

Darren spotted the buyer immediately, a middle class grunger he had met in Lyme some weeks ago. He knew him to be the son of a lawyer with an office in Exeter who had represented Wayne in the youth court on a minor matter of shoplifting. In other words Darren knew enough about his buyer to be able to fuck him if he grassed or set him up with the cops. The two of them exchanged brief pleasantries and sat down in a fairly dark corner of the pub. Josh pretended to watch Sky Sports but in fact watched the door. The student barmaid was oblivious. Five minutes later the deal had been done, an exchange made and Darren and Josh left the Plug and Pipe two hundred quid richer.

50. Stuart Townsend introduced Heather to the Crewkerne Domestic Violence Unit. This consisted of two part-time cops called Suzy and Maxine, both married women with young families who did 30 hours a week each. Heather could tell immediately that neither of them was the

slightest bit interested in the job. They eyed Heather with curiosity but not hostility. It was like they were thinking why a young, good looking girl like her had opted for this backward neck of the woods. Suzy and Maxine aroused curiosity in Heather also – she recognised immediately that they were bright but very bored women who had become inextricably and permanently stranded up shit creek without a paddle. The three of them went to the canteen for a cup of tea and biscuits whilst Townsend went to do some checks at one of the terminals in the CID office. He was worried about what Decker was doing and wanted to get back down to the coast. The last thing he wanted was that bastard being able to say he'd sorted things out himself because his DC was on a jolly with the new bird. It would be just like him.

It turned out that Suzy and Maxine weren't actually from the triangle but were from Bristol and had worked for Avon and Somerset Constabulary before it had ceded Crewkerne to Dorset. Their husbands were both in sales and travelled to London and Bristol a lot and so both families, already known to each other through their kids' schooling, had moved to this fairly central part of the West Country.

'You won't need to come up here much, we have it fairly well wrapped up. It's just the same old drunken husbands knocking about the same old drunken wives.' Suzy was pleasant. As was Maxine,

'Yeah, if there's anything out of the usual we'll give you a call. We've both got cars if you want us down on the coast.'

'Yeah, I could do with getting down to Lyme now and again, nice gift shops, so, me first please.'

'Nah, come on, I need it more than you, the sea air that is, I want to be first to Lyme to help our new colleague here….'

Heather was laughing at their banter, 'It won't be up to me girls, I'm not a sergeant or anything, I'm just like you, I'll do as I'm told….'

'Yeah, but we got to stick together, us girls,' giggled Maxine, 'we could work something out, yeah, now we've got a mate on the coast.'

Heather laughed again and rose, her tea unfinished. 'We'll see. I've got to find Stuart, he's keen to get back to Lyme,' then, quietly, conspiratorially, 'I think he's a bit scared of his skipper.'

'Which one's that then?' enquired Suzy.

'Decker.'

'Oh, that wanker,' sniffed Maxine. 'Yeah, I know him, dangerous bastard, snake, watch out for him, do your legs, he will.'

'Yeah, real nasty bastard,' agreed Suzy.

They said their goodbyes and Heather found Stuart out in the yard standing beside the car like a cat on hot bricks.

'Come on Heather, I need to get back,' then under his breath but audible, '… fuck's sake.'

As Townsend pulled the car out of the yard too quickly he had to brake to avoid hitting a big, dirty white van which had to skid and swerve. The driver glared and then looked away as his passenger obviously reminded him that the car had just come out of the back of the fucking police station.

'Shit!' exclaimed Townsend, then conceded, 'My fault, I suppose.'

Heather wasn't listening, she was trying to place the van driver's face. She couldn't quite remember the last time she'd seen it but had the feeling that the last occasion had been equally unpleasant.

51. The two police officers headed south to Lyme Regis so that Townsend could link up with his sergeant. He was keen to offload his new colleague. There was still something about her that put him off, something neutral, disengaging. She could go and put her uniform on and go for a walk while he went back to catching criminals. The journey was accomplished in silence. He had nothing to say to Heather and she

concentrated on not being rendered nauseous by the narrow high hedged roads that turned and winded ridiculously to accommodate the layout of fields demarked since Roman times.

Just as they crossed the A35 a mile or two north of the sea Heather's mobile phone sounded to signify receipt of a WhatsApp message. She looked at it and saw that the message was accompanied by three colour photographs. Danny Garrigan and the Kelly brothers. The accompanying text read: these not published yet, all yours. exclusive. nothing official for 3 days.

She smiled and put the phone away. This could be a bit of real luck. Might have to give Alex a shag after all.

'You're popular,' said Townsend, flatly.

'Yeah.' she said, in the same flat tone. The distance between the two lengthened.

52. Katie sat at the big farmhouse kitchen table and picked at a breakfast of fried field mushrooms and bacon. She had made this herself, her parents having long gone out to their work and rituals. Her father had been particularly low the previous evening and Katie was worried about him. The sheep were not selling. French produce was stealing the market and local farmers were actually trying to give their lambs away for nothing so that the land could be put to other uses. Quite what they were would vary from farm to dilapidated farm. Some near suicidal landowners were talking of golf courses and paintball shooting ranges. Katie's dad was seriously thinking about a clay pigeon shooting school; he knew a farmer in Devon who was making a small fortune that way. She and her mother doubted that he would do it though, too much of a farmer. He would just knuckle down and work even harder. He was exhausted; Katie could see this plainly and was cross at her mother for being in so much denial. 'Everything will be fine, dear, just a bit of a bad spell. Can you run me into Axminster? Lovely book fair on just now, and

I'm meeting Jane for coffee at that new bistro in the converted old mill....'

Katie pushed the meal aside, half eaten and went outside to roll a cigarette. Out came the Zippo and her mind caved in to the thoughts it had been laboriously denying itself all morning. All night in fact. She wondered what he was doing. Work? She doubted it. Triangle Man with clean, callous-free hands did not work because the only work in the Triangle caused callouses. No, she was unable not to form the conclusion that Darren Pyke was a wrongun, as her father would say. A wrongun.

She spent the day faffing about with an anatomy assignment, usually not a problem to her, the unchallenging nature of the work failed to keep her mind sufficiently occupied and by the time her mother had got back from shopping-lunching-coffeeing Katie had left and was on her way to Lyme Regis in her tiny little Ford. She had not once thought about her horses.

53. WPC Heather Boyle was not due to commence duty until 1400 hours but was in the police station at Bridport at 10am. She had driven down from Dorchester following a bit of a row with her mother. Her brothers were back from college and the house wasn't big enough for all of them. A bit of cabin fever had ensued and poor old Don Pryce had got it in the neck from the eldest boy. 'You're just after mum's money,' had come the usual accusation and Don had raised his eyes skyward. He had started up a one man legal practice in Dorchester and it was doing okay so he was paying his way. This had reassured Heather to some extent but the boys were still suspicious. They still missed their dad, if the truth was known, and Don was paying for that. But he loved Julie Boyle and being with her was worth the aggravation. He had sold his house in Ealing, west London, and the proceeds had paid for a 12 month lease on his Dorchester office, along with a three bedroomed cottage near the town centre. Heather had to admit that the new family home was lovely, with its brand new kitchen, yellow brick wall and a front garden ablaze with pink peonies.

Anyway, Heather was not thinking about all this as she connected her phone to one of the printers in the CID office and ran A4 size copies off of the three scousers. Danny Garrigan and the Kelly Brothers. Sounded like a band. She folded the pictures and stuffed them in her uniform tunic. The she got hold of Reg Bull on his mobile phone. He was on an 8 to 4 shift in his marked patrol car and gladly agreed to pick her up for a drive around the county. She was waiting for him in the backyard when Decker walked through the car park. Seeing her he changed direction and approached with a quizzical look.

'What are you doing here at this time of day Miss Boyle? I happen to know you don't start till two.'

She was a bit lost for words. This guy was scary. Why had he made it his business to know the shift pattern of a uniformed WPC? He, the busiest detective on the south coast of England. She was not flattered and suspected something nasty was on the cards.

'Oh, just keen, you know sarge, just super keen. I'm er, well, just keen to have a look and get to know the roads, and that....'

'You won't get any thanks for it.' He was not impressed. By the time he had finished saying it he was already walking away from her.

54. 'What's the matter with you lately anyways Daz? You got a face like a bulldog chewin' a wasp.'

Darren was driving as usual and Josh was asking the questions. He did not get a response.

'Oi, I'm fucking talkin' to you bruv. What's the matter? We pulled off a good job yesterday and look at you. Anybody'd think you'd just been told you got cancer or sumthin''

'Just leave it Josh. Got a worry on, that's all.'

'What worry Daz?' Josh was concerned. If one Pyke had a worry then by definition they all had.

'Oh, nuthin to do with the family, just me, think I'm, well, getting itchy feet that's all.' As he said this he pulled the van over in the middle of nowhere, switched off the engine and took out his tobacco.

'What you stopped for? We got to be in Lyme by three.'

'Yeah, what are we doing again, remind me.'

'Fucking hell Daz, get a grip. We got a call remember, Jason Willis wants to see us for a pint, that's always good crack. We 'ave a quick couple in Lyme then fuck off along the coast to do some business. He's going to introduce us to a friend of his in Bradstock or sumthin'.'

'I dunno.' Darren was fumbling for matches and thought of his Zippo and what it would be doing this afternoon.

'What d'you mean you dunno? It's all arranged mate, you agreed this morning.'

'What happens if it's a setup?'

'I don't believe you. We ain't even carryin' anything. The van's clean.'

Darren thought of the gun behind him and remembered that he had told Josh that he had put it away somewhere safe until Emmet remembered to ask for it back.

'Yeah, whatever.' Then a pause. 'Tell you what, you meet Willis on your own. I'm having the afternoon off.'

'Eh?! Aw, c'mon on man, you can't do....'

Having just moved off and back onto the road, Darren slammed on the brakes and nearly put his brother through the windscreen.

'I can and I fucking am!' He screamed this with such venom that Josh froze, nodding wide eyed in vigorous agreement. His brother terrified him at times. The journey to Lyme continued in silence. Darren parked the van up in a car park, paid for an eight hour ticket which he stuck in the windscreen before tossing the keys to Josh and walking off in the general direction of the harbour. Josh locked the van up and walked to the Lifeboat. Billy Skimmer wouldn't mind him in there on his own, without Darren. Come to think of it, thought Josh, he could get in pretty much anywhere when Daz wasn't about. It was always Darren who attracted trouble, just something about him. He called Willis on his phone and told him to be in the Lifeboat and that Darren wasn't going to be there.

'Not the Lifeboat,' Willis said, 'full of fuckin' scousers mate, go back up the hill to the Goat. Decent pint in there.' Josh agreed and complied. He liked Willis, they had always seen eye to eye, never fallen out. Setup – what was his brother on?

55. The fact that the Lifeboat was full of scousers meant that Garrigan and the Kelly Brothers were actually not there. They'd been there the night before, three missing handbags testified to that, but were now grazing in fresh pastures nearer the waterside, leaving the old town pubs like the Lifeboat to their entourage of followers who always lagged by 24 hours. The three principal Liverpudlians were having a quiet, mature drink in the Seagull Inn, quietly discussing their plans for the evening and collectively eyeing the fat purse on the table occupied by a lone female smoking roll ups and drinking red wine.

'We could have that away now,' ventured one of the Kelly Brothers.

'Don't be fuckin' stupid,' cautioned Garrigan, 'Too early in the day, she'll raise the alarm the place'll be swarming with bizzies before the sun goes down. It isn't busy enough yet and there's a camera in the top corner over there. Sit back my friends, sit back and relax, there'll be rich pickings later. Our fellow countrymen will be kickin' up a dust cloud in the town centre tonight, and we'll do some nice quiet work here, away from all the limelight. Agreed?'

'Agreed Danny. As usual.' Agreed the other Kelly Brother.

Then Darren Pyke walked into the pub and the three thieves froze. Feral always recognises feral. He didn't see them in the corner at first, so intent was he at getting his approach to Katie right. But he felt them drilling holes in him with their rat eyes, and so he stopped before reaching Katie. Stopped dead in fact, and turned slowly to face them. Garrigan leaned back in his chair and looked Darren up and down - the other two held his eye and glared. They were not frightened of him and Darren sensed this. Invariably grockles would look away when they got the Pyke eye, but these three were different. Darren felt the weight of his asp in the back pocket of his jeans, hidden by his overhanging £60 Lacoste shirt, and had an inkling that he would be using it later that evening, if not before.

Katie did not even look up.

'Wondered how long you'd be.'

Darren just stood there, dumbstruck, staring at her. Then she looked up at him and smiled.

'Aren't you going to sit down then? Where's your drink?' She did not ask for a refill. Not that kind of bird.

'Haven't got one.' Came the lame reply. He found himself behaving like a child. Then he quickly turned and walked briskly back to the bar before she had a chance to speak again like she was his mother. Her tone had angered him. As he passed the three scousers sat in the corner he looked down his nose at them. Garrigan ignored this with a knowing smile. The Kelly brothers were almost on their feet, lips curling.

'Calm down, calm down, he's only a fuckin' conehead just been sent to the bar by his girlfriend who's probably his fuckin' sister.'

It was good job Darren didn't hear this.

Frankie the student barmaid greeted Darren nervously. She knew him and his reputation. She served him a pint of Stella and a glass of red wine. She had already tipped off her boss as to his presence in the pub and Colleen Bradstock, the landlady, was viewing the scene on her close circuit TV in her lounge. Oh dear. She'd been told on the Pubwatch network to look out, or listen out, for Liverpudlians who were here on a thieving mission. And she was always on the lookout for Darren Pyke. This was a win double. Two threats in her bar at the same time. And it was late on a summer's afternoon. The temperature was dropping and soon the place would be full of beach refugees. Stressed out parents with scratchy kids would fill the place, it would become a depository for unguarded handbags and purses, cameras and iPods, mobile phones and sunglasses. And she had one well known thief and three unknown ones just sitting waiting. She didn't even bother thinking about calling the police, it would be, 'Yes Miss Bradstock, we'll have some plain clothes in there with you as soon as possible.' Yeah, she bet, like tomorrow.

She found herself looking at the girl Pyke was sitting with. She had never seen him with a girl before. It was always with his brothers or other villains of the area. She tolerated them nervously. They spent a lot of money in her pub, always showing off their cash. But there was something very different about Darren Pyke today, like he was mesmerised by this young lady. Colleen had never seen her before and noted her striking appearance. Probably a farmer's daughter, home on vacation from university. Spot on, Colleen.

'How long have you been here?' Asked Darren as he pulled up a chair.

'Not long, half an hour or so.' As she spoke she regarded him studiously, looking at various parts of his face and hair, then his shirt. Her head was tilted slightly to one side.

Darren did not like this but was unable to articulate his displeasure. Normally it would have been, "What the fuck are you looking at?!" But this was not normal.

Then her eyes settled on his and she smiled. He felt a warmth sweep over him. The assessment was over. Approval was his, at least for the time being. Their first meeting had been such a random encounter that he had learned nothing. She had been pre-occupied and hadn't given him much attention, just took his wine and went home drunk to mummy and daddy. He had not dared to think he had made any sort of impression at all. Not even a poor one. But all of a sudden there was a change. A sliver of light, perhaps.

'Sorry.'

'What are you apologising for?'

'For being late.'

'You weren't late. We never even agreed to meet.'

'Yeah, well, you've still had to wait.'

She couldn't believe this. 'I wasn't waiting for you Darren, I was just sitting here by myself watching the kids play on the beach.'

Darren looked down and thought for a moment, change direction, 'You sit on your own much?'

'Yeah. I like to.'

'You want me to leave.'

'No.'

'Thank fuck for that.'

'What?! I beg your pardon!' She laughed.

'I said thank God for that, I thought I was going to have to....'

'No you didn't – honestly, your language is....'

'I know, I know, terrible. Dragged up, see, not brought up like some.'

This banter continued as the pub patio filled up. The presence of the scousers in the corner receded in Darren's mind as he continued to fall in love with Katie Pentreath. She was pleasant and played with him kindly, comparing his nervousness and vulnerability to the pomposity and arrogance of Simon Murdoch who she knew would at that time be donning rugby shirt and designer jeans for beer and high jinks in Brighton. Wanker, she thought, and continued to enjoy her more interesting and sinister company.

But as the evening wore on she deconstructed him and after a couple of hours began to feel the old enemy nearby. Boredom. She kept it up though, not wishing to burst his bubble – yes, she could see what was happening – playfully entrancing him, feeding off him and hating herself for it and loving it.

It was around 9 o'clock when something happened to make her think she may have underestimated her companion. It was when he got up and went to the bar for refills. Just as he got to the bar in came Josh and tapped Darren on the shoulder. They were thirty feet away and the pub was quite busy but Katie could see that they were brothers, or sincerely hoped so. Josh leaned forward to whisper something to Darren's ear and it was immediately clear to her that he was being told something important. All of a sudden she was not there. He was gone in a second, half turning round to offer only a fleeting wave goodbye and the thinnest of smiles. Josh had left ahead of him, unaware of Katie's presence on the patio. All of a sudden Katie Pentreath barely existed in his life. She felt humiliated and embarrassed. Stupid bitch, she called herself, who did she think she was.

56. 'They've got in through the back doors, the battery chargers gone, and the bolt cutters, and Wayne's new drill, all the good stuff. All the shit's still in there.'

The van had been screwed. Josh had finished his bit of business in the Goat with Willis and had walked down the hill into town through the car park. Checking the van was just a habit. It usually contained contraband of some sort and the odd walk-by occasionally yielded sight of an unmarked cop car waiting to follow, stop and search if the van was driven away, on which occasions it of course would not be. But there were no cops this time and for once Josh had wished there had been. The back doors of the Transit had been unceremoniously jemmied and their best tools nicked.

'Fucking scousers, Daz, the town's full of them. Where've you been, anyway?'

'Seagull.'

'What for?'

'Mind your own fuckin' business.' They were walking back up the hill to the van, Darren's face was down, eyes ablaze. When they got to their vehicle Darren ignored the busted rear doors and went to the front driver's side, Josh chucked him the keys and he opened up to find with great relief the shotgun was still holstered between the seat and the partition separating the cockpit from the payload area. He then went to the rear of the vehicle, surveyed the damage and decided that the matter would be sorted before they went home that night.

Katie had not been alone for long. Within two minutes of Darren leaving Danny Garrigan had joined her, politely.

'Mind if I sit here for a few minutes? Just waiting for somebody.'

She didn't bother to reply, just shrugged her shoulders and issued a very thin, brief smile whilst looking away. She had not noticed Garrigan and his sidekicks whilst they had sat farther back inside the pub. She still was unaware of the Kelly brothers who were now stationed strategically in separate areas of the bar.

Darren marched at breakneck speed back down to the seaside. Josh almost had to jog to keep up with him. Scousers eh? Josh had updated him on local intelligence, how a band of Liverpudlian scum was taking the town apart. Darren now figured he knew the business of the three wide-boy strangers in the Seagull.

'Was that your boyfriend that just got up left you all by yourself like, you know, just like that?'

'What?' asked Katie. Who the hell was this idiot? It was not until she condescended to look him in the eye that she sensed danger.

'The tall fella, he your boyfriend or wha'?'

She composed herself. 'Would you kindly leave me alone. I said you could sit there, not talk to me.'

'You said fuck all love.'

'What?!' the pub was busy now, and noisy.

'I said, you said fuck all!' This was the last thing Garrigan said before his shoulder was broken. Darren's fully extended steel asp came down on the Liverpudlian's collar bone with great force. The force of a man disgusted with himself for leaving a woman he adored in order to check on a fucking Ford Transit.

Garrigan did not scream, he just rolled off the chair clutching his shoulder, face contorted in shock and agony, as one of the Kelly brothers launched himself at Darren. The glass in his hand was a millisecond from Darren's face when the ledge of Josh's hand intervened and sent it smashing back into Kelly's face. It must have hit an artery in his eyebrow because blood spurted out over Darren. Kelly went down like a sack of shit, holding his wound with both hands. The whole thing lasted about four seconds, the pub went silent, the bar staff cowered and Katie Pentreath sat rigid with her mouth open. Everything just stayed frozen for a further and very long five seconds, the two scousers were persuaded to remain on the floor, both staring at the thirteen inches of high tensile steel Darren wielded menacingly.

'There's another one in here somewhere,' Darren informed his brother who was half crouched ready for more, surveying the crowd, fists clenched.

'Come on, we're going,' hissed Darren to Katie. She nodded dumbly and stood, as if in a trance. The three of them left as a lone, tiny police siren sounded in the distance. The alarm button behind the bar had been pressed.

They walked quickly out of the pub patio and onto the darkening beach which was by then virtually deserted. A low orange sun was still just above the horizon, shade-lighting everything and cast long shadows on the white sand through which they trudged fast and wordlessly. They made their way along the sand which the receding tide had left wet and flat. Two hundred yards east and they were onto the pebble beach when they saw the little police car travel slowly but noisily in the opposite direction along the promenade, pedestrian holiday makers stepping aside grudgingly to allow it to pass. Having cleared the seafront part of the town the three trudged up through some dry, loose sand and re-entered the town at the quietest and least populated end of the beach. They stopped to empty sand from their shoes, just like three regular youngsters at the seaside. Not a word had been spoken. They acted as one and Katie Pentreath was part of that one. She had witnessed a violent assault by her companion with whom she had now fled. Oh my God – complicity.

57. 'You got your car?'

'Yes Darren, but I've been drinking.'

'I'll drive. Where is it parked?'

'You're not insured – and you've been drinking too.'

'Listen love, the cops are too busy at the pub now and we've got to get out of here and I've got to get this blood off of me. We can't use the van, it's too well known. Tell me where the car is and give me the keys.'

She complied, the little Ford was luckily nearby and they quickly drove to the car-park where the van was. Darren jumped out of the car, opened the van, took out the gun, locked the van back up and returned very quickly to the car. He opened the back door of the Ford and handed the .410 to Josh who was almost as surprised as Katie. He put it on the floor as Darren jumped back into the driver's seat and drove off at speed towards the A35.

Katie was terrified. 'That's a fucking gun, you've got a gun in my car and we're on the run from the fucking police! Jesus Christ, I only wanted a quiet glass of wine, just let me out – you can have the fucking car!'

At this she was grappling with the passenger door handle. The door opened but Darren had accelerated up the hill and the car was going too fast for her to be able to jump out.

'Just calm down. You can have the car back in a minute. I only want to get us to the countryside, into the dark. Me and Josh'll walk across the fields. I'll have been named by now and the police'll be looking for my van. I need to get this blood cleaned off me.'

Heather and Reg, both in full uniform had arrived at the Seagull Inn and were administering first aid to Danny Garrigan and Paul Kelly. The blood from Kelly's eyebrow had been stemmed but Garrigan's shoulder was badly broken and he needed to go to hospital. He was refusing to do this.

'I'll be alright, just put it in a sling, it's just bruised, I'll be alright.'

No you won't mate, Heather argued, you need to go to Exeter hospital, you have a bad injury. Who did this to you?'

'Fucked if I know love, I was just talking to a young lady and this chavvy attacks me. He'd been with her earlier on, like, and then he came back with his mate. I think they were locals, mind, I heard him talking and it was like a local accent.'

'Will you make a statement?' Reg asked the inevitable question.

'No way, mate, no way. We're only here on holidays, movin' on tomorrow like.'

'I'm calling the air ambulance Reg, he's got to go to Exeter.'

'You're calling the fuckin' what? The air ambulance? A chopper like?'

'That's right.'

'Here, Paul, do you hear this, I'm going in a chopper, coosty eh?' And then to Heather, 'Can me brothers come as well?'

'Probably' she replied, with an encouraging nod. Reg was looking at her, frowning. He decided to say nothing so as not to contradict her in front of these people.

Paul Kelly was not impressed, he held a wad of cotton wool to his eyebrow whilst looking around for his brother. The pub had returned almost to normal, the barmaid was serving but was glancing over nervously at the two police officers at their work on the patio. Sooner or later they would be asking her questions like 'What happened? Would you recognise them? Do you know them?' She decided that she had seen nothing. Seen nothing, heard nothing, so will speak nothing.

Heather stood up from crouching over Garrigan and turned her back. She appeared to be talking into her radio set.

58. Darren skidded the Ford to a halt in the mud about 500 yards short of Everett House. He and Josh got out of the car and stood on either side of it. Katie sat in the passenger seat, shaking with fear. She looked at Darren standing there in the half-light with the shotgun in his right hand. It was pointing downwards.

'Katie, go on, fuck off home, we're going to walk from here.'

She struggled over into the driver's seat and did what she was told.

The Pyke brothers were soon on the safe side of the Everett wall. The gun was deposited and Darren got cleaned up.

The air ambulance was going to be a while and the crew wanted to land it in the car park behind Lyme Regis Police station. Heather invited the scousers to get into the police car and make the quarter mile journey to that location. They all agreed, the other Kelly brother having joined them. Heather was riding her luck. Reg stayed silent and drove. The three passengers sat crammed in the back seat, Garrigan groaning with pain every time the little car hit a bump during the short trip up the hill.

Once in the back yard Heather invited them into the station for tea whilst they waited for the chopper. The Kelly brothers were not sure about this – having a natural aversion towards police stations – police anything, in fact – but Garrigan talked them round,

'Come on lads, it'll be a fuckin' laugh if nuthin' else.'

Once inside the station Heather left them with Reg and pretended to go and make tea. In actual fact she went up to the CID office and contacted Decker on his mobile. He was in Bridport and when she gave him the news he said he was on his way. Townsend had gone off duty and she was pleased about that. She took the large printed photographs out of her tunic pocket and, unfolding them, spread them out on a desk. Then she really did make five cups of tea and took them downstairs to help Reg keep their three guests chatting until the 'air ambulance landed.' It wouldn't be long.

'Can I just take a note of your names please lads, we've got to submit a report? Just a formality. Predictably, the three thieves lied, giving pre-arranged duff names. Luvly jubbly, thought Heather, as she made dutiful notes in her pocket book. The scousers sipped their tea; Garrigan winked at Kelly.

59. Katie parked her car drunkenly in the farmyard and let herself into the house. Her mother had gone to bed but old Bertie Pentreath was working at his old desk. He looked up briefly at his daughter,

'Hello there, nice evening?'

'Yes thank you,' she replied, trying to appear normal.

'We didn't know you were going out Katie, and you went really early.'

Katie didn't answer and just went straight upstairs to her room. She toppled onto her bed and stared at the ceiling. She thought of Darren, of the way in which he had hit that man with his metal bar thing. She thought of the gun. She thought about the way in which she had, when doubling back along that beach, been one of them. One of Darren's kind, hiding from the police. Had anyone in the pub recognised her? She doubted it. The bar staff were a new lot and anyway she was not known in Lyme, usually preferring to be on her farm and with her horses during vacation.

Darren and Josh holed up at the Everett's for the night, slept in the big attic of one of the outhouses. Darren was fairly sure that the barmaid at the Seagull wouldn't grass, but you never know what happens when the police get hold of people and apply their winning ways. Best they laid low for a couple of days. Their mum would be worried but hey, she should be used to it by now and they were big lads after all.

Decker was just turning off the A35 on the final coastward approach to Lyme when his phone went. It was the police control room at Bridport. He was told that not long after he had left a load of thefts had been reported by people coming off the beaches. The common theme, lads with Liverpudlian accents had been at play. Fucking scousers, he thought. By the time he turned into the backyard of Lyme police station he was just in the right mood to hear Heather's report to him. As he walked through the rear door he heard Heather's guests getting restless.

'Where's this fucking chopper then love?'

'Yeah, thought you said it would only be a few minutes.'

One of them, the uninjured Kelly brother had stood up and was peering out of the window as Decker had parked the CID car in the rear car park.

'Oi,' he observed, 'There's a bizzy just come in and parked his motor where the chopper's going to land.'

The other two went quiet. They heard the back door go as Decker entered the building. The DS had made provisions and, within seconds, two patrol cars from neighbouring Devon pulled in, two cops up in each. All of a sudden the scousers knew what was happening and they were up and trying to get out. Reg jumped on the uninjured Kelly and Heather got hold of his brother. Garrigan made for the door of the waiting room but Decker walked in and pushed him hard back into the room, 'Where d'you think you're going you scouse cunt?'

Barry Kelly broke free from Heather and got to the door behind Decker, only to be stopped by a punch in the mouth from a burly cop who had just arrived. Reg still had hold of Paul Kelly. Thus all three Liverpudlians were under arrest.

Heather saw her chance. 'Danny Garrigan, Paul Kelly, Barry Kelly. You are all under arrest on suspicion of theft. You do not have to say anything but it may harm your defence if you fail to mention something you later seek to rely on in court. Understand?'

Everyone stared at Heather, the scousers, the Devon cop and his colleague who had just entered the room, Reg and, with particular interest, Decker.

Garrigan broke the silence with a bit of welcome Liverpudlian humour, 'Do I take it the air ambulance won't be coming then?'

60. Gabby and Rosie were delighted to see Katie the next morning and cantered to the gate to greet her. She found the decision terrible but opted to take Rosie first.

'Don't worry Gabby, I'll be back and it'll be your turn this afternoon,' she consoled the chestnut horse. She saddled Rosie up and they headed for the bridle path. Gabby moped off back into the middle of the field, disgusted.

Twenty minutes and half a mile later she was getting the horse across the road. Rosie was particularly bad at this and was very nervous of traffic. The rider waited for what she thought was a wide enough gap in the traffic and kicked her heels a couple of times into the animal's side, at the same time giving her a smart slap on the haunch with her hand. The horse trotted forward for a few yards but then froze – right in the middle of the road. A car seemed to have come from nowhere and screeched to halt. The driver, a police woman in full uniform, got out and was not best pleased. Taking the horse by the reins, WPC Heather Boyle led it across the road with a profusely apologetic and thankful Katie still mounted. Additional traffic had slowed to a halt and then moved on when the horse was on the grass verge and out of the way.

'Next time love, get off the horse and lead it across before you get someone killed.'

'I'm really sorry officer, she's nervous.' And so am I if you're going to ask me about what happened in the pub last night, thought Katie, but then calmed down when it became clear that the officer was not about to make any such enquiry. She also felt safe in the knowledge that her appearance was radically different from the previous evening and it was unlikely that she'd answer any description. Her hair was up inside her riding hat, she wore a tight corduroy jacket, jodhpurs and shiny black boots. Twelve hours earlier she had been a boozy long haired scruffy undergraduate.

'She's nervous, how'd you think I felt when all of a sudden I've got a horse plonked in front of me?!'

'Like I said, I'm sorry.' Kate did not want a lecture. This girl could not be much older than her.

Then the cop softened. 'Yeah, okay. Nice horse. Name?'

'Rosie.'

'And the horse?'

'The horse is Rosie. I'm Katie.'

They both laughed.

'Okay Katie and Rosie, I'll see you around.' With that the cop was back in her car and gone.

Katie rode onto the bridle path and made her way north. There was something about the way the policewoman had looked at her that she didn't like. Had she perhaps recognised her from a description from the night before after all? No. It was something else, something totally different, and she found it perhaps a little amusing, but certainly did not like it. Well, well, how odd.

61. Heather managed to get to Crewkerne without further encounters with the animal kingdom and was greeted by her two domestic violence colleagues with some enthusiasm.

'Well,' said Maxine. 'Here's our heroine from the coast, cleaning up our friends from the north, eh?'

'Yeah,' joined in Suzy. 'Only been here five minutes and she's Dorset's top crime fighter.'

There was not a trace of jealousy in the girls' tone; they were genuinely pleased and excited by Heather's success. She went briskly through the morning's DV reports with them – same old shite, same old names – before logging onto the County intranet to catch up the latest from Lyme and Bridport.

Decker and Townsend had been dealing with the three prisoners. Their descriptions were coming up all over the place as belonging to those responsible for numerous thefts from pubs and restaurants along the coast. Had it not been for Heather's informed intervention the gang would have moved on, followed by their diversionary support artists. Regarding the latter, a number of incidents involving drunken Liverpudlians had kicked off in Lyme during the night and there was debris everywhere. One of the plate glass windows of the amusement arcade had been smashed causing a section of promenade to be roped off and declared unsafe to walk along until the mess had been cleared away.

There was little doubt that the scouse mob of about 15 or twenty had gone on the rampage after somehow hearing of their leaders' incarceration.

62. All this action inevitably attracted attention from the media. This came in the ubiquitous form of Jim Ramage, twenty five stone of perspiring Glaswegian in a cream cotton suit and bashed up black Range Rover. Ramage patrolled the Dorset coast, working the pubs and hotels, and jazz festivals and market town fayres and anywhere else where gossip and rumours travelled and wriggled through and around various versions of the truth. So it was no surprise to find the big black vehicle parked outside Lyme nick on that fine morning in early summer. The big man leaned against it and smoked a Hamlet cigar and gulped tea from a polystyrene cup he'd bought from a café on the seafront where he'd just been to survey the damage. There'd been two or three arrests for public order offences and criminal damage during the festivities and those miscreants had been shipped to the cells in Bridport. They would appear in court that morning, get bail no doubt and then fuck off back to Merseyside never to be seen again. Ramage had seen it all before. The courts were under such pressure to save prison space you virtually had to be accused of rape or murder before objections to bail were heeded.

But Garrigan and the Kelly brothers were still in the cells at Lyme, having been fed breakfast and given disposable toothbrushes they now awaited the arrival of the duty solicitor. Which was what Ramage was doing.

'Morning Mr. Gardner.' Said Ramage to Mark Gardner as the solicitor approached the front steps of the police station.

'Morning Mr. Ramage,' he replied with exaggerated routine politeness. The two knew each other from old and got on fairly well, both being fond of beer and football.

'I wonder who got the first call this morning, you or me?' continued the brief.

'I always get the first call, but you always get to jump the queue.'

'Yes, but I've actually got to do some fucking work for a living.' Gardner managed to say this fairly quietly as he brushed past the huge reporter.

'See you in the Goat for lunch?' enquired Ramage of Gardner's back.

'Maybe,' answered the brief over his shoulder as he pushed through the door of the police station.

Mark Gardner had his own legal practice in Lyme. The pickings were not rich, it had to be said, and he'd become something of a jack of all trades. A bit of probate, a bit of conveyancing and a bit of crime. This morning he was duty solicitor for police stations and had been happy to take such a local call. There were other occasions when he would have to travel to Weymouth and Dorchester to sit with miscreants as they were interrogated by the police, usually about various shenanigans of the previous evening.

63. On her way back to Lyme from Crewkerne Heather had to pull over to answer her mobile. It was Decker.

'Sarge?' she acknowledged.

'Go to the Seagull and speak to the barmaid at 11 o'clock, that's when she starts work, okay, get a statement from her. Don't take no for an answer, she must have seen something. I want to know who bashed up our scousers, it won't look good if they stand in court without us having done a thorough investigation into their injuries. The Mags'll think we done it. Okay?'

'Okay sarge.'

Decker had a good point. Danny Garigan and Paul Kelly were themselves victims. Barry Kelly had been lucky, otherwise he would have got a pasting too. She wondered who had done this. Attempts at the time to find witnesses had been a waste of time; everybody was moving on and nobody had really seen anything; it all happened really quickly officer and we were busy with the kids and they were screaming and anyway we're going home tomorrow must rush, bye.

Heather had already telephoned Alex of course and he was delighted. He could put the info on general release now. Heather had stolen the march, had identified three active criminals from information he had sent her and could not have done it otherwise. What had she said was in it for him? Best he arranged to visit Dorset again.

64. Darren and Josh Pyke emerged from the Everett's place warily and with sleep in their eyes. They'd spent the night in sleeping bags in an outhouse and were as stiff as boards. Emmett Everett had been asked to drive them to Axminster where they had thought they would spend the day drinking and lying low. But Emmett had refused. He had seen the blood on Darren and did not want to be seen with the Pykes for a while. He shut the gate behind them.

'Bastard,' muttered Darren. 'Would've only taken him a few minutes.'

'Aw, you can't blame him bruv, we're probably wanted men by now, somebody'll have recognised us last night, I bet.'

Darren said nothing, just turned his head and glared at his brother as they trudged along the narrow lane. They were watched by Carmella Everett, Emmett's green haired sister, from a window at the top of the strange Everett House. She turned her head and looked down on their yard to see her brother walking from one of the sheds with his shotgun, on his way to kill a mixxy rabbit, no doubt.

'Go on then, fuckin' say it.' Darren slowed as he said this, he was not muttering now.

'Say what?'

They both stopped walking.

'Say that last night wouldn't have happened but for me chatting to that bird.'

'I'm not sayin' that bruv.'

'No, but you're fuckin' thinking it aren't you!?'

Realizing what was about to happen he decided to overcome his fear of his brother and deploy a pre-emptive strike. This took the form of his favourite punch, a backhanded upward swing with the edge of his right hand to the throat of his opponent and Darren went down in a similar way to that of the glass wielding Paul Kelly on the previous evening.

'You fuckin' cunt!' he croaked as his knees hit the deck and his elder brother stood ready to deliver more if the need arose.

'Have some fuckin' respect Darren,' urged Josh, watching for Darren's next move, wary of the telescopic asp his brother invariably had in his back pocket.

But Darren stayed on his knees and just nodded. Josh could not remember a time when Darren Pyke had given in like this. Not ever. Was he ill or something?

'You okay bruv?'

'Yeah. Great. Just been felled by me brother. Yeah, great…'

'You were going to do it to me if I hadn't have…'

'Yeah, maybe, how d'you know though?'

'There's sumthin' the matter with you, bruv, you're not behavin' normal, how can I trust you when you do sumthin' like you did last night, in front of all those people?'

Darren got to his feet slowly. Josh backed away a step or two, watching that right hand and that back pocket.

'Trust me? Trust me did you say? Course you can trust me, I'd die for you bruv. I'd fuckin' die for you!'

'Me too bruv.'

With that Darren and Josh threw themselves at each other and hugged close and tight. They had always been up against it and had always come through. The younger boys were just wasters and their elder brother had flown the nest. It had always been up to Josh and Darren to put extra money in their mum's purse and to fight for the family's reputation, such as it was. Nobody ever slagged off the Pyke family for fear of it getting back to Josh and Darren.

65. Frankie Mills was in her first year at Southampton Solent University doing media studies. As with most of the new crop of undergraduates she had taken a gap year to earn some money but had done little else but spend it, hence the job in the Seagull Inn. The nasty business out on the patio the night before had shaken her. She knew the Pykes were involved but had no intention of saying anything to anybody about anything. She had grown up in the Triangle and was not going to get called a grass by her roots friends. That was what she called them, her roots friends. The ones who had never stayed on at school to do A-levels. The ones with no ambition at all, who would be driving tractors and working in shops and living happily in Lyme or Bridport or Axminster or in the outlying villages and farms for the rest of their lives. She kept these separate from her new life uni friends, none of whom lived locally, thankfully.

She expected a visit from the police and was not surprised to see an officer waiting by the door when she opened up the pub at 11am. The officer introduced herself as Heather Boyle and started by asking if she could buy a cup of coffee from her and drink it whilst they had a quick chat. She looked tired and Frankie was taken in by this show of human vulnerability and trust.

'Can I drink it inside so my sergeant doesn't catch me?'

'Yeah, sure, of course. And you can have the coffee free.'

'Cor, thanks. I'll buy you a drink next time I'm in here off duty.'

'No thanks.'

And with that it froze over a bit. Frankie didn't want to get cozy. Roots wouldn't approve. But she poured the cop a coffee into a mug from the already hot pot on the bar and put it down on the table in front of her. Whilst at the bar she had felt the cop staring at her, looking her up and down. Was she a suspect? No, that wasn't it. It was something else, and she didn't like it.

Heather thanked her and sipped. The barmaid sat down nervously at the table, on the edge of a chair.

'Well, what happened here last night then?'

'You mean the fight?'

'What else?'

'I dunno, all I saw was this guy lying on the floor and then another guy wading in with a glass in his hand and then another guy karate chopping the second guy in the throat.'

'Recognise....'

'No.'

'You sound very sure.'

'I am sure. Never seen them before in my life.'

'You can go and bottle up now Frankie, the back bar needs doing.'

Colleen Bradstock had walked into the beach bar in her dressing gown and slippers. Frankie wasted no time, nodded curtly at Heather and left.

'Come upstairs with me please officer. I don't want to be seen in my nightie.'

Heather smiled and rose. She held the mug awkwardly.

'You can bring that with you.'

'Thanks.' Heather was taken aback by this tall, middle aged beauty and followed her up two flights of a winding staircase to a wonderful Victorian room with the most brilliant sea view Heather had ever seen.

Colleen noticed Heather looking around her living quarters, taking in the view, blinking at the contrast between this environment and the one only a few feet below them.

'There's been a pub on this site for three hundred years. Downstairs has to change with the times, up here doesn't.'

'It's beautiful,' said Heather, still looking around admiringly, behaving more like a visitor to a museum than a uniformed police officer investigating a serious crime.

'Thank you. Would you like a top-up?' Colleen was referring to Heather's coffee mug.

'Oh, er, no thanks. Best get on with what I've come here for. You obviously know why I'm here, don't you.' It wasn't a question.

'Yes. Colleen Bradstock, pleased to meet you.'

'Oh, I'm sorry, I... Heather Boyle, I'm new here, recently transferred from the Metropolitan Police in London.'

Colleen smiled. 'Yes, I know where the Metropolitan Police is based Heather. We're not all country yokels around these parts you know.'

Heather was a little taken aback by this; a slight edge had crept into Colleen's voice.

'I'm sorry, I didn't say you were... I don't think you are... I've been made to feel very welcome by everyone. And it's certainly busy enough.'

She was regaining her control of the situation. 'Especially in the evening, where there's alcohol involved.'

Colleen raised her eyebrows and tilted her head slightly.

'Non-drinker are you?'

'No, but...'

'No, I know you're not, you were in here with your boyfriend a couple of weeks ago, I remember you. Never forget a face in this business.'

Heather was taken aback by this.

'Pardon?'

'Sorry, he may not have been a boyfriend, just a young man, had a cockney accent.'

'No, he's a former colleague from London,' Heather now remembered that she had had a drink with Alex in the pub when he was down visiting. This woman did not miss much.

'I don't miss much.'

'No. You don't. How do you do it?'

'Technology my dear. Look.'

With that Colleen pulled back a curtain to reveal a large flat screen on the wall. She stabbed at a remote control and it lit up with six simultaneous pictures of the pub's interior. She thumbed the remote and the pictures changed to include live shots of the exterior and of the kitchen and of the side alley that lead from the beach to the street. The quality was good and in colour. Colleen Bradstock could sit in her Victorian apartment and know everything that went on in her pub below. She continued with the demonstration and Heather became increasingly impressed by this strange lady. She was shown how frames could be frozen, close-ups shot, directional microphones used to eavesdrop conversations, till displays relayed, colour prints produced and how everything but everything was recorded on a hard drive and kept forever.

Before she was finished Colleen became aware that Heather was not looking at the screen but at her. She turned to face her guest.

'Yes, I know, bit of a contradiction, aren't I? I used to be in IT before moving here. Worked in London for my husband. He died.'

'I'm sorry.'

'Yes, so am I. Shall we get down to it then? You want the film from last night. I keep calling it film, stupid really, there's never been film used in years. Should call it material. Material generated during the course of an investigation.' She had walked over to a pc in the corner of the room, behind a Japanese silk screen and was tapping away on the keyboard.

'What's your email address?'

Heather was once again very impressed.

'Er… heather.boyle@dorset.gov.gsi.police, why?'

'I'll email it to you as an attachment, I'll give everything recorded yesterday from opening time onwards, that way you won't have to come back.'

Heather wasn't sure if she liked the last comment. Was she not welcome?

'Don't take that personally. Sorry. Pop in anytime, especially when you're off duty and not wearing the costume.' She looked Heather up and down as she said this, then turned back to the computer and pecked a few keys. She paused, stared at the screen, and tried again, frowning.

'It's not working, says the file is too large to send by email.'

Heather understood this. 'That figures, is it bigger than twenty five megabytes?'

'Yeah, the whole lot is 79MB it says.'

Heather had the answer. 'Ok, send it to my Google Drive account, then I'll pick it up on my laptop.'

Heather gave Colleen her Google Drive address and the publican complied, gladly. The job was now done, as far as she was concerned.

'There. It's done. Need anything else just email me back, okay?'

'Okay. Actually, yes, I'll need a written statement from you at some point, producing the digital material as an exhibit,' then the cop thought for a few seconds before saying, as if thinking out loud, 'or I could just produce it as my exhibit and then....'

Colleen had caught on, 'And then I wouldn't have to make a statement?'

'Possibly,' conceded Heather.

And before she knew it she was being led down the winding stairs to the front door of the pub. They shook hands and the police officer left. Heather felt like she had been dismissed.

66. Bertie Pentreath emerged from Barclays Bank in Axminster in a pensive mood. He'd just had an hour with Jack Fletcher, the manager. They had been fairly close over the years, enjoying a few beers together most weeks. Their wives socialized and they played the odd game of golf. But things were getting tight and Jack was beginning to distance himself. The auditors had been in and were not encouraging managers to lend to farmers; livestock values were decreasing almost by the day and land, unless it had planning permission, was worth bugger all. Bertie had regained a little ground with Jack with his clay pigeon shooting school idea. Jack was a keen shooter and warmed to the proposal. But when they had moved onto money the whole thing began to look shaky. They parted company with Bertie undertaking to look into the planning permission side of things – the town hall would have to have a say, no doubt about that. Christ, what a mess. He tried not to think about it too deeply. But there he was, a farmer thinking of opening a fucking clay

pigeon amusement arcade so he could get his daughter through university. He had always wished that Sally had given him a son, but now he was not so sure. A son would have been ashamed of him. A failed farmer - that was what he was. His only consolation was that he was one of many in that part of the world. He crossed the road and entered the nearest pub which happened to be the Duke of Clarence. He normally avoided the Duke but he wanted a drink and was on his own.

Apart from a handful of what Bertie called dole munchers the pub was empty. It was early lunchtime and the barman was eating a greasy bacon sandwich with greasier hands. Seeing this, Bertie ordered a bottle of light ale. He did not want those hands anywhere near a glass from which he was going to drink. He swigged the beer out of the bottle and gazed out of the window.

'Fuckin' filth!'

Harry Pitt's loud, semi-drunken voice was describing his opponent's safety shot. The language and volume caused Bertie to turn his head, which immediately attracted the following reaction.

'And what the fuck are you looking at old man?'

Bertie, normally a fairly timid man who lacked confidence, was not impressed by this piece of shit.

'Nothing. I'm looking at absolutely nothing.' As he continued to regard Pitt. The young man did not at first follow the subtlety of Bertie's response and had turned away and lined up another shot before it dawned on him. Then the cue stopped dead as the player slowly straightened and turned back towards the old man who had just insulted him. Usually Bertie would have felt fear when confronted like this, but felt nothing of the sort and found himself amazed by his own calmness. Something had happened to him very recently, perhaps even since leaving his bank manager only a few minutes earlier. And there was something about this boy that he felt deep down had to be defeated. Had to be challenged and defeated before it was too late. The hairs stood up on the old man's neck as the young man walked towards him, pool cue in hand, snarl on face.

Bertie waited until the young man was at just the right distance before bringing the right one up sharply and hard, the toe cap striking Harry just under his left kneecap. This caused Pitt to jack-knife forward, his head going down. The old man seized this opportunity, turning and sidestepping, looping his arm around the boy's neck and engaging a very tight headlock. Years heaving bails and bags and heavy machinery had made the old man as strong as an ox and Pitt could not move. He tried to grab Bertie's testicles so the old man brought his knee up into the snarling spitting face of his captive. Then one of the assembled associates joined in and jumped on Bertie from behind. He was dragged backwards and down, but tightened his iron grip on Pitt's neck. Pitt's face was puce and he was making strange gurgling sounds. He had stopped trying to disable Bertie and his arms were just flailing around desperately. Then it all stopped as suddenly as it had started. Bertie released his grip, shook off the other youths and stood up at the same time as Pitt staggered to his feet, coughing and reaching, eyes ablaze.

'I'll fuckin' have you for that one day you old cunt! You just fucking wait.'

As he said this he was distracted by the barman talking on the phone, no doubt giving the name of the pub to the police dispatcher.

'Don't bother with that Seb, it's over.'

Then, returning his glare towards Bertie,

'For now.'

Realizing that the police had been called and that Seb was not about to cancel them Pitt and his hangers on left. Bertie dusted himself down and decided to remain in the bar for a few minutes longer. He did not wish to be ambushed out in the street or, worse still, followed home.

67. It was nearly midday when Heather got back to Lyme police station and was sitting reviewing the CCTV recorded footage emailed to her by Colleen Bradstock. She was kicking herself. She had all this material but no written statement saying who had supplied it or where it had come from. Under the Criminal Justice Act documentary evidence, which is what the emails comprised, had to be exhibited into the prosecution case by way of written witness statements, and she had neglected to obtain one from Colleen. She would go back soon. But first she had to see if the footage was of any use. Garrigan and the Kellys had been banged up for twelve hours now and that left only another twelve before they would probably have to be either charged or simply released. Decker and Townsend were interviewing them in the presence of their solicitor, that much she knew, together with the fact that Decker would soon be on her case for video ammunition to be put to the detainees. She was frantic to find something. Oh, how she needed her luck to hold.

She powered up Windows media Player and used it to open the MP4 attachments emailed by Colleen. They were very good quality and the player software enabled Heather to fast forward the hours of coverage - right up to 36 times normal speed. There was a recorded time on the footage and Heather used it to home in to the period on the pub patio she considered relevant. The first thing she saw was Katie Pentreath sitting alone with a glass of red wine in front of her, rolling a cigarette. She froze the frame and zoomed in. Brilliant quality. Lovely girl. Beautiful hair. She continued and watched in real time. Then Darren Pyke appeared and joined the girl. They knew each other, but not well Heather surmised. There was a nervousness about Darren who she felt she knew but could not place. What she viewed over the next half hour had Heather almost running back down the hill to the Seagull Inn. She had to get that statement, together with a permanent version of the evidence on disc. It was no good her copying it to disc, that would have to be done by the exhibiting witness who she hoped had not gone to the cash and carry or was otherwise too busy to re-engage.

The Liverpudlians had clearly come off second best but Paul Kelly's apparent intention to deploy his beer glass gave one of the assailants a clear case of self-defence. The other one, the one with the telescopic asp (where had he got that from?) had problems; not least so because she knew she had seen him before somewhere, definitely a local. His breaking of Danny Garrigan's shoulder seemed unprovoked. What a psycho, thought Heather, as she walked into the Seagull looking around for Colleen.

68. Meanwhile, Darren and Josh were back in Lyme, checking out their van. Darren opened the driver's door, took his asp out of his back pocket, stuck it under the seat and locked the van up again. They had had the idea to brazen it out, return to the Seagull to find out what had happened after they'd left and re-assert themselves as men who appreciated discretion, so to speak. In other words they were going to intimidate potential witnesses.

The first thing they saw was Heather standing at the bar in uniform. Initially they froze, but only for a second or two.

'No, come on, fuck all happened, remember?' Darren hissed at Josh, and they continued their walk across the patio and into the bar. Heather was trying to get Frankie's attention but the barmaid studiously ignored the uniformed officer, staring instead at the incoming pair. Heather turned around to see what she was looking at and instantly recognised the two assailants. They did not acknowledge, instead politely ordered, paid for and took their drinks out to the patio where they sat down and lit cigarettes.

Heather knew she'd seen Darren somewhere before, before viewing the CCTV footage, but couldn't place him. She's been trying to process so many new faces lately. Anyway, she was going to get to know these two pretty well, pretty soon. She decided not to do it herself and walked through to the front bar of the pub, near the street. From a point at which she could still just see the Pyke brothers – they had looked around when she left the patio bar and had formed the conclusion that she had exited the pub altogether – she pulled out her airwave radio.

Reg Bull was punting his marked police car just along the seafront when the call came out. Urgent assistance required at Seagull Inn, Lyme Regis, by single officer about to arrest two suspects for serious assault. The message dispatcher was speaking from Dorchester, some forty miles away, so the message had travelled eighty miles to be delivered a few hundred yards from its source. No matter, within 45 seconds Reg joined Heather at the front of the pub. She briefed him and they both walked through to confront Darren and Josh Pyke.

'Afternoon boys,' greeted Reg, and they both looked up.

'Afternoon officers,' replied Darren, squiffily. The boys were on about their 6th pint of Stella.

'My colleague would like a word with you.'

They both looked at Heather. Darren actually gave her the once over, starting with the legs and loitering over the breasts. His lip curled as he met her eye. 'Yeah?' he said.

'Were you two in here last night?'

'Yeah' Said Darren. 'No,' said Josh, at the same time.

'So you were and you weren't,' said Heather, nodding at Darren and Josh respectively.

'No we both were. My brother gets confused,' answered Darren, with a light hearted laugh.

'Fuck off bruv,' chipped in Josh, contributing to the lightness, realizing that it was important not to appear nervous or defensive. The two had been through this many times before. Relax, be nonchalant.

Heather decided that she had enough to make arrests.

'I have reason to believe that you were both involved in a serious assault in this pub at around 9 o'clock last night. You are both under arrest. You are not obliged to say anything but it may harm your defence if you....'

Darren rose to his feet and Reg stepped forward, left palm extended, right hand on the handle of his stick. He of course knew Darren, had done for years. He knew that he would probably come quietly if spoken to right. The boy loved his mother and hated dawn raids at home, which was what would happen if the two of them resisted arrest and legged it now.

'Sit down Daz, she's okay, she has a job to do, don't make things messy.' Darren sat down again. He was pleased he'd deposited his asp in the van when they'd checked it on the way down. That would have been damning evidence.

It was the second time in as many days that Heather had felt isolated. She felt once again that her Dorset colleagues enjoyed a closeness with their charges to which she was not a party. 'Sit down Daz, she's okay...,' Heather was momentarily distracted by this and looked at Reg for a second or two, having to drag her eyes off of him as she agreed, 'Yes gents, I'm okay, I won't bite.'

'Who's been saying what about us this time?' asked Josh.

'Nobody has said anything. We've got two bashed up scousers in the police station and I've just seen the CCTV coverage of this place last night. You two are the stars of the show. Let's go, we've got a car out the front.'

Frankie the barmaid avoided eye contact as the boys filed through to the street, Heather in front, Reg at the rear. They all piled into the car and went to the police station. The lads sat glumly in the back seat. Josh was worrying that they may have been followed to the Everett's place the previous night, and if so would it get searched now, and if so would they find the stash, and if so…?

Darren was more focussed. Where were the cameras? Would these fucking scousers make statements? If so would they go to court?

They were told to remain in the car which Reg had driven into the back yard whilst Heather went in to the building to check that the victims of this crime – and the perpetrators of others – were safely locked away. Having established this to be the case Heather returned to the police vehicle and ushered her prisoners into the charge room where the custody officer, Sergeant Evans, sat frowning. In fifteen years at Lyme he'd rarely known it to be this busy. Five prisoners in at the same time? Same officer? Who was this girl from London?

69. When Bertie got home he found his daughter hard at her books. He smiled at her as he walked past the kitchen table to the huge dresser. He opened the bottom cupboard and took out a bottle of malt whisky. Katie watched every move. What the hell was going on here? It was barely 1 o'clock in the afternoon.

But Bertie was in a buoyant mood, his violent confrontation with the local yobbery, from which he had emerged, in his perception, the clear winner, had emboldened him. Life in the old boy yet.

'If you fancy taking, what do you call it, a gap year my dear, you can help me run my clay pigeon shooting school.'

Katie rolled her eyes. 'Dad, if I take a gap year it'll be to go to the Far East or the USA, not to help you run an amusement arcade on our farm.'

'Oh, "our farm" now is it? Wasn't "our farm" when I was milking the cows at 4 o'clock this morning. It was definitely "my" farm then, I seem to remember. Certainly felt like it anyway. Like it certainly felt like it when I was pulling drowned sheep out of the floodwater last year, I certainly seemed to have sole ownership then too. You and your mother like living on a farm, but you don't like the realities of running the damned thing.'

He had obviously been drinking already, surmised Katie, and it would now get worse.

'Yeah, okay Dad, whatever.' Her eyes dropped back to her books.

'No, not whatever, not whatever or what if or maybe or just suppose. It's going to happen. I've been to see the bank manager today and it's on. Planning permission is going through and we'll be open in six months, you wait. To hell with the dairy and the sheep and those bloody cattle. To hell with the EU and the Milk Marketing board. This is going to become a centre of sporting excellence. You wait. Clay pigeon shooting is an Olympic sport I'll have you know, and we'll have the best come here to train. We'll be able to charge top prices.'

He walked over and sat down close to her, plonking his bottle and a glass on the table. As he poured he talked.

'You see, all these failed farmers and golf courses, well, a golf course needs maintenance, and they can't compete with the established clubs, unless they try to open their own clubs which they just simply wouldn't be allowed to do,' he took a long pull of malt, 'but a clay shoot, there's not that many of them anyway and you don't need that much land and the maintenance is minimal....'

'Dad, I need to get on with this work. Please.' She smiled at him as she said this, patiently and pleasantly.

He went quiet for a second and then sighed.

'Okay my dear. I'll let you get on. Remember though, if you fancy that gap year once you've qualified there'll be a lot of money to be made. Then you can set up your own veterinary practice in Crewkerne or Chard or somewhere local.'

Sally and Bertie did not want to lose their only child. They did not want her, above all, to go abroad. Many of their friend's children had graduated and had not only left Dorset but had left the country. Sally and Bertie were terrified of that happening to them. It was bad enough Katie being at University, and she was back most weekends, for God's sake, to get her washing done.

70. 'Well, well, well,' Sgt Evans said as the Pykes had strolled into his charge room. 'Darren and Wayne, is it?'

'Josh,' said Josh.

'Eh?' said Sgt Evans.

'Josh. I'm Josh, this is Darren,' said Josh. Darren was disinterested in this stupid conversation his brother was having with fucking sergeant Bilko. He was more interested in the names written up on the wall board - the names of detainees already in the cells: GARRIGAN D, KELLY P, KELLY B. Beside each name was a number, 1, 3, & 4, denoting the cells they occupied, presumably. Darren wondered what the matter was with cell 2.

The Pykes knew the score, giving their names and address and emptying their pockets. They were asked if they wanted anyone informed of their arrest and declined. They were asked if they wanted a solicitor and accepted. They jointly nominated a man called John Witchelow, a solicitor from Chard who, in their estimations, knew the score. Sgt Evans smiled as he tapped Witchelow's name onto the computerised custody record. He reckoned Witchelow was on some sort of retainer with the Pykes, they kept him busy enough.

Their detention authorities pending ongoing enquiries; the brothers were put in cell 2 together to await interview when the brief arrived.

71. Upstairs in the police station canteen Heather and Reg were writing their arrest notes and sipping tea. They were nearly finished when in walked Decker and Townsend.

'Here she is – our new superstar,' announced Townsend. She looked up and smiled at them. Townsend was grinning at her. Decker had his eyebrows raised and his head cocked to one side.

'Don't take the piss DC Townsend. PC Boyle is obviously a worker. We could do with more of her type.'

Stuart Townsend's eyes went down for a second. He had misjudged the situation; had expected Decker to join his gentle ribbing of the new officer. Instead he had made him look foolish. It went quiet.

'Get the teas in then Townsend, come on, and ask these working officers if they need a top up.' Decker was enjoying this. Stuart Townsend obeyed. Both Heather and Reg accepted the offer of more tea. It would have been rude not to.

The teas were brought over from the hatch by the obedient Townsend – Heather was enjoying this – and the two detectives sat at an adjacent table.

'We'll let you get on with your notes folks. Don't mind us.' Decker was polite and respectful.

Heather and Reg got on with their notes, conferring only when necessary and in the lowest of voices, mindful that the CID officers were within earshot. Not that they were conspiring or anything, just that they did not want any clever comments coming from Townsend.

After five or ten minutes, their clerical work complete, Reg and Heather rose, gathered up their notebooks, radios and other police paraphernalia and made to leave the canteen. As they walked towards the door Decker twisted around in his chair,

'I'm sure you've already thought of this but we need to find out who the girl is, she seemed to be the centre of attention last night if the video is anything to go by.'

Townsend was nodding.

'Okay sarge,' said Heather, as she walked out with Reg. She realized Decker must have viewed the MP4 she'd received from Colleen Bradstock which she'd then attached to the electronic crime report. It occurred to her that she had still not obtained a written statement from Colleen, exhibiting the material.

'We have to go back down to the pub Reg,' she told her older colleague as they walked down the stairs.

'Why's that then?'

'I've yet to get a statement from the landlady.'

'Best we go now then. Decker and Townsend'll want to start interviewing those two soon. They'll want a statement first; the video'll probably be their only evidence.'

'How d'you mean?'

'Well, those scousers won't want to say anything, will they?'

'No, suppose not.'

'Not as they're getting charged with a load of thefts. They'll just want to get bail and fuck off out of the county, if you'll pardon my French.'

'French pardoned.'

And Reg was pretty much spot on. The scousers were held for the full twenty four hours. Decker applied to the Superintendent for more time but the alleged offences, thefts of handbags and purses and the like in pubs, were not serious enough to warrant additional detention. So Garrigan and the Kelly Brothers had to be released on police bail to return at a later date by which time enquiries would be complete. Some chance of that. Merseyside Police did checks on the Liverpool addresses they gave and, of, course these were verified by people who probably did not reside there full time themselves. Decker invited Heather to take a long look at the scousers as they were being given back their belongings by the custody officer before leaving the station. She would not, he informed her, see them again. Heather responded like a brand new probationer. She thought it would be unwise to remind Decker that she had actually just spent a very busy four years in the Met and knew all about people jumping bail. She was not much bothered about not seeing the scousers again. It was a matter of job done, really. They would scoot back to Merseyside and the hangers on would either join them or carry on down the coast. Either way, Dorset was well rid. Heather was much more interested in the Pyke brothers. They had committed the more serious offences and the departure of their Liverpudlian victims meant a dearth of evidence. The video footage was good, but such material rarely proved to be enough by itself in court. Juries liked human witnesses, and there was really only one to this offence. The girl. The girl who had actually left the scene with the assailants. So, not only was she a witness, she was also a possible accomplice. Or could be treated as such until she provided a witness statement. Heather looked forward to meeting her again. Especially as she was sure that she'd seen her somewhere before, very recently. Why did she keep getting that feeling about people? Were they duplicated around here? Were they all related look-alikes?

72. Darren and Josh got bailed out as well, a respectable while after the scousers to give the latter time to clear town. John Witchelow had, as usual, advised them to say nothing when questioned until the police had finished their enquiries. It would only be then that they would see what sort of case they faced and what they had to deny. But the brief interview gave Heather a chance to meet these two again, see the whites of their eyes. Not that they looked at her much, they just kept their eyes on their brief, waiting for signals and prompts like a couple of child actors. Having signed for their belongings and having agreed to return three weeks later, they walked up the hill to their van. The parking ticket had long since run out and had been replaced by a fixed penalty notice. It joined the others in the glove compartment. They would have to sell the vehicle soon, replace it with a 'clean' one. The Pyke brothers went home to get some of their dad's cider down them and then some decent sleep. Lay low for a while.

73. Decker and Townsend were in the CID office drinking coffee. They had interviewed the Pyke brothers separately, each interrogation taking place in the presence of Witchelow, the brief. Both boys had refused to answer any of the questions, even when shown the video footage from

the pub. They were experienced lads and knew that the legal warnings about silence at the police station not always being the best alternative was a load of shite. Okay, yes, a judge later could invite a jury to draw adverse inferences regarding a person's refusal to answer questions put to him by the police, but it rarely happened. And anyway, Witchelow had told them to remain silent – who were they to ignore good legal advice?

'Who is that fucking girl?' said Decker, half to himself as he threw a half full polystyrene cup of coffee into a bin.

'She has to come in. She's an accomplice. Has supergirl found her yet?'

'Dunno,' said Townsend. Probably will though, knowing her. She seems to be pretty lucky.'

'Yeah, often the same with newcomers. It soon fizzles out though. She's keen to impress now but she'll slow down. Let's have another look at the video.'

With that the two detectives sat through over an hour of unedited electronic material. It could always be that they'd missed something the first time round. But they had not, and the only chance they had to progress this was to identify the girl with the red wine and the hand rolling tobacco who left the pub with the Pyke brothers. She was the key. Danny Garrigan and Paul Kelly had both made victim statements which could be read out in court in their absence. Their wounds had been photographed and the medical evidence would be provided by the doctor who had treated them in the cells. Hospitalisation had not been necessary, but there was still enough for a malicious wounding charge against the Pykes. They just had to find and turn that girl.

74. That girl was riding Gabby. The usual bridle path, on her way to her usual place on the ridge from which she would be able to see a long winding stretch of the Dorset coast. It had been a few days now since the nasty business in the pub. She had stayed out of town, spending time with her parents and her books and her horses. The studying was going

well and she was becoming enveloped in that lovely feeling of timeless relaxation that can be found in the deep countryside.

Not today though.

'Afternoon.'

He'd been waiting for her. Lying propped up against the steep bank of a hedgerow with his hands clasped behind his head and his legs crossed, he was also relaxed. He had been waiting for her; that was clear. And she found herself pleased to see him.

She pulled the horse up. Gabby snorted with derision. She wasn't going to get all the attention today after all.

'Good afternoon.' She replied, pleasantly, quietly.

'Can we have a talk?'

'Yes, of course.' She dismounted and tied the horse loosely to a gate before sitting down alongside Darren Pyke. They were quite high up. Across the road from where they sat there was a rare gap in the hedgerow through which they had a grand view of the sea, about two miles to the south. The weather was beautiful. The blue sky and blue sea turned misty and pale as they met each other, blending in, joining, as one; they were, after all, made of the same stuff.

Nothing was said at first and they both got out their tobacco and made cigarettes. There was a familiarity between them which she found comforting and scary at the same time. The violence in the pub that night seemed a long time ago, even though it was less than three days previously. She lit their fags with what was now her lighter and they both exhaled long plumes of blue smoke into the still summer air.

'Sorry about the other night.' It had to be said.

'It's okay.'

'That bloke was being a pest to you.'

'Yes, but there was no need....'

'I know, I know, I went in hard. But we have to you see, me and my brothers, we have to go in hard otherwise we come off worst.'

'What do you mean?'

'Katie, we are the Pyke brothers. People hate us.'

'I don't. I've never even heard of you.'

'Dunno how not.'

'Well, I've only recently started going out in Lyme and places like that. I was always a swot at school.'

'Which school did you go to?'

'Colleton Girls. Private school. Boring.'

'Oh.'

There was then a thirty second pause whilst Darren decided to get something over with.

'Listen, Katie, me and Josh got pulled in the next day, arrested and questioned that is. We never said nothin' but one of the questions they kept asking was who you were. "Who was the girl with the long hair" they kept asking.'

'How did they know I was there?' asked Katie, alarmed, sitting forward and turning to him.

'CCTV. They showed me pictures of you and me sat there. Some film, like, we were chatting fine. Then I left, then that idiot came and sat with you, then I came back and it all kicked off.'

'Do you think they'll want to speak to me?'

'Yeah. I reckon the two scousers have gone, they won't give evidence.

Nobody else in the pub'll have seen anything, I promise you, and the CCTV stuff can't be relied on in court....'

'Are you sure?' She was working with him. They were together in this.

'Yeah. My brief'll tear it to bits. It's easy for us to see because we know what happened but all a jury'll see is the gaps, the bits not covered. They need a witness and they'll be looking for you Katie.'

'Shit.' She felt sick and looked away. All of a sudden it wasn't such a lovely summer's day. A lone cloud moved across the sky, got between them and the sun and everything around them darkened.

'We left together,' Katie continued, 'I'm an accessory.'

'Nah, you didn't do anything, remember that. The CCTV backs that up okay. But I'm worried they'll try to bully you into giving evidence against me... like by saying if you don't you'll get charged as well.'

'Are you charged? Are you going to court?'

'No, not yet. Bailed to go back to the police station. They need time to do more enquiries. Which means they need more time to find you. Stay out of town.'

'Pardon.'

'Just stay out of town for a good while. Keep your head down.'

She did not like this one bit.

'Now just hold on there Darren. I didn't do anything. I was sat minding my own business when this happened. Having some peace. Yes, you and I have become friends, but that's where it ends. I'm not some sort of moll who does what she's told....'

She trailed off, she did not like the way he was looking at her. He flicked away his cigarette and turned to face her square on. He did not touch her, but was very close.

'Look Katie, it'll just be for a few weeks then you can go back to university and after a few months the whole thing'll be forgotten. Just do it for me.'

'No,' she got to her feet. 'No, I will not behave like some sort of fugitive. What if my mum and dad want to take me into Lyme for a meal, or to the theatre? What have I got to say to them? Oh, sorry, can't come, the police are looking for me to interview me about an assault committed by a man I was seen drinking with? You must be joking Darren!'

He was still sitting, and now was gazing out to sea. Like many of his kind, he would never give eye contact when he was being admonished or questioned or criticised.

She walked over to the horse and with that he was on his feet. Just as she was about to put her foot in the stirrup she felt his hand on her shoulder. She turned and saw a very earnest Darren Pyke. His hand dropped from her shoulder and now both hands held her by the upper arms. Not a tight grip, but firm.

'Listen Katie. You come from the right side of the sheets. You've got a chance in life. Now give me and my brother a chance.'

All of a sudden it was him and his brother, she thought. How people can realign themselves when the chips are down. Thicker than water.

'It's got nothing to do with me.' She pulled away from him and put her foot back in the stirrup. She was frightened. He let her get onto the horse.

She gathered the reins and looked down at him. She pulled the horse around but he grabbed the halter with his left hand. His right hand held her by the thigh, just above the knee. She froze.

'Don't worry Katie, I won't let anyone harm you.'

Then he let go, eye contact between the two lingered for a second and she moved off. He stood watching her. The horse picked up a bit of speed and was trotting away within ten yards. Jesus Christ. He thought,

Jesus Christ, no. She's frightened of me. What a mess. And he walked away. Five minutes later she was up on the ridge looking back. There was no sign of him. No white van, nothing, and she had a view of every road and every field for miles.

75. It was a Saturday, and Dorchester Town Football Club were playing Arsenal in a pre-season friendly. Every copper in the county, and some, had been drafted in. There was a carnival atmosphere in the town. Thousands of Londoners in red shirts filled the pubs; many had been there since the previous evening. Trouble was not expected but contingency plans had to be in place. A marquee had been erected at the rear of police HQ and in this was a huge makeshift police canteen. Officers sat at long trestle tables drinking tea and eating pre-packed sandwiches. A few huddled to play cards. It was relaxed and easy. Everyone was cheerful, most were getting paid overtime.

Heather and Reg sat at a table with the Bridport lot. A bit of piss-taking was going on.

'Hey Heather, brought your dad out of the day centre for the afternoon?'

'Oi Reg, wait till I see your missus, you've been teaching that young girl the county roads for three months now, she a slow learner or are you fucking' stalkin' her?'

'Leave it out, they might be in love, you never know....'

'What would you fuckin' know about anything Spratt, you don't know what it's for.'

'Yeah Spratt, never 'ad your skin back, I bet.'

Darkie Spratt usually ended up on the receiving end of any piss-take, no matter where it started, because he always had to try to join in. Heather jumped to his defence.

'Leave Darkie alone, he's better looking than you Rumsey.'

Eric Rumsey swivelled around in alternating directions a few times, 'Sorry, someone talking to me – oh, a woman, one of those things, quite few in the police nowadays....'

'Fuck off Rumsey,' bantered Heather, 'I'll deck you any day.'

There was laughter, without irony. It was going to be a good day. They would all be off duty by 6 or 7 and would go and get drunk together. It was days like this that made being in the police almost worthwhile. In a few days' time they would be at each other's throats again mind, or stabbing each other in the back, such were the jealousies.

A little bit of this surfaced there and then.

'Hear you getting fast tracked into the CID Heather.' This was from Jack Mordecai, a young, ambitious PC from Crewkerne. Rumour had it that he was having a little fling with Maxine, one of Heather's domestic violence colleagues.

'Leave it out,' intervened Reg, 'We're 'avin' a nice day, don't need....'

'No, It's okay Reg,' said Heather, before turning to the smirking Mordecai, 'No Jack, I applied for it but I got told I had to slow down, nick a few less people, or I would show you up and you would play the 's' card, sue the job for sex discrimination if I got in the CID before you.'

'Who told you that, the Chief Constable? She's a right one to talk about that. Gets her cock cut off to get up the ladder....'

'Ah fuckin' leave it out Jack, for fucks sake, I'm havin' my sarnies.' Rumsey re-introduced the humour to the day, they all laughed, including Mordecai.

76. Carmella Everett drove the big Land Rover to the bottom of Rockham Ditch and then up over the other side. At the top of the other side of the valley was a copse of oak and holly trees. A strange mix that

gave the small piece of woodland a rich and dark density. Carmella liked to sleep rough occasionally and she kept various items of camping equipment, including a tent, under a tarpaulin at the centre of the copse. A strange kid, she had never really been to school after the age of fourteen, the teachers sort of wrote her off as a country girl who would never really be a statistic. She cooked for her brothers and looked after her mum. And she did other things as well.

At the other side of the copse was an old military road. This separated the Everetts land from that of a Mrs. Walters who had a few sheep and who lived with her many cats and large inheritance. Mrs. Walters was no bother and her land provided a nice buffer zone between the Everett's and the real farmers of the region. The first of those, adjacent to Mrs. Walters, was the Pentreath lot. Fuckin snobs, they were. The old woman always in Axminster talking posh over cups of frothy coffee, the old man with his nice 'drover and subsidised tractors. And now this latest development – Darren shagging their stupid student daughter. Carmella couldn't bear to think of it. She had part learned and part surmised this version of events by listening to local rumour and adding bits of her own to feed her own self-pity and loathing of the outside world. She parked the Land Rover up at the edge of the copse and walked into it, through to the other side. He was already there, up in the hide. The treehouse was built about twenty feet up in an old oak and had been erected to help direct the local fox hunt, when it had been legal. Now it was used by Darren Pyke to watch Katie Pentreath. Before that it had been used by Darren Pyke and Carmella Everett for... just being together. Darren would now sit up there with his binoculars for hours and look straight into the backyard of the Pentreath farm. He wasn't so much looking out for her leaving the place; he was looking out for people visiting her, particularly if those people just happened to be members of the Dorset Constabulary. That was his story, anyway.

There was a rope ladder attached to the trunk of the oak and Carmella pulled herself up it. She was fit and strong, her calloused hands and muscular arms doing most of the work, her legs barely taking part.

He had been there all night, it was plain to see, and was still in his sleeping bag. Lying on his stomach he was propped up on his elbows looking through the binoculars. He didn't even acknowledge Carmella.

'You been here all night you sad fuck?' She pulled out a dog end from her jeans pocket and fumbled around for a light.

He made no reply.

'You got a light?'

He shook his head.

'Where's your lighter?'

He shrugged.

'I gave you that lighter years ago Darren, you're never without it.'

He remained silent, just looked at the Pentreath farm. She followed his gaze and her intuition prompted a wild guess.

'Suppose she's got it, has she?'

He nodded, almost imperceptibly.

Oh, that's fuckin' great, isn't it? She's got the only thing I ever gave you stuffed in her pocket next to her fanny. That makes me feel fuckin' great.'

No reply. She lay down beside him, on her side facing him, and put her arm over his shoulders and her leg over his backside.

'You're fuckin' in love with her aren't you?' she accused him as she hooked her leg around his body and pulled herself against him. He dropped the binoculars and unzipped the sleeping bag. She wriggled in beside him. She was surprised when she got an answer.

'It's not that I'm in love with her, I just, well, it's like I'm scared Carmella. I keep thinking about her all the time. She could have me locked up for a long time if she talks to the police, gives a statement like, it's like I want to warn her from doing it but all I know is how to threaten people and I can't threaten her. She's better than me, she's....'

'She ain't better than you Darren Pyke, she ain't better than nobody, she's just a fuckin'....'

With that his hand came up from where it had been at the small of her back and gripped her throat.

'That's enough,' he hissed. She closed her eyes and let the moment pass. She had been putting up with his temper since they were infants. His gripped slacked, she breathed again and his hand slipped down to her breasts and then down and around to her backside. Her hand was busy too and they kissed each other like they always had done. Carmella had never kissed anyone else. Darren had not kissed very many others. Then all of a sudden he pulled away from her and pushed her hand away from his groin.

'We got to stop doing this. It's not right.'

'Why isn't it right Darren? We've being doing it for years, hasn't harmed anybody. I'm on the pill, there won't be a baby now.'

'It's not that.'

'What is it then? It's her isn't it, fuckin' snobby arse over there.'

'No.'

'Yes'

'No!'

'Yes!' she thrashed out of the sleeping bag and sprang to her feet. The hide shook as she stomped on the wooden plank flooring.

'You tell me you're watching for the police, fuckin' liar, you're watchin' her fuckin' bedroom. Don't lie Darren. Tell the truth and I won't mind, it's not like we're married or anything....'

'Shut up,' he had his hands over his face, 'shut up, shut up, shut the fuck up!'

Carmella Everett did shut up. She stood there, hand on her hips and looked down at her half-brother. She had idolised him since they had played together in nappies. He was a year older than her and the only boy she'd ever known, apart from her full brothers. They were rarely seen out together but looked a good couple when they were. Despite sharing a father they did not look alike apart from both being tall and athletic. He had dark hair and hers was the copper green of a deep country girl. His skin was the barroom suntan of a low life liver, and hers was tanned bronze. He wore chav shell suits and trainers; she was never seen in other than faded jeans and washed out tee-shirts. Always braless.

He got to his feet and wiped his face with his sleeve. She backed off to give him space as he rolled up the sleeping bag and stowed it in a polythene bag which he then jammed in one of the roughhewn rafters of the tree-house. She watched him. Watched how her life partner – a term she'd got from one of the many American novels she read - seemed to be disintegrating. It had been three weeks now since he'd told her about the incident in the pub. He'd spent increasing amounts of time up in that old oak, often sleeping there overnight. She had spent a few of those nights with him at first, but had stopped making herself available when she realised he wasn't thinking of her when they made the tree-house shake in the moonlight.

77. 'You got a statement from that girl yet?'

Decker was ever anxious for results and knew that the Pyke brothers could not be charged with the assaults without their female companion turning on them. The scousers had predictably not answered their bail and could be written off as witnesses. Under fairy recent legislation however you do not need a victim to prove an assault. If you've got medical evidence, photographs and corroborative evidence you have the victim statements read out in court as if they were giving evidence live from the witness box. The CCTV footage was good but would not stand up on its own. That girl was a must.

'I'm still looking for her sarge.'

'Do you know who she is?'

'No, but I'll find her.'

Decker's eyebrows moved upwards as he walked away across the floor of the canteen to get a cup of tea.

And Heather knew that she would find that girl. It had taken a couple of days before she had realised that she had an answer to the problem. She had been on late shift and was at home, trying to relax before going to work. Whilst flicking through some TV channels she alighted on a horse race, and she had it. Rosie. Or was it Katie. One was a horse and the other a girl. A beautiful girl with tasty thighs and a lovely arse, she remembered. It had to be her. She would find her, oh yes, now that it was an obsession.

78. Reg Bull parked his little police car halfway onto the steep grass verge of the narrow road. The vehicle was tilted at such an angle that when he opened the driver's door it hit the verge and jammed there. When he'd finally managed to extricate himself from the car he walked across the road to a gate. One foot on the bottom bar he leaned on the heavy wooden frame and surveyed the steeply declining paddock that fell away before him. In the paddock were two horses. Reg had viewed the video footage of the Seagull Inn affray and he'd had an idea. An idea that he was keeping to himself for now. After a few minutes of rumination he struggled back into his car and drove to Lyme. At the police station he strolled into the canteen and got himself a cup of tea which he took to a table by the window. He sat down by himself. There was no one else in the room until Heather Boyle walked in a few minutes later to begin her scheduled refreshments break. It was exactly 10am.

'Hiya Reg,' said Heather, cheerfully, as she walked to the serving hatch.

'Can I get you anything?'

'No thank you.' The response was terse.

'Oh. Right.' She noted his mood and it worried her. She had been very busy and had been spending increasing amounts of time with her CID colleagues, almost behaving as if she was one of them. She was concerned that this would be perceived badly by the uniformed officers and to varying extents her concerns were well founded, but hey, she had a career to think about. Having said that, she didn't want to upset Reg Bull. He had parented her for several weeks after her arrival and she wanted him to think that she was grateful and regarded him as her friend and confidant.

She got a coffee and walked slowly, tentatively, towards where he was sat.

'Can I join you?'

'Yeah, suppose so.' He was looking out of the window.

She sat down opposite him, a small table was all that separated them, but he would not look at her, just gazed out of the window.

'What's the matter Reg?'

'I know who the girl is.'

Heather feigned ignorance.

'What? What girl?'

'Your girl. The witness.'

Heather kept her powder dry, waiting to see if Reg's idea corroborated her own.

'Oh, that's great, let's go and see her. We'll go together.'

'Not yet.' Now he turned to face her.

'What? Why not yet?'

'I've got a few more enquiries to do, just to make sure.'

'Well let me in on it, it's my enquiry.'

'Oh, is it now?'

'Look Reg, I haven't got time for this, the domestic violence unit I'm running at Crewk....'

'You're running? You're running? Oh, so Maxine and Suzy are just your helpers now are they?'

'I didn't mean it like that, I meant....'

'I know what you meant young lady,' Reg was rising out of his seat as he said this, 'I know what you meant.'

With that he was gone. She sat there, staring at her coffee and his untouched cup of tea.

As Reg Bull ambled across the car park to his police car he allowed himself a little smile.

79. There was nobody at home when Reg drove the liveried police car into the courtyard of Lower Brooklands Farm. Bertie Pentreath was in Axminster with his bank manager again, Sally was shopping in Dorchester, accompanied by Katie. Reg strolled around the yard for a few minutes and was greeted by numerous cats and chickens. It was a clean and tidy farm. The cows had been milked and put back out to grass, eight or ten piglets scuffled about cheerfully, annoying their huge mother who lay in mud against a wall in the sun and a big bull called Barton bellowed triumphantly from the top of a nearby field he shared with

twelve pregnant cows. Idyllic. But not for long, thought Reg. As he drove away from the farm Reg decided that he would return later. He figured it would not be long before Heather worked out for herself who her witness was and get there before him, now that she knew he had a head start. He need not have worried. Things were going to move on very quickly by themselves now. Watching Reg Bull was Carmella Everett from the hide in the oak about three hundred yards away. She was alone and had been reading, not paying much attention, just enjoying some peace. But she had noticed the police car and the little hairs on the back of her neck bristled. She was talking to them. She would be a witness. She would send Darren down. Carmella made her mind up there and then to save the love of her life; no way were they going to lock her Darren up in a prison. No way.

Carmella swung down from the tree house and trudged through the copse to her Land Rover. She drove up the hill to the Everett homestead to find Darren, Josh and her brother Emmett working in the silage pit. She couldn't work out whether they were burying something or digging something up. She knew better than to ask. But she knew generally what they were up to. They'd been away overnight with the horsebox attached to the back of Darren's van. There would not have been any horses involved though, that was for sure.

She went over to where the boys were working and took hold of Darren's arm and started to pull him to one side. Emmett pretended he didn't see this and continued working in the pit. Josh watched with open suspicion. He did not like Carmella and had suspected her of corrupting his brother from an early age, which was a bit rich.

Having got him out of earshot she whispered urgently into his ear,

'The police have been to Brooklands Farm.'

'When?' Darren was startled by this.

'Just now, about ten minutes ago. A cop in a blue and white car. Just on his own.'

'Ah. Prob'ly nuthin.' Darren was keen to set her mind at rest.

'Does she know your name? I mean your full name and where you live.'

'No, she doesn't. And that's a fact.'

'But she saw what happened and the police have had you in. If she….'

'Yeah Carmy, I know all that, stop worryin' it'll be fine, she won't grass, I've spoken to her. She won't even go into Lyme now. I've dealt with it. Now fuck off, I've got work to do.'

With that he pulled away from her and re-joined Josh and Emmett at the silage pit. They had been working hard lately.

80. Heather lay on the sofa in Dorchester reading the Sunday newspapers. Her mother and Don Pryce were out for the day so she had the house to herself. She had the idea to call a friend in London when her mobile went off. It was a friend in London, but not the one she'd had in mind.

'Oh Christ,' she thought.

'Hello Alex,' she said.

'Where's my shag then?' he laughed.

'Dunno. Think I might have lost it down the back of the car seat, or left it a pub or something.'

'Shoddy. Listen, something's come up….'

'Yeah, I bet it has, put it away!'

'No, seriously Heather, you'll not believe this, you couldn't make it up.'

'Probably not, but I bet you're going to.'

'That's fucking unfair girl, what about the scousers, they were real enough were they not?!'

She was done on that one. 'Yeah, suppose so, sorry.'

'Right then. One of my mates' snouts does a bit of drugs work down in Bristol. He reckons there's a team down there uses a horsebox to transport gear in. A horsebox on the back of a white van.'

She was off the sofa.

'Jesus! I think... nah, could be anybody.'

'I've got a registration number.'

'You're kidding, wait till I get a pen....'

'And what, might I ask, are you going to do with a pen?'

'Write down the registration number that you are going to fucking give and yes, whatever, you can have as many shags as you like!' She lied.

'Bollocks!'

'Yours or clean ones?'

'You're going to have me over again.'

'Oh Alex, when are we going to stop this silly game. When are you going to find yourself a girl? A girly girl that is.'

'Not until I've given you a good seeing to. Only then will I be able to move on in life my love. Only then.'

'Registration number.'

'No.'

'Yes.'

'No.'

'I've seen a white van pulling a horsebox down here, I know I have, and I know whose it is as well.'

'Okay, here it goes, ready?'

'Yeah.'

'V345 ASU.'

'Is that the horsebox or the van?' she realised what she had said before the last word was fully spoken, but it was too late.

'Ha. Ha ha ha ha ha ha ha ha haaaa – well now. I think I'd better come on down there and hold your liddle bitty hand sweet missy, jes' in case you get yourself a bee sting or a liddle biddy mud on your liddle biddy pop-socks, eh?' Alex delivered this in a southern redneck drawl. Heather was puce.

'Fuck off.' Was all she could muster, not very loud either.

'Ah's comin down and ah'll be there tonight missy.' With that he hung up.

She smiled. She sort of loved him a bit really, and hey, this sounded interesting.

81. It was a grand day down on the seafront. Lyme was awash with day trippers and there was a brass band playing on the beach. The fishing boats were doing fine business taking families out to sea for an hour and coming back with bunches of fresh mackerel. The pubs were buzzing and everything was hunky dory, just like the English seaside should be.

Darren and Josh had left the van well out of the way, behind a church in the old part of town, about half a mile from the front. They walked in silence along the busy promenade. Their pale skin and dark nylon clothing set them apart, but nobody looked at them. They did not look like they would appreciate being looked at too much. They eyed everyone with derision. Fucking happy families. They walked into the Seagull Inn to find Colleen Bradstock working behind the bar, helping her staff during the busy part of the daytime session. She would not be there during the evening session; she could watch that from upstairs.

'Everything alright Colleen?' Asked Darren, quite pleasantly.

'Everything's just fine Darren, thank you for asking.' She began her reply before he had even finished the question.

'Good,' said Darren, 'Just checking.' And they turned and walked out. Colleen watched them go and shook her head. She had been in the area a good while now and new that the jolly exterior concealed not far beneath a pretty nasty underbelly. There are cockroaches beneath the floorboards of the best of kitchens.

Having made their presence known the two youths walked slowly up the hill to the police station. They had an appointment and could not really afford to be late. Witchelow would be waiting.

And he was. The middle aged solicitor hated these two pieces of shit and the fact that he's had to turn out today for a hundred and fifty quid. Legal aid work paid little these days, but old lags like Witchelow couldn't be fussy in a competitive and overcrowded profession.

'Alright lads?' he greeted them.

'Alright John,' they answered in unison.

'It's going to be a no comment job again, unless I say different, okay?'

They nodded.

'If they start asking who the girl was that was with you, you don't know, okay?'

'Well, we don't know, that's the truth, she was just sat there, that's all.' Darren was protesting a little too much.

'Yeah, save it Darren. Like I said, volunteer nothing and don't answer any questions unless I advise otherwise.'

They went in.

Heather Boyle and Stuart Townsend were waiting. The Pyke brothers were booked in by the custody sergeant. Darren was searched and put into a cell, his possessions sealed in a polythene bag. Josh was taken straight into the interview room. He and Witchelow sat at one side of the table and Heather and Townsend at the other. A few meaningless pleasantries were exchanged and the recording machine was switched on. Heather introduced herself and her colleague for the tape and Witchelow did the same for himself and his client. Heather cautioned Josh,

'You are not obliged to say anything but it may harm your defence if you fail to mention now something you later seek to rely on in court.'

Then she went straight to it.

'Who was the girl?'

'On my advice my client does not intend to answer any of your questions officer.'

'Yes, but I intend to ask them,' snapped PC Boyle,

'Who was the girl?'

'You've already asked that question officer.'

'Yes, and I'm asking it again – who was the girl in the pub Josh?'

'Officer,' Witchelow was beginning to raise his voice, Townsend was looking at Heather whose face was reddening,

'I've advised my client not to answer any questions until we have had full disclosure. You have not even shown us the video footage....'

Heather interjected, 'That's coming now.'

She flicked on the computer and dragged the keyboard towards her. A few taps and some edited footage of the Seagull Inn on the night in question started to roll.

'Are we going to get a copy of this?' asked Witchelow.

Heather nodded. Townsend was still looking at her, he was impressed.

They watched the coverage of the alleged assaults. They watched as Darren's weapon, was it a length of steel or stick or something, it seemed quite flimsy, was swung downwards. It was not possible to see where it actually connected as some people stood up in front of the camera at that point, probably to vacate their seats to get out of the way. Then they saw Josh being rushed at and swing his backhand chop in defence, and then there was glass and then there was blood and chaos. The only clear, consistent feature of the video was the girl with long brown hair who sat at the centre of it all, motionless.

'The video you've just seen is exhibit CB/1, do you want to see it again?'

'No thank you,' said Witchelow, 'It's clear already that you have little to ask my clients about. A pub fight during which they appear to be defending themselves.'

'Not what the victims claim Mr. Witchelow.'

The statements of Danny Garrigan and the Kelly brothers, for what they were worth, had been served on Witchelow on the previous occasion, when he had attended the station following the arrest of his clients. They were unimpressive, clearly made by witnesses who had no intention whatsoever of attending court or even being called to do so. But the statement of the doctor was good, and those of the ambulance crew. The injuries were quite serious, definitely grievous bodily harm. The Crown prosecution Service would undoubtedly reduce the charges to common assault to render them incapable of Crown Court trial, thereby keeping the trial, if there was one, at the Magistrates Court to save money.

'If the witness statements are so good officer then why don't you charge my clients now?'

Heather was a bit stuck here. The fact was that there was not enough. The video had too many gaps, no matter how many times she reviewed it. If she could only locate that girl. Then she had an idea.

'It looks like I'm going to have to if I can't find that girl. We consider the video evidence is enough to give this gentleman here,' she nodded in Josh's direction, 'a case to answer. I only ask for the girl's identity because, as you know, we have a duty to trace and locate all witnesses, even if they end up giving evidence for the defence.'

This did the trick. Josh could not contain himself, he'd been thinking all along that his brother's posh new mate would be a good witness for them, impressive in court like, say she only saw the scousers attack us and that one of them had been bothering her anyway.

'Ask Darren.' He said.

'Josh, there's no need...' Witchelow was cut short by Heather.

'Yes, thank you Mr. Witchelow, don't you interrupt your client. What is it I've got to ask Darren, Josh?'

Josh looked at Witchelow who glared at him. The boy collected himself.

'Nuthin.'

'I'd like some time with my client now please officers.'

'What d'you mean 'nothing', Josh?'

'Officer!' Witchelow raised his voice.

'The tape's running Heather,' warned Townsend, 'we'd best give them a break.'

'We've only just started.' But Heather stood up. She was still flushed. She was furious with Witchelow but knew she could do nothing about it.

They left Josh and Witchelow in the interview and closed the door behind them. Outside in the corridor Heather stood with her hands on her hips, feet apart, and stared at the floor.

'What's the matter,' asked Townsend, 'We're nearly there.'

She liked the 'we'.

'How do you mean?'

'We've established a connection.'

There it was again.

'Go on.'

'Darren and the girl, there's a connection.'

'We already know that from the video.'

'Yeah but Josh, his reply to you implies that there's more. He hasn't seen the full video yet and didn't see Darren sitting with the girl. There's more to this than meets the eye Heather. Darren knew the girl before that night in the pub. Trust me. I bet she's been getting in the way, getting in between Darren and his brothers. They won't like her, I'll bet.'

He had a point. She was definitely the key.

They did not bother to interview Josh again that day. They swapped him for Darren and went straight into it.

After the usual rigmarole with the caution, the tapes and the action bit of the video and the proclamations from Witchelow Heather came to the point.

'Who's the girl?'

No reply from Darren. She repeated the question a few times to the rising protests from Witchelow but got no reply. Darren was obviously not going to say a word.

Both brothers were released for another three weeks on police bail pending further enquiries, the sole purpose of which being patently obvious.

82. There was no moon and a light breeze in the hedgerows made enough noise to cover any sound she made as she crept up to the farm buildings and moved around the side of the barn to where the farmhouse stood slightly apart. She sat down against a wall and waited and watched. Carmella wore dark overalls, black boots and a black woollen hat which when rolled down over her face became a full face ski-mask.

83. Heather was making paella for her mum and Don Pryce. One of her brothers was home from university and the other was arriving the next day so the house was full.

'What time is Alex arriving?' asked Mrs. Boyle.

'Oh, won't be till late,' answered Heather, 'He probably won't get off duty till 10 then the drive will take ages in all this mist.'

A thick fog had descended on the West Country and was reported to have backed up towards London enveloping all of the west bound roads.

'I hope he's a careful driver. Do you like him?' The question was tagged on the back of the last sentence, not as an afterthought, more of a surfacing of an irrepressible curiosity.

'Yes mum, I like him. He's a friend of mine.'

'You know what I mean Heather, Don and I were thinking....'

'Don and you can think all you like mum, it's just a friendship, nothing more.'

'You're a good looking girl Heather, is there no-one special, I would have thought....'

'Mum, I'm a busy career girl. I get on with people great, I'm not a loner, and I get on really well with blokes. It's just that I don't have time for a serious relationship at the moment, okay?' She said all this in a smiling, affable manner, determined to avoid further examination. She was not ready.

84. Reg Bull booked off duty that evening and went straight to the Goat pub in Lyme. He was aware that Heather had not been on duty all day. Their shifts had become increasingly disparate as her involvement with domestic violence and criminal investigations made her less available for the mundane business of patrolling the county with an old codger. Reg was getting pretty bitter about this and most other things in life. He had become yesterday's man. But then what man does not?

He got a pint and sat down in the corner. He took a few gulps until the beer was half gone, took a deep breath and pulled out his mobile.

85. Heather was serving the paella when two things happened at the same time; her mobile phone rang and the door knocker was rapped. The former was Reg Bull who she greeted as she opened the door to greet her other admirer, Alex Miller.

'Reg, hi, just a sec, there's someone at the door....'

'Hi. I'm on the phone, go through to the kitchen....'

'Sorry Reg, I've got a visitor and I'm serving dinner, can I call you back?'

'Yeah. Call me back. It's about the girl.'

With that Reg rang off.

'Hello, hello, Reg....'

'Come on Heather, take Alex's coat – she's very rude isn't she....'

'Mum, give me two minutes, don't worry about him, he can wait a minute!'

Alex was used to this sort of abuse. Enjoyed it. One day, one day.

She got last received call up on her screen and pressed to call it.

'Hello.'

'Reg, where are you, what's the info?'

'Can't talk right now. Have to switch the phone off. It's quiz night in 'ere.'

'In where?'

Bzzzzzzzzzzzzzzzzzzzzzzz.

'Oh bloody hell Reg!'

She pressed re-dial but the number was unreachable.

'Come on Heather, Alex is standing here not knowing what to do.'

'Aw, poor Alex, poor, poor Alex,' she went back into the kitchen and pecked Alex on the cheek as she passed him.

'Cor, Mrs. Boyle, did you see that, I got a kiss. Maybe I should arrange for her phone to go off more often when I'm at the door.'

'Do you mean to say you actually arranged for that to happen?'

'Don't be so thick mum!'

'Oh, alright, I'm divvy, I know.' Then to Don as he walked in from the lounge, 'They're taking the pee out of me Don.'

'Can't say I blame them.'

The banter continued. Alex was relaxed with this family and only wished that there was real substance in his presence. Heather's brother Sam joined them and he and Alex talked about football as dinner was served and consumed at the big kitchen table. Heather managed to keep her mind on the proceedings. She of course realised that old Reg was having his bit of fun and knew that he would be sitting in some sad old pub somewhere waiting for her to interrupt her Saturday evening at home 30 miles away to try to find him. She most certainly would not.

Less than an hour later Alex was sat in the front passenger seat of Heather's car whilst she assured him that he could drink as much as he liked because she was driving and that what they were doing linked into the information he had for her. He had by now given her the number of the white van that pulled the horsebox. No trace on the PNC, well, only to a builder's firm in bath that had gone bust over two years previously. So they had to try to find the van that pulled the horsebox that had been seen in Crewkerne by her about three weeks ago and if that pale, somehow always familiar face belonged to Darren Pyke then, well, did she have a job on or what!

She guessed it would be the Goat and of course she was right. And she was right when she had guessed that there would be no quiz on. That was just Reg's excuse for not being able to give any information over the phone, having to hang up so she would come looking for him. At least he had assumed correctly that she would pick the right pub. What he hadn't bargained for was Alex Miller being in tow.

The pub was quite busy by the time they got there and Reg was in company with some fellow middle aged male beer swillers. He had a bit of a flush to his cheeks which deepened when he managed to focus on her then faded when he got sight of Alex.

He stood up face her and swayed a bit. Some of his cronies nudged each other and exchanged winks.

'Hi Reg, this is Alex.' Heather sounded sociable and cheerful, as if the meeting had been pre-arranged or expected.

'Hello.'

'What can I get you Reg?' Heather had briefed Alex about her 'uncle' Reg and the Met officer was under strict instructions to be polite and respectful. He wasn't in Shepherds Bush now, she reminded him.

Heather managed to coax Reg into a corner where the three of them sat down. Reg could not look at Alex and just stared at Heather.

'I've been telling Alex all about you Reg, about how you've taught me the county, shown me the ropes and that.' Silence.

'She says you know the place like the back of your hand Reg.'

Reg ignored these overtures. 'Brooklands Farm. The name's Katie Pentreath, checks out on the voters register. Got the lead from a mate of mine. He's a vet. Most of the pet horses around here have medical records. Took me about ten minutes to find her.'

There was a pause for a few seconds whilst Heather took this in. Alex was watching her and then looked away, keen not to cause embarrassment.

'Bloody hell, why didn't I think of that?' She exhaled the words, rather than spoke them.

Reg had to have a dig. 'Because you're too bloody keen to show how much you're doing without actually doing anything.'

This was unfair and the old man knew it, but he was too drunk to care.

'What's the matter with you? I'm here now aren't I? On my night off? Because I got a call from you.' Then she got off the ropes. 'You're enjoying this aren't you Reg. Got one up on me. Well I don't look at it like that, I couldn't care less mate. You go and bring her in. I'll tell DS Decker on Monday that you have located the witness and possibly co-suspect in the Seagull Inn assaults and that it would be unfair of me to bring her in and steal the glory. You have it Reg, I couldn't give a fuck!'

With that she was on her feet and on her way out of the pub, Alex in tow. She pulled the door open and turned to face Reg who looked a bit shell-shocked by this, 'I've got bigger fish to fry Reg, so you get on with your silly games.' With that she stormed out.

Out on the street Alex had to catch up with her.

'Are you sure that was wise?'

'I'm sure it fucking wasn't but what the fuck. That's this place all over Alex, jealousies and backstabbing,' she fumbled for her keys and sprung the central locking of her car.

'C'mon,' she said, 'we've got a white van to find love.'

He liked the 'we' and really liked the 'love.'

86. At that very point in time the white van they sought was in the town of Staines, next to Heathrow Airport just to the west of London. Darren was driving, Josh in the passenger seat wrestling with a map. The roads were confusing them with right-turnless dual carriageways, numerous roundabouts, dazzling lights of all colours and heavy, fast traffic. Darren tried to remain calm but he felt his temper rumbling.

'Fucks sake, where the fuck d'you want me to go?'

'Just wait, wait, pull over, I can't see the fuckin' map like this, it's dark… pull over.'

Darren pulled over into a lay-by, the near side wheel of the horsebox hit the kerb and the empty contraption bounced about crazily for a second or two before they came to a standstill.

'Give me that,' said Darren, snatching the map from Josh. No sooner had

West Country

he focused his eyes on the confusing spaghetti picture before him than he got a sharp tap on the leg from his brother. He looked up to see the police officer dismounting his motorcycle in front of them. The brothers froze. The watched the cop as he swaggered towards them, talking on his radio and looking at the index number of the van as he did so. He made for Darren's side and Darren wound down the window, breathing deeply to settle his nerves.

'Lost lads?' asked the officer, reasonably.

'No.' Darren replied, unconvincingly.

'Just thought you'd stop over for a read of the map then eh?'

No reply. Both boys stared ahead of them. He liked this. And he liked the way the boys looked, as well. Baseball caps, nylon tracksuit tops, pale skin. Hardly the farmer types. Hardly horsey.

'Where did you get the horsebox from lads?'

'It's ours,' volunteered Josh from the passenger side.

'Yeah.' Agreed Darren.

'We come from Dorset.'

The officer was even more impressed. He caught the accent.

'Jump out, let's 'ave a look, make sure you ain't rustling.'

Darren opened the door and slid out of the van, keen to get that cop to the rear of the horsebox and away from the driver's side of the transit. He couldn't stop thinking about what would happen if the cop searched the cab and found a certain piece of hardware lurking behind the seat.

He walked with the cop around to the back of the horse box, sprung the bolt and let the door swing. Apart from about a foot of manure on the floor it was of course empty.

'Where's the horse then?' came the predictable question.

Darren had the answer. 'Haven't got one. We're just taking the box back down to Dorset for a friend.' That accent again.

'Okay lads, that's fine. Let's have your names to record the fact I've spoken to you.'

Darren and Josh gave Emmett Everett and Dean Everett respectively, along with the Everett's address. This was pre-arranged and would stand up to any enquiry. They did not want their real names on record and the Everett brothers got a little drink for the cover they provided, on top of the little drink they got for the loan of the box. A radio check on the names satisfied the cop and he was on his way. Darren got back into the van and watched as the motorcycle roared off. It did not occur to the boys to wonder why the cop had not queried the registered ownership of the van; even though they knew it was still in the name of its previous owner, a bankrupt building company in Bath.

'Fuckin' hell bruv,' he said. 'Let's get this done and get out of here. That was a real let-off, if he'd been a bit keener....'

'Nah,' assured Josh, who had more knowledge of the various forms of police life, had made a bit of a study of it, 'just a traffic cop, wanting to get finished his shift and home to wifey.'

What they didn't know was that the traffic cop was talking to the mike in his helmet, relaying the location of the van and the description of its occupants. It had not been a routine stop.

They did a tug of war with the map for a few minutes and managed to get their bearings. Within twenty minutes they were where they wanted to be; on another lay-by on which stood a mobile burger bar. The Volvo was already there. Darren got out of the van and went to the serving hatch. It was just after 9pm and was getting dark. Josh went to speak to the driver of the Volvo, a middle-aged cannabis dealer who went by the name of Mutton. The deal was done quickly, as it had been on two or three occasions in the past, in the same area but at different locations.

Darren chucked two hotdogs onto the dashboard of the Transit and gunned the engine whilst his brother hid a parcel under the manure in the box. When he climbed into the passenger seat he stank. Good. They were off, westwards ho. What they did not realise was, that so was a three vehicle surveillance team from the Met's South West Area Drugs Squad.

The team followed the boys down the M3 and along the M27 towards Southampton. The officers had been briefed to the effect that the Transit was part of a bigger concern trafficking drugs to and from the port towns on the south coast. Their instructions were not to stop and search the vehicle, just to see where it went. In modern day British policing, intelligence was everything. Surveillance would be conducted at the expense of results if it held the promise of leading to bigger things. And the intelligence about this van was that it was operated by a small fry with bigger connections. Mutton, the driver of the Volvo who now had £450 on him, was driving east into London and to his flat in Paddington. They knew all about him too, another piece of small fry. Where was he getting the drugs from? The police were not sure, probably a Turkish connection. But the pieces were falling into place. They had some names now and an address that checked out, even though it was probably false, it was progress. To have given that address and those names the boys must have some knowledge of the rightful owners of those identities. The surveillance team pulled off and stood down when it became apparent that the Transit was not going to Southampton. More intelligence in the bag; back to base, debrief and end of the shift. Darren and Josh made their way home, blissfully ignorant.

87. Heather could not quite make the connection between the Pyke brothers and that white Ford Transit. But she somehow knew that it existed. She had been trying to memorise so many likeness, names, descriptions, places and connections over the previous two months that her brain was addled. As for white vans, she couldn't stop seeing them. There was one on every corner of every road. But now she had a number.

She drove hard and the journey made Alex feel quite ill. He had rushed his pint in the Goat and being thrown around on country roads gave him the serious hiccups.

'Fuck's sake Heather! What's the rush?'

'I just want to get this job done.'

'What job? Driving like a lunatic isn't going to find that van any quicker, and we ain't doing anything about it tonight if we do find it.'

'I'm not looking for the van. We're going to see that girl.'

'Aw, come on, you don't have to do that now, I'm down for the weekend remember, I'm not fucking helping you take statements.'

'Don't worry, I'm not going to take a statement tonight, just going to let her know I know who she is, that's all.'

They had crossed over the A35 and were heading north towards Brooklands Ridge when Alex's mobile let off an irritating ring tone - the Benny Hill theme tune.

'Hello… Gibbo… yeah, okay, not bad… you're fucking joking! Yeah? Nice one mate, cheers…. How long… yeah? Two…. I haven't got a pen, text me mate, WhatsApp me with them. Cheers mate… yeah, I'm down here now…. No chance… would be a fine thing….Okay mate…. Nice one. ta.'

The call over, he turned to Heather, 'Right, which road would you take to here from London, the quickest route?'

'A303 I suppose, why?'

'That was Gibbo – remember him, Peter Gibbons? On the divisional crime squad?'

'Yeah, didn't he want to go to surveillance?'

'That's exactly what he's doing now and he's got our white van.'

She slowed right down, as if coming to a halt. She was looking at Alex, waiting for instructions. She was in the driving seat but he was very much in charge now.

'What, right now?'

'No, they let it go half an hour ago, he couldn't make the call right then, but it looks like it's on its way down here. Head for the 303.'

88. It was a lump of flint about the size of a man's fist. It arced upwards and across the moonlit farmyard. It hit Sally and Bertie Pentreath's bedroom window with a crash that started a cacophony of animal protest. Dogs barked, geese shouted, hens scattered, screeching from their roosts and even the old bull roared. The shrillest sound however was Sally's scream. It was primeval. Bertie said nothing; he was up and out on the yard with his 12 bore shotgun within seconds. But Carmella was already well gone. Over the wall and along the shadow of a hedgerow she sprinted like a big cat. Bertie Pentreath was left with the feeling that the rock had been propelled for over half a mile from the other side of the ridge, such was the total absence of suspects. He went back in to the house to console his wife. She was clearing up the glass from the bedroom floor. At the other side of the house Katie had slept through it all. Her father looked into her room and decided not to wake her. He had already made his mind up that it was nothing to do with his daughter and the least she knew about it the better. Those yobs in the pub in Axminster must have either recognised him or found out who he was. He would report the matter to the police the next day. He did not want any fuss now. But they spent the rest of the night sitting in the kitchen drinking tea.

'I cannot believe that this has happened,' said Sally.

'Oh, I bloody can. They were a right bunch of horrible bastards. Never seen them around before. Probably come from Stockard or Chard. How the hell they've found out where I am I do not know.'

'Are you sure it's about that Bertie? Perhaps it's about something else.'

'What else could it be? We don't go out much, we don't socialise very often, we don't have any enemies. This is the first time I've been involved in anything since we moved here.'

There was then a few minutes silence.

'Maybe it's about Katie.' Sally gazed into space as she said this.

'Who has she upset so much that this happens? She hardly knows anyone in the whole county, and I can't think it's any of her uni friends.'

'She has been going out a bit on her own, drinking – and driving, I might add – she's been a bit strange, a bit withdrawn....'

'Sally, she's an undergraduate with a heap of stress and big decisions to make. She needs a bit of space. No, this has got to be down to the boys from the pub in Axminster, as simple as that. I'll put a report into the police tomorrow and that'll probably be the end of it.

89. The A303 is a fairly fast dual carriageway that runs in an east-west direction across the northern part of Dorset. The A35 is a slower road that runs in roughly parallel but along the south of the county, near the coast. Heather and Alex were parked up on the A303 waiting for the van which, of course, was being driven westwards along the A35. They gave up at 3am and decided to go back to Dorchester. The night had become cold and they were each starting to feel a bit silly, waiting for a van to come from London for fuck's sake! There'd been a few, obviously, but not with the right index number and not with a horsebox. As the traffic got lighter and lighter they each came to the conclusion there was probably not many more effective ways by which to waste the weekend. If only they had chosen the A35.

90. Josh jumped out of the van and opened the Everett's gate. Darren drove the van in and they both set about uncoupling the horsebox before taking the Transit back to Stockard where they parked it a respectable distance from their home address. Once indoors they started to talk about

what had happened, running ideas past each other. It was how they worked.

'D'you think the cops'll check out the address we gave?'

'They already did didn't they? I heard him on the radio, something about a voter's register.'

'You mean the Everetts vote?'

They both laughed at this.

'Yeah, the old woman will I think. She's kind of respectable.'

'Hope Carmella doesn't.'

'Yeah, bet you do.'

'What d'you mean by that.'

'Nuthin.'

'So the next thing that happens is that the London old bill'll tell the Dorset old bill that we've – or the Everetts I should say - have been stopped in our van.'

'Yeah, suppose, so what. The van isn't registered to us anyways. No problem bruv.'

And with that they both fell asleep, one in the armchair, one on the sofa.

91. Katie Pentreath woke the next morning oblivious to the night's events and the fact that two people very important to her future were thinking very carefully about her. She felt angry with Darren for his ultimatum and worried for her parents and any repercussions they would suffer once she returned to Brighton.

The first was Heather Boyle. She had woken early, still buzzing from the recent developments. Alone in a different room was her frustrated male suitor, memories of the previous evening had quickly dissipated and had been replaced by thoughts of a different kind. She did not know how Reg had located the girl, if indeed he had, nor did she much care. Suffice to say she felt pretty confident in Reg's ability to get things right and hey, even if he hadn't, she now had an excuse to visit one Katie Pentreath.

The second was Darren Pyke, who was now addressing himself to Carmella's information. He could not rely on the possibility that the police visit to Upper Brooklands Farm was unrelated to the Seagull Inn incident.

92. Katie got up and went downstairs, both her parents were up and at the breakfast table. They both looked exhausted. 'What's the matter with you two?' asked their daughter, visibly shocked by their appearance. Sally and Bertie looked at each other. Sally shrugged and Bertie spoke.

'Someone threw a rock through our bedroom window last night. I think I know who it was.'

Katie was at once sure that she knew as well. 'Who?'

'Oh, don't know their names, I got into a bit of a fight in a pub in Axminster the other day, gave a lad a thick ear, hurt his pride a bit, he must've known who I am, that's all.'

'You've called the police?'

'Yes. They're sending someone out. Can't see the point mind. They said it might be a while. Short of manpower or something.' He took a long pull from his tea cup. Katie sat down at the table.

'You okay Mum?'

'Oh, lovely dear, just had a boulder come flying through the bedroom window in the middle of the night that's all. All these years I've know your father, this is the first time he's brought trouble....'

'Oh, leave it out Sally, the lout deserved what he got.'

Katie went quiet then. It was very unlike her father to get involved in anything like this. Very few people knew them and he did not normally socialise in pubs. So Katie was a bit concerned as to how some tearaways from a pub in Axminster, over seven miles away, recognised Bertie Pentreath as the owner of Brooklands Farm. It didn't stack up. There was of course another very distinct possibility.

She had a quick bowl of muesli and went out to check her horses. As she walked out of the farmyard a police car pulled in. It was being driven by Jack Saunders, a Special Constable who she had never seen before. He was there to take the details of the rock through the window incident she correctly surmised and she could be of no assistance. Nor was she going to hang about to be asked. She was anxious to check out Rosie and Gabriel and hurried on foot to the paddock. Her best friends met her at the gate and all was well. She saddled up Gabriel and rode him out of the field, much to Rosie's disgust. She was getting angrier by the minute. If that bastard had done this she was going to have to deal with it. She was not going to allow her parents to suffer just because she had had a drink with the wrong guy at the wrong time in the wrong place.

93. 'I'm going up to the Everett's' said Darren to Josh. They had both woken at about the same time and Darren had made a pot of tea. Before he and his brother supped a mug-full each he had taken two cups to their parents who slept separately but in the same room upstairs.

'Yeah,' said Josh, 'Best you do before they get a visit.'

As it happened there was no rush. The details they had given to the motorcycle cop had not yet been circulated as criminal intelligence; the only trace of the details having been given to the police lay on the message log at police HQ in Dorchester. It was from there that the check on the voter's register had been carried out and the results relayed back to the Metropolitan Police control by the dispatcher. Two boys called

Everett had been stopped in a white van in west London. The van had a 'drugs interest' tag on the computer and in two or three days' time that information would find its way to Lyme Regis police station and would be circulating the roll call of each shift for a day or two. There would be no real effort made to search for the van, apart from the odd drive past the Everett's place maybe – and it of course would not be there - there were simply not the resources available. To be on the safe side Darren parked the Transit up a side track about a quarter of a mile from the Everett holding. The five or so miles from Stockard had been driven alone and he was wary of being stopped, wishing he had left the shotgun behind at the house. It was in its usual position, jammed behind the driver's seat. He cursed under his breath at his own risk-taking; if the van was found and searched now he would be in the shit; his and his brother's dabs were all over it. So he hurried along, keen to get his errand done and get the Transit back to a safe place in Stockard.

94. Heather Boyle got dressed quickly and left the house without any breakfast. It was late, almost ten, and she had decided that Alex was better off staying in bed than getting under her feet. She had a job to do and, although off duty, she could not wait until after the weekend. She did not ring into the police station to book on, nor did she put her uniform on. She simply packed her mobile phone and jumped into her car to head for Brooklands Farm and what she thought would be her first meeting with Katie Pentreath. As she pulled into the farmyard SPC Jack Saunders was just leaving. He did not recognise her in plain clothes but she knew him having been briefly introduced by Reg Bull in the backyard of Lyme Police Station several weeks earlier. At first she thought she had been beaten to it and her lip curled at the possibility of jealous old Reg deliberately giving someone else the information just out of spite. Anyway, she'd started so she'd finish, she'd just say she was doing some follow up enquiries. Something was not quite right though; why would an unpaid Special want to get involved in a GBH enquiry. Everything soon became clear.

'Oh, Hello,' said Sally Pentreath as WPC Boyle showed her warrant card, 'You've just missed your colleague, have some wires crossed?'

'Well, I'm actually the officer in charge of the investigation, just checking that everything is alright. Is Katie in?'

'No,' said Sally, frowning, concerned by the interest in her daughter.

'Oh, so my colleague didn't get a statement from her then?'

'No. Why would he want to, she was asleep at the other end of the house when it happened?'

What the hell was going on?

'Mrs. Pentreath, I need to talk to Katie please, it's quite important.'

Sally was worried now, it was her turn to wonder what the hell was going on.

'She's down at the paddock, seeing to her horses. What's this about please?'

'We believe she may have witnessed a serious assault two weeks ago in Lyme Regis. I need to speak to her.'

'Two weeks ago? What are you talking about? I thought you were here about the window.'

'Excuse me?'

'I think you'd better come in young lady.'

Heather followed Sally into the house and they sat down. Heather listened to the story about how a rock had come crashing through their bedroom window not eight hours earlier and how they thought it had something to do with some youths Bertie had had an altercation with in an Axminster pub. As they chatted Sally formed the impression that the episode was more to do with her daughter than her husband and immediately started forming plans for her to return to Brighton ahead of schedule or to spend the rest of the vacation in Cornwall with relatives.

Heather assured Mrs. Pentreath that everything was in hand and that the matter would now be treated as urgent. She had made it clear to the lady that her daughter was merely a witness to the assault and that she was in no trouble herself and all possible efforts would be made to protect from any further attempts to intimidate her. Sally was not assured and insisted on accompanying Heather to the paddock to find Katie. They both got into Heather's car and Sally gave directions. By the time they got there Katie was of course gone on Gabriel and where to, was anyone's guess.

'How long does she usually go for?'

'Depends a lot on how the horse is, could be half an hour could be a couple of hours.'

'I can't wait in that case. I'll take you back to the farm. I'll give you my mobile number, let me know when she returns and I'll be right back.'

Having dropped Sally back, Heather decided to return to Dorchester to continue her weekend. She could not and would not be expected to do all this work in her own time, indeed it would make her even more unpopular with her colleagues – pushy ambitious London cow etc. – and furthermore she was not over keen on leaving Alex with her family to become over communicative on the social life of cops in London. He was such a gobshite, he really was. But then if Darren Pyke did chuck that rock through the Pentreath's bedroom window and . . . She slowed to a halt about fifty yards from the A35 and tried to think things through. She decided to ring Alex and ask him what he thought. His number was not for some reason on her phone's contacts list although she knew it by rote. As she tapped in the number a fast vehicle passed by so close that it rocked her little car. She looked up to see a white Ford Transit van receding in the distance, clearly being driven by a lunatic. It was not disappearing so fast that she could not see the registration number. It was.... She knew that by rote as well.

She threw her phone down on the passenger seat, it bounced around and ended up in the footwell. She gunned the engine and lurched off of the verge into the road and after the van. It turned left on the A35 and Heather was held up by eastbound traffic before she could also pull out and follow. When she did manage to get onto the dual carriageway the Transit was a quarter of a mile ahead. But she could still see it, and saw it as it turned off again onto the Crewkerne Road. She made some ground and followed, just keeping the vehicle in sight, she could see the top of it just above the hedgerows as it wound its way north. Then it was gone. She got to a small crossroads and had not a clue which way the Transit had turned. By then the hedges were fifteen feet high on either side of the road and she was completely unsighted, like being in the middle of a maze. But she had had a sighting, and that was better than nothing. She would report it on Monday. Now she would go home to Dorchester and the job could fuck itself for the next thirty six hours.

95. Darren had not realized he had been followed, so intent was he on getting to the Everett's place. To save time he had actually gone the long way round so that a chunk of his journey was on the A35. But now he was back in deepest Triangle country and pulled up on a bridle path a good 500 yards from the Everett's place. It was one of his favourite parking spots and the van was out of sight to all but the most diligent of searchers. He locked the vehicle and trudged down the road and through the Everett's gate. Carmella answered the door and Darren could tell from her smirk that she'd been up to something.

96. Reg Bull was working the weekend and sat in the unstaffed canteen eating a pasty he'd bought from a stall on the Lyme seafront. He was of course thinking about Heather and whether she had already followed up on his information, in spite of it being her weekend off. He decided that he would be surprised if she hadn't. His thoughts were interrupted when he was joined by another old timer, Norman Hogg.

'Alright mate?' Asked the Groundhog as he sat down opposite at the small wobbly table.

'Yeah mate, not too bad. Yourself?'

'Yeah, I'm good.'

'Good.'

The two men were not close and never really had been. Their similar ages, length of service and backgrounds served not to bring them together; on the contrary, they were rivals. Furthermore, Reg was married to Norman's sister. They had never actually fallen out, but quietly competed for influence over both management and their younger colleagues. It was like that with old PCs who'd never taken promotion. It was like they wanted to compensate for their lack of advancement through the ranks by way of power in the canteen. Norman had always looked upon Reg as someone to keep an eye on, his brother in law would not have been his choice to marry his younger sister, she could have done better, the silly girl. So Norman looked after Reg from a distance, made sure he didn't go astray.

The big difference between them was that Norman was much more powerful and he had achieved this through the Federation. The Federation exists basically as the national cops' union. Each of the forty three forces in England and Wales has its own Branch and each of these has its own full time officials and representatives. Norman was not a full time official but a working cop who was given considerable leeway in terms of shift allowances and free time to represent cops in trouble. And cops frequently get into trouble by way of criminal allegations against them from anything to assault during the course of making arrests to organised corruption, not that there was much of the latter in Dorset. Aside from criminal matters there is the discipline code to which all officers must adhere on pain of dismissal. And the efficiency code to which all probationary officers, that is those in the first two years of their service, must comply. In short they must demonstrate that they are well presented and efficient police officers. Norman never made any secret of his love of being a Fed Rep. He enjoyed the respect it brought from younger colleagues and the notoriety it earned him among the senior ranks. He knew the job well and was renowned for his advocacy skills when conducting the defence of officers at disciplinary hearings. He rarely needed the services of a qualified lawyer, even though officers were entitled by law to professional representation. No, the Groundhog was quite capable of swaying the Chief Constable and his performance on behalf of PC Cozens a few weeks previously, was a demonstration of this. The Chief Constable liked him, and he quite liked her. He especially liked the way she enjoyed it when he made fools of the sycophants who surrounded her, those senior officers who regularly tried to make names for themselves by disciplining members of the junior ranks.

'Nice job on young Cozens the other week Norm,' offered Reg.

'Cheers mate, it's always a pleasure. Fucking Superintendent Barratt. Anyways, it's not over yet, still a bit of work to do for the lad.'

'Do you think you'll save him?'

'Yeah, should think so, got the Chief on my side I think.'

Then there was a pause before the Groundhog spoke again.

'This new girl from London.' It was like he was announcing the heading of a conversation, an item on the agenda of a meeting.

'What about her?' Reg asked, eyebrows raised.

'You and her pretty close?'

'What d'you mean?'

'You givin' her one or what?' Norman was grinning.

'Fuckin' chance'd be fine thing mate. Why, is that the rumour?' Both men were chuckling now.

'Nah, sorry mate, nobody would be daft enough to believe it.'

Reg put on a crestfallen look, 'Oh, that's nice, here's me thinking I was getting a big reputation like you Norman.'

'No chance mate. In fact, rumour has it that you're a bit of a sad bastard.' The words cut into Reg like a knife in the guts. The laughter stopped.

'Who's sayin' that then?' Reg tried to pretend to be unfazed but Norman was far from stupid and saw he had got to his rival.

'Don't worry about it. Just the usual rumour mongers. They'll get bored and move on to something else.'

Another pause. 'She's doin' well I hear.'

'Yeah, dead keen, bright kid, ambitious, wants CID.'

'So I heard. A bit of jealousy brewin' mind mate. If she gets made up to DC before some of the others there'll be fuck on.'

'Nothin' to do with me Norman, I showed her round the county for a few weeks, that's all. She spends most of her time in plain clothes between the DVU at Crewkerne and helping Decker and Townsend with enquiries.'

'Yeah, so I hear. They're talking about her as far away as Bournemouth.'

A few minutes silence followed again whilst they supped their tea and listened to the chatter on the airwave radio system. Then DI Kevin Packington sauntered into the canteen looking for someone. He called over to the two old timers.

'Mornin' chaps, either of you seen DS Decker at all?'

'No guv,' was the chorused reply.

Packington turned and ambled back to his office. There'd been quite a bit of shit come in overnight – criminal damage to flower pots, burglaries at a caravan site and a fight in Charmouth between two locals at a pub skittle match. Each was alleging assault against the other and both wanted to make statements. Packington was bored but felt he couldn't go to the pub until he allocated the night's crime wave to his detective sergeant who could then delegate it to who the fuck he liked.

97. Heather booked on duty at 2pm on the following Monday, strapped on her utility belt and pulled the keys to a patrol car. Then she made her way to Upper Brooklands Farm. Fifteen minutes later she had parked and was walking across the farmyard to the back door of the Pentreath's house. She was still about five yards away when it was opened by Katie who had seen the police officer approaching.

'Hello Katie,' said Heather in an overly casual tone, as if they were just passing in the street.

'Hello officer. We meet again.'

'Call me Heather. I expect you know why I'm here.'

'Yeah, let's go for a walk.'

Katie had taken control of the situation and Heather found herself not minding one bit.

They strolled in silence for a few minutes, around the back of the hayshed and onto a track that led up the hill and away from the buildings.

'Lovely day.'

'Yeah.'

They were both a bit out of breath when they got to the top of the slope. They turned around and sat down on the grass, facing across the valley and looking directly at the copse on the other side of Mrs. Walter's farm. Heather was sweating so she took off her tunic and utility belt.

'Bloody gear they give us these days. You'd think I was off to Iraq, not Dorset.'

Katie laughed politely. She seemed cool and composed. Heather noticed that she wore no bra beneath her tee shirt.

'Right. It's about the Seagull Inn assaults. We have you on CCTV as being there, witnessing the whole shebang. Agreed?'

'Agreed.'

'D'you know Darren and Josh Pyke well?'

'No, hardly at all. Had a few drinks with Darren. That was the first time I think I'd ever seen the other one.'

'Josh you mean.'

'Do I? I didn't even know his name was Josh.'

'You left with them after the fight.'

'Yes.'

'Why?'

'Don't know really, just seemed the best thing to do. Suppose I felt kind of responsible for what had happened….'

'Why was that?'

'Well, Darren had been with me and he left, then the Liverpudlian guy started making a nuisance of himself to me, then Darren came back and sort of protected me. I suppose I wanted to demonstrate loyalty. Does that make me an accessory?'

'No, but it means you've got some explaining to do Katie. Just to me though.'

'Why just to you?'

'Because if I'm happy that you're not involved with them and that you're just a witness then all you do is have to make a witness statement.'

'What, and go to court?'

'Probably, but to give evidence for the Crown, not as a defendant.'

'Yes, I realise that,' there was an edge creeping into Katie's voice. Did this copper think she was some sort of child? 'But what happens if I don't actually want to go to court to give evidence for the Crown?'

'Then we'll wonder why Katie, perhaps we'll think that you were involved, egged the Pykes on or something, then you might get charged.'

Katie was on her feet. 'Are you threatening me?'

Heather was startled by this reaction. She was beginning to think that she may have misjudged this young lady.

'No, sorry, sit down.'

'No, I won't sit down, you've come up here to my home to enlist my help to do your job and now you're saying like I have no choice but to put my neck on the line for you. If you do make me go to court I will make my concerns about your behaviour known to the judge. Can you leave now please.'

Heather was on her feet now. This had put the fear of God into her. A hostile witness; something to be avoided like the plague.

'Katie, I'm so sorry, please sit down again. I'm sorry. Please, we'll work something else out.'

But Katie was not impressed by all this. 'No, I'm going back to the house. The interview is over officer.'

And she was trudging down the hill. Heather followed in silence, her tunic and utility belt under her arm. Made a right mess of that, she thought.

When they got to the farmyard Katie went to the door of the house and turned to face Heather.

'In future telephone before you come, but I'd really rather you didn't come back. I don't want to get involved.'

'Why not Katie, you scared?'

Then Katie was walking towards the officer, anger renewed.

'Aren't you forgetting something?'

'What?'

'We had a rock put through our window on Saturday night. It could have seriously injured my parents.'

'D'you think it was the Pykes that did that?'

'Of course it fucking was, what else was it about?'

'The crime report says your father had a fight with some locals in the Duke of Clarence pub in Axminster a few weeks ago, it says he thought that it must have been them.'

'Yes, well, I have a different theory.' Then she began to walk across the yard toward one of the sheds. 'Come over here a minute.'

Then they were talking again, as if the spat had not occurred. Heather felt relief. She did not want to leave this girl's side at that moment. She could sense that opportunities were going to open.

Katie spoke in a low voice. 'How the hell can I help? Darren is not the sort who would not take it personally is he? Me standing there giving evidence against him and his brother. D'you think he'd put up with that after what you say you've seen on your CCTV?'

Heather had to admit she was stumped by this. She did not for one minute believe what she was about to say but said it any way.

'But he won't be able to do anything – he'll be in prison.'

'Yeah, for how long, life? I don't think so, and that's supposing he gets convicted.' There was then a pause as the two women looked at each other. Katie cocked her head slightly to one side, questioningly, and said, 'Do you think I'm stupid?'

Heather was on the defensive again. 'No,' she replied, quietly, 'of course not.' She turned and walked to her patrol car, head down. Katie watched her drive away. There was something she did not like about this police officer.

98. Josh was washing his bullet. He'd been to Chard the night before and had done some brisk cocaine business. The thing had been in and out of his rectum four times and needed a good clean. Each wrap of Charlie had earned him £15 clear profit and there had been twelve wraps in the shell when he'd gone out. Now there were none. A good night's work and Mrs. Pyke would have a good birthday the following week. He would make sure of that. There was a rap on the bathroom door.

'Come on mate, for fuck's sake.' It was young Wayne. He'd been spending a lot of time with his girlfriend lately and was keeping out of trouble. The other younger brother, Joe, seemed to be under control too, big into surfing on Charmouth beach with some Lyme boys.

'Aw Josh, I'm burstin', come on, what you doin, avin' a wank?'

With that Josh was out of the bathroom and had Wayne by the throat on the landing of the little house.

'You cheeky little fucker, I'll have your balls off for that.'

Wayne giggled as best he could and got his brother around the neck. They both ended up on the floor, punching the shit out of each other and roaring with laughter.

'Oi, pack it in.' It was the old man bellowing from the front bedroom.

'Ah, shad up you old git!' shouted Wayne.

'I'll fuckin' old git you in a minute you little bastard...'

'Little bastard am I? Well that'd be down to you then, eh?'

The boys were on their feet and Josh was laughing at the banter between his father and brother. It came to an end and the boys went downstairs. Leaving their father demanding that a cup of tea be taken up. It would be done.

Then Darren came in. He had been out all night and looked shattered. Josh guessed he had spent the night with Carmella.

'Been shakin' the tree house bruv?'

'Fuck off,' was the response.

Josh did not agree with his brother and half-sister's incest, but he was the only one who knew about it, although old man Pyke suspected but chose not to say anything. Anyway, there was no harm done, so what the fuck. That's what Darren told himself, anyway.

Yes, he had been in the hide overnight, but Carmella had not been with him. He had been watching the Pentreath farm and had seen everything he needed to see. His and Josh's date to return to Lyme police station was ten days later and he feared that Katie Pentreath would soon provide a statement that would send him and his brother to jail, if she had not already done so. He was going to have to act fast. He still did not know about the fist-sized lump of flint that was now in the exhibits cupboard at Lyme police station. It had been examined for prints but without result. If no-one was arrested for the offence within three months the rock would be discarded. For now it just lay there on a shelf, with a sticker on it bearing the crime reference number.

99. Heather looked at it as she contemplated the attack on the Pentreath house. If the Pyke brothers had been responsible, and she had no doubt that they were, then they would do more if it was necessary to stop Katie giving evidence. They would stop at nothing, of that she was in no doubt and she decided that she would have to do something about it. She had

told Decker but he had referred to the crime report and the fact that the victim, Bertie Pentreath had stated that he suspected some youths from Axminster to be responsible. Heather had responded to the effect that the Pyke brothers presented altogether better suspects.

'Well go and bring them in then,' Decker had countered, 'but if they deny it, which is a distinct possibility, then what have you got?'

She could not argue with this. The brothers were back in the station anyway in just over a week and pulling them in early would do no good at all if she did not have additional evidence. In fact it could harm the assault enquiry by giving them reason to guess – correctly – that she was having trouble getting Katie's co-operation. She simply had to get that statement from Katie, otherwise the job was going nowhere. And she had a host of other things to be getting on with. Maxine and Sharon were struggling with an influx of domestic violence in Crewkerne and there was still that white van to find. It was the latter that had been occupying her thoughts mostly. What a hot one that would be in terms of enhancing her chances of a CID job. She was actually almost scared to turn the information into success because of the jealousy it would cause. But then, that information was on daily records anyway, every cop in the county had access to it. Lazy bumpkins didn't want to know. Rather just harass motorists and litterbugs, thought Heather in her more superior moments. She was sitting in a marked patrol car eating a sandwich in a layby on the A35, watching with amusement as the traffic visibly slowed on seeing her. But she was not on traffic duty. From where she sat she could see the Everett's place, or part of it at least. It was well hidden, but Heather had come upon this vantage point to which she had sight of the front gate to the property about 500 yards away on the other side of a cow field. She hunkered down to watch, having decided to waste an hour on it. Her airwave was on if they wanted her, but it was a quiet mid-week afternoon and she anticipated that she would have some peace. Her eyes glued on the gate, her mind wandered. Alex had gone back to London at the end of the weekend, still without his shag. (Surely he must have given up by now.) Heather thought about Caroline and the bad business. How it was in the past now and how lucky she was – so far. That had cost her a lot of money and she hoped the matter was dead and buried. She suspected somehow however that it was not. Buried, maybe; dead, no. She thought of Reg. Poor old git. Sad old git. What had he done to deserve his life? A real yesterday's man. Just there to give others a leg up, nothing in it for him anymore. Just work, booze, a stagnant marriage and the whole world taking the piss out of you. What a way to end up. She knew he had probably fallen in love with her and was keen not to hurt him. The best way to do that, she decided, was to stay clear of him. Keep out of his way. Or she could tell him.

She thought about her mum and Don Pryce. She had mellowed toward the lawyer over the previous couple of months. Perhaps he was not such a gold digger after all. Perhaps he did love her mum. Anyway, it was a good cover for her being there, for having transferred from the Met to work and live in Dorset. They did not know about the bad business.

Then she saw it. The roof of a white van moving about on the other side of the Everett's wall. It was too big to be the roof of a tractor and too flat to be a horsebox. She was out of the car and over a style and into the field. Keeping close to the hedgerow, she made her way down the slope to get a better look. That van was in there alright. But that meant the driver had given the Met cop correct details when he was stopped. That did not really add up if they were up to tricks. And the Everetts had no markers, no traces of having been suspected of anything seriously criminal. Strange bunch maybe, but then there were plenty of those in the Triangle. All they really did was brew hooch, poach a few fish and pheasants and breed horses, and good ones at that, apparently. As she closed in she switched off her airwave to maintain a silent approach. And then she was up against the high wall. Having come down the slope from the road she was no longer able to see what lay on the other side. All she needed was a glance at the number plate. That was all. She started climbing. The wall was of flint rocks, tightly rendered, and there was little purchase. She managed to get her hand onto the top but then her toe slipped from its shallow foothold and she was down again. She walked along a bit, looking for a better place to climb, but there was none. She heard voices and an engine running. Normal agricultural sounds. She was making her way along the wall, the gate to the property receding behind her. Then she heard the gate being opened and she hit the ground, managing to get a bit of cover behind a clump of nettles. The white Ford Transit roared out onto the road and Heather Boyle saw her career in the Dorset Constabulary take a big leap forward.

100. It was Lyme Regis Carnival Week and the town was buzzing. There was a bit of overtime available and Reg Bull took advantage of it and worked all the hours he could. His drinking had got him into financial difficulties and he had two kids who, although in their twenties, still milked him dry. Mrs. Bull was at home, as usual. Plotting against him. She had recently conned him into signing their house over to her so that when he died before her – note the 'when' – she wouldn't be liable for so much tax. That was her story anyway. Reg wasn't really bothered what the truth was, he just did as he was told. He was mulling these things over in his mind as he punted his panda along the busy seafront. He would park up and have a walk for a while. Do the friendly Bobby bit for the holiday makers and kids. Then he would sneak into the Seagull Inn for a couple of sly ones, hat and epaulettes in plastic bag.

When he got there Colleen Bradstock was bottling up and briefing her staff. On seeing Reg they slunk into the shadows and left Colleen to deal with the officer. Colleen knew that Reg was only after a beer and that at 11:15 in the morning in Carnival Week she had better things to do than idly chat with a bored and drunken policeman. But she liked Reg and wrote off ten minutes for him.

'You spoken to that girl yet then?'

'I haven't but one of my colleagues has.'

'Which one, Heather?'

'Yeah, I think so.'

'Strange girl, that.'

'Who?'

'Heather, Heather Boyle. Strange.'

'What do you mean?' Reg had begun supping his first pint but it was now suspended between bar and mouth.

'Oh, you know, us women have ways of knowing things.'

The pint glass finished its journey as Reg began gulping, eyes glazed, unfocused. Three-quarters empty, the glass came down again to its midway point.

'I never thought of her as strange, ambitious maybe, but not strange.' He was addressing the surface of the bar, frowning.

'Doesn't matter. What'd did the girl say to her, the Pentreath girl?'

'Dunno, wasn't there. How did you know that Pentreath girl, anyway? You never did tell me.'

'Oh, that doesn't matter Reg. Put it down to publican's local knowledge.'

101. The Pentreath girl was sitting at home in her parent's farmhouse wishing she was back at university and away from all this. It was claustrophobic, and the claustrophobia was following her, tightening up. All this space, all this free time, all this peace, but something finds you, latches on, and then tightens. This had all started with getting a light from someone and a quiet drink down at the Seagull. Then Darren Pyke had brought his world to her, and now she was being asked to go to court.

102. Carmella Everett had watched Darren leave Rockham in the van from her bedroom window. He had spent the night in the tree house and had forbidden Carmella from joining him. Her jealousy consumed her.

He was hers and that bitch was stealing him from her. She had still not let on about the rock through the window and had no intention of doing so. He would half kill her for that and she knew it. Darren had used his temper on her on many occasions in the past and she was not about to invite another hiding from him. She remembered the time that he'd blackened her eye during one drink fuelled Christmas and had then beaten up her brother Emmett for making an issue of it.

She sat on her bed and tried to read but could not concentrate. Hundreds of paperback novels were strewn about the little room; the walls were adorned with grunge rock posters and her own bizarre paintings. She had a liking for red and black and for daubing slightly macabre abstractions with thick acrylic paint onto big squares of hardboard. A psychologist would have a field day if one ever got near her. She sat and stared at one picture in particular. It was a blown up black and white photograph of her and Darren standing next to a tree in the middle of a field. She had accomplished this with a photocopying machine in the post office in Axminster. Then she had coloured the picture in red and black. The image had thus taken on a strangely artificial appearance, unpleasant to look at; it was as if the two figures had fallen from space. Like Carmella was trying to dehumanise herself and her lover, so that earthly rules would not apply to them.

103. And Darren Pyke knew about Carmella's jealousy. He was thinking about it as he drove the van towards Stockard. He was going to pick up Josh and drive on to Crewkerne where his brother had a deal going down. It was a particularly dangerous job, especially in broad daylight. He now hated using the van. He knew the careful thing to have done would be to have dumped the vehicle and acquired something else. He could not be sure but had to assume that the registration number had been logged and, following their stop in west London, circulated on police records. He would have a story ready and the shotgun was safely hidden in one of the Everett's outhouses. But he still did not want to be seen in this van; he did not want it known that he and his brother had

been in London or anywhere near it. He managed to light a cigarette as he drove with a box of matches. He thought of his lighter and where it was at that minute in time. As he drove over the ridge he looked for her. He took a circuitous route to check her pony paddock. The two horses were grazing peacefully as he slowed past the gate, looking across at the stable. No sign of her. He was torn. He understood that he loved her, and understood that not only would she never love him but was in a position to put him and his brother in jail should she want to. He remembered that she had told him that she would be going back to University at the beginning of September. It was barely August yet and he and Josh were back in the police station during the following week. If she gave a statement and got them charged they would not even get bail the next day at court. They would spend the rest of the summer in Dorchester prison awaiting trial. Then would they get off in front of jury? Witchelow had advised them that it did not matter if the scousers were never found. The law allowed victims to go missing. The CCTV footage and the girl's evidence would be enough to convict, Witchelow had warned. Darren decided that he could not risk doing nothing.

104. Chief Constable Joanne Bache read the county crime intelligence input every morning. She was interested by the London drug surveillance team input and suspicious about the way it had been picked up and developed by her transferee from the Met. The Chief Constable did not believe in coincidences and decided to have words. If that girl was up to something then she wanted to know about it. She had read Heather Boyle's file and there was nothing untoward, but files did not contain everything. She rang Packington.

'Yes Ma'am,' answered the aging DI, wondering to what he owed this pleasure on a Monday morning.

'Your new girl at Lyme Kevin, Heather Boyle.'

'Yes Ma'am, what about her?' Packington was intrigued, but after less than a second's thought he knew what this was about. He had read the intelligence input as well and he also found it suspicious that the ex-Met officer had inputted the van onto the system before the information had filtered through from the dispatch at Dorchester. Heather had been on at him to get a surveillance team onto the Everett place to look out for the van, but of course there were not the resources.

'She certainly seems to know more about this marker on the white Ford Transit than anyone else. Do you think she'd hold back on us, saving it for herself?'

'I don't think so Ma'am, she's pretty ambitious but I don't think she'd go that far. She put her input onto daily records pretty much as soon as she could and the information from the Met has not added to it.'

'Okay,' said the Chief. 'Just checking, I don't want any prima donna's in this county Kevin.'

'What, other than the ones around you at headquarters ma'am?' Packington judged that he could get away with this bit of familiarity, and he knew how Bache hated her crawlers.

'Now, now Kevin, don't be nasty.' She hung up and stood up at her desk. Something told her that there was more to this Heather Boyle, much more. It was as if she was still working with her Met colleagues, so quick she had been in inputting that surveillance product. She was still talking to them and not only to them but to a surveillance team, advanced cops, she was well connected and therefore had probably been doing well. This begged a big question; why had she moved to Dorset? Bache decided to have a meeting with her new girl from the smoke.

105. Music, if that's what you could call it, by the Cardiacs blasted out of her little hi-fi as Carmella mixed the concoction. She crushed fruit, she added sugar, honey, cream, eggs and mushrooms. The substance had bulk yet was fluid. It was the first time she'd ever used the pestle and mortar, utensils that had been bought for her by her mother in a junk shop in Taunton. Carmella wondered if her mother had been moved to purchase the present by some unknown hand. A hand that perhaps knew

the use that would be put to the tool many years in the future. The additional ingredients were added generously and once mixed, the whole litre or so of soup was decanted into a flask. She was in her room and a right mess she'd made of it. She could hear her mother rattling about downstairs in the big scullery, making the boys their dinner. It was getting dark and she would go out that night.

'Carmella,' it was Emmett shouting to make himself heard above the ridiculous music, 'Carmella, you're needed down here.'

'Who by?' she replied, shrilly, nervously clearing the debris in case of a surprise visit. There was fruit peel everywhere, including on her counterpane.

'Come and see.'

She knew at once that it was Darren. She had not noticed him arrive across the yard of the homestead but knew it was him and her heart quickened with fear and lust. She quickly wiped her hands on a towel and brushed her long, thick green-blonde hair, and then opened her bedroom door to go downstairs. There was no need to – he was in and on her in a trice. He had her gently by the throat and pushed her back on the bed, straddling her. She giggled with fear, he was angry about something but the sex between them would neuter that anger, she knew. It always did.

'Don't you go fucking near her!' He hissed, 'Don't even think 'bout it!'

At first she thought he must know about the rock through the window. But then had he done so he would have come right out with it. No, he was guessing, just taking precautions.

'I've no intention of going anywhere near the fucking bitch so don't you worry. I wouldn't piss on her if she was on fire.'

'No, because you'd be the one to set fire to her!'

She started to giggle and he slapped her, which made her giggle more.

Then he stuck his lips over hers. She stiffened, thinking of her mother and brothers downstairs, her eyes twisted round to see the flask on the little dressing table. She was thinking about what it contained as Darren drew back from her face, looking at her quizzically, she look back into his eyes. Keen not to have him follow her gaze to the flask.

'We'd better go down.'

'Tree-house tonight?' he breathed this, rather than spoke it.

'Maybe.'

She got up from the bed and went downstairs. The table was set, Darren having accepted an invitation to stay for dinner. As the pair walked into the scullery Mrs. Everett looked at her daughter and then at Darren, her daughter's half-brother. She had always known, if she was honest with herself, she just hoped they would grow out of it.

106. It was mid-August and a heat wave had descended on Lyme Bay. The holiday season was in full swing and the region was making the most of it. Lifeboat Week followed Jazz Festival Week and was in turn followed by Carnival Week, back to back events to keep the tourists busy and spending. Dorset youth gravitated to the coast to get what it could out of the visitors from London and the buzz they brought. The pubs and restaurants did a belting trade, as did other entrepreneurs like Darren and Josh. They had relaxed caution in respect of their use of the white van and horsebox; had the stop in London meant anything then the Everett's farm would have been searched by now. Nothing had come of it. Or so they thought. They had thought nothing of it when Reg Bull had called at their house several weeks beforehand to cancel their bail. They were no longer expected to attend Lyme police station to answer further questions about the fight at the Seagull Inn. That could mean only one thing, they had decided, and that was that Katie Pentreath had not made a statement. Which was of course true, she had not made a statement, but then the police had not really persisted in their quest to get her to do so. The police being Heather Boyle, Tom Decker and Stuart Townsend.

And it was those three cops that dined on seafood one balmy Friday evening in a busy bar on Lyme's Silver Street. It had been Decker's idea, to go out and relax as a team. Heather and Stuart Townsend had thought it odd; not like Decker at all to have time for socialising with his colleagues, but they had gone along with it. Decker had not told his two young charges but he had been tipped for promotion, or at least that he was neck and neck with a Bournemouth DS for promotion. He was being watched and he wanted to leave nothing to chance. He needed to be seen to be a top notch skipper, out with his troops and getting results. Well, he was out with his troops alright; he was even going to pay for the meal. Team-building. Results? Heather Boyle was going to see to that. The three of them had discussed at length alternative strategies for catching the Pykes at the drugs game. Her observation at the Everett's farm had ensured that she did not even have to think about putting her uniform on. She was on permanent secondment to Lyme CID, with a twice weekly visit to the Domestic Violence unit at Crewkerne.

Knowing that Darren and Josh Pyke were dealers and proving it to the point of a sustainable prosecution were two different things. It was nigh-on impossible to conduct organised surveillance on narrow, thinly populated country roads. Technical surveillance was equally as challenging. Try getting a camera vehicle parked up anywhere near the Pyke residence and it would be sussed within minutes. Likewise with the Everett's place. No, Decker was having to dig deep and use his imagination.

The conversation was desultory but not unpleasant. Townsend did not want to appear too pally with Decker in the presence of Heather. He was not sure how to play this. He knew Decker was up to something, so out of character it was for him to spend any out of hours' time with his colleagues, let alone buy two of them a meal. But he couldn't work out what it was, beyond a mild suspicion that he was sounding them out for something a bit dodgy. This would of course entail trusting Heather Boyle. During one of the frequent lulls in the fairly banal chatter Townsend regarded his new colleague who sat diagonally opposite him. She was dismantling a king prawn, frowning, pretending to be completely absorbed by the task. Townsend looked at her wet, ringless fingers, then at her thin, pursed lips, and then at her pale blue eyes which immediately met his as she sensed his interest. Her fingers kept working the prawn as she held his stare. He found himself feeling uncomfortable and averted his attention to elsewhere in the room, looking at this and that, pretending to wander as he could still see that her eyes were still on him. He looked back at her and she still had him, looking up from her plate, her head still angled downward so that the white of her eyes were prominent above her bottom lids. But the prawn was now ready and making its way towards her mouth. She popped it in and grinned at him as she chewed. He grinned back, relieved.

'What are you two up to?' asked Decker, having watched this little dance being performed before him.

Townsend got in quick. 'I was just thinking when she was going to actually eat that prawn and stop tearing it to pieces.'

No you weren't, thought Heather. You were thinking whether or not I was to be trusted and to what extent I was a danger to you. But she said nothing; just let her eyes fall back to her plate. The grin turned into a pleasant smile.

'This food is lovely.' She wanted to keep it light.

'Yeah, thanks Tom, nice of you to bring us out. You want a beer?'

'Yeah, why not, er, there's something we need to get straight.'

Here we go, thought Townsend. There was then a short pause as Heather and Townsend waited for their sergeant to swallow a lump of herring and wash it down with a gulp of Peroni.

'I need to know how committed the pair of you are to nailing the Pyke brothers?'

Heather and Townsend looked at each other and then back to Decker.

'Very.' This was from Heather. 'Yes, very,' agreed Townsend.

'The reason why I ask is because, and I'm sure the pair of you have thought of this, because we are not going to get them by orthodox methods.'

Silence.

What I mean is we're going to have to use our heads and do something proactive.

Silence again. Decker looked at each of them in turn. They were both just staring at him.

'Jesus Christ, come on, I'm after ideas, don't just stare at me. We can't follow the white van, we haven't got the facilities to mount technical surveillance, the Met won't follow them any further west than Hampshire, and the two little fuckers are supplying our coast with dope, what are we going to do about it?'

Heather saw her chance. 'We need a UC job.'

Townsend countered this. 'We haven't got anybody to do it. The Pykes know every copper in Dorset, including you.'

'Yeah and they laugh at me. I couldn't even nail them for the Seagull Inn assaults. Bet they think I'm a right pancake.'

Decker was looking thoughtful. He asked Heather, 'was it you that told them they didn't have to return to the station the other week?'

'No, I sent Reg Bull, he was over in Stockard, said it was no bother.'

Decker continued exploring. 'How many times have you been to see the Pentreath girl?'

'Just the once. There's no way she's going to make a statement sarge, no way. And she doesn't like me either.'

'Why do you say that?' asked Townsend, keen to make a contribution to the storming session.

'Not sure.' (She was fairly sure).

Decker changed direction. 'Where's the van just now?'

'Holed up at the Everett's place we think,' answered Heather.

'That bunch of throwbacks.' Decker did not like country folk very much.

'He loves her.' Heather announced this in a low, detached tone. The two men looked at her and then at each other.

'Who loves who?' Decker asked the question, intrigued, not smiling as Townsend was.

'Darren Pyke loves Katie Pentreath.'

'How d'you know this?' continued Decker.

'Just do. Excuse me.' With that she was up and off to the lavatory, the two men turned to watch her as she walked across the room.

'What the fuck's the matter with her?' said Townsend.

'Don't know. But I like it.'

107. 'Oh, I really find that very fucking difficult to believe!' Chief Constable Joanne Bache could feel her face burning with anger. She did not often use bad language but there were occasions when even she lost her cool. The Chief had been through too much in her own life to be able to put up with the petty expectations of other and whilst she was normally quite good at managing those expectations there were some who pushed the boundaries too far. And this was one of them. Philippa Lavelle owned a patch of land just inland from Bridport. On it she bred strange birds that were a cross between chickens and turkeys or some such fucking thing, the Chief was not interested. But Philippa Lavelle had friends in high places. She dined in fashionable West Bay, co-wrote satirical comedy and played the cello for various orchestras and bands.

She was rumoured to have had audience with the Prime Minister and to be involved with the Independent Police Complaints Commission.

The Chief listened to more. It was from a very mischievous-sounding DI Kevin Packington.

'Why are you coming direct to me Kevin, you've got at least three ranks to go through before you get to this office you know.'

'I'm sorry Ma'am, but I didn't think you'd want everybody knowing about this before you did. I'm getting it from the horse's mouth. She rang me direct, it's not been reported to anyone else and it's not on the computer system yet.'

The Chief sighed. 'Well just put it on then. Don't treat her any different from anyone else. And get that smirk off your face inspector – I can actually hear it.'

'Yes Ma'am.' Packington put down the receiver and burst out laughing. He was alone in his little office in Lyme and halfway through a half-bottle of Dewar's scotch.

'Prize cross-bred Guinea fowl. Rustled. On the missing list. Including the prize cock.' He was talking to himself. He was glad he hadn't mentioned the last bit of detail to the Chief – she might have taken it the wrong way. He roared at this last thought.

108. It was three o'clock on a Friday afternoon and the weekend's drinking had started for Reg Bull too, as he settled down in the Goat. The first couple of pints barely touched the sides as he thought about Heather's failure to get that statement from Katie Pentreath. He thought about the sneer with which Darren had greeted the news that he and his brother were no longer required to attend the police station to answer further questions about the Seagull Inn massacre, as it had become known. Fucking scum, thought Reg. They always got away with stuff. Fucking gangsters. But what should he care. Sad old Reg Bull, retiring in eighteen months, full pension, mortgage paid, what should he care?

But he did care and he seriously cared about Heather Boyle. Not that she was particularly good looking or anything, too young for him anyway, just that there was something about her. She was certainly different and there had been no talk of a boyfriend. There was that DC from London who had come to stay with her a couple of times but she had made it clear that there was nothing in it, just friends. What was the matter with her? Why had she not been able to get the Pentreath girl to make a statement against the Pykes? Was she not bothered? Had she really tried? He had given her Katie on a plate, having located her identity by simple local knowledge and basic deduction. She had been seen at the Mermaid Theatre in Lyme and one had to be a member to get there had one not? From there it was a simple matter of having a quick look at the attendance register, courtesy of the admissions clerk who was an old buddy of his and who worked part-time behind the bar in the Goat. Basic stuff. What was the matter with these young coppers? Too far up their own arses planning their own careers. Humph!

109. It was just after 2am when Carmella slipped out of the house into the fierce moonlight. She actually found it too bright and kept close to the hedgerows and stone walls as she made her way over the fields. She was about to do a terrible thing, she knew that, but it had to be done. She wore dark combat clothes and her ski-mask, rolled up like a hat but ready to come down over her face when the need arose. Under her bomber jacket she concealed the flask. Her stomach churned with nerves as she neared the paddock. Gabriella and Rosie stood together and watched her arrive; it was as if they expected her, as if they knew that they now had a part to play. Carmella could see the two horses watching her as she walked up to the paddock gate. A silence descended and she felt the urgent need to urinate. She put down the flask on the ground and backed away from the gate, seeking the privacy of the tall hedge. Satisfied that the horses could not see her she slipped down her trousers and squatted. The temperature had dropped markedly and her steam rose into the moonlight and her piss rolled down the hill. Bladder empty she rose and pulled her pants up. Returning to the gate she saw that the horses were

still watching, waiting. She hoped they had not seen the steam. She stowed the flask and climbed into the paddock. She walked past the ponies and headed for their feed trough at the far end, near the stables. They followed her, heads lowered. Rosie and Gabby each had a stall in the little stable, and in each stall was a feed trough. In each trough there was some leftover meal. Carmella divided the contents of the flask fairly between the two, and mixed it with the meal. The two horses waited patiently for her to finish the job and exit the stable. Then they entered and ate, almost dutifully.

Carmella sprinted back across the paddock. As she did she threw the flask high into the air and over a hedge into an adjoining field. When she reached the gate she vomited, thinking about what she had done, about what was going to happen. But it had to happen. It had to. Half an hour later she crept into the tree house, took off all of her clothes and slipped into her sleeping bag. She held herself tightly and wished Darren was with her.

110. But Darren was at home with his parents and brothers, sleeping soundly in his dirty little bed. He and Josh had spent the evening very profitably in Chard, doing deals with the locals and staying away from the coast. Joe and Wayne had joined them and they'd had a laugh. Even done a bit of copper baiting when a local panda turned up following reports of rowdiness in the town centre at kicking out time. 'Fuck off coppers' they had chanted as the two old specials drove around nervously, not stopping to challenge them. Then they had gone to a curry house and spoiled the evening for other diners before the hapless Bobbies were called upon again to provide some completely ineffectual uniformed presence. Then the four lads had set off to walk home to Stockard; the van was holed up at the Everett's in Rockham Ditch and would not be coming out unless absolutely necessary. The shotgun was still hidden in one of the outhouses.

As they trudged home Darren had become quiet, subdued, leaving his three brothers to do the noisemaking, shouting at the full moon, throwing stones at sheep and cattle in the fields. Darren thought of Katie, what would she be doing now? Getting shagged? He doubted it, probably a virgin, posh cow. But he longed to see her again. Quite reasonably capable of a fair degree of stoicism, Darren had hoped the feelings he had for the middle class student would pass, it had been fun and had given him a bit of confidence in himself - perhaps he wasn't such a small town petty criminal after all. Perhaps he did have something to offer. But he would never know for sure because she was gone. She would go back to her university and that would be it. Well, at least she wasn't going to give evidence against him, that was a bonus. But all that meant was that she was frightened of him, not that she liked him or respected him or felt any affection. A depression fell over him as he trudged the last half mile back to the scruffy little council house. His brothers were up ahead of him, still whooping and yelling, waking up all and sundry. Darren just felt like crying. What was it all about?

111. The two horses began coughing together, and together they made their way to the water trough, about twenty yards from the stable. They did not seem to be afraid or surprised by what was happening to them. It was enough that they were together and they walked slowly and closely side by side in the moonlight towards the trough. Rosie was the first to go. As she leaned forward to take a drink her front legs went from beneath her and her head went into the trough with a dull thud and hollow splash. Gabby seemed to try to help her, nuzzling her head under her neck to get some leverage, but then her legs went as well. She let out a high-pitched whinny and joined her partner in death.

Katie heard her horse cry and leapt out of bed. What the hell had happened? Dogs? But there was no barking. Horseflies? Not at this time of night. She pulled on her clothes and left the house. She could scarcely believe the brightness of the moon. It was like daylight. There were even shadows and the stillness was uncanny. And she knew it was bad. As she approached the paddock she started to run, by the time she saw her dead horses she was sprinting. And then she screamed.

112. And Carmella lay in the tree house and sobbed, not being capable of understanding why she had done this, just knowing that deep down there were things in her body, chemicals, molecules, fluids that were not right, especially when they mixed with the stuff inside Darren's body. That was what had caused this. Chemicals. We all have poison in us she decided, all of us, and sometimes it just boils up into an anger, a rage. Carmella listened to Katie wail in the moonlight and hugged herself tighter and tighter, rocking herself violently.

Katie sprinted back to the house and phoned the emergency vet. She had managed to get Rosie's head out of the water trough and thought there may have been a pulse in each of her horses, but she knew she was kidding herself. Still, she called the emergency number, what else was there to do? Her parents heard and both joined her on the ground floor of the house. Bertie got into the Land Rover and made for the paddock. The dogs barked. Sally boiled the kettle and wrung her hands, not knowing what to do for her frantic daughter. Bertie got to the horse corpses to find out that that was just what they were. Not a sign of life. But the vet could come anyway, perform an autopsy and give them the cause of death. Rock through the window, now this. It did not occur to Bertie that it was anything other than poisoning and he knew it had everything to do with his daughter and her associates in Lyme. What was she up to her neck in to cause this? What would be next? Would they have to sell up and move? These were the questions Bertie Pentreath was having to ask himself as he felt over the horses' stiffening bodies for wounds. It had occurred to him that they could have been darted. Then he checked the food trough and smelled a strange sweet odour of fruit and honey.

113. 'You'd better get up to that Brooklands Farm now my girl. The shit's hit the fan.' It was Decker talking to Heather on the telephone.

'What's happened?'

'Some bastard's poisoned the girl's horses. Just been reported, happened in the night. You get up there and get that girl to the nick to make a statement as quick as you like.'

Heather was in Dorchester, it was eight o'clock on a Saturday morning and she had not expected to be back on duty for another twenty four hours. Her mind reeled.

'Yes sarge, but... ' But he was gone.

Decker sat at his desk in the CID office. He had tried to get hold of Townsend but the DC was not picking up his phone. Decker lit a cigarette contrary to the no-smoking rules. He opened the window. This had to be down to the Pyke scum but there was no way he wanted to pull them in. He needed that drugs job badly and investigating the poisoning of horses was not going to suffice as a substitute. Locking the Pyke brothers up would spook them, they'd ditch their business; put it to sleep for months if they had to. And he didn't have months. Anyway, how would he prove anything? The scene would be forensicated but fields and stables were not renowned for smooth, print-bearing surfaces. He sighed as he exhaled smoke from his fag.

Heather pulled her car into the Pentreath farmyard and was not even out of the driver's seat before she saw Katie marching across the muddy concrete towards her. She wore jeans and gumboots, a fleece wide open at the neck. Her hair was greasy, her face tearstained and she had dark bags under her eyes. She was clearly in some sort of emotional shock.

'I want them fucking dead!' she screamed at the policewoman.

'I'll make as many fucking statements as you want, I'll say anything, I just want them dead!'

Heather wore her most sympathetic look and held her arms out.

'No, don't start that old shit PC Boyle. Just get your pen and paper and come with me.' With that the Pentreath girl wheeled around and headed back to the house. Heather bent into her car and took out the spare clipboard she always carried. It had in it statement forms, accident report books, arrest report books and exhibit labels. Every off duty cop should carry a spare such clipboard – you never knew what you may come across. Then she followed the farmer's daughter into the big house.

'Did you see what they've done?' She had turned and stood with her back to the wall shouting at Heather as if this were all her fault.

'Er, no I came straight here, I didn't go to the scene....'

'Scene. Scene is exactly what it is. We've got the vet doing an autopsy now. He reckons they gave them fruit and honey laced with strychnine....'

The last words were high pitched as she started sobbing.

'My poor horses. What harm had they done? What harm had I done? It wasn't as if I'd made a fucking statement to help you with the pub fight enquiry. They'd got away with that....' More sobbing. She stood there, shaking and sobbing. She looked small and broken by the night. Her hands were red and shook. She backed into a wooden kitchen chair, her knees buckled and she sat down hard. Her head came forward into her hands and Heather tried once again to get close. This time Katie let the police woman touch her. Put an arm on her shoulder.

'Can I make some coffee?' Asked Heather in a whisper, as if she was asking permission to do something vaguely naughty. Katie nodded her tousled head, still looking down. Her parents were in the paddock with the vet and the scenes of crime officer who was trying vainly to get fingerprints from the wooden surfaces of the stable. A young PC and a civilian Community Support Officer were kicking about in the paddock for clues. A footprint in the mud perhaps, a DNA bearing fag end? But there was nothing in the immediate vicinity. It would not be long before they gave up and went back to Lyme to greet the morning weekend day-trippers. Would they check the next field and find the thermos flask? Unlikely.

'He must have seen me in Lyme the other night.' Katie was talking to the floor as Heather filled the kettle. The police officer said nothing, just listened.

'He told me not to go there but I went to the theatre with my parents. I didn't see him or his brothers but they have watchers everywhere.'

By this time mugs of instant coffee had been put on the table and Heather was sat taking notes.

'When did he tell you not to go into town?'

'Soon after the incident in the Seagull Inn.'

'What, before I came to see you last time.'

'Yes.'

'Why did you not tell me then?' It was a stupid question but one that had to be asked. The dark circled eyes came up from the flagstones on the kitchen floor for the first time since they had entered the house. They fixed Heather with a stare that was accompanied by a slight curl of the lip. Heather got in first, 'I have to ask these questions Katie, even if the answers are obvious.'

'I don't want you to ask any questions at all. Why don't you just fucking listen to me? Stop trying to shoehorn this whole thing into your agenda all the time, your way of seeing things, your neat little picture of life. Just let me tell it how it is.'

Heather Boyle was stumped by this, she had to admit. This was one bright young girl who had everything. A good brain, doting parents, chosen career, then she had been nudged off course. In the middle of nowhere, in a backwater English seaside town where nothing much happens at the best of times, nothing unusual anyway, she had been drawn into another sphere of influence. Only for a short while, but it had been enough. And now everything was going wrong. And now she was going to tell it in her own words, how it felt to be touched by the dark side of life.

'It was like it was destined to happen. I was bored with my coursework a few weeks ago and my parents were getting on my nerves. No real problems, I needed some space. The farm isn't doing well and dad is thinking of opening a shooting school on the land. He keeps going on about it and mum is dead against it. It has nothing to do with me. I'm going to be a vet and I have my finals next summer. So I need some space to keep my head together, not listen to those two bickering on. So I went down to the Cobb in Lyme, walked around there, enjoyed the light and the movement. I like red wine so I went into the Seagull Inn and got a large glass full of it. I did this a couple of times and found myself attracting some unwanted attention. Most of it from Darren Pyke. Then we met a couple of times when I was out riding. I smoke and roll my own. I didn't have a light one day so he gave me his lighter. Said I could keep it.' As she said this she fumbled in the pocket of her jeans, having to stretch one leg outwards and move her weight onto the opposite hip to do so. She withdrew the Zippo and threw it on the table with a clatter. Heather picked it up and examined it whilst continuing to listen. A battered old brass Zippo with the letters DP scratched on it.

'It was like he was finding it very strange to talk to me. He wasn't rude, or pushy, nor did he try to touch me at all. He asked me a lot of questions about myself, what I wanted to do, what I wanted from life, what I liked and disliked and how I knew what I disliked. But he wasn't really interested in knowing about me. He was more interested I think in how people began to answer such questions, whether they actually bothered to even try to. He was I'm sure asking himself whether or not he should bother asking himself these questions. Do you follow me?'

Oh, yes, Heather Boyle followed alright. No problem there at all. But she wasn't sure how she was going to incorporate all this in a witness statement.

'Yes, I follow Katie. Go on.'

The farmer's daughter looked up again and stared hard at her listener. 'I'll go on when I'm ready to go on.'

'Sorry Katie.'

'Sorry? What are you sorry for? My horses? My life? Your life? Interrupting me?'

Heather did not respond to this.

'Come on Heather, what are you sorry for?' A pause, still no response from the police officer.

'Let me help you. You're not sorry at all. You're just anxious to get this fitting snugly into your plans. Your career plans. Is that right?'

Heather stayed silent and held the Pentreath girl's stare like her life depended on it.

'Come on, is that right?'

'What's it got to do with you what my thoughts are? I'm here to do a job and protect you from this idiot who you seemed to have formed a liking for, don't try to get clever with me Katie, I'm not stupid.'

The farmer's daughter was on her feet at this, flouncing around the kitchen as she started to shout. Heather remained calm, for some reason perfectly sure that all this was some sort of act, a sham. A cover-up of some kind.

'No, you just think everyone else is. Because they won't readily process their problems to your liking. Won't make neat little statements, packaging everything up to give you nice court cases and nice neat results.' She was sitting down again and rolling a cigarette. She did not offer Heather a smoke. The police officer stayed silent and let this run. She was not even making notes. This woman was hysterical; she would come back another time, just now she would simply listen.

'On the night of the trouble at the Seagull he was very dignified. It was this that had me somehow spellbound. I've never met many rough men in my life, but I know generally what they are capable of. I see enough of them in Brighton, they target us students. They don't care what happens, as long as they have a good night out. I've no doubt Darren is just like that when he's with his mates and his brothers. But I felt I was having some sort of effect on him. Not that I was trying, because I wasn't, I was barely even listening to him half of the time. But as the hour or so wore on that evening I became more aware of him, I felt like he was dragging me into himself. Everything else going on in that busy pub patio was like it was somewhere else. He was mesmerising me. Mesmerising. That's the word. And I think I was doing the same to him. And that, officer, that is where the problem lies.'

I know the feeling, thought Heather Boyle.

114. Half a dozen miles away in Bridport another woman was talking to the police. This particular woman had two police officers in attendance, DS Decker and DI Packington, both of whom were very bored but heavily mandated.

'As I said to Chief Superintendent Jarvis this morning, these birds are very rare, each worth thousands of pounds, especially the cock.'

Oh fucking hell, thought Decker. Jesus Christ, thought Packington. The two detectives just sat there, not bothering to hide their glazed eyes. Word had come down from above to deal with this as a priority. This woman had contacts in the Rotary Club, the County Council and probably the Royal Naval Lifeboat Institution and the fucking Independent Police Complaints Commission. She went up as high as Perry Jarvis, a Bournemouth Chief Super with a house near Bridport. He had contacted Sherrell at Headquarters who in turn had made the job a priority. Somebody, probably Lavelle's employees, was systematically relieving her of prize livestock, namely exotic guinea fowl. Additionally, building materials were disappearing from one of the blasted woman's numerous property projects and one of her husband's precious vintage sports cars had been criminally damaged by way of the old brake-fluid-over-the-bonnet trick.

Philippa Lavelle had many enemies. She had upset a lot of working class local people in the county with her selfish property development and money grabbing attitude. But she had friends in high places whom she either bullied or implicitly bribed. Philippa Lavelle always had to have her own way - that was the bottom line. And she was making that fact quite clear now.

'I want these people caught gentleman, and quickly. Why should they get away with this, after all the hard work I've put into the community. I've given these people jobs, provided them with livelihoods and they've thrown all that back in my face. I'm hurt and angry.'

'We'll do our best Mrs. Lavelle.'

It was Packington, hoping to wrap things up, the time rapidly approaching beer o'clock. Decker, who had been writing furiously on a statement form, chipped in, 'Yes Mrs. Lavelle, if you'd just like to read this over and sign at the top and at the bottom of each page.'

'I'll probably have to have my solicitor check it over first before I sign,' came the infuriating reply.

'Fine,' said Decker, 'Let me take a copy of it so that I can be getting it typed up while you have it checked over.'

'Very well, sergeant, but what if it's not right, then your typist's work will have been wasted. That's public money is it not?'

Decker had to fight to restrain himself. This woman was monstrous.

'Not a problem, it'll be easily changed on the computer.' Then he stood up and walked to the other side of the office, glad of the need to get to the photocopier. He just had to put some distance between himself and this thing. Packington yawned and looked at his watch.

'Oh, I'm not keeping you, am I?' observed the woman.

'Yes Mrs. Lavelle,' answered Packington, laconically 'as a matter of fact you are. I need to be in Lyme in five minutes. There was a fight in a pub last night, someone got a black eye. I need to investigate.'

Decker froze. He was having no part of this, Packington was in his dotage and could afford to be rude, but he still had a career to worry about.

'I'll see to it that your matter gets top priority Mrs. Lavelle. May I offer you a lift anywhere?'

'No thank you sergeant,' replied the woman to Decker, whilst still looking venomously at the plainly disinterested and insolent Packington. He cocked his head to one side and returned her glare with an exaggerated smile.

'I'll show you out Mrs. Lavelle,' said Decker. With that Philippa Lavelle stood and walked out of the door of the office, followed by Decker. Two minutes later the detective sergeant was back.

'All due respect boss, but we need to be a bit careful with that one. Friends in high places and all that.'

'Ah, fuck her and her stupid birds. What do I care? Haven't we got better things to do?'

'Yes guv, I have to do those as well. I've got drugs information waiting to be acted on, I've got drunken assaults every other night on the coast, I've got car thefts, burglaries, domestic violence and to top all that I've got two poisoned horses up on one of the farms.'

'What?' Packington appeared for the first time to be interested.

'Two horses belonging to the Pentreath girl, the one who was the witness to the Seagull Inn assaults when the Pyke brothers done those scousers over.'

'So now the Pyke brothers have poisoned her horses?'

'Not sure really. Doesn't fit that neatly. She refused to make a statement. We cancelled the Pyke's bail. They were off the hook. No need to threaten the girl. No need to kill her horses. Doesn't make sense.'

Packington sat slumped in the chair and fiddled with a paperclip, bending it this way and that. He was thoughtful.

'That's interesting. Maybe we should have the Pyke boys back in again.'

'Yeah, suppose, wouldn't harm, would it. Rattle their cages a bit.'

'D'you need a hand?' asked Packington, staring at his paper clip which was now almost straight. Decker found this question difficult to believe. Packington offering to do some work for a change. Too good to miss.

'Yes please. We'll hit them tomorrow morning. I'll get a search warrant out for their address. Can you get some more troops together, say from Crewkerne or Dorch?'

'I'll try, no promises though. We could do it ourselves couldn't we? We've got Townsend and the Met girl, what's her name, Boyle.'

Decker was not sure about this. 'We'll need more than that guvnor, those Pykes can be a handful, and there are a lot of them.'

'I'll see what I can rustle up,' said Packington as he looked at his watch and rose. As he walked out of the office he mumbled, 'I'm going for a pint.'

115. The meeting between Heather Boyle and Katie Pentreath had ended with predictable acrimony. Heather's statement pad contained about two pages of meaningless product about Katie's ownership of the two horses, how she had given nobody permission to feed them and how she had no evidence as to who on earth had killed them. She had added, however, that if the perpetrators were caught she would assist police in every possible way. Funny how horses seemed to take precedence over scousers.

When Heather got back to Lyme, Decker and Townsend were waiting for her.

'Okey dokey Heather my dear, are you ready for some action?'

This was from Decker and she liked the sound of it.

'Of course.'

'Get up to Chard Magistrates Court as quick as you like and get a warrant for the Pyke's home address. Section 8 of PACE, evidence of an indictable offence namely animal cruelty and criminal damage to over five grand's worth of stupid animals.' Criminal damage had to have a value of over five thousand pounds before it became indictable, in other words sufficiently serious to merit a search warrant to seek evidence.

Heather was stunned by this. They were trying to get the resources together to mount a surveillance operation on the Pykes and this would not help one bit.

'How do we know the horses were worth over five grand?'

'You tell me, you've been taking a statement off of the girl, what did she say they were worth?'

Heather looked down. 'I forgot to ask. Sorry.'

'Great. Ring her up and ask her now.'

Heather was unsure how to handle this. Decker clearly wanted to get on and do something about this but she thought he was being rushed by the need to be seen to be doing something, as opposed by any real operational urgency. If they spooked the Pykes the drugs operation would go down the pan. Surely he should be able to see this.

'How do we reasonably suspect the Pykes have anything to do with this? We've long since given up on getting Katie Pentreath to give evidence against them and they know it, they were NFAD nearly a month ago.'

Decker would not normally have put up with such questioning of his own judgement and authority, but he decided to play along.

'They don't know we've given up on the Seagull Inn enquiry, and if they think we have they cannot be sure so they thought they'd better make sure young Katie doesn't change her mind.'

'So they kill her horses? I don't think so. Anyway, the Pykes rather like horses, they help the Everetts deal in them, when they're not dealing in drugs, that is.'

Decker had had enough.

'Look Heather, I'm not asking you to get that warrant, I'm telling you. Now sign up the information and get over to the court and swear it out.'

Heather reddened. 'So you want me to commit perjury, is that it?'

'What the hell are you talking about?' Decker was losing it and Townsend squirmed.

Heather was now puce and beginning to shake, either with anger or with nerves.

'Sergeant, with all due respect I do not have reasonable suspicion that there will be evidence of horse poisoning at the home address of Darren and Josh Pyke.'

'No? Well maybe PC Boyle you should not be assisting the CID. Maybe you should be returned to full-time uniformed duty so that you can help old Reg with his ice cream vendors and tourist traffic.'

Heather just stood there. She was being blackmailed and no way was she going to cave in. Decker saw this and, still holding the blank warrant and accompanying documents, turned and walked out.

There followed an uncomfortable silence between Townsend and Heather, which was broken by the former.

'Oh dear Hev, I think you've blown it.' He said this fairly pleasantly, with a sympathetic smile which she appreciated.

'Seems so. Fuck it. I'm not swearing on oath something I don't believe just because he tells me to. If he's so sure the Pykes are involved why doesn't he go and do it. Come to think of it, why didn't he ask you?'

This was a good question and one that had just occurred also to Townsend. 'I dunno. Maybe he was testing your integrity. Anyway. He's taken the paperwork so maybe he is going to lead from the front and get that warrant, in which case we'll be hitting the Pykes tomorrow morning.'

'Is that his plan?' asked Heather.

'Yep. And he'll carry it out, I know him.'

116. Superintendent Perry Jarvis was, as per usual, annoying the Chief Constable.

'I am sorry Ma'am, but the evidence is frankly overwhelming. The Lavelle property is being targeted by current and former employees trying to get their own back on her. She's been an absolute bitch to them. Failing to pay wages on time, sacking them for going sick, not recognising their employment rights, so they've formed a band of vigilantes and they're knocking our crime figures for six.'

Although an annoying little twat, Jarvis had a point and a significant one at that. The 43 police forces of England and Wales are judged every year by Her Majesties Inspectorate of Constabularies. One of the parameters by which they are judged is the crime figures, or, more importantly, the detection rate. The more reported offences that are cleared up the better.

'Philippa Lavelle has currently 37 unsolved crimes on our books. That's more than the rest of the west of Dorset put together. Only in Bournemouth do we have a worse situation.'

'Yes, and that brings me to another point Perry,' interjected the Chief. 'Why are you so interested in this, it's not even on your manor?'

Jarvis was prepared for this and unfazed. 'Agreed Ma'am, but I'm a neighbour of Lavelle and I have her in my ear all the time. And she hassles my wife every time she sees her. It's really getting us down.'

'So your interest is not just professional then? A bit personal as well.' The Chief pressed on, more for the sake of it as she knew that this was a bright boy who would not be put off.

'I suppose I wouldn't even know about it if I didn't live near Bridport so yes, there is a personal angle, but the fact remains that we have the Inspectorate in three months' time and there are 36 crime clear ups waiting to be had, but they won't wait forever. We need to mount an operation as a matter of urgency before evidence deteriorates and suspects move on. Most of the workforce involved are itinerate pluckers living in caravans. They'll be here for a few weeks more and then leave as the summer ends.'

The Chief smiled at the 'itinerate pluckers' label, but Jarvis was unaware that he'd been humorous. He was right of course. This had to be sorted and fast. Joanne Bache realised that she could not miss an opportunity to clear up 36 crimes under fairly conducive circumstances. Easy pickings.

'Yeah okay Perry, I'll speak to Rob Sherrell, stick it on paper and we'll get cracking. Thanks for your input.'

The meeting had been in the Chief's office and as Joanne Bache said these final words Jarvis knew it was over and that he had got what he wanted and that Philippa Lavelle would be ever so pleased with him and his wife. He stood and walked to the door. His impeccable manners saw to it that as he closed the door he turned and addressed the Chief,

'Thank you for your time, Ma'am.'

She smiled thinly as he disappeared. She picked up the phone to Sherrell. 'Can you come in a minute Rob?'

117. Reg was already in the Goat when Packington ambled in.

'Ah Mr. Bull sir,' saluted Packington amicably, 'How the devil are you?'

Reg was not bothered about being caught in the pub by the DI at this time of the day, especially whilst off duty. And he knew Packington couldn't give a toss anyway, off duty or not.

'Not bad, guvnor, not bad at all, and yourself?'

'Tickety boo Reg, tickety boo, and call me Kevin, Want a drink?'

Reg's pint was nearly empty.

'Don't mind if I do Kevin. Thanks. Youngs please.'

Youngs bitter was Reg's favourite, and the Goat was the only pub in west Dorset that did it.

Packington got two pints of the stuff and carried it across to where Reg was sitting in his usual corner of the pub.

'It's lucky I've bumped into you really.'

Reg was intrigued by this. 'Really?'

'Yes really. You've been helping young Heather Boyle with this Pentreath girl business, is that right?'

'Yeah, suppose, I was her 'parent PC' for few weeks I helped her with all sorts. Not anymore though.' The last sentence was muted, almost under his breath and he looked away as he spoke it.

Packington did not miss this. 'Why not anymore?'

'Well, she's with your mob now, isn't she, don't need an old codger like me showing her the ropes when she's got the West Dorset CID trying to get inside her knickers.'

Packington burst out laughing, not so much at what Reg Bull had just said, but more at the fact that he seemed actually serious.

'You reckon? Who's tryin' to get inside her knickers then? She ain't all that, pretty plain I remember thinking.'

'No she's not plain, she's fucking gorgeous.'

'Ah,' exclaimed the DI, his laugh growing louder, 'the green eyed monster, eh?'

Reg realised he was going to get the piss taken out of him something rotten if he didn't put this right.

'No, no, no, not at all Guvnor, I couldn't give a shit, I'm a married man....'

'Not very successfully, by all accounts.' The DI had stopped laughing.

'What d'you mean by that Guvnor?' Reg was on his guard, taken aback by the last remark.

'Oh come on Reg, you're always on the piss, never at home, you hang around the nick when you're off duty, and now it seems you have a crush on a young WPC.' The DI wasn't even smiling now.

Reg needed to nip this in the bud. Leaning forward he made sure the DI knew he meant business: 'Look Mr. Packington, all we see in this fuckin' force is some people getting the good work and some not, some people getting promoted and some not. Some people getting disciplined for the same things that other get off with....'

The DI was too quick for him, 'and some people getting the attention of young women and others not. Is that right Reg? That's what it is, isn't it?'

And Reg Bull was silent. 'Come on', said the DI, 'Relax and drink your beer. We're the same age you and I Reg, we shouldn't be getting ourselves wound up about these things.'

'I like the 'we'', replied Reg, sitting back in his chair again, 'You never seem wound up about anything.'

'It's all in the mind mate, all in the mind.'

'Yeah, suppose.'

There was a pause then for a few minutes whilst the two middle aged men supped their pints and watched the locals come and go, returning stares to anyone who offered them. The silence was broken by the DI.

Anyway, whilst we're on the subject, did you give her one?' Reg should have expected this from the cruel CID sense of humour, but he had not, and nor did he find it funny. 'Fuck off guv'nor.' And with that he drained his beer, put his glass down quietly and left the pub, leaving Packington giggling like an idiot.

118. It was a week before Katie stopped crying. The carcasses of Rosie and Gabby had been buried in their paddock in a deep grave dug by Bertie Pentreath with a borrowed JCB. There was no head-stone or anything like that and there had been no funeral. But the carcasses had been laid out on their sides facing each other on Katie's instructions. That way they would keep each other company, at least.

It was mid-August and Katie could not believe what the summer had brought her. The murder of her horses would, she knew, affect her for life and she wondered if she could face her veterinary studies again. To work in the business of saving animals lives when she had been party to the killing of her own would be an irony difficult to live with. And oh yes, she firmly believed she had been the cause of Rosie and Gabby's deaths. Flaunting her arse around the pubs of Lyme Regis like that. What had she thought she was doing? Enjoying being the subject of adoration and infatuation of a man she should have known would have been incapable of dealing with rejection. It would have taken her about two seconds to work out that Darren Pyke was going to be trouble. But she enjoyed the attention and the power it bestowed upon her. So she had cast caution aside. And now look where she was. Bereft and damaged. Moreover, she instinctively knew that it was far from over.

119. It was a shade after 5.30 in the morning when Heather drove her car into the back yard of Lyme police station. Predictably, she was the first there. She went upstairs into the CID office and put the kettle on. As the old contraption brought itself to the boil she yawned and thought of the day ahead; not without trepidation. Next in was Decker.

'Morning Heather, everything teed up?'

'Yes sarge, everything's fine. Did the magistrates ask any awkward questions?'

'No, of course not, they looked at the paperwork and signed, good as gold. Would have done the same for you if you'd had the bottle to apply for the warrant.'

So he was going to be like this was he? The bully boy was back.

Decker raced on. 'Radios charged? Control room at Dorchester informed? Custody officer given the heads up?'

Heather was able to answer in the affirmative to all of these. She had done the lot.

Then Townsend walked in with a couple of uniformed officers.

'Mornin' sarge, mornin' Hev.'

'Ah, good morning DC Townsend', replied Decker, looking at his watch. Townsend was not late but Decker had to make the point that the junior officer had been there before him. It didn't matter that she'd been there before him also.

Townsend managed to pretend to ignore this. 'The dog van's outside. The handlers want to know where the briefing is.'

Decker had thought of this. 'Bring them up here. How many of them are there?'

'Two handlers, two dogs sarge.' Heather got in with this one. After all, it had been her who'd arranged them. Townsend opened a window, leaned out and whistled into the back yard. Within minutes two burly uniforms were in the office. The dogs could be heard barking in the van, excited by the forthcoming deployment.

And that was it, seven of them. Decker bade them an official good morning, told them all to be seated and started an unfriendly briefing.

'Okay. This morning we are going to Stockard to execute a search warrant at the address of Darren and Joshua Pyke....' At that the dog handlers, two of a rather testy section based at Dorchester and unfamiliar with Lyme and in particular Detective Sergeant Decker, turned to look at each other, one of them raised his eyes heavenwards.

'What the fuck's the matter with you?' snapped Decker. The errant handler was taken aback by this. They were a much sought after resource and their transgressions were normally forgiven.

'Nothing sarge.'

'Yes there is, share it, what do you know about the Pykes?'

Luckily for the handler the phone in the DI's office rang and Decker had to go to answer it. It was not often that the DI's phone rang outside office hours and Decker knew that it would be to do with the present job. As soon as he was out of sight the handlers looked around at the others for some sort of explanation. All they got was a warning from Townsend. 'Be careful, he doesn't fuck about.' Any response to this would have been drowned out.

'You're fuckin' joking boss!' Decker, usually composed, had received some unexpected news. Everyone waited in stunned silence for the next instalment.

'But I've got....'

Another pause. 'Yes sir. Not a problem. I'll re-assign.' Another pause whilst the DS received further instructions. 'No problem sir. Eight o'clock, see you there. Oh, what do I do with the dog van? Yeah, fine. See you there.'

The troops waited for him to emerge for the DI's office, which he did a very long ten seconds later. When he did he bore a subdued announcement.

'I suppose you've gathered we're not going to Stockard now.'

120. But one policeman was already at Stockard. Despite talk of including him in the operation, Reg Bull had originally been left out of the plans to raid the Pyke house. There had been nothing sinister about this decision, just logistics; he was rostered on a late shift, the late shift sergeant could not afford to lose him and the money was not there to pay the overtime. But Reg had persisted and had told the shift manager that he would do the job as overtime but not for payment, provided that he could claim the time back within six months. This was an alternative and the shift manager relented. So Reg Bull had booked out an airwave radio the night before and had gone directly to Stockard, missing the briefing. But he was then not himself missed; another job had taken precedence before the Stockard briefing had even taken place, so he would not feature in the redeployment.

So now he sat in his car listening for CID activity on the airwave that would signal they were on their way. At least if it kicked off in the house he would be nearby to help. Albeit old, pretty fat and at the end of his so-called career, Reg found himself intrigued by certain situations that arose from his job. He was for instance intrigued by the relationship between the Pykes and the Everetts. Something was not right about this, had never been. The Pykes were urban low-life; on the other hand the Everetts were regarded as a bit strange but generally law-abiding and pleasant, in a Bohemian sort of way. Reg had researched their horse-breeding and it appeared to thrive, and this in an era when you could hardly give a horse away. They kept a clean farm because they simply had to in order to maintain their reputation and breeder's licence. So why was the Pyke's van always around there and why had Darren Pyke given the Everett address when he and his brother had been pulled in west London? Were they setting the Everett's up for something? Reg doubted this, they had every reason not to. Reg decided that the Pykes were probably paying the Everetts for the use of the horsebox and the parking space so that they could conduct their drugs business in comparative safety. You could hide drugs a lot better on an agricultural smallholding than in a small council house.

So Reg sat and waited with genuine professional interest. It was turning out to be a lovely morning, his favourite part of the day; before all the shit and backstabbing started, before the civilian bitches arrived at work to jockey for male uniformed attention, before the canteen tea became stewed.

121. Emmett Everett was making poached eggs for his mum and sister to eat in bed. It was, after all, Saturday morning. Mrs. Everett got hers first, and she sat up in bed wearily but gratefully as her son presented the tray of breakfast.

'Could I have some orange juice as well my old mate?' Her broad Dorset accent seemed to be stronger when she had just woken, as though she'd been using it in her dreams.

'Comin' up, my old mate.'

'Don't be takin' the piss now, just 'cos you've managed to get yourself out of bed in the morning for once.'

They both laughed and Emmett went back downstairs to get the juice. Only when his mother was sorted did he deliver a meal to his sister's room. Carmella was on her 110th crunch when her brother backed in through her bedroom door with the breakfast tray.

'Mornin' sis, breakfast is served.'

'Cheers mate,' grunted the girl. Her feet were jammed under the bed and her knees were bent and her hands were clenched behind her neck. She ground out five more repetitions of the exercise before allowing herself to collapse backwards onto the floor. She was naked from the waist up and her small breasts seemed as firm as her six-pack abdominals. Emmett admired her body as he put the tray down on her bed. He was a keen trainer himself and spent a good hour every day, often accompanied by his sister, in a homemade gym in one of the numerous outhouses. Carmella had always been stronger and faster though, and sometimes Emmet wondered if she had been taking those steroid things that he had seen on the telly. If she was then she would start growing a beard. He would watch out for that. In the meantime there was something more pressing on his mind.

'Sis.' He ventured, as he watched her sit on the bed and attack the eggs.

'Yeah?' her chewing slowed – she recognised the pre-question tone.

'Are you and Darren still 'avin' sex in the tree-house?'

The girl quietly lifted the tray from her lap and placed it to one side. The she slowly stood. As she did so her head was still inclined downwards, so that as she looked up from under her brows, her eyes gleamed with a lot of white beneath the irises.

'Why do you ask bruv? You jealous?' She said this calmly, almost pleasantly. But Emmett kind of knew what was coming.

'No sis.'

'You sure bruv? You sure you don't want to fuck me bruv? You like looking at me.'

Emmett had heard all this before and genuinely did not want to have sex with his half-sister. Theirs was and always had been a perfectly natural sibling relationship, and they had always got on reasonably well. Unless of course Darren was on the scene or whenever his name was mentioned.

'No sis. And you fucking know I don't want to do that to you. But I'm worried about you and Darren. We get a lot of money from 'im an' Josh. We need to keep them happy. So don't you go fallin' out with Daz, eh.' The girl was speechless. And there she was thinking it was going to be the old protective big brother sketch again – "You sure you doin' the right thing lettin' your brother shag you? You be sure to be on the pill... I wish you an' Daz would pack it in... You don't need him, you could pull any bloke in Lyme." – But no, he was telling her to keep Darren happy by giving him sex! Her own half-brother, to shore up their business relationship.

'You cunt!' screamed Carmella as her knee went up into Emmett's groin so hard he screamed with her. 'You fucking scabby fucking cunt!' She punctuated each word with a punch or a knee or a kick at her brother, who was now on the floor in the foetal position. It was a good job for him that she did not have her shoes on. Then she jumped up and landed on him with her knees. Then she prised his hands away from his face and got a hold of his throat. Bearing down on him she demanded some information.

'What's he bin sayin'?'

No answer. 'What the fuck has he bin sayin' Emmett, to fuckin' bring this on? Tell me!'

'Nuthin' much sis,' choked Emmett, just said you haven't bin very 'appy lately, that's all.'

'Yeah, that's true enough, for fuckin' sure that's true enough.' She loosened her grip and rolled off of him. Far from amusing her, the emergent irony hurt Carmella badly.

122. It was after 7am before Reg realised he'd been left high and dry. He tried to raise Decker on the airwave. No response. Same with Townsend and Heather. Little did he know that their radios had never been switched on and that they had been diverted to Bridport on another job. He used his mobile phone to call the desk sergeant at Lyme who told him that the CID, dog van and a couple of uniformed PCs had been seen leaving the

station over an hour previously and were on their way to meet Dorchester units on another division. That was all the desk sergeant knew. So Reg had been either forgotten about or deliberately kept out of the way. His self-pity preferred the second interpretation. Yesterday's man, he thought, and was close to tears as he drove away from Stockard. Yesterday's man. He felt completely empty, foolish and angry. Worst of all, he knew why. At 48 years of age nothing was about him anymore. Everything was about other people. He would be retiring in little over a year. To what? Gardening (his boring wife already had plans for the new patio and Japanese style gazebo). Beekeeping? No money in honey any more. Drinking? His pension would not stretch to it. No, he could barely cope with the wasted past and contemplating the future as it currently stood was just impossible.

123. Heather sat in the back of the CID car and seethed. They were going to fucking Bridport to be briefed by a Bournemouth DI before going on to arrest people for stealing fucking exotic wildfowl. She just could not believe it. But then of course she could believe it. It had been the same in the Met. Clear-up figures were paramount and what Decker was now saying from the front passenger seat to her and Townsend was straight out of the police management handbook.

'This is, believe it or not, proper deployment of personnel in a cash strapped policing era. Turning the Pykes over can wait. The search warrant is valid for a month. The job we're going to is urgent because the suspects could move on any day, and there are fifteen to twenty of them. The victim, if you could call her that, is a woman called Philippa Lavelle and she's a big noise with contacts on the West Dorset Council, which is where we get a lot of our money from. There have been forty three reported thefts or, put it this way, forty three birds have gone missing and each can be recorded as one crime, so that's forty three clear-ups for the books. If we charge the Pykes, or anyone else, with poisoning two horses that's only two criminal damage clear-ups....'

Townsend could not resist it, 'So a fucking chicken is worth the same as a horse?'

'Yes,' continued Decker calmly, refusing to let this get to him, 'more in fact because stealing a chicken is theft whereas killing a horse is only criminal damage.'

Heather just sat and listened to this bollocks. She thought of those two lovely horses and that distraught gorgeous girl Katie Pentreath. She had thought of little else but Katie Pentreath all night in fact, as she'd lain in her bed worrying about not oversleeping. It pained Heather that Katie plainly disliked her. Perhaps it was the uniform. Perhaps it was that Katie, possibly a rebellious student, just did not like cops. Or perhaps she just did not like women with short hair.

The CID car led the convoy with the dog van and marked car with the two uniformed cops following behind. As they pulled into the car park at the rear of Bridport police station Decker's professionalism deserted him. The first thing he saw was Perry Jarvis and Rob Sherrell standing talking to each other.

'Fucking hell, what are those two doing here? Does money talk or fucking what! A Bournemouth superintendent and a Dorchester commander in Bridport at this time in the morning. I don't believe it!'

Townsend was equally incredulous as he pulled the car to a stop. 'Can't be our job sarge, must be something else going on.'

'What else? A terrorist attack?' Decker's face was crimson and there were bits of spittle on his chin. Heather decided to keep quiet. Then there was a tap on the passenger-side window. Decker looked around and upwards to see none other than Detective Inspector Kevin Packington winking at him with a mischievous smirk on his face. Packington beckoned and Decker got out of the car. Townsend moved it forward and parked in a vacant bay. He and Heather stayed in the car to await instructions, neither wanting to get caught in any political crossfire.

'What's occurring guvnor?' asked Decker of Packington, almost accusingly.

'Settle down Tom, settle down. I told you on the telephone what this was all about. Don't start whinging.' Packington was actually chuckling, he loved to see cool-headed professionals get their knickers in a twist. It amused him greatly.

Within five minutes they were all in the station canteen being briefed by Superintendent Perry Jarvis. There were more than thirty cops crammed into that small room listening to Jarvis try to make an important job out of the arrest of seven seasonal farmworkers from a local caravan site for the thefts of wildfowl from a local poultry farm. They listened to how the birds were the personal pets of the farm owner, a Mrs. Philippa Lavelle, how they were not kept for commercial gain like the chickens and egg laying hens and how they would have suffered great cruelty in the course of their being abducted. Decker looked around at the faces in the canteen. All were equally unimpressed; all knew what the patronising, condescending Jarvis was up to. There were going to be seven arrests and forty odd crimes 'solved.' That should keep Her Majesty's Inspectorate of Constabularies happy for a while. Keep the Chief in a job for a bit longer. Make sure the Home Office and the Dorset County Council keep the purse strings open.

124. And Darren Pyke opened his eyes to the new day. It was 06.30. Not that he had slept much. The whole triangle knew about Katie's horses being poisoned and a piece had been hurriedly put together by the intrepid reporter, Jim Ramage. Although never too bothered about factual content, Jim had gone to the bother of trying to get an interview with the Pentreaths, had actually driven up to their farm. Katie had been unavailable for comment but old Bertie had provided Ramage with a story about how he was being targeted by some local youths from Axminster and that he thought it may be in connection with his current plans to turn his farm into a clay pigeon shooting centre. He told the reporter – and there was a lot of truth in the story – that a hard core of locals were against his plans and were possibly paying a couple of hoodlums to give him and his family a hard time. Ramage bought the

story. Bertie knew damned fine that it was nonsense and also knew instinctively that all this had something to do with his daughter and her little associations of late. She was in danger and he just wanted her away and back to Brighton. None of these idiots would follow her there; they wouldn't even know where it was.

There were only two people who knew who had killed those horses. One was the horse killer and the other was Darren Pyke, who also knew that he would end up taking the blame for it. He would of course deny it and probably would not be charged for lack of any real evidence, but he would get the blame all the same, condemned by his peers and West Dorset population alike. The truth, of course, would never be known, for if it did then another truth would emerge. He knew that if he blew the whistle on his sister and she was interviewed by even the most inept police officer there would be only one outcome. He and she would end up in the dock of Dorchester Crown Court facing an incest indictment. Not good for the rep. Not good for business.

He and Josh were due to go to Bristol later that day to do a pick-up and he knew he would therefore have to go to the Everett's place to pick up the van and the horsebox. He really did not fancy it. So he slid out of bed and into his clothes, crept out of the house and started walking towards Upper Brooklands Farm.

And Katie Pentreath was waiting. She knew that one day soon he would turn up. She somehow knew that the police would never arrest him for killing her horses. She was not even sure that he had killed them, so why should the police even suspect him. They would always do their best not to do any work anyway. But she was sure that once Darren found out about the horse killing he would visit her, just to make sure she didn't finger him for it. She had not been sleeping too well lately, believe it or not, but it was not because of the horses. She was very sad about them and very angry as well, but found herself strangely detached. Whether this was part of the process of dealing with the incident or her veterinary training telling her that horses were just animals and that animals were killed in the hundreds of thousand every day in much crueller circumstances having led terrible lives, she was not sure. Anyway, she decided after a quick breakfast to walk down to the stable in the paddock and clean it out. She would not be getting replacement horses, she had already decided that, but at least she could make sure the place was tidy; a mark of respect for her two dead friends. It was going to be interesting to see how she would cope with this. As she turned a corner on the lane she saw the fresh earth mound of the double grave. Any lump in her throat? No, so far, so good. She entered the stable and the smell of her two dead friends was still about, this nearly set her off but she still hung on to her emotions. She busied herself tidying up some tack and raking some loose straw into neat piles and then she sat down on the floor with her back against the wall. She sniffed a couple of times and wondered why she wasn't bawling her eyes out.

And then there he was. 'Have you got a light please?'

She looked up and to her left to see him standing in the doorway. The she looked forward and down at the floor again, and wondered why she was not up and going for his throat. 'Yes, of course,' she replied, and fumbled for the lighter. He walked forward and sat down on the floor near her, his back against the same wall but about two yards to her left. She handed him the lighter and he held it in his hand, looking at it as if it was something he'd never seen before. He did not light a cigarette.

'You know it wasn't me, don't you?' he said this quietly, politely.

'Of course it wasn't you, I know that Darren. I don't know how I know but I just do. The question remains though, who killed my horses? I believe you may have the answer to that question. What do you think?'

Darren Pyke sighed and remained focused on the Zippo in his hand.

'I may have an idea, but I can't say nuthin', not yet anyway.'

'Let me know when you're ready Darren.' As she said this she reached out and put her hand on his, the one holding the Zippo. It was their first physical contact. It electrified him. He felt that someone inside him, someone he sort of knew but did not, was trying to get out. This other person, this parallel Darren Pyke, was not a friend and not an enemy. That itself was an alien concept for Darren. You were invariably one or the other in his world. He froze and just stared at the lighter. Katie leaned across and kissed him on the cheek. This caused Darren to turn his head towards her. She noticed for the first time a certain sadness in his eyes, the sadness perhaps of someone who had been born into the wrong body and who had fought to adapt to that body, and to express himself within its limitations. She moved over to him and placed a hand on each side of his face and pressed her open mouth over his closed lips. He opened his mouth and folded his arms awkwardly around her. His heart raced.

Then Katie pulled back from him for just long enough to say, 'You poor boy,' and then swung herself around to face and straddle him. That did it, as she knew it would. She was playing a very dangerous game. She knew the violence of which he was capable but somehow she also knew the power she had over him. She played with this. As he tried to roll over on top of her she removed her weight from him, using her strong thighs in a squatting motion, she pulled her face back from his and placed a finger over his lips.

'Not here,' she cautioned. 'I'm very noisy and my parents are within earshot.' Darren could hardly bear it but knew any attempt by him to use force would mean very serious trouble indeed. He had committed rape once or twice in the past on unwilling girlfriends and got away with it. But he knew that this was a different scenario altogether. He was shaking and lay awkwardly, half propped up against the wall. She stood, legs astride him and looked down at his troubled face. Under normal circumstances Katie would of course have enjoyed this moment of complete domination. And if Darren had been anything other than the completely normal young male that he was, then so would have he. But these were not normal circumstances. Katie Pentreath wanted to know who had killed her horses, but she also wanted very badly to know what was going to happen next. What had she or anyone else for that matter done to bring this on her family? First a rock through the window, now this. It had nothing to do with her father, she knew that. Those who objected to his plans for a clay shooting farm would not do this. The altercation in the pub? No, that may have explained the lump of flint through the window, but not this. People in these parts generally liked animals, especially horses. No, this was the work of a complete nutter, and Darren would know all the nutters in these parts, she was sure of that.

'Who killed my horses Darren?' She still stood astride him, looking down her nose.

'I don't fuckin' know Katie.' He started to get up and she sensed that it would not be wise to try to stop him, so she moved back, gave him some space. She was not yet sufficiently confident to corner this wild guy.

When they were standing facing each other she moved close to him and put her hands on his shoulders, looking at him square in the eyes, her elbows bent to 45 degrees and held there so as not to permit contact between their torsos.

'Find out for me Darren. Find them for me. I'm relying on you. You are the only person on earth who can help me.'

Whilst Darren Pyke knew exactly what this middle class bitch was up to – sex for information then whistles for the sex – he found himself spellbound, compelled to comply, or at least to pretend to. It was as if his genes, or the genes of his parallel self that wanted to escape, were commanding him to go along with this as it represented their best chance of progression to a higher social level. The consequence was that he was in love with her.

'Okay, I'll do my best for you. When can I see you next? Tonight?' He knew he was showing too many cards. He knew that by saying this he was telling her that he knew the answer to her question. But then if she did not believe this then he would get nowhere. At least he did know, at least he was not deceiving her totally. He was surprised when she answered in the affirmative.

'Okay, yes, tonight, in Lyme.'

He was wary about this, 'Where in Lyme Katie?'

She shrugged and took out her tobacco. 'I dunno, you choose.'

He laughed. Never in his life had he enjoyed being in control but feeling out of control. He threw caution to the wind and decided to make as much out of this as possible.

'Okay then, I'll see you outside the Mermaid Theatre. Away from the sea and the tourists and the shit. We can have a good chat there.'

'Okay. See you there then.' As she said this she backed away from him and inclined her head back a little so that she could look just slightly down her nose. 'What time?'

'Eight?'

'Make it eight thirty.' And then she was gone, leaving him standing there in the straw.

125. By ten o'clock that morning both Bridport and Lyme police stations had their cells full of detainees, arrested at various locations. Mainly caravan sites in the county, on suspicion of stealing expensive wildfowl from the farm of Ms. Philippa Lavelle. The uniform custody officers at both stations, awoken from their customary early slumber, could not believe it. They were endlessly harangued by management about the overtime their troops incurred doing necessary, often emergency police work. Then they see thousands of pounds being spent on an operation to detect and clear-up the theft of a few chickens from a rich woman with a farm and a seat on the local Rotary Club. It made them sick.

Superintendent Perry Jarvis held a briefing in the canteen at Bridport and was just about to start by thanking the twenty or so officers present when in walked PC Norman Hogg. He had been on routine patrol in his little panda car when he'd got wind of the 'chicken run', as it was being called already. The sound of the name Jarvis had angered him. What the fuck was Jarvis, a Bournemouth superintendent, doing in this part of the county. It stank, especially as Norman knew that Jarvis lived near Bridport and was a neighbour of Lavelle. And Norman knew something else about Jarvis that was not common knowledge; he was on the shortlist to take command of the Dorset Police Professional Standards Department. Internal Affairs, as it was called by the media. The enemy of the Police Federation, Professional Standards Departments up and down the country were populated by ambitious cops who would happily make scapegoats out of basically innocent cops if it got them a foot on the promotion ladder. Norman Hogg knew Jarvis of old and had done battle with him on numerous discipline hearings when, as an inspector, Jarvis had constructed misconduct cases against junior officers. It was true that most, not all but most of those junior officers had misbehaved. That had not been what had upset Norman. The problem had been the zealous attitude of Jarvis. Like he was doing God's work trying to rid the force of corrupt officers, when all the young cop had done was to sleep in for early shift on a couple of occasions, or given some drunken yob in Bournemouth a fucking good hiding for being lippy.

Jarvis watched Norman walk into the canteen and did not take his eyes off of him as he spoke.

'Ladies and gentlemen, so far, so good and this morning's success has been all down to you. This county must not become a soft touch for every itinerant worker in the south of England who fancies his thieving chances. What we've done this morning will send out a clear message to the rural low-life. Mess with Dorset and you'll get messed back with.'

He then paused as if awaiting a round of applause. None came.

'Right, okay, those of you who have been selected to conduct the interviews please stay to be briefed by the DI, the rest of you - thank you sincerely for your hard work this morning.'

There followed a two or three second silence before chairs began to scrape and those dismissed rose and shuffled out of the room, most thankful to get back to their normal duties and away from this bullshit.

Norman Hogg stayed and stood at the back, staring at Jarvis. Jarvis looked at him and held his gaze for a few seconds before smiling a tight lipped smile and looking back down to shuffle his briefing sheets. He was not going to be intimidated by this silly old Constable who thought he had a friend in the Chief. These old Federation reps were usually the same. It was like the Federation had provided them with a career to replace the one they might have had in the police force had they been bright enough to pass the promotion exams. They were usually not so they volunteered for a task that few wanted - looking after miscreants and lame ducks in the job. In return they got generally cushy duties and a wide berth from their superiors. Plus of course expense paid trips up and down the country to meetings and conferences – a bit like senior officers, really.

Norman did not fancy a tea any longer so he turned and went back downstairs to his car. On the way out he bumped into a very cross Reg Bull.

'Alright Reg?' Norman enquired, casually.

'No I'm fuckin' not, where's fuckin' Decker, and that slapper Heather Boyle?' Reg was pushing past Norman as he said this, his eyes already mounting the stairs.

'Steady on Reggie,' Norman could see there was going to be trouble if he didn't do something, so put his arm up and stopped Reg at the door. 'What's the matter with you?'

'Left me high an' dry, they did. Sat like a daft cunt in Stockard. We was going to turn over the Pykes and then I hear they came here instead. Never told me fuck all.'

Norman could hardly contain himself, but he managed to keep a straight face because he could see Reg was very, very upset.

'Fuck's sake mate, don't take that personally, happens all the time. You know what they say, if you can't take the jokes then….'

'Yeah, I know, don't join the job. But I've taken enough fuckin' jokes over the years.'

Reg then tried to push past Norman Hogg but the bigger man would not let him.

'You're not going up that canteen in your state of mind. They're up there getting briefed and I've got too much on my plate at the moment to take on another cop on a board for insubordination. Come on Reg, let's go for a walk on the sea front.'

Reg Bull could see the sense in this. If he was let loose on Decker now he would only regret the consequences. He relaxed a few notches and nodded. There were others trying to get through the door and the situation was attracting attention. Reg moved away and the two old policemen walked out of the yard together and down the hill to the sea.

126. Alex Miller swore as Heather's ring tone gave way to an invitation to leave a message. He had no way of knowing that she was being debriefed following her assistance with the arrest of some chicken thieves. Alex was busy as usual brokering jobs between mates, sharing information, stirring up shit with the 'guvnors', getting pissed and generally being a normal lad in the police service. He was also still thinking occasionally of Heather Boyle and how he still missed her and hadn't given up on getting her knickers off. He had to admit to himself that he was a little bit in love with her. Oh, he'd heard all the rumours, had even helped in their dissemination on occasions, but he still had a massive crush on her. He couldn't understand it really. It wasn't like he was short of offers and he had two or three birds he could fuck any time he wanted. But there was just something about his friend Heather. Something out of reach to others yet just possibly within his.

Anyway. He had good news for her. It had gone dead on the 'White Van Job' for about six weeks because those country bumpkins had no way of plotting the vehicle up, no resources to conduct meaningful surveillance.

Not that Alex thought that that would matter too much. These jobs could to go to sleep for months and then be restarted. Drug dealers went quiet from time to time if they thought the heat was on, but would always go back to the trade, so much money involved, you see. So much very easy money. Alex had been talking to Gibbons at a football function on the previous evening. A lot of beer had been downed and Gibbons had let slip that some tracking equipment had gone missing from the surveillance team stores. A couple of pints more and Gibbons confided in Miller that he might know where that equipment was located. Stuff went missing all the time, and often ended up being flogged to ex-cop private investigators who were just starting up and couldn't afford to buy on the commercial market. There was invariably a bit of a fuss made at the outset before new kit was taken out of the box and the nicked stuff was declared obsolete anyway. Gibbons knew that Alex Miller had friends in the private eye business and was obviously touting for trade. Alex decided to accommodate.

'How much?' he asked.

'Three hundred for the lot, three lumps and the receiver.'

'Make it two, I only need one lump.' A 'lump' was an actual tracking device which would be covertly placed on or in the target vehicle. The 'receiver' was simply a DVD or data stick containing the software which could then be downloaded onto any PC or laptop.

'Done.'

And they had another pint each, this time with whiskey chasers.

Alex knew exactly where this equipment was going to end up. It was just ironic that he was having to purchase and handle stolen goods to get a job restarted in another Force. But then he did after all have his own agenda, and it wasn't all about police work.

About an hour later he tried again and got through, her phone was back on.

'Hi Hev, it's Alex, what's occurring?'

'Oh, hi. Don't ask.' She was obviously pissed off.

'What's the matter mate, what are they doing to you down there? Got you milking the cows or something?'

'Not bloody far off it. What d'you want?'

'Uh, that's nice, what do I want. Why do you always think I want something?'

'Because I know you do and I know what you want.'

'Why ask then?' Then he went on before the banter got out of hand, 'Look, I've got something for you, something a bit technical.'

'Go on.'

'Not over the phone, we need to meet.' Here we go, she thought.

'Yeah, whenever, you know where I am. When do you want to come down?' She found herself surprised by her invitation. She was obviously in need of a bit of sanity, a bit of the old cosmopolitan life that Alex reminded her of.

'I'll be down tonight, at your house. Eight o'clock.' She agreed to this and they both hung up.

Alex was genuinely pleased about this from a professional point of view. If he could get that lump on that van and have access to the data it generated then he could put in a good bid for a Dorset-Met operational link up. It would be interesting in itself and might yield results on his Heather-shagging ambitions.

127. He would not have been able to attach a tracker on the white Transit at that moment in time though; it was doing 50 on the M4 to Cardiff. Darren was driving and had only just relaxed having got halfway across

Somerset. He hated being in that vehicle now, especially with the horsebox in tow. He had wanted to leave the trailer behind but Josh, who sat silently in the passenger seat, had insisted. For extra cover they'd actually put a horse in the box. A pony called Eddie who had not been impressed when shoved into the cramped space to be bounced along a motorway and made to breathe noxious fumes. Eddie's presence in the box held them up considerably and being stuck in the slow lane they often had to crawl along with big loads at frustratingly low speeds. But then that was what made these two so good at their job. No flash Mercs, no Armani suits, no handguns. Just an old van, a horse in a box and a sawn off rabbit gun should things really get desperate.

As Darren pulled off the motorway and down through Newport towards Cardiff docks Josh gave directions. They were to meet a guy called Larry who had made contact with Josh by way of a card in the window of an Axminster newsagent. 'Flat share for Japanese students in Cardiff', then a mobile number. It was one of the current communications systems. Talk about low tech. They were pretty good at their jobs, were the Pykes. Imaginative. No overuse of mobiles. No emails. Guarded language at all times. The window card trick had been dreamt up by Josh and the word was around Cardiff that was the way to start a deal up with the Dorset boys. It had obviously occurred to Josh that word could reach the wrong ears and they could get set up by competitors or cops. So there was a security vetting system in place. Before the Pykes travelled to Cardiff to make a purchase, their seller (Japanese landlord, as they would call him) would have to make a trip to Axminster, alone, for a game of pool. During the game and over a pint or two the Pykes would gently grill him. One of the younger brothers or perhaps a follower would hang around outside the pub smoking, watching for backup boys and noting unfamiliar index plates. Not until they were satisfied that they had a genuine dealer would they progress the business, either there and then or, as was the present case, by way of a trip to Tiger Bay.

Anyway. The two Pykes met Larry and a deal was done. They handed over four hundred quid whilst pretending to show Larry the teeth of a confused and anxious Eddie and in return got a couple of parcels. One was a handsome block of cannabis resin wrapped in cling film. This went straight to the bottom of a healthy pile of shit Eddie had deposited on the outward journey. The other was much smaller and had to be decanted into Josh's .303 bullet case. Where that in turn went does not have to be rehearsed. Ten minutes later and they were back on the motorway eastward bound.

'Fucking alright, innit. Fucking half a ton of gee-gee in the back and it's me with a .303 bullet stuck up my arse. Next time the horse gets it. Just think, we could get a fuckin' Howitzer shell up there.'

They both laughed, relieved the day's business was almost over. They would go back to the Everett's place now, let Eddie out into his paddock with a reward of fresh hay and cool water, bury the gear, put the van in a shed and lie low for few days. That way if they'd been followed a surveillance team would probably get bored and go home. The boys knew that if they didn't get pulled on the road then they were unlikely to get spun once they'd gone to ground. No decent cops were going to search a farm with multiple occupants living there with varying degrees of permanency to look for drugs that were probably well hidden. Not when they had the chance of stopping a vehicle on the road with cargo on board and two occupants who couldn't really argue that it had nothing to do with them. So they both breathed sighs of relief as Carmella Everett pulled the gates closed behind them and they trundled in with the van and horsebox.

128. When Tom Decker got home that evening he was very cross indeed. He and his wife Lucy had no children, but to compensate they had a big house overlooking Lyme Bay on one of the new developments. It was well furnished and they both drove nice cars. Lucy did not work and Decker wanted it that way. He saw her as his support team – her career was helping him with his. Lucy put up with this quite cheerfully. There was not much in the area in the way of decent jobs for women. She had qualified as a legal secretary years previously, but had packed it in when she realised that the hours she worked for a local conveyancing firm

were so long so as to reduce her salary to the equivalent of the minimum wage. No, she was happy enough looking after her husband and looked forward to the day when he would be a very senior officer. The money would be good, she told herself, as would the posh dinners in Dorchester and Bournemouth to which she would accompany him. She already had a good wardrobe and worked daily on her figure to suit.

'I'm putting in for a transfer to the Met.'

Lucy had heard all this before. 'Are you dear? That'll be nice. I'll stay here and you can come home at the weekends.' There was no way she was going to move to a rabbit hutch in London, which was about all they'd get for the money they would raise from the sale of their house in Lyme.

'Look, it's alright for you, lolling about here, coffee mornings and aerobics and all that bollocks. It's me that's got to put up with these arseholes. Fucking chicken thefts, that's what me and my team have been investigating all day, fucking chicken thefts. This place is a goldmine of serious crime if you have time to dig for it, a fucking goldmine. But what do they want, clear-up figures. So when fucking Lady Flaunteroy gets a few of her prize budgies nicked by her slave workers everyone has to jump to it. And who's there in the thick of it? Fucking Jarvis. Not even on his manor. Fucking careerist.'

Lucy did not fail to see the irony, but said nothing but 'Oh, that creepy crawly man who keeps getting promoted?'

'Yeah, that's the one… are you taking the piss missus?' he was looking at her quizzically, not sure if she was baiting him.

'No dear, just that it seems you're doing all the work these days and others are getting promoted.'

'Fucking tell me about it.'

Then he felt stupid all of a sudden. He was standing there, sweating profusely with his tie down and one of his shoe laces undone, like a schoolboy having a tantrum. And his wife was humouring him. He let out a little laugh and looked down at the floor, unashamed to be embarrassed. She went to him and held his hands.

'Tom, don't worry, you'll make it. I know it must be frustrating for you, but we have a good life and good health. We've got plenty money and a nice home. Don't be so hard on yourself.'

Decker nodded and gave his wife a hug. But he was still hurting, her warmth and love did nothing whatsoever to appease him. On the contrary, she had been so patient, so understanding, so emotionally unselfish. He owed her so much and he was determined to give her what she wanted. What they both wanted.

129. Alex had arrived at Heather's home in Dorchester his usual cheerful cockney sparrow self. He found her morose mood a challenge and, when he discovered it was work related and not stemming from female hormones, he set about putting things right.

'Heather, you know very well, it's part of being a cop, whether it's the Met, Dorset or Albania, now and again you've got to eat shit.'

She was not impressed. This was all so predictable. This would not have happened to her in the Met – there weren't any chickens there for a start - she nearly laughed at her own joke, but managed not to – and the resources were available to actually tackle difficult problems and clear up serious crime. Well, sometimes, anyway. But here, fucking hell, it was like going back twenty years, or so she guessed. If the truth was known it was probably more like forty.

'Anyway,' went on Alex, unfazed by the negativity he faced, 'I've got a present for you.'

Oh shit she thought. What the hell was he going to do now? She was mindful of his obvious and admitted agenda. Then he went out to his vehicle and came back with a box containing the equipment. She recognised it immediately.

It consisted of a grey metal box about the size of a cigarette packet that was the transmitter, a plastic envelope containing a DVD, and an instruction manual. Heather was not in the slightest bit technical, but she knew the value of these things and the intelligence they could yield.

'Is this yours Alex?' The question was the same as 'Are you entitled to have this, Alex?'

'Yeah, paid for, cash.'

'But why do you need to have one of your own?'

'To give to you as a present.'

'But why do I need one?'

'Because your shit-kicking force can't provide you with one to do your job with, that's why.'

He was right of course. She had asked Decker if they could put technical surveillance on the Pyke's Transit. He had agreed that that was going to be the only way they were going to be able to conduct meaningful surveillance on the vehicle and made a few calls to HQ. The answer was as he had expected. All the equipment was deployed and there was already a queue. Forget it for at least three months. And there was the little matter of RIPA. The Regulation of Investigatory Powers Act forbade government bodies such as the police from conducting covert and intrusive surveillance on citizens without express authority from very senior officials. In Dorset the Chief Constable had decreed that she would be that senior official. So, no putting trackers on cars or microphones in peoples' houses or businesses without the Chief's prior authority. Did Decker really want to antagonise Chief Constable Bache with an application for an expensive, speculative and politically sensitive operation right in the middle of the summer period when her resources and patience were stretched to breaking point as it was? No. So nothing more had been said about it. They would carry on with more conventional methods, like executing search warrants and stopping the van every time it was seen on the road. Unsubtle crap, but it was all they could do. Such methods rarely gave up good, trial worthy evidence unless the police just got lucky and did a search or a stop at the right place at the right time. What they did do was disrupt criminal activity, make life difficult for villains, and harass them out of business which was better than nothing. But nobody went to prison. It had crossed Decker's mind more than once that that was what they wanted, the powers that were. The prisons were full anyway.

Heather caressed the device. They were sat on the sofa in the house in Dorchester. They were alone. The present Alex had just given her pleased her. She leaned over and pecked him lightly on the cheek.

'Thank you,' she said, drawing back before he could return the kiss. 'But what if Decker won't let me use it?' Alex decided to quickly change the subject.

'Come on', said Alex, 'enough of this, take me to the pub, I want to go to Lyme.'

She could hardly not agree to this, so off they went in Heather's car.

130. Katie and Darren met outside the Mermaid Theatre. She felt she was on her own territory. It was a good distance from the fashionable pubs along at the Cobb end of the promenade, and she could watch Darren's approach as he walked along the beachside road to where she stood. He was quite well dressed, for him. Gone was the black and grey shell suit and white leather pumps. He had on clean blue jeans and a red polo shirt. On his feet were brown moccasins. Not exactly colour coordinated, she thought, but not chav either. He was making an effort. This worried Katie a bit and she had to remind herself not to lead this lad on too much. Yes. She would have to earn his confidence because she had no doubt that he knew who had killed her horses, or at least could find out. And she did not waver in her total belief that he had not been responsible. Not

knowingly, anyway.

'Hi', she greeted him as he walked up to her, his eyes everywhere but on her. 'What's the matter, afraid some of your friends might see you near one of the local centres of culture?'

'Eh?' he genuinely did not know what she was talking about.

'Never mind Darren. Come with me.' She put her hand into the crook of his arm and led him around the back of the theatre and into a quiet cobbled street. She had seen that a small Italian restaurant had recently opened there and was hungry. She had decided that Darren would have no choice in the matter.

'Where are we going?' She suspected that Darren had never been in a restaurant in his life. She was right.

'We're going to eat some Italian food. I'm paying.'

'No problem.' Darren was determined not to reveal his ignorance.

They walked into the tiny bistro and were shown a seat near the window. The place was empty and the proprietor wanted it to look otherwise from the street. He was a fat Albanian called Mergen who did his best to appear to come from Rome.

Mergen showed the couple his basic but not unattractive menu and asked what they would like to drink. Darren looked at Katie for guidance; she ordered a bottle of Italian red.

The wine came and they were not given the opportunity to taste it, Mergen realising that such a formality may have caused embarrassment for the young man. Katie poured and Darren was the first to take a gulp from his glass. It was not true to say that he had never had wine before, but this was the first time he'd drunk it from a glass.

'Well,' said Katie, breaking the silence that was about to become awkward, 'here we are again, having a drink together in Lyme Regis.'

'Yeah, no scousers this time though.' Darren laughed nervously as he said this, keen to distinguish this occasion as some sort of fresh start. Not that he would have been able to articulate what he thought it was a fresh start of, if anything.

She cut to the chase. 'Have the police given you any more hassle about that night?'

'No,' he answered hurriedly to get the subject dealt with and out of the way. 'Not a thing, cancelled our bail so me and Josh, don't have to go back. Nothing will happen now, unless you pipe up.' He regretted the last bit before he'd finished saying it.

'If I was going to 'pipe up', as you call it, I would have done so before now Darren.'

'Yeah, sorry, I know.' There followed a pause before he went on, 'What did you tell them, anyway?'

'If by 'them' you mean that butch police woman called Heather, I told them the truth, what had happened, how you protected me, how I left with you out of a sense of loyalty and how I was not going to give evidence against you in court.'

Darren had assumed that this was what had happened, but it did not explain why he and Josh had not been charged on the basis of the CCTV footage alone. There surely must have been enough compelling evidence on it.

'Is that all?'

'No. She threatened me, said that if I didn't cooperate I could get charged as an accessory. I said I would tell the judge about this if she made me go to court. That seems to have done the trick.'

Darren looked at his companion in awe. So this was what education was all about. He took out his tobacco tin and started to roll, more for want of something to do than the need of a smoke. She went on.

'Did you throw the rock through my parent's bedroom window Darren?'

His fingers stopped working and he looked up at her eyes.

'No. I didn't do that Katie. Like I didn't kill your horses either. The only thing I ever did was ask you to stay away from Lyme for a while. I would never harm you or your family. I think you know that.' He remained quite still as he waited for a response.

She let him suffer for a few seconds and tilted her head slightly to one side as she regarded him.

'You know I believe you. What I want to know is why.'

Darren surprised himself with his reply.

'I think you know the answer to that as well.' He was still motionless and watched with satisfaction when she blinked and looked down.

'Yes, I suppose I do.'

131. Not three hundred yards away Heather and Alex walked into the Goat. The first person Heather clapped eyes on – probably because she was looking for him, was Reg Bull. He was sitting with a couple of the locals playing crib. His eyes met Heather's and he looked down immediately, pretending not to be interested in her arrival, to be engrossed in the game. In truth his heart missed a beat.

'Lager Hev?' Alex had led through the door and turned to his companion to ask this question. He just caught her looking at Reg.

'Er... yes. Yes please Alex. Stella.'

'Pint?'

'Please.'

Reg watched the two youngsters sit down and begin to talk earnestly about something that seemed very important to them. Neither would see him looking at them. They were engrossed. Like they were planning something that was more important than the evening ahead. Reg knew without any doubt that it would be about the Pykes. What was that Met fucker doing down here otherwise, aside from trying to get Heather Boyle into bed? And why was Heather so very keen to get at the Pykes? Perhaps, thought Reg, perhaps she just wanted to get a decent job that was going to enhance her CID prospects. Perhaps she thought they should be doing more important things in the Dorset Police than chasing around after stolen chickens. Yes. That was all there was to it. Heather was milking this young man from the Met for information and advice that she could not get from her own supervisors. And if he was getting a shag out of it then best of luck to him. Reg smarted but consoled himself that there was nothing sinister going on. Nothing he wouldn't find out about in due course. So he accepted when one of his cronies offered him another pint of Youngs, got involved in another game of crib and tried not to think about the two young people sitting plotting something on the other side of the room. Halfway through the next pint he stopped kidding himself and got out of his seat and walked over to them.

'Hello my little chickadees.' He slurred.

Heather and Alex looked up. 'Hi Reg,' said Heather. Alex looked down, instantly sensing trouble. He did not like Reg's tone, nor the look on his face.

'What was that all about this morning then? Left me in the lurch a bit didn't you?'

Heather was on her guard now as well.

'What are you talking about Reg?'

'I'm sitting in Stockard like a prat and the next thing I know you bastards've fucked off to Bridport. Nice of you to tell me.'

Heather was looking around, aware and troubled by the fact that the local populace were sharing this debrief.

'Come here and sit down Reg, and keep your voice down,' she implored,

'Come here.' She got up and took him by the arm, guiding him onto a luckily vacant stool at their table. The crib school were looking across the room, Heather glared at them and they looked back down at their cards.

Reg allowed his knees to give way and he crumpled onto the stool. He still held a half finished pint, some of which had deposited a brown stain above his top lip on its journey into his mouth. Heather sat down facing him, trying to get eye contact, but his were glazed and he appeared to be focussed on a point in space between them.

'Christ Reg, I'm so sorry, I'd no idea that you hadn't been told. To tell the absolute truth I forgot all about you....'

'Hah,' exclaimed the old cop, a bitter and somewhat theatrical smile playing on his rubbery, drunken lips. 'Good of you to be so honest with me....'

'No, what I mean is....'

'You've said what you mean Heather, and I thank you for it, you forgot about me....'

Heather raised her voice a little, 'We forgot about the fact that you were there, don't take it so personally and stop feeling fucking sorry for yourself for a change.'

It was Reg's turn to worry about who was listening to this, and he looked around nervously. At once he was ashamed and angry with himself for allowing this to happen. He looked down into his pint glass and waited for the lecture.

'Reg, now listen to me.' Her head was close to his. The pub had returned to its business, although it was lost on no-one that there was a bit of trouble between a couple of the local Bobbies. Tongues would wag, no doubt.

'People are going to talk about this. Pull yourself together. We were redeployed at short notice. We were very annoyed, we had to drop the Stockard job and rush to Bridport just to please some wanker called Jarvis who is up the arses of the local gentry….' At this Reg looked up at her. Not quite liking her disrespectful reference to anything local; who did she think she was? Fucking incomer. Then he looked down again, inwardly laughing at his own parochial servility. She went on, 'you were best off out of it mate, I can tell you. We had to go around a caravan site and nick a dozen chicken pluckers, all called either Ward or Smith. They were laughing at us.' Then Reg started to see the funny side of it for a few seconds, he even smiled a little, this time without the bitterness.

'Yeah, I know all this, and I was glad I missed it, but I still should have been told you were standing down from Stockard Heather, Decker should have told me, why didn't you tell me?' He was serious again.

'Reg, like I said, it was all rush, rush, rush. We didn't mean to leave you out or anything, sat there in Stockard at that time in the morning waiting for action over the airwave radio….' Then she saw him in her mind's eye, sat there in his little car, all tense and ready for action, and then smirked, just a trace, but it was a smirk and he saw it. 'Honest mate, it was a mistake….'

'You think it's funny don't you.' He had seen it.

She recovered, the smirk disappeared, 'No, not at all….'

He was in her face again, spitting bitterness, hatred even.

'Just remember Heather, if you got one ounce of pleasure out of leaving me out, then that pleasure comes from nothing but spite.'

She was taken aback by the intensity of his message, the almost manic look in eyes, suddenly very sober. Alex intervened, sensing that something had to be done pretty quickly about this.

'Oi you two, I haven't come all way from London to listen to stories about carrot cruncher's cock-ups. Youngs Reg?'

'Yes. Why not.' The old cop did not take his eyes from Heather's as he said this. She, of course, held the stare. Spite, eh? Oh, she knew all about that all right.

The landlady observed the minor drama from behind the steam that rose from the glass washer she was busy loading.

132. Bertie Pentreath was sitting in front of a roaring farmhouse fire. He had always liked a big open fire. It was one of the best things about being a farmer. Sally fussed in the kitchen, pretending she had lots to do when all she was doing was trying to expend nervous energy. They had been married twenty seven years and most of that had been spent accommodating each other's diverging interests. Sally just wanted a normal life. She had never wanted a farm and when they had moved east from Cornwall Bertie had had his daughter's love of horses to help persuade Sally that a farm was the only viable way to achieve happiness. But of course it had not worked. Not really. Oh, there had been good times of course. The milk had kept them in a living for a while, and the wool from the sheep, and the rapeseed fields were economically productive for a while. But these threads of relative success were invariably down to favourable political breezes from the EU that could not be controlled or maintained. Whichever crop received a subsidy from Brussels the Pentreaths could normally make a success of, even if they knew the harvest would be wasted or destroyed, they would produce their quota, just to get the subsidy.

As he stared at the burning embers he reflected on this and the falsity of the last ten years. He thought of the future and the silly clay pigeon idea. What the hell was he doing, he asked himself? Was he going mad? And now there was this. The rock through the window and the poisoned horses. Why did Katie seem so unperturbed? He heard his wife go into the kitchen and decided, there and then, that he had had enough.

'Sally.'

She stopped dead still. She could not see him but froze at the tone of his voice. Oh no, please not that.

133. Darren struggled with his pasta and veal escalope. He'd wanted steak and chips and could not believe the waiter's attitude. Who did the little eyetie think he was, looking down his snotty nose at him like that? He mentally noted to pay this place another visit sometime, when he was in different company. On several occasions during the meal Katie wondered if she had done the right thing, bringing this boy in here. But she emboldened herself with the knowledge that it was the correct strategy. If he was going to soften up he would do so quicker on away territory. The last thing Katie wanted was his brothers in tow, he would only show off to them, act the big man.

The wine was working fine, although Darren made it clear that he would want a few pints afterwards to take the taste away, so to speak. She agreed, but first a bit of business.

'Why do you think I know you did not kill my horses?'

Oh, he thought, not this again. They had spent the forty or so minutes talking about anything and everything that Darren was able to talk about, football, films, television, rock music; but now it was back to the real point of the evening.

'Dunno.'

'Why do you think I know that you did not throw that rock through my parent's bedroom window?'

'Dunno.'

'Well think about it Darren, please, try to think about it….'

He became suddenly angry, 'Yeah, alright, alright, I'm thinking about it! I suppose it's because you know… you know I would never harm you or your family… why would I… look, we've been through all this. What do you want me to say? What d'you want me to do?'

'Nothing, just stay by my side while I find out who did these things, that's all.'

Darren liked this. He was her minder; he was to look after her. That, in his book, was a relationship. He felt warm all over. It was like she'd asked him to marry her. He had feared that all she was going to do was buy him a meal and task him with finding the horse killer. That would have been difficult, especially as he knew but could never reveal the identity of the perpetrator. But this, this was a turn up for the books. All he had to do was watch her back. Let her do the leg work, ask the questions, listen for names.

Katie paid the bill and let her new mate take her into the Regis Arms. As she expected Darren's younger brothers were in there. Joe and Wayne looked at their older sibling and then at Katie, and then back and forth again, almost in unison. It was that posh bird Josh had told them about. Darren gave them both a quick glare each – stay away from me – and led Katie to the narrow bar.

'What d'you want?' This came out a bit too gruffly, more so than he would have liked. It was as if he wanted to make up for being uncomfortable in the bistro. He was in charge now.

'Oh, er, red wine please.' She was all of a sudden timid, under his control.

'Large red wine, pint of Stella,' ordered Darren Pyke.

134. Aware that the atmosphere in the Goat had changed somewhat since the locals had been treated to this rare display from three of Lyme's finest, Reg left. As he lurched out of the door he turned to Heather and Alex and slurred what he hoped was a loaded farewell.

'Be seeing you two very soon.' What he quite meant by that neither Heather nor Alex were sure. Nor was Reg really, only that he knew that it meant something. Something was going to happen, he didn't know what but he knew it, all the same.

'Sorry about that.' Heather apologised to Alex but would have done so to the whole pub if she could have. There were only about thirty people in there at the time – a full house for the Goat – and they all knew who she was, who Reg was and what Alex must be. She found it stifling. It took a good ten minutes for people to begin talking normally again and even then the couple were the subject of lingering glances. They finished their drinks as slowly as they could bear, and then left to make their way down to the Seagull pubs where they could be relatively anonymous.

Katie Pentreath was also leaving the pub, but she was alone. She had decided that enough was enough for one evening and had excused herself. Darren had offered to accompany her home, but he hadn't really meant it. By that time a number of the local pond life had entered the Pilot and he was keen to keep up appearances. They had all seen him with his new posh bird and that was enough. He could not be seen to be under the thumb. He walked as far as the door with her and all eyes were on them. Was he going to get a kiss? Yes, as she pulled open the door she turned and pecked him on the cheek. Their first public kiss. He wanted more and followed her out onto the street.

'How you getting home?'

'I'm going to get a cab Darren, you go back inside with your mates, go on.' She was being friendly, accommodating. She wanted to get away. As she turned his hand went to her shoulder, he leant forward to try to steal another kiss, but she laughed and pulled away.

'See you Darren, I'll give you a call. Try and have some news for me.' The last sentence came out with an edge that she had not intended. The emphasis was on the try. He just stood there and said, 'I'll try.' His tone was earnest, as if he was responding to some sort of contractual requirement that he desperately wanted to fulfil. He watched her walk quickly up the hill, body inclined forward, hips waving him goodbye, towards the 24 hour cab office. Darren joined his drinking mates to enjoy their admiration. But he didn't enjoy it for long. Within ten minutes he was gone from the pub. Something she had said had bobbed to the surface of his addled mind like a corpse to the top of a lake, suddenly buoyed by its own decomposition.

135. Simon Murdoch had telephoned Katie's home number earlier that evening just to find out how she was. The start of a new term was approaching and he was keen to reaffirm their relationship. Although bright he was a fairly simple minded guy, was our Simon. Middle class and privately educated he was bored with his veterinary studies and would have preferred a life in the city making loads of money. But he was keen to impress his father by qualifying as a professional so he soldiered on. One more year to go and then he would take a well-earned year out and would have a look round to see what was on offer. At the present getting his degree and having Katie were important to him. She was good in bed and was a good friend. He was choked when her mother told him about the horses. It was the first he had heard of it and jumped immediately into his car and headed for the West Country.

By the time he got to Upper Brooklands Farm two hours later Katie was already in Exeter hospital. She had managed to call the ambulance herself, not wanting to disturb her parents. She was not too badly hurt and did not fear for her survival. Nothing was broken and she tasted no blood. She was going to live but needed treatment, she guessed, for concussion. She had got out of the cab at the gate of the horse's paddock. There had been a bright moon and, sentimentalised by the wine, she wanted to visit the grave. The attack had been from behind and she had gone face down in the mud made by a cloudburst that day.

The A & E staff nurse had called the police as what she had before her was a strange assault on a girl who would not normally be the kind to get into fights. The patient had been drinking, but was not drunk. She was sobbing, but was not hysterical, she was worried, but was not frightened, she was shaken, but remarkably stoic and maintaining that she had no idea who her assailant was. The staff nurse did not believe her and so called Exeter police control room. Within minutes a Devon and Cornwall cop was there, notebook out, taking details. Katie gave her university campus address in Brighton and asked to be left alone. The officer protested for a short while, went through the motions, before shrugging and reporting back that the victim of an apparent assault in the neighbouring force area of Dorset did not want to make any allegations against anyone. He had done his job and so had the staff nurse. The statistical crime report would be electronically transferred to Dorset that night, for the attention of Lyme Regis CID the following morning.

She discharged herself from hospital at about 2.30am. She did not call her parents and was satisfied that they would not know where she was. The ambulance had thankfully arrived at the paddock gate silently, albeit with its blue light flashing. She had kept her mobile switched on throughout her journey to hospital and during her stay, against the regulations about it interfering with equipment. There had been no calls. Her parents had slept through. She got a minicab from the A&E back to Upper Brooklands; she had to get the driver to stop at a cash point before leaving Exeter so that she could afford the fare. Then she crept into the house and slid into her bed, unaware that Simon Murdoch lay awake in the guest room, listening to her every sound. She had not spotted his car in the yard behind one of the tractors.

Her back and neck ached like hell where she had been hit from behind. It had not been a weapon but her assailant had been very strong. At first she had thought she was about to be raped as the attacker held her face down in the mud with one hand whilst with the other felt around the tops of her thighs, crotch and buttocks. But then it was obvious that it was the contents of her jeans pockets that were of interest. Her wallet came out, her keys, her phone, her handkerchief, loose change, tobacco; all these were left in the mud. The only item to be stolen was the Zippo lighter with the letters DP scratched on it. Before leaving her the thief gave her a kick to the belly and rammed her face right down into the ground to ensure her eyes were full of mud and her dead horse's shit.

She had been cleaned up on arrival at hospital, and had tried to finish the job before leaving, but she still stank in her bed. She began to sob again as she lay there, but finally drifted off to a troubled sleep.

136. Heather got a call on the following morning on her mobile from Reg Bull. It was a Saturday and her weekend off. It was his as well and she was to later wonder why he had gone into work. He told her about the crime report. She was up and on her way to Lyme before Alex had awoken. She knew this because, for the first time ever, she had allowed him to sleep with her. That had been as far as it had gone through. No sex, no groping (not for the want of his trying) but she had allowed him to be there and had not found it too abhorrent.

When she got to the CID office she looked at the crime recording system entry. The attack had taken place just about midnight. The location was exactly the same as that of the horse killing. What the fuck was going on here, she thought, what sort of fucking God forsaken place was this?!

The case had not been allocated to an investigator yet so she put herself down for the job, she would answer questions later. It was 9am and she picked up the phone and dialled a mobile number.

Katie answered groggily.

'Katie, I'm so sorry, it's Heather Boyle....'

'Get over here now.'

'Pardon?'

'You heard. Get on your way over here Heather.'

'I'll be twenty minutes Katie.' And she put down the phone. As she picked up her clipboard and made for the door she noticed that Reg had been standing by the window watching her. She had not heard him come in. He was silhouetted but she was sure that she saw the trace of a smile.

She had crossed the A35 and was on the Crewkerne road when her phone went. She pulled over. It was Katie.

'Don't make a fuss, just come to the door and I will be waiting for you. My mum and dad don't know about this yet. We'll talk in my room.' There was a faint tone to her voice that puzzled Heather, not unpleasantly.

Having driven into the farmyard she walked up to the door, clipboard in hand, dressed in full uniform. The door opened before she could knock and Katie Pentreath showed her upstairs. Once in the bedroom Heather noticed the assault victim's hair was damp and freshly washed. She wore a long T shirt and nothing else. She bade heather sit down, but not before she had offered to take the police officer's tunic, it was a hot morning. When they were both seated she began.

'I'm not going to mess you about. I was attacked by someone who wishes to disassociate me from Darren Pyke. I had been with Darren in a pub in full view of everyone not twenty minutes before I was attacked. I left the pub – the Regis Arms in Lyme, at about 10pm. There was still plenty of light, and the moon was bright. I got a cab and had it drop me by the paddock. I was a bit drunk I suppose and I wanted to see Gabby and Rosie's grave. They were my….'

'Yes, I know.' Heather was business-like, making it clear by her tone that she did not want any waterworks. Katie got the message.

'Right. Anyway, I had barely got across the field when bang, he got me from behind. It was a cross between a rabbit punch and a hard push to the back. He was very strong and did not say a word. I just froze, I….'

Then it all came out. Up until that point she had tried to look upon the whole thing as if it were happening to someone else. The murder of her horses, the rock through the window, the assaults in the pub, the strange relationship with Darren. This was all happening to a lonely girl who lived with her parents in an isolated farm in the middle of Dorset, not a bright veterinary undergraduate who would shortly be returning to the city and to her studies and sophisticated friends. It was like she was acting out a play that would only last a few months and that relieved the boredom of the long tedious summer. But just then she realised that she was that lonely girl; she was that vulnerable only child of the failing marriage of a pair of miserable dreamers. That it was happening to her and that she was actually in great danger. So she started to shake. She shook and sobbed and wretched. She was sitting on the bed and the officer moved from her chair to sit beside her. Her first instinct was to recoil, but she relaxed and let the officer put her arm around her shoulders.

'I'm scared Heather, I'm so fucking scared,' she whispered, the tears were streaming down her face.

'He held me down with one hand and felt me with the other. I thought he was going to rape me but he just took my lighter – Darren's lighter. That's how I know it's something to do with Darren. Darren was the only one in the pub I told where I was going. None of his brothers or horrible mates knew where I was headed. I don't know who this was. It certainly wasn't Darren. Darren would not do what he did, not...' there was a pause as she choked on her tears, not able to describe something. 'Not what Katie. What did he do?'

'Oh, he was after the lighter, but he made the most of it. He had a good feel whilst he was at it.'

'Where did he feel? Did he touch you indecently?'

Despite her distress Katie was able to reason that this was an unnecessary question. But she sobbed a 'Yes' anyway.

Heather decided to strike whilst the iron was hot. An hour later she had a full statement covering the scouser incident, the killing of the horses, and this latest incident which was clearly by Darren Pyke or one of his associates to sever evidential contact between him and Katie Pentreath. The testimony was not detailed and a further statement would have to be taken in due course to add feature, but it was enough to be going on with and when Katie had added her signature to the bottom of each handwritten page, Heather felt secure in the knowledge that she had her witness thoroughly on side.

137. Decker and Townsend sat opposite each other at a small table in the Bridport police station canteen. They listened to two uniformed colleagues at another table talking excitedly about how they were going to spend that month's overtime payments, enhanced considerably by the labour intensive chicken rustling operation in which they were currently involved.

'Fucking wankers,' muttered Decker, 'They'll get the dough and then go back to nicking motorists and drunks. It's us that then have to fight crime in the county with fuck all resources.'

'Yeah, how many more interviews have we got to do today?' Townsend was seriously pissed off. He knew that this would never even come to anything. The seasonal workers would be either charged with the thefts or bailed to return to the station at a later date. The ones that were charged would go to a specially convened court the next day, plead not guilty and be remanded on bail. The alleged offences were not serious enough to warrant their being remanded in custody. So they would all end up on bail and then they would all abscond. End of story. They would stay away for a couple of years and might even come back another time. They all had the same or similar names and they all looked remarkably alike. They could all be identified by way of fingerprints or DNA, for sure, but who would be bothered to deploy such methods to chase chicken thieves, even if they were exotic chickens. No, the object of the current exercise was purely and simply to improve the detection statistics. Everyone knew that.

'About six, maybe seven. Depends if Witchelow's client stumps up any more information.'

The local briefs were milking it too. John Witchelow had managed to get himself the most talkative detainee and was hoping that his client would get charged so that the job would run on. He would see if he could get him to grass up his mates and get protective custody so that he would be sure not to leg it and so be sure to go to court. Witchelow would persuade him to elect trial by judge and jury and then public funding would flow nicely, thank you very much.

'And all because that prat Jarvis is bridge-buddy with that fucking bitch Lavelle. What a shit-hole county this is. Like the middle ages.'

Decker was letting his bitterness flow. Perhaps a bit too much he thought, so he stemmed it. He was talking to an officer junior to himself and reminded himself to be more professional.

'Not to worry, it'll all be forgotten tomorrow Stuart, and we'll get onto more serious stuff.'

Decker drained his tea and stretched. It was just after ten in the morning and they had not finished until ten the previous evening. Townsend had gone for a drink after that and was bit jaded. But Decker had missed out on the pub and was fresh as a daisy. As usual.

138. Carmella froze as she felt the tree house shake. She slipped back into her sleeping bag and pretended to be asleep. Darren hauled himself onto the wooden flooring and, in one motion, got hold of his half-sister's green hair and pulled her out of the bag. She did not scream. Screaming was forbidden in the tree house. Her face, although contorted with pain, bore at once a cheeky smirk.

'Whassa matter Tarzan, your posh bitch not givin' you nuthin?'

With that he punched her in the mouth. Her feet were still tangled in the sleeping bag and she went down fast. In a trice she was up, blooding trickling off of her chin, going for the counter strike. She hit him square on the nose, at the same time her knee came up hard into his groin, her free hand around his neck. He yelped and hit her again, this time on the side of her head. A clump of hair had come out and they had a hold of each other, each trying to hurt the other badly. They went down in a heap and both knew that this was going to end in only one way.

139. The Chief Constable's Suite at HQ was buzzing with sycophants.

Jarvis was in his element and had with him a uniformed sergeant carrying a laptop. Amazingly he had managed to prepare a PowerPoint presentation of the previous day's operation, complete with detainees' photographs, overtime breakdowns, clear-up figures, interrogation outcomes and proposals for sharing information with neighbouring forces and even beyond. Upon being invited to do so, Jarvis delivered a very well prepared performance. Both he and the uniformed sergeant looked tired. They had undoubtedly been up most of the night putting this together.

Chief Constable Joanne Bache could not believe it. But then again she could. This lot would stop at nothing to get the next rank. But then nor had she.

She suffered the meeting and thanked Jarvis and the other contributors. She announced that she was very pleased with the way that things had turned out and that she had no doubt that the positive statistics generated by the investigation would, in turn, generate enhanced financial support from the public fund, which, in turn, would enable the Force to deliver a better service to the population of the county without having to over-stretch existing resources. She thanked those present and invited them to leave, save for Superintendent Jarvis and Mr. Sutherland, her legal advisor. Eight senior officers filed out, including DCI Sherrell who seemed a little put out that he had not been invited to stay. He was after all, HQ crime liaison officer. He would later remember thinking that this second meeting was not just about the chicken job, if at all.

He was right. Within a few minutes Jarvis and his uniformed sergeant were also dismissed. Their being asked to stay behind had been merely a decoy to make it look like the Chief was still occupied by a legal problem arising from the chicken job. In fact the second meeting had nothing to do with that, not directly anyway. Sure, she passed the time for a few minutes with both the Force Solicitor Sutherland present with Jarvis and his uniformed skipper, but the conversation was inconsequential and merely touched on the expected allegations that the pluckers had been targeted because they were travellers, that the warrants had been unlawfully applied for, that the paperwork had not all been completed properly and so on. Jarvis assured the Chief that everything was in order and he and his sergeant left with the laptop.

That left Mr. Craig Sutherland LLB. His and the Chief's eyes followed Jarvis and the Sergeant out of the room and both pairs lingered on the door for a few seconds after it was closed. Then they turned to face each other. The Chief began predictably with a flash of a brilliant white smile and beautiful green eyes. Sutherland adored her, he would do anything to please her and she knew it.

'Well Craig, here we are again. In the middle of another summer season with upsides and downsides.' She stopped and regarded him with open amusement. He was not the sort of man she found attractive. He was skinny and had a pinched look about him, as if always thinking how he could get his own back, get even. A churlish little man who relished his position of power as an addition to his persona, rather than a tool to get his job done. His job? To advise the Chief on matters legal, although if the truth were known she probably knew more about the relevant law than he did; she certainly had the instinct as to when and how to apply it. But the rules said that she had to have an in-house solicitor to give advice, that way the Force was insured against her own possible mistakes or misfeasance.

'Er, yes Chief, here we are again.' She had long since given up trying to get him to call her Joanne. She suspected that he might suffer from some sort of innate gender reassignment discrimination thing, or whatever the libbies would call it. She found the thought amusing.

'Well, we have a problem – you got my email?'

'Yes Chief.'

'So, what are we going to do about her?'

'God knows Chief, she's here now, but it's not surprising that the recruitment lot didn't pick it up.'

'Oh, I'm sure they did, I have no fucking doubt whatsoever that they knew about this before they waved her in. They'll be laughing their tits off now. You know it.'

Sutherland should have been used to the Chief's occasional profanity by now. She did not swear all the time but, when the occasion demanded it, did so with an obscenity that bordered on the erotic.

'Oh, I don't know, it wasn't on her record, it only came to light during the current investigation of one of her former colleagues, Caroline Sherry.'

The Chief looked thoughtful. 'Remind me why Sherry is being investigated.' Sutherland was sure that this did not need to be asked. Joanne Bache was renowned for her photographic memory and would have read the strictly confidential report on the relationship between Heather Boyle and Caroline Sherry in detail and in about four minutes flat and would have remembered every word.

'She was on attachment to a technical surveillance unit and some kit went missing.' At that point Sutherland referred to a file he had in front of him, 'Tracking equipment.' The report says that this sort of kit would not normally go missing by accident as it could only be installed with RIPA authority and the inventory control was consequently quite tight. It was just a case of one day it was there and the next it wasn't. When she got pulled she made out she was being targeted because of her unfortunate history with our recruit. It was nothing of the kind; she was fingered by one of her colleagues.'

140. And two hundred and fifty miles away Caroline Sherry combed her short black hair. She regarded herself in the mirror and did not particularly like what she saw, but then that was the deal in Andersonstown where she came from. West Belfast was somewhere where no-one really liked themselves – they were all a product of something big and nasty. Coming to live and work in London had solved

little; possibly saved her life – if that was a solution. But she had not been happy ever in her life. Did not know how to be. Whenever she encountered that strange feeling that she suspected might be called happiness she would immediately experience an overwhelming sense of guilt. Happy? How dare she. She had not seen her father in three years, his choice after he had found out about how she lived her life. About what she had chosen to be. Who did she think she was? Eschewing the love of her family and loyalty of her clan to go to London to behave like she did. And of course there had been Heather. No, what did she mean, 'Had been'. Heather was still very much part of her life. Very much indeed. Dorset her arse. The moon would not be far enough away my dear. It's not over yet Heather, she assured herself. We're still full on.

Caroline had got a friend of hers to make the phone call. She had a London accent and was totally trustworthy. The call was to the effect that a certain PC Caroline Sherry had stolen surveillance equipment from her employers the Metropolitan Police. Nothing more. Nothing less. The information however just happened to coincide with the tracking device going missing from the South West London Surveillance Team office.

The idea was securely based on Caroline's well-founded belief that Alex Miller had nicked the gear, aided and abetted by Peter Gibbons. It hadn't taken long for Caroline to work this out. There was the usual furore when the kit went missing; a little enquiry by senior officers, bored with it before they started, then it all fizzled out. The stuff was near to the end of its shelf-life anyway, so if it fell into the wrong hands it would soon be superseded by the next generation of intrusive technology. Alex had always been a bit dodgy and when he and Gibbons got together things happened. Now, add this to the fact that Caroline had learned through the grapevine – 'rumour control' they called it in the police – that Alex was visiting Heather in Dorset and was trying to give her a leg up in return for a chance at getting his over and a picture emerged. Caroline knew about the van and the fact that the Met was now following the trail to the West Country. She had no doubt that the Dorset Constabulary would not have the technical resources available to do the job; it was bad enough getting hardware to do anything in the Met. So that gave young Alex a starting point, a tasty morsel with which to lure his impossible target, the subject of his unrequited love. For fuck's sake, didn't he know? Getting someone to grass her up for the theft was, in her own estimation, a necessary subtlety. She was a beat officer with no interest in or knowledge of technical surveillance. They could investigate her all they liked but would not find anything and would surely conclude that the information was a smokescreen, thrown up out of spite; their former relationship and acrimonious split had been an open secret. Another interesting – and even better – outcome would be that they would form the suspicion that she had in fact stolen the kit for Heather, and that therefore Heather was handling, and using, the nicked tracker. That would certainly stir things up a bit. All grist to the mill.

She stopped combing and put her hand to the nape of her neck. The scar was still numb and raised. They had told her that it would take some time for the nerves to knit together and for the feeling to come back.

141. Heather got back to Lyme police station just as Decker and Townsend were about to restart their work on the bird thieves. 'How's it going?' she asked as she saw them in the corridor next to the secure area.

'Why should you care?' answered Decker. 'Anyway, what're you doing? It's supposed to be your day off.'

'Kate Pentreath got attacked last night. It's got something to do with Darren Pyke, if it wasn't him it was his brothers or his mates, no doubt about it.'

'You been to see her?'

'Yeah, got a statement, she wants to know and she'll give evidence on the scouse assaults as well.'

Townsend was impressed. 'Well now, you lucky cow, we're doing all this shit work and you stumble on that, how did you get to know about it so soon?'

'I got my snouts Stuart.'

Decker was able to put a positive spin on things. 'Well, maybe this chicken shit job was all for the best – we've actually got something to nick Pyke for now, as opposed to just spinning his hovel with a warrant on a wing and a prayer.'

'That's what I was thinking sarge, but couldn't we still use the warrant?'

Crawling cow, though Townsend.

'Yeah, course, we'll hit it Monday morning….'

Heather was afraid that this might be the response.

'Monday? Would tomorrow not be better sarge? He'll assume Katie's made a statement, he'll be cleaning out the house already I would have thought…?'

'Well then even tomorrow will be too late, won't it. That girl never made a statement last time so he'll have no reason to think she's going to give one now.'

Heather had to admit he was right. There was never a best time to do these jobs; then again there was never a bad time. These scumbags were always up to something and if you hit their homes at 5 in the morning you'd never know what you'd find. This was an even better situation: if they drew a blank on the actual search they still had Darren Pyke and his brother to arrest for questioning in connection with an indecent assault on Katie Pentreath. Later that morning Heather told Reg and invited him along. He agreed to be there and said he would do as he did before and be in his car nearby the Pyke address at 5am with an airwave on board. That way he could claim the overtime even if he did not have to do anything. Whilst these preparations were taking place Katie Pentreath sat at home in her room and did a lot of crying. She had managed to conceal the attack from her parents; there was no visible bruising and she had managed to explain away Heather's visit on the police having another go at getting more information from her on the attack on the Liverpudlians;

just a follow up visit, she had said.

But Katie was alone and feeling it. The fact that Simon Murdoch was there and was fussing around like an old hen did not help in the least. More, it actually reminded her how detached she had become from her normal, other life. She could barely talk to him and he spent more time with her mother. Her father had gone to the paddock to look for clues, to do anything that would be seen to be of help. Bertie felt useless. He knew he should not contact the police because that would be seen as interfering, he knew he could not try to comfort his daughter because that would be seen as silly and patronising, so he decided to keep out of the way and conduct his own investigation. She rolled a cigarette and fumbled for the lighter.

142. The Chief was thoughtful but knew she was doing the right thing. This had to be nipped in the bud. If this girl was trouble she still had eight months to get rid of her, which was what was left of her 12 month probation period. Sutherland advised that if she was going to invoke that procedure she ought to do it sooner rather than later. She did not have evidence to start misconduct proceedings, only a strong indication that Heather Boyle was unlikely to be a fit and proper Constable in the Dorset Police. The fact that a former colleague in the Metropolitan Police had named her as a suspect for assault and handling stolen surveillance equipment was almost enough. The Chief decided to take some additional advice from a rather unlikely source.

'Okay Craig, thanks for your help. I fully understand my obligations under Regulation 13, I've got to give her a chance to improve and have her supervisors set up a personal development plan, is that it?'

'Yes Chief, if you don't then she could appeal and we'd end up with egg on our faces.'

Well, I would, thought Joanne Bache.

143. Heather was in a rather testy conversation with her duty inspector,

an ineffectual little man called Askew, about the re-rostering of her duties.

'But sir, I was recalled to duty on Saturday morning by Reg Bull, he said you knew about it.' She did not mean to drop Reg in it but could not understand why he would have lied to her. Katie Pentreath had been assaulted and there was no CID to deal with it because they were all out chasing chicken thieves.

The inspector was relentlessly boring. 'You must seek supervisory authority before you work on a rostered day off.' As he said this he made a note in his pocket book and walked away. Katie thought this odd, why had he made that note? Was he collating evidence against her like this? What was going on? Anyway, she did not have time to think about it. Maxine and Suzy had been sending her emails from Crewkerne, there were a lot of domestic violence matters to sort out and she needed to get up there. So she did just that. Left Lyme to its own devises and headed north through the Triangle. It went without saying that she would call in on Katie on the way.

'Have you got him in yet? I'm scared to go out of the fucking house.' Katie hissed this at Heather, as they stood in the hallway; she was nervous of her mother hearing her from the kitchen.

'No, not yet.'

'When then?'

'Soon, I can't actually tell you, it's confidential.'

'How soon? Look I know I've been a silly cow getting involved with that piece of shit, but the fact is I need protection Heather. My family need protection. I'll go to court, don't you worry about that. I'll make a stand. I've had enough.'

Katie was trembling and Heather could not resist putting her arms around her. They went up onto her shoulders and round the farmer's daughter's neck. As Heather pulled her towards her Katie resisted at first and then allowed herself to be pulled into the embrace. It was very close. Ridiculously close. Katie's arms remained by her sides for a few seconds before coming up to hold the police officer loosely around the waist.

'Don't worry. It'll be very soon,' whispered Heather into Katie's ear. Katie was all of a sudden concerned about what the cop was actually talking about, so unprofessional this behaviour seemed. She pulled away and regarded Heather with that quizzical tilt of the head.

'Who killed my horses?' The question was flat and business-like and as soon as she had asked it, she turned and walked towards the door to open it.

'How do I know? I haven't asked anyone yet.' Heather stood there feeling rather silly; one second she had had a lovely girl in her arms, the next she was being shown the door. She collected herself and walked out.

'I'll ring you tomorrow,' said the police officer.

'Do.' said the farmer's daughter.

144. When she got to Crewkern about 30 minutes later she found both Maxine and Suzy stressed to the eyeballs. They had both been required to stay on for extra hours during the previous week because of the pressure of work and this had a domestic impact on each of them. They both tried to be pleasant to Heather, but could not really conceal their shared frustrations.

'The thing is,' said Suzy, getting straight to the point as usual, 'you've got a career in the police service, we have got jobs to do.'

Maxine jumped in, trying to take the edge off of this rather aggressive approach, 'It's not that we're jealous or anything, it was our choice to get married and have babies and all that, but we need our time at home, that's the whole point of being part-time, we don't need to be getting in a state about what's going on here, that's why we thought you'd been sent in to help us...' Then Suzy chimed in again, 'Yeah, but you keep getting caught up doing stuff for the CID in Lyme. We don't understand Heather?'

Heather surveyed the scene quickly. Both women looked exhausted. They sat in the cramped little office and were clearly up to their necks in work. Heather had checked the domestic violence figures from a terminal in Lyme before she had left that morning and they were high. Too high for two part-timers to cope with. What was it with this place, eighteen assaults by husbands on their wives in two weeks? And the CPS always wanted to prosecute. It seemed to be getting worse as the summer drew on. In London the wife beating season was generally the winter or when bad weather prevailed; families were forced indoors together. But here there was some other factor at work. The only pattern that Heather could discern was that adultery was more rampant in the good weather and people always got to find out. The whole Triangle was occupied it seemed by one big extended family, with everybody but everybody knowing each other's business. If a bloke went over the side, his wife would know about it before he got home that night, if indeed he did get home before daybreak. It was like nothing else was important to them, sex was God.

Heather remembered reading once that in rural areas working class people were often depressed because of their poverty and their lack of status and education, this meant that sex and booze were all they had to look forward to. And once adultery became established it was for everyone to get involved. The only real way for a wife to get her own back was to do it herself and take the kicking then do it again. The husband would continue as if it was his right, and so it went on. The odd thing that occurred to Heather was that the men rarely fought with each other, they just shagged each other's wives and beat up their own when they found out about it.

Anyway, the girls needed help and had obviously been disappointed by Heather's prolonged absence. She set about mending her damaged reputation and spent the rest of the day, and the following one, at

Crewkerne taking statements from the bruised wives of farm workers.

Half way through the second day she got a call from Decker.

'Heather, we need to hit Stockard, where's that warrant?' She had it in her clipboard, not wanting it to be executed in her absence.

'I've got it with me sarge, I'm in Crewkerne at the DVU.'

'Yes, I know where you are. When are you coming back?'

'Tomorrow, I'll be back in Lyme tomorrow, I'm on a late shift.'

Decker paused, he did not like the way she seemed to be taking charge of the situation. 'Right, when you finish tonight come back here and bring that warrant with you. If I'm not here leave it in my middle tray. We'll execute it tomorrow morning whether you're here or not.' Then he rang off.

Heather could not leave Crewkerne as soon as she would have liked that day. She soldiered on with phone calls to victims and witnesses, a visit to a newly opened women's refuge and giving some urgent attention to numerous requests from the Crown prosecution Service for additional material for use in court. Frequently domestic violence case did not get as far as court because spouses cannot be compelled to give evidence against each other. The preferred route is protection from harassment notice which is served on the assailant and prevents him, or her, from going near the estranged partner. As soon as such a notice is transgressed then the offender can be taken straight to the magistrates' court and sent to prison for anything up to six months without the need of a trial. This had happened a couple of times already, that same year before Heather's arrival in the county and the two individuals concerned were due to be released at around the same time. One was a man who had made a hobby out of inflicting invisible damage to his wife of twenty years, the other a woman who had become besotted with her now adult son and would not stop paying him nocturnal visits and causing criminal damage to his car and the exterior of his house. The worry was what happened when they got out of jail. Heather had considered applying for anti-social behaviour orders against them with conditions attached to keep them away from the addresses concerned, but she was told that the local authority for some reason would not do this to people who have just got out of jail. So it was one headache after the next. She slumped back in her chair in the chaotic little office and did a quick survey of the situation. She had certainly never been busier in her whole life; she found the supervision in the Dorset police, piecemeal and fragmented. She was working for Crewkerne DVU, Lyme Regis D Shift and at the same time she was on what seemed permanent attachment to the CID. She came to the conclusion that she was either both highly valued and sought after, or she was having the fucking piss ripped out of her. Of course, she suspected the latter.

She got through the day and then telephoned her Lyme shift inspector to request that she be allowed not to have to work in uniform the following afternoon as she was assisting the CID with a search the next morning and for her to have to work through afterwards would mean a double stretch of over 16 hours - her request was denied. She slumped back in her chair again. It was Sunday evening and she needed a drink. She called Alex who had been staying at her house in Dorchester, thoroughly ignored by his hostess. Heather's mother had taken off with her partner for the weekend and her brother was away on a cricketing tournament in Yorkshire, organised by his school. Alex, having the house to himself, kept busy by playing with the tracking equipment. He would have rather been playing with Heather's equipment, but he had to make do with a transmitter and his battered laptop.

The equipment was a T48 tracker and was GPS orientated, which means it operated by reporting its location in real time with reference to 24 satellites that orbit the earth. About the size of a packet of ten cigarettes, the T48 had to be located in or on a vehicle in such way as to afford it direct line of site with the satellites unobstructed by thick metal. So it was not just a simple matter of reaching under the target vehicle and allowing a strong magnet to do the work. The vehicle had to be broken into and the device had to be installed covertly somewhere under the dashboard. This made it an unpopular piece of kit which was being phased from use by the police and security services. But once installed it was deadly accurate and could be accessed by way of mobile phone or internet connection. Alex had bought an untraceable SIM card and had put this inside, thereby severing ints connection to its previous owner, the Metropolitan Police. He now had Google Maps up on his laptop which was synced to the tracker and was supplying the exact location of the T48 by telling him that it was poisoned at 41 Mason Avenue, Dorchester, UK, DT3 4AD, which was the address of the house in which he presently sat. That was the easy bit. Now to get the tracker into that van. How was he going to do that? Alex asked himself this question several times over, just before Heather came in through the door. When he looked up from the sofa at her something told him that she would have the solution to that problem.

145. By ten o'clock that evening Katie had had more than enough red wine. She was sat in the Seagull Inn with none other than Mr. Simon Murdoch. Why she had taken him there she was not really sure. He suspected that she was testing him, testing his courage. She had told him more or less the full story about Darren Pyke, about the fight with the Liverpudlians, the rock through the window of the farmhouse and the fact that her horses would still be alive if she had never met the piece of shit. She told Simon how she felt that Darren had become emotional about her; how he may react if he saw her with him and that he was also a very violent man. All the time she watched Simon for some sort of reaction, a sign of fear perhaps. But Simon Murdoch gave no such thing. In fact his lip curled into a slight but perceptible sneer as he listened to this tale of parochial imbecility. Simon had insisted that they went to the Seagull; she, nor he, was going to be intimidated by this low life.

'So, I suppose he'll beat me up, will he? You're young Darren.'

'Oh, I don't really know what he would do if he saw you with me. He's very tough though. Can we go in a minute please?'

'No, I'll take him on if it happens. He doesn't frighten me one bit.'

This risk assessment by Simon frightened Katie. He was going to meet this bloody nonsense head on and her estimation of whom she had always regarded as a middle class buffoon had changed dramatically. His valour immediately threw the whole affair into very sharp relief. Why had no-one got hold of the Pykes, roughed them up, had them arrested? Why had nobody written to the police chief, or the county council, or the local newspaper? Why had no one taken out proceedings against them and their team of scruffy chavs from Stockard? An ASBO perhaps, an exclusion order. But no one ever tried to do anything. It was all a lot of pussy-footing about. This sort of thing did not happen in west Dorset, and if it did there would not be a fuss because fusses cost too much money and gave the place a bad name. So, prevarication was really just a way of life in these parts. That way everything seemed to be okay, there was always a sense that things were being done about problems but all was really being achieved was that the symptoms were disguised, given a gloss. The real badness was there though, just below the surface, writhing away like a mass of maggots. There was no community, although everything was called that; community bowls match, community anti-vandalism initiative, community jazz week, community beach clean, community neighbourhood watch, community this, community that, community the other. But there really was no such thing. Just a population of competing interests held together by a common state of denial.

Simon stood up and walked over to the bar with the empties. He was taking control of the situation. As he stood with his back to Katie she noticed for the first time that he had a broad back and a thick neck. Simon was a heavily fixtured rugby player and had confidence in his own physical ability. Katie yearned for the new term to start, away from this horrible place and back to a life in which at least people knew where each other stood. Intelligent people who were unashamed of their ambitions and prejudices, who saw the world as what it was and were prepared to take it on.

146. Simon was still at the bar when Darren Pyke walked into the pub. He took in Katie and Simon in one glance and knew that this was it. He

was sick of not being himself, pretending to be someone who had suddenly found a chance in life. Now here was the naked truth. Simon Murdoch turned round with the drinks in his hand and saw Darren standing at the door and Katie looking from one to the other with wide eyes and open mouth. Simon saw immediately that he was about 2 stone heavier than his adversary and a lot stronger and fitter.

He also knew immediately that he had no chance whatsoever. He had just time to drop the drinks onto the floor and raise his arms in self-defence before Darren's asp broke his left arm. Katie screamed and the pub just froze. Simon went down on his knees. Darren took a step back and used the rugby player's head as a football. Just one kick, a volley, laces first, through the ball like he'd always been taught. Simon went back and was unconscious before the back of his head hit the bar. Darren turned to face Katie Pentreath, her scream exhausted and replaced by terror. The look Darren Pyke gave her was simply murderous. And then he was gone. Katie Pentreath wanted to go over to her injured companion but her vanity prevented. She was wearing light blue jeans and she had urinated. So she just sat there and sobbed, loudly and uncontrollably. A couple of pub customers were attending Simon and were ignoring her, not even aware that she was with him. The barmaid called the ambulance. Upstairs Colleen Bradstock had been watching on screen. She had pressed the alarm and Dorset's finest would be there sometime. Useless bastards, she thought, this should never have happened.

Darren instinctively took the beach route, just like the last time he'd used his asp. He got a cab up into the Triangle, got out at a cottage belonging to someone he did not even know, and walked half a mile to the Everett's.

147. The next morning saw Heather at the Seagull Inn trying in vain to procure witnesses. Decker was driving around the country lanes looking for Katie. She had left the farmhouse to ostensibly get some tobacco. That had been an hour previously and Decker was worried. He had dispatched a couple of big lads from the Bridport crime squad to

Stockard to nick Darren Pyke, along with anyone who tried to stop them, but he was not at home so they were just parked up there on the off chance he would return. There were not enough troops to search the area or to visit any of the likely Pyke haunts. Decker was also worried about something else; this whole business had got out of control because Darren Pyke was not already in custody awaiting trial for the first Seagull Inn assault and he could see the blame coming his way if he did not start boxing clever.

Katie was sitting on top of the ridge crying her eyes out. What the hell was happening to her? Her horses were dead, her studies neglected, her parents cracking up. She had been attacked, threatened and harassed. And now Simon Murdoch, her boyfriend, had been badly injured by this man called Darren Pyke who was quite evidently obsessed with her.

She rocked back and forth trying to console herself that everything would be back to normal; soon she would be back at university, would finish her studies and would then get a pair of horses during the Christmas break. She would be away from Pyke and all this madness would be dispatched to the past. But she could not kid herself. She missed Gabby and Rosie dreadfully and could not understand how anyone could have murdered them. Darren would not have done it. Surely not. But who then? Someone who was jealous of her, a business foe of her father? But he didn't have any, and who could be jealous of her? No one in the area knew her well enough.

148. Darren shivered in the tree house, even though Carmella hugged him tight inside the sleeping bag. He shivered with fear. That had torn it. No doubt whatsoever. He would be banged up within hours, he knew it. Katie would not keep her distance from the police this time. He was going to have to disappear or he would be going away for a good few years. Unprovoked attack with a lethal weapon. GBH with intent. Carries maximum of life imprisonment, and he would be sure to draw five to seven, with his form. Carmella, snuggled up and hugged him tighter from behind, reading his mind.

'You need transport, food, supplies, clothes and money. Stay here today and let the heat die down a bit, they'll be crawling all over the place looking for you. That bitch'll have made a statement by now and I bet she'll include the first business as well, the one with the scousers.' He had not considered that. Seven to ten.

The Pyke's white van was parked just inside the curtilage of the Everett farmland. Alex Miller had found it, gained entry with a skeleton key – good cops are often good burglars - and had stuck the tracker under the dashboard, wiring it up to the vehicle's own power supply and fixing the aerial in the best possible transmitting position. He had accomplished this at three o'clock the previous morning, blissfully unaware of the drama unfolding and the frenetic police activity about to take place. Mission accomplished, he sat quietly for a few seconds in the Transit's passenger seat and surveyed his handiwork, making sure that everything – old newspapers, parking tickets, empty fag packets were more or less back in their places. The he decided to have a rummage. He clambered into the payload area and used his tiny pocket torch to do a quick spin of the contents. Nothing of any real interest. It was as he struggled back into the front of the vehicle that he noticed the whittled down butt of the gun protruding diagonally from behind the driver's seat. He extracted the weapon with his gloved hand, inspected it and saw that both short barrels were loaded. Then he replaced it carefully behind the driver's seat, got out of the van and made his way back to his own vehicle which was parked up unobtrusively at a 24 hour transport café on the A35, about a mile away. On the way there he sat in a field with his back against a stone wall and rolled a cigarette. He blew the smoke at the moon and thought about what he had just done - and what he had left undone. Having awoken about three hours earlier he had formed the belief that nothing was going to happen unless and until he got that tracker into that van, that the longer he put it off the more difficult the task would become and the less point there would be to it. It was only a matter of time before the Pykes got swifted and then the game, his game, would be over. Heather would have no real further need of him. He would be redundant and the window of opportunity would have passed. Go for it, he had demanded of himself, now. And now it was done. And he had the massive bonus of knowing the exact location of an illegal firearm.

He took out his mobile phone and thumbed a number. It was the number of the sim card in the tracker, which he now activated. Within seconds he received a text of the location of the van: 'rockham valley dt7 3ty, 2k A35'. Spot on. He felt powerful.

Alex had crept back into Heather's house in Dorchester just after 4am and was fast asleep in the downstairs guest room when Heather rose to the sound of her mobile phone shortly after 5.45am.

'Heather can you come in to work please,' was all she needed to know that it was open war on Katie Pentreath's tormentors. All plans of a sophisticated, intelligence-led operation against the Pykes would now have to be abandoned. What a waste of time that had been, she thought as she got dressed. Little did she know that she was wrong about that.

149. Whilst most of the west Dorset police were running around after the Pyke boys, two of their elder statesmen were in another county altogether. Constables Reg Bull and Norman Hogg were in leafy Surrey, attending a seminar at the Police Federation Headquarters. Norman had invited Reg along with him as he needed help occasionally with discipline cases and wanted to recruit him as a part-time representative. Reg was up for this, it was a way out of doing as many late shifts and 6am starts. Norman also had something to gain in that he might just be giving his brother-in-law something useful to do to divert him from his apparent self-destruct mission, thereby possibly improving his sister's chances of retaining her husband's pension.

The Federation headquarters in Leatherhead was a new, purpose built structure of glass and steel. It had cost £27m and was a major bone of political contention between the Central Committee and the 43 satellite force committees, of which Dorset was one.

'Fucking hell, look at it,' said Norman as the two old timers approached the building on foot from the nearby railway station.

'This is all about egos mate, not about the members,' ventured Reg, hoping that Norman would agree and that he had not gone overboard with this comment. He need not have worried.

'You've got that right me old mate, you're spot on the money there.' Reg had just gone up in Norman's estimation.

The seminar was on the subject of scapegoating. Once the 50 or 60 delegates were comfortable in the huge central meeting room, they were addressed by the General Secretary of the organisation, Ian Blenny, a weasely, buck-toothed man from one of the north western forces who had made it to the top of the Federation by making sure he was in the right place at the right time to say the right things. A real political reptile.

As Whitehead dished out a string of platitudes to his captive audience Norman leaned towards Reg,

'He's never repped a copper at a disciplinary hearing in his fuckin' life.'

'Don't surprise me one bit,' came the inevitable reply.

Then Blenny introduced his first speaker, a civilian employee of the organisation called Dan Fraser. He was the manager of the legal services department and was well liked for his proactive stance on funding lawyers to not only defend the organisation's members but also to attack those who maliciously prosecuted, blamed or defamed honest, hard-working cops. He had committed large amounts of money to suing Chief Constables up and down the country and many newspapers were well aware of his name and his eagerness to engage in high court proceedings if they so much as dared to publish defamatory material about rank and file cops without making sure they got their facts dead right.

Fraser talked passionately for about an hour on the need to use the Federation's money effectively and to attack its enemies at every opportunity. Real fighting stuff, which Norman liked. Reg was also impressed. He had always thought that all Norman and other Fed reps did was represent Bobbies at discipline hearings and mediate on workplace grievances. But this took the thing to a new level and he found himself feeling keen to get involved.

150. 'What the fuck is going on down there? Lyme is supposed to be the jewel in our crown, the place people go when they're sick of Bournemouth!'

Rob Sherrell didn't reply, he did not have answer. The Chief was right. Lyme had been ignored and only got knee-jerk policing when something happened.

'Well? What are you going to do about it?' The Chief was struck by Sherrell's dumbfounded silence. Was this county so much out of control? Were there no contingency plans? What were these clowns she called her senior management team up to?

'Ma'am,' Sherrell thought he had better offer some sort of an excuse, 'We've got so many balls up in the air....'

'Ha!' the Chief could not resist it, 'I suppose two of them are yours are they?'

Sherrell thought of a good reply to that one but he had a mortgage to pay, so he just said, 'It sometimes feels like it Ma'am,' and he did not stop there,

'Crime feeds on itself, the word gets out that we're struggling to cope and we end up getting targeted by every scumbag in the county, in the country even. We're a soft touch in West Dorset and you know it Chief, so stop blaming your own people.'

Sherrell could hardly believe that he was saying this, but it had to be said. She was losing the plot. Not that it was her fault really, the economic deficit was taking its toll on the public purse and many domestic services were suffering as the recession bit hard. Policing in west Dorset was not a Whitehall priority at the best of times. Right now it was not even on the radar. Chief Joanne Bache and her detective chief inspector just stood looking at each other for a long five seconds. They both knew that this was all pointless. There was nothing to pull out of the bag. There were no reserve resources to call on. Hell, the night shift around the Lyme and Bridport area was staffed by Special Constables, unpaid volunteers.

'This lad Murdoch that took the beating last night, I've had his father on the phone this morning, says he can't get any reply from Lyme CID. I told him to email them and he blew his top.'

'Hardly surprising, he wants to speak to a copper about a serious assault on his son and you tell him to try email, hell Rob, what do you think...?'

'All right, all right,' Sherrell was on the point of raising his voice at the Chief Constable, his mortgage becoming less important with each second; he would not be blamed for this but sensed blame settling on him like a pigeon on a statue. And he was not having any of it.

151. Heather Boyle was with Caroline Bradstock upstairs in the Seagull Inn. They were viewing the CCTV of Darren Pyke felling Simon Murdoch. The level of violence, although consisting of a single blow and one kick, was sickening. They agreed that Murdoch was lucky to be alive.

By the time she got back to the station Heather was livid that Pyke had not been in custody after the assault on the Liverpudlians, after the poisoning of the horses, after the robbery of the lighter from Katie – what the fuck was he still doing walking the streets? And now this had happened. At that moment the seed of an idea began to form.

152. Carmella Everett lay in her bed and positively glowed. She had spent the night alone but was nonetheless pretty ecstatic. It was all pretty much coming into place. Soon things would be back to normal. It would just be her and Daz again. Like it should be, naturally... well, she knew what she meant.

153. Katie Pentreath had never really known exhaustion. Real

exhaustion. She knew it now. She sat with Heather Boyle in the CID office in Lyme Police Station. Simon Murdoch was still in Exeter Hospital, having been detained overnight for observations. The news was not bad but was not good either. He had actually fitted during the early hours, a sign of possible brain damage. But the doctors were confident that this would heal and were worryingly keen to point out that the outcome could have been very much worse.

'It won't be long before he's in custody and you'll be safe and sound. He won't be coming out for a long time.'

'Where have I heard that before?'

'I know, I know, but we've just never had the opportunity to catch up with him. As soon as we put the job together something else comes up. Resources problems....'

'Resources problems? My boyfriend is lucky to be alive Heather and you talk about resources problems!?'

It was the first time that she had called the cop Heather and the cop liked it.

'Let's get out of here Katie, let's go for a drive down to Exeter, then we can be on hand for visiting or to pick up Simon if he gets discharged before visiting, which he probably will.'

'His parents are down there with him, what's the point?'

'To show support, I think we both need to do that.'
Both?

So Heather drove her private car, off duty, with Katie in the passenger seat, under circumstances which they both knew were pivotal. Statements would have to be made this time. Evidence would have to be given. And it was going to be horrible. Katie could not bear to think about what was going to be said about her in court. How she had been unfaithful, two-timing, etc., etc. She could not bear to think about how this cop was manipulating her, just so that she could solve the case. She could not bear to think what Simon was thinking about her, what his parents were thinking about her.

But as they drove through the rain Katie began to feel a warmth. This came from her female companion. She glanced across at the driving cop. Her face was taught with worry and responsibility. Perhaps Katie had been a bit hard on her, and she admitted this to herself. And just because Heather looked a bit butch, a bit athletic, didn't mean that she was a lesbian. And so what if she was, thought Katie. So what if she was. Katie was confused, frightened and very, very alone. She was, worst of all she knew, about to face terrible exclusion from her friends and university colleagues. She had been cavorting with scum, had seen the outcome coming and had done nothing about it. Had probably facilitated it, they would say. And had then looked on like a spectator.

They parked up in the hospital's leafy grounds and walked to the garish entrance. The middle class girl was so glad she had the cop by her side. It sent out the right message to Simon and his parents. But also there was a strange familiarity growing between the two young women. Just before they reached the ward where they had been told Simon lay, their hands came together. One did not grab the other, there was no leader, no follower, they just came together and squeezed, and then parted just before the two of them rounded the corner and stood before Simon's bed, Simon, and his doting parents. The visit was brief. The way back along the coast was silent but intense and the two decided to take a walk on the beach.

154. Reg Bull pulled his little car into the car park of the Goat. He was looking for any sign of the Pyke brothers. Any one of them would do. He felt that he was up against it, up against the clock. Something was eating away at him, he felt a deep urgency that he was on a mission to save a life, of whom he was not entirely sure, but nearly 30 years as a cop in this part of the world told him that just sometimes a certain configuration of events, people and time conspired with very unfortunate

consequences. In short he felt that one or more of the Pyke brothers was about to kill someone, and that someone would probably be Heather Boyle. He'd often heard that Darren bragged that he'd 'go down for a copper', i.e. get sent to prison for murdering a police offer, but it was a common brag, drunkenly slurred by many of the county's low life.

Reg had advised Heather to stay out of the way, stay in Dorchester for a few days; she had a good bit of leave owed to her. She did not know what the hell he was talking about and actually thought he'd gone a bit potty, gone on a bit of a propriety trip, taken the parent pc thing a bit too far. Whatever, Heather had not heard that Darren Pyke was going to kill her, there had been no risk assessment, no hard intelligence, or even soft stuff for that matter; the only soft thing seemed to be Reg Bull's brain. Nonsense.

155. The longer it went on the worse it got. And the worsening was not just a steady decline, it was exponential, accelerating. It had been a slow burn at first, a niggling lump in the back of his throat, accompanied by a bad taste in his mouth and a dull ache in his belly. But now it was growing at a ferocious rate, consuming him so he could barely function. His last 22 years now seemed pointless; the next 22 certainly so. It was what he had just witnessed on the beach. The kiss. Right in front of him. It was as if she had meant him to see it, although he was sure she had not, judging by her reaction when she saw that the incident had been witnessed by him and two others. She had freaked out completely, called the cop a fucking bitch and had taken off across the soft sand, stumbling and falling about all over the place and sobbing and howling. The cop had just stood there and gawped, not knowing what to do, before just turning and trudging in the opposite direction, head down, looking pretty embarrassed and upset herself. But nothing compared to Darren and the betrayal and humiliation he felt. So the anger grew. Into fury. Into rage. She had tricked him, made him love her when there had been no intention on her part other than to use him and abuse him. That was how he chose to see it anyway. It did not

matter to Darren that he was actually conscious of what he was doing, of the flawed logic; all that mattered was that he had to somehow exorcise the raging mutant tumour of self-loathing that was growing inside him.

156. And so he did what he had done many times before as a growing boy – he cried into her lap, into the lap of his divine goddess, his sister-mistress-lover. She understood hatred and love and despair and above all total confusion. And Carmella purred and spat with satisfaction and ideas and decisions. Ideas and decisions about what to do to fettle the bitch who had so wounded her little soldier. Darren looked up from her moist crotch where his head lay and caught sight of her twisted face. And he too made a decision.

157. Heather rang Alex, she needed him with her, it was part of the plan. Alex could not believe it and actually thought for a minute or two that he was being set up. No sooner he had parked up his filthy vehicle outside the house in Dorchester he was being dragged in and upstairs by a scantily clad police woman who smelled like a fucking perfumed garden. Had she been on the piss, he asked.

'No mate, just celibate for too long, me waters have finally broken and you've been very patient.'

He was not impressed and glanced about the house for signs of hidden cameras. She had him by the sleeve and actually was pulling him up the stairs, giggling.

'What you up to Hev? Why can't we go out first? What's this all about?'

Shut up Alex, get your kit off. And with that she stripped as if she was just taking a bath, so unsexy was the act. She even folded her clothing up as she did this and laid the garments on a chair by the bed. Alex just stood and watched; he felt like a peeping Tom but could not avert his eyes. Then she stood naked in front of him and put her hands on her hips, her legs apart. She scowled. What was the matter with him?

158. On the coast the sky was actually clearing as Reg lurched out of the Goat and made for his car with a sense of urgency he could not quite understand. Fuck the drink-driving he thought. If I get caught I get caught. This was not like Reg.

159. It was the hand squeeze that Heather had thought about as she lay alongside Alex, her crotch wet and her left nipple sore from where he had bitten too hard. She shuddered. Alex wore a smirk but knew he was not entitled to it. She was up to something, or had been up to something for which she was trying to make amends. For the want of it Alex formed the suspicion that Heather had just let him fuck her because she had recently been fucked by that old codger Reg and she needed to get back on track, so to speak. Re-establish herself in the real world before she fell totally into the nether world that was west Dorset. Yeah, that would do, thought Alex, that's what it was, but not to worry, she had seemed to enjoy it so perhaps there would be more. The precedent had been set. He could not have been more wrong.

160. Reg hit the A35 and crossed without even looking, an extremely reckless bit of driving. He sped up the Crewkerne Road as if on an emergency call. Which he knew he was. He had to get to that farm. How the hell could that girl not have 24 hour police protection? The aging cop was seeing a whole vista pan out before him; the girl would get killed and Heather would be blamed. It wasn't her fault Darren Pyke had never been arrested, charged with the Seagull assault and kept in custody. That had been the fault of Dorset fucking Police for getting its priorities wrong. Looking after a rich bitch and her pet fucking chickens when they should have been banging up violent criminals. And now Katie Pentreath was in mortal danger and Heather Boyle was on offer.

It was two minutes to midnight as he slowed for a vicious bend in the road, the rain stopped. And he heard the gunshot.

And so did Katie's parents, before lurching out of their bed and wordlessly to the door, knowing that their daughter was not in the house because they had both heard the door go as she had left not three minutes before, just before they both bundled into her room to see the empty bed.

161. The rain hammered down. The noise inside the van excluded logic. Just a loud, incessant din, like the roll of a mad drummer. Darren ground his jaws together. The gun lay across his lap. He glanced across at Carmella. Her profile was at once beautiful and hideous. Her eyes bulged and her nostrils were flared. She smelled blood. They saw the little car begin to wind its way up the hill from the A35, the headlight beams turning this way and that, like searchlights, following the contours of the road. Darren began to shake, his mouth went dry, she had to be given the final ultimatum.

The van was parked diagonally across the road and within a few short minutes it was blocking the path of Katie's car, within a few more seconds she became worried, another second and she was terrified, ramming into reverse and trying to drive backwards up the winding hill as she watched Darren Pyke get out of the van with a gun in his hand. She knew she was going to die, but then she had known that all along really. If only she had thought about it. The story had been falling into place since that first night in the Seagull Inn, followed by the steady growth of intertwining circumstances, the police involvement, the fucking lesbian cop, her parents. And the little beach episode was the catalyst. The defining moment. The slipknot that pulled it all together. And now she was trying to run, the survival instinct taking over, but too late. The steering wheel slipped from her trembling hands and the car hit the high verge and stalled immediately, its exhaust pipe blocked with mud. And then the rain stopped, and there was silence.

She froze like a statue as she watched them draw near. The water on the windscreen diffracted the images so she could not see their faces. She stared ahead. Steam rose off the bonnet. She locked the doors. And then the butt of the gun came through the driver's window.

Katie tried to scramble across to her left but couldn't free her feet from the footwell. Then the passenger door was pulled open and Darren Pyke grabbed her by the hair and started dragging her out of the car. She tried to scream but no noise came out. She held the steering wheel with her right hand and managed to hook her left arm behind the passenger seat.

'Get out of the way Darren!' screamed Carmella, who had snatched the gun from Darren's hands, opened the driver's door and was now almost inside the vehicle and on top of Katie with the gun pointed at the terrified girl's head.

'No, don't shoot her, don't fuckin' shoot her!'

Still holding Katie's hair Darren also got a hand on the barrel of the shotgun and pulled sideways and downwards. But Carmella was strong and viciously determined, snatching the weapon out of Darren's grip and giving him no choice but to let go of Katie's hair and lunge at his half-sister to take the gun from her. He failed. Momentarily freed, Katie tried to arch her back to somehow get between the seats and into the rear of the car. In doing so she raised her head – and Carmella pulled the trigger.

The crash and flash of the gunshot stopped the world. Katie went rigid and then slumped, half of her face gone; one eye grotesquely staring and blinking, Carmella and Darren froze facing each other across the dying girl. Then at once they both sprung backwards out of the car, crouched, still staring at what they had done. Then they got in the van and drove, in silence. After about half a mile Darren braked and stopped, got out and walked quickly round to the passenger side, leaving the keys in the ignition.

He spoke quietly and calmly, 'Take the van to Wales and keep driving, go to Cardiff....'

Carmella was shocked, 'I can't drive to Wales, I never been to fuckin' Wales, I..., where are you goin?'

'If you don't do as I say we'll both be in prison for life, you'll never see your family again. I know people in Cardiff, call me when you get there and I'll tell you what to do, just get there and dump the van in a side street or somethin', you got enough credit on your phone?'

She nodded frantically.

'Here', he shoved some cash in the top pocket of the denim jacket, about £40. She shuffled across into the driver's seat, gripped the wheel and just stared ahead, transfixed by the horror of what had just happened and what she feared lay ahead.

'Go!'

She revved up, engaged a gear, took her foot off the clutch and the van stalled and cut out.

'For fuck's sake get a grip!'

She took a deep breath, started the engine and tried again; the van lurched off into the night. It had started raining again. Darren turned heel and started walking. Within a hundred yards he was over a style and onto a waterlogged public footpath which took him to the top of a hill from which he could see the lights of Lyme. The butt of the .410 was in the back of his belt, the barrel between his shoulder blades.

162. Townsend got a call from Decker at 4.31am. The DS sounded strained but very controlled. 'Get into Bridport by five please, we have a problem.'

'What problem?', but Decker had hung up.

When Townsend pulled into the car park at Bridport police station he looked up at the second floor of the building and saw that the CID office was in darkness. He got out of his car, puzzled, not a sign of life. He had expected the buzz of expectation following a major incident and had been trying guess what the incident would be on his way over from his flat in Charmouth.

'Right, come over and get into my car.' Decker's voice was flat, professional and uncompromising. Townsend was bewildered. He did not like the look of this one bit. What was Decker up to?

He did what he was told and as soon as he was in the passenger seat of Decker's Volvo the DS gave him the facts. Katie Pentreath had been murdered about four hours previously. The main suspect was Darren Pyke but there may have been others. The incident room had been set up at Lyme and the Chief Constable and all her merry men were on their way. The shit had well and truly hit the fan and they would be looking for a scapegoat. Decker told Townsend that they had to get their heads together. Townsend was totally gobsmacked. Get their heads together for what? If Pyke had gone to ground no amount of getting heads together would find him, it had to be scorched earth – every scumbag's house or hovel in the county had to be spun and spun deep. It had to be a manhunt.

But that was not the point. They were looking for someone to blame.

'There's going to be a stewards enquiry my son, and we'll be in the frame, you and me Stuart. The DI'll get out of it and upwards from him they're fucking untouchable, but you and me are in this together, the DS and the DC, you wait and see, by the time they're finished anybody'll think we killed the girl.'

Decker wanted to hear it from Townsend, but the young DC was not stupid, he could see it was coming and deliberately chose his next sentence.

'No sarge, no way, they can't pin anything on her... we - they can, but I'm not helping them.'

With that Townsend got out of the car and walked to his own vehicle, got in and drove home, his mind numb with shock at the murder and moreover, by far moreover, at what had just taken place. Fucking Dorset's finest eh? Good traffic stuff and launching a major investigation into the theft of some fucking hens. But a murder? Too difficult, so blame a cop for not preventing it. Terrific.

163. Heather had just received her early morning call from the DI who had for some reason been unable to reach Decker, the latter's phone being unusually turned off. Having hung up she just sat on the edge of her bed and stared at her reflection in a large dressing table mirror. She wore a singlet, her hair was tousled and there was some serious luggage under her eyes. Alex had not woken and snored on a duvet on the floor to which she had relocated him following their sexual combat session. So, a pretty weird start to the day. Having been fucked by a bloke she had now just been told that the person she really wanted to fuck had had her head blown off. The worst of it was that the two incidents had probably happened at the same time. She just stared at the mirror and wished she could move. But no, she just stared back at herself, muscular neck and shoulders, tight belly and tender vagina. The DI had sounded cold, had said he wanted her to hurry up and get to Lyme to take on a central role, probably as office manager. He had sounded tired, but there was also something else she could not put her finger on. She stripped and got into the shower, soaping herself thoroughly everywhere, mildly disgusted by what she had done she was keen, but not desperate, to get Alex's smell off of her. It hadn't been that bad, just a bit sore now. She thought of Katie and how this had happened and then it dawned on her, she froze in the hot water, stood still like a statue as the soap suds drained down her body and the realisation sank in – it was her fault. The murder was her fault, that had been the message in Packington's voice – get into work now, you're on trial. That was it. There was no doubt who had fired the shot, it had to be Darren Pyke, there was no one else, no other possible suspect. And what else had the DI said? Not much left of her, face gone, not much head left, brains all over the fucking place, Jesus Christ, her poor parents. Alex was still sleeping smugly when she left, disgusting man she thought, filthy fucker like them all.

164. The canteen at Lyme Police Station had been opened up especially

and the place was buzzing. Brown gloved inspectors shook hands with each other, young detectives struggled with hangovers, old detectives struggled with hangovers, senior officers traded buzzwords and worried about the looming overtime bill, crime squad rookies assembled in the incident room, techies plugged in the kit and Alsatians barked in the vans in the yard whilst their handlers smoked roll-ups and moaned about everyone else. It was the typical start to a murder enquiry. Whether it be the chance to impress peers and governors, the chance to get off of shift work for a few weeks, the chance to earn good overtime or just the chance for a change, it presented opportunities for everyone.

Sherrell made his entry. He now carried the title of Force Head of CID – a position seemingly created by the Chief Constable for her trusted charge – and he wanted to make an impression. Of all the opportunists he was one of the best, particularly when the grasping was at relatively low risk. And this one could not be better. A young woman had been brutally murdered by a known suspect who had been harassing her for some time whilst most of the Force's resources had been engaged on the investigation of the theft of poultry from a friend of an East Dorset Superintendent. It was West Dorset's chance, and West Dorset was Sherrell's home region and career base.

He tapped a spoon on a table and launched into what he mentally prepared on his journey from home. He had visited the control room at Bridport and had snatched the CAD printouts which gave a staccato account of the incident. He had not visited the scene.

'Right, listen up. We have the murder of a young female on the Crewkerne Road about a mile north of the A35. The weapon appears to have been a small bore shotgun. Not found at scene. The shot was at close range and the motive is unknown. The victim was shot whilst at the wheel of a motor vehicle registered in the name of Katherine Pentreath of Upper Brooklands Farm, there is little doubt that she is the victim but the body has not yet been identified. The only suspect at this stage is a 22 year old male called Darren Pyke, a well-known petty criminal in these parts. The first action is for an armed team to attend his home address in

Stockton, will the armed officers please see the office manager D/S Decker now.

Three men and a woman, bleary eyed from their early wake-up and dressed in navy blue fatigues, shuffled over to where Decker was sitting at a hastily made workstation with a sheaf of papers in front of him and two IT bods working around plumbing in a terminal to be linked to the national major enquiry system.

'WD01 and WD02 go with them and follow DI Packington's briefing downstairs in the lobby. He will tell you to be careful so I won't bother. The rest of you stay seated and rested, it's going to be a long day.'

Heather was downstairs in the lobby with Packington. She watched and listened as he delivered the worst briefing she had ever witnessed. The burly sergeant in charge of the armed team was used to this sort of shambolic start to a major job and was quick to rescue the aging DI.

'Aye folks,' – broad Ulster accent – 'this is the layout and this is the approach.' He then went on to hold up an A4 sheet of paper on which was drawn a sketch of the Pyke house location with adjoining streets. He gave short, clear instructions as to what he wanted done and his officers nodded their complete understanding. They were from Dorchester force HQ but their remit was not confined to Dorset and they often found themselves deployed in various parts of the West Country. Packington thanked them and wished them luck for which they politely thanked him before moving off swiftly followed by the personnel carriers and dog section.

165. That left Heather alone with Packington. They both headed upstairs without a word and went into his office. She knew that there was something very nasty brewing for her. Packington looked confused and troubled. He was not really sure why he was doing this, so close to retirement and a nice pension and beery days in his garden. But he could

not bear scapegoating.

'I said go to Lyme and you went to what you thought was the scene. Why?'

'Like I said guv, I....'

'WHY!?'

Heather was stunned. She had never heard the DI raise his voice and would have bet he was probably incapable of it. And he didn't raise it, he virtually screamed. She was dumbstruck.

'Alright, I'll fucking tell you why. You're in on it.'

'What?'

'You're in on it. Complicit. An accessory to murder. I should arrest you now.'

She just stood there and stared. She knew he wasn't joking.

'You've been following Darren Pyke for a long time. You've known about the danger he presented to Katie Pentreath for a long time, you've faffed about and done fuck all about it except hoard intelligence about them and their connections and movements. We've been doing a bit of backtracking. You're getting shagged by a met cop, aren't you?'

It was not a question.

Her faced burned like a furnace.

'No. If you must know I'm...' Then she thought better of it and looked down, on the point of tears.

'You're what? What?'

'In a relationship with someone else, Alex Miller is just a mate, a friend....'

'Dodgy fuckin' bastard, that's what he is. I've been talking to his DI, I know all about him and I don't like the fact that you are associating with him, whatever the basis. I wouldn't mind betting that the pair of you have been trying to set up something big, just so you can get a fast route into the CID here. You should have stayed in London Heather. You're going to fucking wish you had. Now go home and stay at home. I don't want you anywhere near this incident room. I'm coming over to see you tomorrow with some work I want you to do on domestic violence. You can work at home. It's research.'

'Is this... am I suspended?'

'No, call it restricted duties. You work from home until I tell you otherwise. You're not to go near anyone or anything. Go on, fuck off.'

Her mind reeled. Packington had been succinct and had made the situation clear. At worst she could get done for gross negligence manslaughter, at best she could get disciplined for neglect of duty. A manslaughter charge could be braught on the basis that she had a duty to act to prevent what had happened from happening but had instead played cat and mouse with the main suspect in order to bolster her own career.... gulp. She got home but could not remember the drive.

166. Alex was up and brewing coffee in his boxers. The sight of his body disgusted her. To think....

'Get dressed can you.'

'What's the matter with you? Where have you been?' He made towards her but she drew back, looking to one side pointedly.

'Yeah, okay, okay, I get the message'. He could not help think that he had enjoyed the previous night a lot more than she had. That her mind had been elsewhere. That she had been thinking of something else. Or someone else.

'Have you heard any news, I mean on the radio or anything,' she asked this still looking to one side, hugging herself, pale and nervous.

'What's the matter Heather?' he made toward her again but she backed off further.

'There's been a murder. Katie Pentreath. Darren Pyke's the main suspect. Along with you and me.'

Alex immediately knew exactly what she was talking about and the matrix of the situation was instantly before him.

'Got it. They're going to say you, we, fucked about with this job in the hope of catching something big whilst ignoring all the warning signs.'

'And that we kept the warning signs to ourselves.' She had stopped looking to one side now and was giving him full eye contact. There was now real communication between them; between two coppers. Back to normal.

167. Reg had been first officer on scene and questions would no doubt be later asked as to what he was doing there off duty in the rain at that time of night. Packington had sent him home having smelt the beer on his breath and had made a mental note of the fact that an old off duty cop had come upon a murder scene within minutes of the crime when it wasn't even on his way home from the pub or work or any other place where he had a normal reason to be. The more Packington thought about it the word normal became inappropriate in this growing mess. He knew Reg had a thing for Heather, whatever a thing was, the dirty old git, but the fact was he had always had an unhealthy interest in the girl's betterment, like he wanted a bit of the action by supporting her. Anyway, he would see Reg soon enough and have a heart to heart with him.

168. The scene had been pretty horrific. Half of Katie's face was gone

and her head for some reason was almost severed from her body. She had taken the full force of the blast in her neck - as she had tried to lunge for the passenger door she had presented a backward and sideward leaning target to her killer. The pellets had hit just below her right ear, some going upwards to destroy half of her face and the rest glancing at a right angle to cut through her neck. Packington thought of this and the very many murders he had helped investigate. No matter how clean one would think the killer blow should be there was always a mess, always unexpected surprises of breaking knives, misfiring guns, victims selfishly having heart attacks before their murderers had quite finished; always something to spoil it, to spoil a good, clean murder.

The armed search of the Pyke home yielded nothing, as expected. The old man was drunk in his bed, the old woman was away visiting her sister and the two younger boys were at Reading festival, probably doing a bit of thieving. Only Josh was at home and was capable of giving a good account of himself. Darren had not been seen for some days, it was claimed.

169. Katie's parents had visibly aged 20 years each in the five hours since their daughter's death. They had not been allowed to see her body at the scene and were not being allowed to see it at the hospital yet. But they would not accept that Katie was dead until they had actually seen her body. At 7.15am they were allowed in. Sally fainted and Bertie pissed his pants.

Nothing could have prepared them for this horror. It crucified them both there and then.

The photographs were going up on the incident room wall and no detail had been spared. Officers gasped and swore when they first set eyes on the images of a beautiful life reduced to butchered muck. It focused their minds, they would get that piece of shit Pyke, he was going down for the rest of his life for this.

By breakfast time the investigation had slipped into a rhythm. Actions were being issued to individuals and teams of cops, statements and information were coming in, generating more actions. Door to door enquiries as to the whereabouts of Pyke, CCTV footage of Lyme, Bridport, Chard, Axminster. Major all ports alert for the white transit van; the list grew and grew.

170. And Alex and Heather just sat and stared at each other. They were both thinking about that van and the tracker under the dashboard. If they came clean Alex would get done for theft, no doubt about it and he would be prosecuted and imprisoned, no doubt about it. They powered up the laptop and watched as the little red dot made its way into the Severn tunnel and blink out. Nice one Darren, escape to Wales.

Alex was thinking fast and logically.

'We've got to let them know where that van is – there must be a way we can do that without letting on how we know.'

She was with him, 'Could the information not come from London, or even Wales, there must be an ANPR out on the registration number.'

'Yeah, but who looks at those, and half the cameras are switched off in some of these shit-kicking counties. Something about they can't afford the staff to watch them. By the time the backlogs are checked the vehicles are miles away, hundreds of miles sometimes.'

'Like I say, could you not get someone from London to find it, anonymous info perhaps?'

'Yeah, yeah, let me think.'

Heather sat and shuddered; Alex got dressed and prepared to leave. He was due back on duty in Shepherds Bush the following day so there was no rush, but for some reason he did not want to stay here. She could get a visit from a bunch of her colleagues at any minute. They would suspect her of knowing something that they didn't and, after all, they were right, bang on the money. He made for the door, gathering his things. She just sat there, not looking at him.

'Eh tu Brute?'

'Eh?'

'You as well? Turning on me?'

He turned abruptly, flung down his bag and in two strides he was upon her, he pulled her up and flung her down on the bed, landing on top of her.

'NO! Never, Heather. It's obviously escaped your notice but I happen to love you! What do you think last night was all about? Just sex?'

'Yes.'

'Well not to fucking me it wasn't! I would ask you to marry me tomorrow if I thought I had a cat in hell's chance....'

'I'm a fucking lesbian Alex, last night was just to say thank you, just to express....'

'D'you think I'm stupid? I know you're 80% gay but, you know, hope springs eternal, I always think that perhaps....'

'I wish I could change things Alex. But you are missing something, something really big....'

She was interrupted by the sound of the front door opening.

'Hello, anyone at home?'

It was her mother. Alex picked up his pack and resumed his journey out.

'I'm just going Mrs. Boyle, nice to see you, short and sweet as they say. Ta ta.' And he was gone.

He drove out of Dorchester, but instead of turning east to London, he turned west – he had an idea. The laptop lay on the passenger seat.

171. To his amazement Reg was teamed up with Maxine from the Crewkerne DVU to do the job of family liaison. He was told that his local knowledge and recent involvement with the Pykes and the victim gave him the edge over anyone else. He was pleased but somewhat daunted. But he liked Maxine and they could both make good overtime out of the job.

The pair pulled up at the farm in Reg's private car. They wore civvies and sombre expressions. It is part of the self-preservation instinct of most coppers; they can distance themselves from their emotions and those of others. Nothing to do with training, just years of thick skin development.

There were a number of other cars in the farmyard, probably relatives and friends, come to lend support. The door was answered by one such face, a blue rinse busy body from Sally's coffee club.

The two cops introduced themselves and were allowed quietly in.

Bertie and Sally sat ashen faced and exhausted at the big kitchen table. A few people fussed about at a distance, making coffee and writing lists of things to do. The local vicar was there in close attendance even though both bereaved parents were known non church goers. Bertie and Sally had been sent away from the tiny Axminster hospital where what was left of their daughter lay.

'When was the last time you saw her?' It was Maxine, she spoke quietly, addressing them both.

'Yesterday.'

'How was she? Did she appear distressed or worried about anything?'

Sally, 'No.'

Bertie, 'It was that bastard Pyke, we all know it. Have you got him yet?'

Reg replied, 'We are looking for a suspect with that name Mr. Pentreath, but there have been no arrests yet. It won't be long though, I'm sure, he won't get far.'

172. Decker was briefing a team of young crime squad officers. They were to descend upon the farm of the Everett's. The armed team were to provide backup, having now returned from the fruitless exercise at Stockard.

'These are a bunch of real hillbillies, but be careful, there are dogs, geese, pigs and crazy horses in there. And a crazy bitch – the mother is known to be very anti-police and there's every chance they'll be expecting us. A few more operational warnings followed and the team filed out to the waiting vehicles. As they did so they passed Mrs. Everett who was standing at the public counter of the station waiting to be seen. She was obviously very distraught and had something to offer the enquiry. But she was ignored by the preoccupied cops. After about a further ten minutes of waiting she shouted and banged on the counter, 'My daughter went out with Darren Pyke last night and has not come back yet, will someone please help me, I've heard what's happened!'

And so had most of the West Country. The media has its tentacles in every corner of the police establishment, sometimes formally, mostly not. When a suspicious death occurs one of the first departments to be informed is that of the local Coroner, in this case located in Dorchester. The Coroner's office is staffed by a small group, usually two or three, badly paid ex-police officers. Invariably they supplement their incomes by tipping off a local journalist when someone gets murdered, commits suicide or dies in any other unusual or unpleasant way thereby attracting a post mortem examination and inquest. Thus Mr. Jim Ramage, the sleuth of the manor, got his very own early morning call and, complete with fag ash on crumpled grey suit, rubber soled shoes and beaten up Range Rover, he had arrived at Lyme police station at about the same time as Mrs. Everett. He stood behind her as she tried to make herself known to any cop who had the time to listen. He saw his opportunity.

'Excuse me love, but has your problem got anything to do with the murder of the girl last night? I'm....'

'Yes. Yes it has. My daughter is missing this morning and she was out with Darren Pyke last night. I'm bloody terrified and these fuckers don't want to know.' The last few words were in a raised voice and directed back over her shoulder from where she stood now with her back to the counter in order to face Ramage.

'You reckon this Darren Pyke bloke did the murder?'

'No doubt about it.' She was shaking, wide eyed and tearful, she hugged herself and tugged at her rough, country clothing, moving her weight back and forth from one scuffed brogue shoe to the other and back a again. She was frantic with worry, anticipation and, most of all the need to unburden herself of secrets and suspicions with which she had lived in silence for far too long.

Ramage was riveted. For a second it was just him and her with a yard between them, the rest of the world oblivious. She was giving information about a murder out loud in a police station but no copper wanted to listen, so preoccupied were they with their programmed tasks, none of them heard. Ramage took Mrs Everett by the arm and led her out into the street.

'Where are we going?' she was sobbing now.

'Let's find somewhere quiet, you need a seat and a cup of tea.'

She nodded eagerly and they walked down to the seafront. It was deserted; too early in the morning. He led her into an empty cafe and sat her down, ordering a pot of tea from a disinterested Polish girl who brought it over to them and set it down sullenly.

'Right love, who are you and who is your daughter?'

She took a deep breath and let it all flow. 'I'm Kitty Everett and my daughter is Carmella. She's er... she's different, a bit of a tomboy to be honest, never really went to school much which was a terrible waste but the other kids used to take the piss out of her and then she would lose her temper and bash em up like and she was... is a brilliant artist, got a vivid imagination like....'

'Slow down Kittie. Did she say where she was going last night?'

'Nah, course not, she's 23 years of age, she went out with Darren when he came round to pick his van up. Nothing unusual about that, they were always together, like brother and sister really, too much like brother and sister....'

'What do you mean by that?'

'I'm sure they've been shagging each other for years but it's like not a real relationship, they're just still like a couple of kids. It's like them having sex was just like they were going fishing or scrumping or something.'

She was talking so fast now that Ramage wondered if he was wasting his time with this gabbling woman.

'Look Kittie, you've got to tell me where you think Carmella and Darren are now, and I will make sure the Chief police officer is told within a few minutes, they listen to me.'

'I haven't a clue where they are but they are in that van of his, I bet, and he'll be driving like a lunatic as usual, unless... I know, they could have holed up... in the tree house, that's it, they may be laying low in the tree house.'

'Where's the tree house?'

She told him and he reached for his phone.

173. The Chief was in the incident room smiling and nodding her greetings at her officers as they went about their business. She sauntered across to where Decker was sat. He had been given the job of office manager and was pecking away on his keyboard, frowning, looking rather distracted.

'Hello sergeant Decker.'

'Hello Ma'am, good to see you.'

Chief Constable Bache was not sure how to take this rather familiar greeting,

'Is it now? Why do you say that Sergeant Decker?'

Decker was going to hold his own. 'Because I find it good to see you Ma'am, I'm only speaking my mind.'

'Hmmm. Okay then. And it's good to see you too Sergeant Decker.'

'Thank you Ma'am'.'

The Chief moved off towards a brace of uniformed Superintendents who were trying to look busy but basically had nothing whatsoever to do other than prepare themselves for daily bollockings about the impending overtime bill. Senior management in the police is all about money. They are paid to know the price of everything and the value of nothing. They have their careers depending on it their appraisals may as well be done by accountants. They have their coppers brains knocked out of them at an early age and replaced by pocket calculators. But always at the top of the list of calculations is that which relates to their pensions; the carrot on the end of the stick that keeps them going. Keeps them sharp and ruthless, cutting back on staff, on overtime and on resources such as cars and protective clothing, on dogs and air support, on canteens and expenses. The list went on and on. And now a young woman had been murdered because of this financial obsession, this lunacy in which policing and the investigation of crime, not to mention prevention, is reduced to function, instead of being about the roles of police officers working as part of society and taking a holistic approach to prevention, detection, intelligence and evidence.

Where the financial blame culture exists in the senior ranks the operational fault-line is directly under the lower ranks, inspector and downwards; when something goes wrong they are the ones that get the bullet and even sometimes locked up, and that was what was troubling Decker. He knew it was only a matter of time before the press got hold of this. That weasel Ramage would be sniffing round already, no doubt. The fact that he had been visibly upset when his troops had been diverted to Bridport on that sunny morning not more than a week ago when they should have putting the Pyke's front door in would count for nothing. The fact that the order to redeploy had come from Dorchester would count for nothing. The only fact that would count for anything at all was that Decker had not presented senior management with a written and articulate argument on the risk Pyke was posing to the community in general and Katie Pentreath in particular, thereby ring-fencing the operation in Stockard that morning and preventing the redeployment.

Ramage specialised in rural problems and had been the star reporter during the floods of 2005 and the foot and mouth epidemic that had followed. Although his police and court contacts were excellent his most coveted informant was a man called Gavin House. House was one of three observers on the Virgin air ambulance and could mobilise that brilliant machine from Exeter at an hours' notice. The Virgin air ambulance is a private service and is not staffed by public servants with duty of care towards the government or the taxpayer.

House was already up and about when he got his morning call from the journo.

'Yeah, got it on the radio. Bad business. Nothing for my machine though – we don't work for the Coroner.'

Ramage had expected this bovine response, or rather seemingly bovine response because he knew that House knew that this was just the opening conversation. The rules House worked under, although not within any statutory framework, were pretty strict on divulging confidential information to third parties. The opening call therefore between the two was merely a marker for House to expect a second call that he could only receive by switching on his unregistered, pay as you go mobile, bought for him for the purpose by Ramage. And, as soon as the meaningless empty chat had concluded he rang off from the first call and switched on the other mobile phone.

174. Having respectfully excused themselves having left their details and assurances that they would return to give any and all support they could, Reg and Maxine left the shell-shocked parents of Katie Pentreath to their trauma. The grief would come later. Reg drove Maxine to Crewkerne where he dropped her off to do some catch-up work in the DVU. They arranged to meet later in the day at Lyme.

175. Unlike Norman Hogg, whilst Reg was getting slaughtered Norman was making hay. He was in a large office at police HQ in Dorchester with James Sprake, the Deputy Chief Constable in charge of the force's professional standards inspectorate. Sprake was little known in Dorset having transferred in from another force somewhere in the north. Rumour had it that he had come from Cleveland where he had blown the whistle on the allegedly corrupt Superintendent Ray Mallon during operation Lancet, the investigation launched to rid that force of its fathomless corruption. But no one had actually been able, or been bothered, to check this out, such was the apathy of the south coast towards the irrelevant north. But Sprake was known as a very cold fish and a man not to be trusted one bit.

'Sit down Mr. Hogg', it was more of a command than an invitation, delivered by Sprake from behind his desk without looking up to greet the federation representative. Norman sat down, eyeing the Deputy Chief with caution, deciding to play his cards very close to his chest.

Sprake sighed and looked up from his desk upon which Norman was annoyed to see a copy of the Daily Telegraph open on the sports page. Arrogant bastard, thought the police constable.

'Bloody Pakistani cricketers, caught chucking a game. Corrupt wankers.' Sprake was sharing his opinion with him, thought Norman.

'What can I do for you Mr. Hogg?' Sprake was still distracted by the article and kept glancing down as he spoke.

'The Pentreath murder sir, I have concerns that….'

Sprake's eyes were on the paper again, but that did not prevent him interrupting,

'That one of your lot is going to get the blame for it?'

'Yes sir, if you like.'

'Mmmm, I'm one step ahead of you Mr. Hogg, and I share your concern. I've had the Chief onto me this morning, she's told me to line up an internal enquiry already.'

Norman was impressed by the Dep's candour, but the 'your lot' bit had not gone unnoticed. The battle lines were being drawn up.

'Will you keep me fully informed sir?'

'Of course I will, we'll need you if there are to be any interviews of officers, and obviously a solicitor or solicitors if the interviews are to be based on criminal allegations.'

'What criminal allegations might I ask sir?'

The Dep was relaxed, almost academic in his assessment. 'Well, gross negligent manslaughter is the obvious one. Then there's misconduct in public office of course, and if we come across anything else in the trawl it'll have to be dealt with too.'

Norman was taken aback by this brutally clinical assessment and waited for a reassuring smile to tell him that the Dep was humorously exaggerating the situation. None came. Trawl? That meant if the impending enquiries unearthed naughty overtime claims, unverifiable expenses, unauthorised absenteeism or any other contravention, no matter how trivial, the full force of the inspectorate would be brought to bear on the unfortunate transgressors.

A few seconds silence passed. Sprake raised his eyebrows and spread his palms outwards.

'Will that be all Mr. Hogg?' Meaning that the meeting was at an end. Norman smiled and rose. 'Thank you for your time sir.' He waited for a response but Sprake's eyes were back on his paper. Norman left the room, closing the door quietly and respectfully behind him. He left the building feeling pleased with himself that he had taken the initiative, but a worry was developing in the back of his mind that he may have put Sprake on higher alert; flagged up that the lower ranks were already getting their heads together, making up their stories. Norman decided not to tell anyone back at Lyme or Bridport about his meeting. The time on his duty sheet would just be down to 'federation business.'

176. Carmella Everett was five miles east of Cardiff when the van started to shudder. Fuel. The needle was well past empty and she had been half - well, fully expecting this setback. There had been no point in pulling into services because she had no money, having spent the last of it at the Severn toll and on a bottle of vodka and some pork pies and tortillas. She allowed the old van to glide to a halt and die quietly on the hard shoulder. She had decided that it would be its last ever journey. She jumped out and without hesitation she climbed the steep embankment at the side of the motorway, clambered over a fence and began to jog across an open field to where she saw some rooftops about half a mile south. A plan was forming in her mad survivor's mind. There was nothing in there to connect her to the crime. Her prints had never been recorded. She was free. Free from everything, score settled, only one more job to do and it

had to be done quickly. She needed some petrol, at least a couple of litres, that would do it. Then it would be job done. As she ran she began to sob; something was not right. What about her mum and her brothers, what would become of them? But the more her mind churned the more entrenched she became in her flight. Mad music began to play in her head. The sweat soaked her clothing and her long muscles began to ache. A cold sun broke through the clouds and seemed to burn her tanned face; she wiped her mouth and tasted the blood on her hand. Then she saw the old mill. A stubby tower with the remnants of an old wooden water wheel. There would be a pond there she thought, and she was right. Coming upon the secluded water she saw that it was fairly clean, if a little overgrown with water plants. She stripped and waded in. It was freezing and she almost cried out loud as the water enveloped her body. A few minutes later she emerged, gleaming and shivering, completely clean. She pulled on her clothes and continued her journey towards the buildings, now only a few hundred yards away.

177. Having identified the tree house with the help of Google Earth and his friendly helicopter crewman, Ramage telephoned the incident room. He knew enough about murder enquiry setups to know to ask for the office manager, and was promptly put through to Decker.

'Have you looked in the tree-house?'

'Who is this?'

'Your favourite sleuth Sergeant Decker, have you looked in the treehouse?'

'What treehouse Ramage and what for?'

Ramage gave a full account of the location of where he thought Darren Pyke might be holed up. Decker thanked him tersely, recorded the conversation on the database and wrote an action to deploy armed police to the copse at the edge of the Everett homestead. The large team did not have to go far; they were already combing over the Everett's home and outbuildings. One of the sniffer dogs was getting very excited at a spot near the silage pit. It turned out that the particular spaniel was omni-competent and did a sideline in drugs as well as people searching. But his canine entreaties were ignored when the order came to redeploy part of the team to the location of the tree house. Five of them set off on foot, two armed, a dog handler and two young DCs.

They approached the big tree in muffled silence, their approach being assisted in this respect by a fairly strong breeze which rustled the undergrowth and leaves.

The dog handler entrusted his charge to one of the DC's and began the ascent, he being the more adventurous and impatient to get off duty. One of the armed officers went up behind him – it should have of course been the other way round. Anyway, they did not reach the top because the dog handler stopped dead, motioning frantically backwards with his hand and attempting to reverse quickly down the rope ladder, the DC having to climb down backwards behind him. They both jumped the last few rungs and landed heavily in a heap together, swearing, the dog handler the loudest. It then became apparent why he had retreated. He was soaked in piss.

'Fucking hell and shit.' He spat, the others not quite knowing what had happened in the dim light, then they all smelled it.

'Someone up there piss on you?' asked the armed officer who had stayed on the deck.

'Yeah, just glad it's not petrol, that's all.'

They all looked up at the dark hulk of the tree-house and wondered what to do. The firearms sergeant decided to take the initiative.

'Right, we're armed police, make yourself known and come down out of there, or we'll....'

'Or you'll what, spray the tree with bullets? I don't think so.' The voice was familiar to one of the DCs who had worked at Lyme quite recently.

'Reg, what the fuck are you doing up there, apart from pissing on us....'

This was answered by stifled laughter, laughter tinged with hysteria.

'I was just passing when I saw a light on, though I'd check it out, sorry about the piss, had a couple in the Goat, got caught short....'

'Reg come down, you're drunk, and you're fucking up evidence, get the fuck down from there,' demanded the DC, Langham was his name, annoyed by this old fart getting in the way. This was a serious murder enquiry and there was no room for clowns.

178. Alex sat behind the wheel of his car and stared down at the laptop. He had tracked the Transit as it had progressed westward and was now wondering why it had stopped. He could not believe how three police forces with ANPR technology had not spotted the vehicle. It was that very fact however, along with the heavy dollops of creosote tar that Darren habitually applied to certain characters on the front and rear plates, which had secured the vehicle's safe passage. The existence of NPR technology and cameras had precluded any sort of human vigilance and the creosote had fuddled the cameras. That was how Darren Pyke's Ford Transit had made it to the last knockings of the M4 in south Wales.

It was to this location that Carmella Everett returned less than half an hour following her decamp from the van. She had in her hand a five gallon can full of petrol she had stolen from the first farm she had come to. It had been an easy crime, so at home was she on agricultural premises. The can had been conveniently located right beside the 40 gallon drum full of fuel, situated like on most farms on a 4ft brick structure not less than 50 yards from the nearest building. Health and safety.

But instead of putting the petrol in the tank of the van, she opened the rear doors, clambered in and doused the interior of the vehicle with the stuff. She then got out, opened the passenger door, stood well back, took Darren's lighter from her pocket, lit it and chucked it in. It was actually a full ten seconds before the Transit became a fireball, long enough for the woman to turn and tear up the embankment. She still felt the heat on her back and the fear of death in her heart. She screamed as she ran, tears spouting from her eyes.

And the little flashing light on Alex's laptop went out.

179. DC Clive Langham had taken charge of the treehouse incident and was duly reporting it to Decker.

'He did fucking what?' The office manager was incredulous; his raised voice had the effect of summoning Sherrell from where he had been standing at the widow of the incident room which overlooked the seafront.

'What's happened?'

'That fucking old dickhead Reg Bull, well known drunk of this manor and lazy bastard, got up into the treehouse first guvnor, probably wankered any evidence we may of had in there and then pissed on one of the dog handlers who was trying to gain access.'

Following his summary Decker just cocked his head on one side and held his palms outwards, as if to say, 'What the fuck am I meant to do with this kind of staff?'

Sherrell was bewildered. 'Reg Bull is supposed to be on family liaison, how did he know about the treehouse action, did you allocate it to him?'

'No, course not. I gave it to this lad and his mate. They took an armed unit and a dog handler.'

'Did PC Bull perhaps overhear about it?'

'No...' then Decker caught on, 'no, that old twat knows things and is holding back, where is he now Clive?'

'Sat in the back of the CID car, pissed as a fart.'

Langham was beginning to wish he had not been given the treehouse action; he was fast becoming involved in an internal discipline investigation and, like most detectives, wanted none of that sort of thing.

'Right, place him formally under arrest and take him to Bridport, let him sleep it off and then I want to speak to him.'

Decker was pretending to be furious for the benefit of Sherrell. The DS could smell a possible way out of taking the flak if this enquiry turned into a witch-hunt, which it inevitably would, and if he could not pin anything on Heather Boyle. Reg Bull was emerging as plan B.

But Sherrell was not convinced. 'Hang on, hang on Sergeant Decker' – the use of the word sergeant was to remind Decker of the fact that he was not in charge of the murder enquiry, or anything that flowed from it or into it – 'Don't turn this into something it isn't,' turning to Langham, 'I'll come down and see him in a minute, keep him in the car, is he complaining about anything?'

'Like what sir?' The DC was genuinely confused about this question.

'Like being brought in by you, being detained, falsely imprisoned, you know, is he in a reasonable mood?'

'Oh, yes guv, good as gold, thinks it's all a big laugh.'

'I'll big laugh him'.

180. The South Wales police traffic unit were taking their time. Another round of teas had been ordered following their assignment over the radio to investigate an apparently abandoned white van on the hard shoulder of the westbound carriageway. They could see the thing on one of the screens in the control room. The initial footage was just of the stationary and abandoned van on the hard shoulder. Nothing exciting about that. But they stopped sipping tea when the lone figure of a girl in jeans ran

down the bank, filled the thing full of petrol and turned it into a fireball.

181. 'What the fuck is your game PC Bull? No, don't answer that. Save it for when we've got the tape switched on. In the meantime you're under arrest on suspicion of perverting the course of justice. You do not have to say anything but it may harm your defence if you fail to mention something you later wish to rely on in court. What you say may be given in evidence.'

They stood in the backyard of Bridport police station. Reg had stopped laughing and joking and DC Clive Langham had been deadly serious from the start. A uniformed PC called Graham Dodd stood with them awaiting instructions which he duly got from Langham. Dodd was 6'7" and a black belt in karate. Not that Reg would've ever tried anything, but he was certainly exhibiting strange behaviour and had a pretty wild look in his eye. He had stopped laughing. They took him in front of the custody sergeant who knew Reg and could see that he was pissed.

'I've heard what Clive has had to say Reg I'm going to put you down to sleep it off. I'm going to have the doctor come and look at you straight away and if I get half a chance you'll be off in an ambulance to Exeter hospital. The last thing I need is drunken cops 'avin' 'eart attacks or stuff in my cells.'

'Whatdya mean shtuff sharge?' Reg through his drunkenness obviously perceived that they thought he'd gone round the bend and was likely to top himself.

'Just stuff Reg, you know, all this is for your own protection until you're fit enough to be interviewed.'

It's a weird thing when a copper gets nicked. They invariably slip straight into role. Like they've rehearsed it a thousand times. Likewise with the custody officer, so keen is he or she to conceal any emotion and to be seen to be fair and impartial, they treat the cop like they would anyone else. The trouble is that anyone else is treated like a suspect, which of course they are. The overall effect is that the participants in the dance are stunned into automaton-like behaviour. They go through the motions, the implications of what may or may not unfold (but probably will) are too great and unpleasant to contemplate.

So Reg Bull trudged down the cell passage, turned into the first available open door which was closed behind him by the reluctant custody officer who did his best not to slam it. Reg sat down on the bench with his head in his hands and tried to work out the answer to the first question that had already been asked him – what the fuck was he playing at? The alcohol was wearing off now and he remembered having done his statement about finding the bouquet of flowers at the scene and then going to the Goat to shake off the depression that had followed his humiliation when Decker had showed him up. From the Goat he had gone the treehouse because he thought he would find Darren Pyke in there and he was going to arrest a murderer. But all that he found was a used condom and some pork pie wrappers. Then they had found him and he had thought bollocks, I'm pissed aren't I? I am an old fool aren't I? Well, might as well act like it. Act the part and you are the part, that's what his old dad had always said. Good advice that, never pretend to be what you're not; pretend to be what you are – or at least what people like to think you are. Keeps them happy.

182. The white van was almost black and still hissing hot when the South Wales Police traffic division car got there. They had taken their time. At first it was put up as a possible terrorist attack with the danger of secondary devices. So they'd left the top brass to argue about that one. When it became apparent that they would have to close the M4 to run that little drama they decided the risk was not so high after all. It became a vehicle used in crime and the approach went ahead. When the half-melted registration plates were finally deciphered and a PNC check done they congratulated themselves on this assessment and informed the murder room ay Lyme. 'We have your van,' was the proud announcement from the valleys, as if they'd performed some sort of

investigative alchemy. Their fucking about had cost the enquiry another two hours and had let Carmella Everett find time to hole up properly in a disused outhouse on the fringe of an old trading estate just south of the M4 between Newport and Cardiff, not far from the farm from where she had nicked the petrol.

'We've been told not to touch it.'

This was Dave Rice to his sidekick Alun Davies. The two sat in their patrol car just behind the burnt out wreck.

'Suits me,' came the taciturn reply.

They had just sent the VRN over the radio and the response had been excitable. They were going to send a pick-up grabber and put the undrivable van on the back of a low loader and take it to Cardiff Central police station to await forensic examination by Dorset. Suited the Taffs, that did. Why should they get their hands dirty and get caught up in the evidential chain of another force's job. The murder had taken place in Dorset boyo so let Dorset do the fucking work boyo.

183. Carmella sat in the concrete and tin shed and shivered. She still had the stench of petrol in her nostrils and ached all over from either the recent exertions, stress, fear, she did not know what, but she was stripped down to her bare survival mode. All that rough sleeping in Rockham Valley was going to pay off now. She knew how to build a fire without smoke, feed off of the land and stay invisible and this was what she intended to do for the foreseeable future. She knew they would be looking for Darren and that a lot of them would be looking for her. Even if and when they found Darren, he wouldn't tell them where she was of course but then he couldn't, could he. But they would figure she had been there. Whenever she had ever left the homestead it was with Darren and her mother had seen them leave together the night before. Yes, they would be looking for her alright.

She concentrated on keeping warm. Finding some hessian sacks she fashioned a bed and managed to get off to sleep. Sleep away. Lay low, save energy, she knew she was going to need it.

184. When Norman Hogg found out about Reg Bull's incarceration he was for once stuck for words. His first instinct was not to get involved. This was serious shit with no bottom to it. What was going on? Reg Bull trying to fuck up a manhunt stroke murder enquiry? This was such serious shit that his mind worked immediately on how to get out of becoming involved.

'So I heard guv, on the grapevine. Look, I was with him a few hours before this all happened, just before he must have found the scene and the body and that. I was buying him beer. I'm too close in Guv and I'm already on notice sort of to represent other officers in this, such as that Met girl Heather Boyle. So there might be a conflict, in fact there's sure to be a conflict, so I can't rep Reg guv. Sorry.'

Superbly done Norman. He had given Sprake this story and had crafted it without notes, just by instinct. The conversation had taken place on the telephone as Sprake was keen to get couple of Professional Standards officers down to Bridport on the hurry up to serve Reg with his reg 9 notice – drunk on duty would do for starters then suspend him pending the outcome of the investigation into perverting the course of justice. Sprake was a bright snake and knew that Reg Bull was probably not the blundering old fool he was making himself out to be. Anyway, let's get him out of the way and move up the food chain a little, that was Sprake's thinking.

185. Simon Murdoch had been detained for a further 24 hours in Exeter Hospital. His mother was by this time by his side, his father was in the Far East on business. A laptop was on the bed and the two of them talked to the old man on Skype.

'Can't just have a punch-up these days son, these scum always resort to weapons... and Katie was there, watching it?'

Simon's mother answered the old man whose face appeared even redder on the little screen.

'Yes, she just sat there watching it, but it wasn't her fault... she....'

'She what...?'

At this point Gladys Murdoch began to shake and sweat, she could not take this. She knew that Katie Pentreath was dead. Simon did not. Nor did the old man. She had been advised not to tell Simon until he was in the clear. His blood pressure was still quite high and they did not want him getting too excited until they were sure he was fit enough to take the shock.

'She called the police I think and made a statement....'

'Have you seen her?'

During this Simon was just staring at the ceiling. He then just reached forward and closed the lid on the machine, cutting the connection.

'What did you do that for son?' Asked his mother.

'Where is she?'

His mother did not answer, she just looked down and trembled.

'Where is she mum?'

'How would I know? I'm not her mother too, I've no idea, I don't know....'

'Just tell me she's alright, she should be here, fuck's sake mum, she left here last night with that copper woman, what was that all about, is she getting protection? Why does she need protection? I've tried ringing her this morning but she's not picking up....'

He stopped when he saw the tears rolling down his mother's face.

186. Carmella slept for two hours. When she woke she was lathered in sweat. The hessian sacks stank and were rough on her bare arms and face. She had slept out of exhaustion and had awoken out of fear. Where the fuck was she? How was she going to get home? What was happening back there? She had been part of a murder. She had helped him do it. Finished off the job. The whole job, once and for all.

She had tried to get away. Tried to reverse back up the hill to her farm and her nice warm house and her nice cosy parents and all that, but the stupid bitch duffed it into the mud and got stuck and stalled and then couldn't start it and then she tried to get out and run... she could never have outrun us anyway, city girl, no muscle. Carmella sobbed as she thought.

Darren was thinking twice. I wasn't. I was sure of what we woz doing. Darren woz going to let her go, I swear it he woz. Not me. It was too late for that with all that gone on before. She was going to put him away, no mistake about that, put him away for a long time, if not for ever. No way woz that going to happen. No way.

Then the door of the shed opened, slowly at first and then quickly, and in walked the silhouette of a man. She jack-knifed upwards to free herself from the sacks and get to her feet, but he was on her in a flash, holding her by the shoulders and forcing her backwards.

'Ssshh, it's okay, it's okay, I'm not going to harm you....'

She kicked out and tried to wriggle free, but he was stronger and heavier and used his weight to control her. He was worried about noise and put a hand over her mouth.

'Keep quiet, I'm not after you or anything, just calm down!'

She just froze and stared upwards with bulging eyes.

'Are you going to keep quiet?'

She nodded and he pulled his hand away.

'I don't know who you are love but I'd rather you hadn't seen me. Now that you have though we're in this together.'

'In what together?' she hissed.

'In running away together. You're definitely on the run from something and you might as well know that so am I, so let's stick together. Deal?'

She nodded.

187. The incident room was quiet, most of the day's actions were either done or being done and Decker was on his own, catching up with the inputting of the data, his civilian indexer having gone home for the night. It was 0034 when Stuart Townsend walked in. He had been in charge of a team of woodentops doing door to door enquiries around the farms and villages. Waste of time. The weather had been atrocious at the time of the murder, rain bashing down on rooves, nothing heard, nothing seen. Townsend perceived door to door as a punishment posting dished out by Decker following the exchange at Bridport before the day had even started. That was not true actually. The office manager had been too busy to think of that, he had just allocated what was quite a responsible job to an experienced man. Door to door rarely yielded results but it had to be done and it had to be shown to have been done properly. Otherwise the defence in any subsequent trial would accuse the investigation team of not unturning every stone and therefore not discovering potential defence witnesses or at least witness who might give an alternative interpretation to that relied upon by the Crown.

Decker looked up and down at his desk again. 'Evening Stuart, or is it morning now?' He wasn't trying to be unpleasant, it just came out that way and he was too tired to care. He could be unpleasant one day and make up for it the next.

'Why me on door to door?' No 'sarge' or 'Tom' even.

'Why not you?' He didn't even look up.

'You worked out how you're going to stitch up Heather for this shit yet?'

Decker stopped what he was doing but still did not look up. He felt like he was going to have to nip this in the bud, and fast before he had a serious problem on his hands. He stood up and faced Townsend, eye to eye; they were a couple of yards apart.

'No. How can I with you clearly on her side? I'll end up with both of you against me, it'll be me carrying the can by myself.'

A pause as Decker stood, turned away and began to walk slowly across the otherwise empty room.

'But I'm used to it Stuart. I'm used to taking the blame for others and getting fuck all credit for the things I do for people and the service. No Stuart, you go ahead and moan to the brass about me, complain away, but remember I'll fight like fuck. You try to make anything of that conversation we had in my car this morning and I bet you that my interpretation of what was said by each and both of us will win the day and you'll come out of it looking like a cunt. You want to place a quiet bet now Stuart?'

Townsend knew he was well beaten. Decker was calling his bluff, or what he thought to be his bluff. Decker had genuinely perceived this approach to be that of Townsend saying give me some good postings on this murder squad or I'll grass you for this morning when you were going to row for the shore and blame Heather. As it happened Townsend had never thought of that angle. He was actually just worried about Heather.

'That just shows how your fucking mind works doesn't it Decker. It's all about you, all about your fucking career and fuck everybody else, cover your own arse and fuck anybody else but it don't work, it don't work 'cos every cunt hates your guts, everybody thinks you're a wanker but at least I say it to your face....'

'Finished?'

'Eh?'

'I said are you finished?'

'Yeah, I'm finished, finished working my bollocks for you that's for sure.'

With that Townsend turned and left the room. He knew he would have to be back the next morning for more actions issued to him by the man he'd just insulted and been insubordinate to, and it would be interesting to see what those actions would be - can't get much lower than door to door though. As regards to the longer term, he would put in for a transfer up to Bournemouth maybe, get away from this sinister fucking place. Yes, sinister, that was it, no longer a shit-kicking backwater; sinister now, maybe there's just a knife edge between the two.

188. Eight o'clock the next morning and the incident room was buzzing again. Or that's what they liked to call it. It actually was humming more like, humming with suppressed tension, in the way that an electricity sub-station hums with a lot of pent up energy with nowhere to go. Sherrell was going through the actions as returned by officers the previous day. Decker sat their ready to generate more, but waiting for the go-ahead to do so. Each action had to be signed off by Sherrell before it went out.

When most of the squad had rolled in Sherrell stood up and banged a spoon on a table.

'Listen up folks, good day's work yesterday, thank you all for your commitment. Keep at it but try to keep your overtime down to 3 hours a day, that way you don't have to claim extra for a late meal on your expenses.'

He paused and looked around at the tired eyes and thoughtful expressions, they were of cops waiting for leadership, waiting to be guided through what would be one of the most important enquiries of their careers given they were in west Dorset and all they were getting was prattle about overtime. Sherrell sensed this and moved on as best he could.

'In addition to the main suspect Darren Pyke we are also now looking for a second person believed to have been with him at the time of the murder or at least shortly before. She is a 23 year old female called Carmella Everett. Pyke is known to associate with the Everett family as you will appreciate but, more interestingly, Carmella has not been seen by her mother since the evening of the murder. We may actually assume that she is with Pyke at this very point in time. The board will be updated and actions raised this morning. But even if you don't get actions to do with either suspect please keeps your ears and eyes open 24/7. These kind of people never stray far, they get nosebleeds if they leave Dorset for more than 24 hours. Okay, good luck and thank you.'

Having got back their attention and a bit of respect Sherrell sat down beside Decker and the two started to rattle out actions which were then issued on paper by the indexer and allocated by Decker.

189. Old Kitty Everett stood at her kitchen window and sobbed. Jesus Christ what had she brought into the world. They weren't bad kids her lot but Carmella had always been a worry. Took after her dad probably, a real Pyke.

And then there was a slow quiet knock on the gate. Kitty knew, think of the devil and he shall appear. She walked out of her kitchen and spoke to him through the wicket in the gate.

'What do you want old man? Come to find that fucking daughter of yours? You're too late old man, she gone off with her brother, gone and killed somebody now they have, puts all the other shit they done to shame, eh old man....'

'Let me in Kitty, we got to talk about this, av'e the old bill bin 'ere yet, they turned our place over yesterday?'

'Yeah, they bin 'ere, had a dig around found nothin' and buggered off. Will that be all old man?'

'Yes Kitty, I'll leave you now.'

And he was gone.

190. Post mortem examinations are gruesome affairs at the best of times. Sherrell hated them, some cops loved them, revelling in the black humour that invariably emerged. The examination of Katie Pentreath's body was no exception.

DC Langham had been nominated exhibits officer for the whole enquiry. Langham was an unfortunate looking character who tried to compensate for this with what he thought was a wicked sense of humour. He wasn't a bad cop, just a bit of a wanker, that's all, said stupid things at the wrong time, such as:

'Nice snatch eh guv?'

Sherrell froze, the almost headless corpse of Katie had just been wheeled out and uncovered and this twat had to say something like that. The morgue attendant, a young lass in her early twenties, went red and stormed off, just as the pathologist, Dr. Darja Reitober, walked into the room with her Dictaphone and toolbox. She had not heard Langham's remark and Sherrell thanked God for that.

'Will you excuse us a minute Doctor, I just want a word with my colleague outside.'

He pulled Langham by the arm out into the corridor of the cold old brick building annexed to Axminster hospital.

'Right DC Langham, no more of that, no more funnies, just do your job and keep your mouth shut, okay?'

Langham got the message. 'Okay sir.'

The two of them went back in and the examination began. 40 minutes later and what was left of Katie had been filleted, dissected, held up, looked at, prodded and sewn more or less together again. Throughout the procedure the pathologist muttered into her Dictaphone. This would later be formulated into a report, once the results of the blood and other body fluid tests had come back.

191. Gladys Murdoch could not conceal the truth from her son. She wept as she gave in to his insistence,

'She was murdered the other night son, only a few hours after she left she was murdered with a gun. They're after the same guy who did this to you... I'm so sorry son....'

She held his hand tight but could not quell the violent trembling that began to rack her son's entire body.

192. Heather walked around Dorchester, aimless, preoccupied and distressed. She had never experienced feelings like these in her life. Even the death of her father, although very sad and the end of a lovely relationship, was the start of a new beginning, doors opening. She remembered hating herself for thinking that at the time, thinking that her father's death gave her the opportunity to spread her wings, be herself. But this, this could really be the end of everything. Bad karma. What goes around comes around Heather. She smiled bitterly to herself. Perhaps this was atonement. Perhaps this would finally be freedom from the selfish mind. Almost like death itself. She considered the worst possible outcome. Five years for gross negligent manslaughter. She had arguably concealed evidence, perverted the course of justice for her own ends. She had selfishly hived off an important investigation in order to spring it later with maximum positive effect on her own career aspirations. The fact that she had done none of this deliberately or with the slightest aforethought meant nothing. Meant nothing because

ironically her downfall would result in the elevation of others, others who would seek to lay blame and claim moral high ground. If they couldn't get her for manslaughter they would certainly try for misconduct in public office. Indictable only, carries a maximum of ten years but she would probably get off with three, 18 months for good behaviour. She actually stopped walking as it suddenly dawned on her that this theorising was actually taking the form of a basically accurate prediction. She was going to be tried, convicted and sent to prison in the most dreadful circumstances. What would it be like for her inside, especially once the old dykes in there found out she was one of them. Would that be good or bad?

Exhausted with all this she tripped into a pub. Suspended cop alone in a dirty old pub at 3 o'clock in the afternoon in a boring provincial town.

193. Meanwhile another suspended cop was doing the same. Reg Bull sat in the Goat in Lyme Regis. He was on about his seventh pint and his mind was just a total mess. He had heard that Heather had also been suspended, or as good as, and he had also been told on no account to contact her and if she contacted him to report the fact immediately. He was on bail, albeit only police bail, to return to the police station pending a decision as to what to do with him. Heather was not on bail having never been arrested in the first place. For her then to contact Reg would be a serious breach of trust, so much so that she would probably be pulled in and fast-tracked on discipline procedure and out of the force. So Reg was actually being used as a potential prosecution witness against Heather, he prayed that she would not ring him, bearing in mind that they would be applying for user trails of both of their phones.

194. The murder hunt charged on all over the place but no one had any idea of the whereabouts of either suspect. Four days, then five. The negative material poured in, no trace this, no trace that, no witnesses. The van was still in Cardiff and Sherrell had decided to have it brought back

to Lyme for examination. They had not managed to get a pair of cops down to Cardiff and besides they also needed a SOCO to look at the burned out scrapheap. Sherrell didn't want a South Wales SOCO in the evidential chain. He had experienced that before and the kerfuffle was awful; different forms, different exhibiting methods, hassle getting the out-of-town guy to go to court.

A surveillance camera had been mounted opposite the Pyke address in Stockard. The technical team from Dorchester had been called in and they had managed to get a device deep planted in a telegraph pole opposite and just down the street from the target premises. It gave a reasonable picture transmitted to a dedicated screen in the incident room. The trouble was that it needed someone to be on that screen 24/7, not a job that attracted volunteers. Usually a low level civilian clerk got the task, which was to keep a written log of all comings and goings, of which there were quite a lot. Stills were snapped of all events, including old Ma Pyke leaving and entering on her interminable cleaning expeditions and the old boy staggering in and out laden with gerry cans of cider. Decker took an interest in this log, and kept his watchful eye on the civilian loggist lest he or she showed an inclination to fall asleep or judiciously ignore mundane sightings. Decker rightly considered that all the sightings of whoever came and went were significant. These low life were keen on family values, it was their only real point of reference. Family was their society, even if they spent most of their time knocking lumps out of each other. It would be most surprising if Darren was to make an appearance there, but his brothers would be in touch with him and their movements had the consequent potential of being significant. For that reason Decker had insisted at a policy meeting that the footage of the product should be stored in its entirety, both to secure evidence and to satisfy disclosure requirements should there ever be a trial.

And he was sure that there would be a trial. They would catch Darren Pyke, he had no doubt, and there would be enough evidence to charge. But a conviction required a lot more evidence and was entirely another matter. So Decker was quite relaxed about the progress of the murder investigation. But he was not in the slightest bit relaxed about the other investigation. The dark side of the job. The laying off of blame. And there were probably more resources being expended on that than were allocated for the capture of the killers. The figures would be certainly comparable anyway, when you considered the rank and pay scales of the brass currently spending their entire waking hours engaged on damage limitation. This aspect was not being helped by the seemingly omnipresent Ramage. The wretched man had made it his business to be in every pub in Lyme at the same time, on top of being constantly parked up outside Lyme and Bridport police stations and even popping up on the steps of the constabulary HQ once an hour on the hour.

The press office at Dorchester had issued him with the standard fodder about police being in pursuit of a man and woman, both in their 20s, whom they needed to speak to urgently in the course of enquiries. This frustrated Ramage because he was keen to name the suspects, which of course he was perfectly able to, but he was gagged by the implicit threat of trouble from the police if he was seen to interfere in any way. Naming the suspect in a newspaper could of course in theory bugger up an inquiry, if for instance the police wished those suspects to relax into thinking that the heat had subsided and that they could venture back onto their patch.

195. One of the first actions to be raised by Decker was a full forensic examination of Katie's mobile phone, found at the scene in her jeans pocket. Almost instantly the examiner had isolated what was surely the suspect's number. It had been from this that Katie had received several texts in the weeks leading to her death. The tones of the messages had become more terse and ominous – 'stay away from town', 'don't go to harbour', 'be careful who you speak to,' and, more sinisterly, seven days before the murder, 'im watchin you'. The number was unregistered and the SIM card had been part of a cash purchase at the Axminster branch of Tesco's.

Decker gave this evidence some focused thought. If Katie had become cooperative – as Heather had claimed – then it could be assumed that she would have shown the officer these texts as giving credence to her fears for her safety. Yet there was nothing logged on any of the crime reporting or intel systems and no checks, until after the killing had been done on the number. Well, no recorded checks anyway. Which made it worse. Had Heather Boyle been given this information and had not done anything about it, that was disciplinary negligence and, had she somehow made enquiries and then kept the result or conclusion under her hat, that was deliberate concealment. This was good news to Decker, the case against PC Boyle was coming together nicely.

196. Norman Hogg had decided to be proactive. This was unusual for a fed rep. They normally waited until a cop was served with discipline papers, arrested or interviewed under caution before they ventured into the arena. Such was the nature of most of these semi-retired careerists. Norman was certainly a federation careerist, and almost fully retired from his role as a police officer serving the public, but he was full on in his role as a fed rep and keen to personally reap the rewards.

He pulled up outside Heather's home at just after 6pm on the fifth night of the murder enquiry. He had not got to the bottom of PC Boyle's current status; was she suspended, off sick, on annual leave or what? DI Packington had told Norman that the officer was working from home. Well, there was actually not really any such thing these days – a cop had to book on at the police station or at least at a police station and be accountable at any time during that tour of duty until he or she booked off at the end of it. She was constructively suspended, he decided.

The door was answered by Don Pryce, Heather's mother's partner.

'Yes?' Norman was casually dressed in slacks and sports jacket.

'Hello sir, I'm PC Hogg from Lyme police station, is Heather in please? I'm her federation rep.'

'Can I see some ID please?'

Mmmm, thought Norman and then remembered that this guy was a solicitor.

'Yeah, sure,' and he produced his warrant card.

'Come in. It's a good idea that you see her.'

They entered the lounge. Heather was sprawled on the sofa, eyes unfocussed hair in a mess and, as soon as she spoke, clearly pissed.

'Well hello Norman, come to check on my welfare 'ave ya?'

At which point Don made his excuses and disappeared off into another room.

'Hello Heather, I'm here as your fed rep, yeah, so I suppose I am here to check on your welfare, but also to give you the heads up on what I think might be happening in the not too distant future.'

'Yeah, yeah, I'm ahead of you Groundhog, you're probably talking to a manslaughterer, ain't ya?'

Heather had managed to get herself up to a sitting position and she positioned herself on the edge of the sofa, legs apart, elbows on knees and head down. She looked up at Norman through tousled hair. She wore a singlet, showing her muscled shoulders and arms and the entirety of her small pert breasts. Norman was not sure if she intended this or just was not bothered. He decided on the latter but averted his eyes anyway.

'What have you been told to do just now? I mean in terms of your duties.'

'DI Packington just told me to go home and not contact anyone, I'm not suspended or anything, I've no idea what the fuck's going on. I know one thing though, if I get a sudden recall to duty I'm going sick, that's for sure.'

'You would bloody have to in your present state Heather, how much have you had today?'

'Few beers, that's all. D'you want a cup of tea or coffee or something?'

Norman saw this as an opportunity to get her on her feet and get her tits out of his sight.

'Yes please, tea would be handy, could murder one.'

His hopes were a bit dashed because when she stood up the duvet under which she had lain fell away to reveal she had nothing on apart from the singlet. So her breasts became covered but the vest barely covered her backside. Norman again began to wonder if she was doing this on purpose. He felt himself redden, wishing that the brief would come back into the room.

'Heather you're not really dressed for this, could you go and put some clothes on please?' He pointedly looked out of the window as he said this.

'Nah, what for, I'm covered up Norman. Blimey, if it was Reg Bull standing here instead of you it would be a different matter. He would probably 'ave a stonker on.'

She laughed for the first time.

'I'm not Reg Bull Heather and you are plainly losing the plot. I'm leaving now, forget the tea.'

'Can I just say one thing Norman, before you run off...?'

'I'm not running off young lady, I've come here to help you and I find you drunk and lewd and unreasonable....'

'Just find out for me what's happening, tell me a bit about the enquiry, has Darren been nicked yet? I'm getting to be interviewed... just tell me what's happening!'

She yelled the last bit and burst into tears.

Norman just stood there and watched her sob and shake. He was unable to avert his eyes as she pulled up the bottom of her singlet and used it to quell her tears. Her six-pack and bush momentarily mesmerised him.

Tearing his eyes away to focus on the window and the garden scene beyond, Norman decided to play his cards very close to his chest; he was clearly dealing with someone on the edge here and he wanted out of this house as soon as possible.

'To be honest I don't know Heather. You're not suspended, you haven't been interviewed, you haven't been arrested, you haven't been seen by anybody concerned about your welfare – until now that is – oh, I'm assuming no one else has been…?'

She shook her head fast, vehemently, the bottom of the singlet now down but not far enough, Reg caught the shake of the head and looked away again.

'No, I don't know what they're thinking Heather, and that's worrying for me because I can usually read their minds. I can usually tell exactly what step PSD are going to take in any situation, especially if I know the people involved.' He fell quiet for a few seconds, eyes still averted.

'Packington just told me to stay here, not to contact anyone. He rang me yesterday, or it might have been the day before, repeating the instruction and telling me that I must not try to contact Reg Bull as he is now on bail – yeah, what's that all about?'

'Can't say too much about that Heather, except that it's not really anything for you to worry about, it was a drink related incident and he'll no doubt get nothing more than a slapped wrist will old Reg, he's just a silly old codger.'

'Do I assume they're watching me?

'Might be an idea Heather, yes, good thinking, just in case….' There were footsteps and he was on his way out of that room.

'Right, I'll give you a ring if I hear anything, you likewise, eh?'

'Yeah, okay Norman.' Like fuck, she thought.

And he was almost out of the door, just as Don Pryce came back into the room. Heather made sure her singlet was pulled right down then soon enough and Norman noticed this as he turned to say goodbye before disappearing.

He closed the front door behind him and headed down the garden path for his car, but not before stopping to admire the peonies.

As he drove back to Lyme Norman considered all the possibilities and alighted on the most reasonable one for all concerned. She was going to have to go, and as soon as possible.

197. Colleen prepared for bed. The last of the bar staff had gone and she threw the switches, plunging the bar, patio and kitchen into darkness. She made her way up the narrow staircase. Upon reaching the top she heard the quiet tap on the patio door. Some drunk coming off of the beach wanting a late one she thought, and decided to ignore it. Having reached the front room she heard the gravel on the window. Who the hell was that? And again, not too insistent, just a request; look outside please, I need to talk. She looked out and could see nothing in the bright moonlight but a deserted beach. She turned away and made for her sofa. Then another soft handful on the leaded panes. Who the hell was out there?

As if she didn't know.

198. Carmella had heard stories about tramps and raggedy men, but she had never seen one, never mind get attacked and held hostage by one. The bloke in the combat trousers and navy blue donkey jacket was not going to let her go anywhere, which was actually fine with Carmella as she would not have been able to decide where to go had she had the freedom of choice.

He had made her sit down with her back to the rear wall of the building; he sat opposite, near the door, confident that if she made a run for it he could get her. He needn't have worried, she had no intention of running and was now strangely unafraid. She instinctively knew that he was not going to harm her... was he a cop?

'Are you a cop?'

The man laughed, 'Hell no, me no cop. I used to be in the army though, if that's any good.'

Carmella felt at ease with this scruffy fella with the cockney accent and cheerful face. He looked ever so tired, but quite fit, she thought.

'Why d'you want to keep me here?'

'I think you may be able to help me, I need to get away from here and you could be my passport. You got wheels?'

She shook her head.

'Shame, it would have been good to have a lift with you. I could have paid you a lot of money for that. You sure you're on your own?'

'Yeah. You asked me that five minutes ago, what makes you think I'm with anybody?'

'Young girl like you, wandering around on your own, seems strange.'

'Like I said, I was hitchhiking and this guy got a bit fresh so I insisted he drop me on the hard shoulder or I was going to make a complaint to the police. So he dropped me, about a mile over there. What's your name?'

'Jack. And yours?'

'Carmella.'

A brief silence fell between them. She felt like she'd entered another world like in one of her fantasy books. Like Alice in Wonderland. Like Lilith. What happened barely 48 hours ago seemed to no longer have any relevance. Like those events were from a different life which had been left, departed from.

'Right Carmella, let's get down to some business.'

Silence from her.

'Let's see how we can help each other.'

This worried her, he'd already shown that he was more than her match physically so a run for it was out of the question, besides the fact that, she had nowhere to run to. But she need not have worried, he was after something different.

'I don't believe you're a hitchhiker. I think you and me have something in common. I think we're both on the run. Am I close?'

She nodded, almost imperceptibly, but she nodded, believing she had nothing to lose.

'Okay, so am I. We have more chance if we are together, nobody is looking for a couple. (He could not have been more wrong). I say we make our move when it gets dark tonight, we get some clothes from somewhere, smarten up and... you got any money?'

She shook her head.

'Yeah, well I have, plenty to be going on with, so we'll get a bus or a train somewhere and lay low like a couple, just like a happy couple on holiday, in Wales, say, how d'you feel about that Carmella?'

'As long as you're not wanting to fuck me, that's all, I'm not into that shit, not just with anybody anyway.'

'Don't worry, my intentions are perfectly honourable and, to be honest, I don't fancy you Carmella, you're a bit too skinny for me.'

She laughed and he laughed with her. She felt all of a sudden warm and secure and just a tiny little bit disappointed that she was not his type. That was for the best though, she told herself.

199. The police had not been wrong, as it happened. Darren Pyke had

returned to Lyme. In fact he had never left the district. And now he sat there, in the lion's mouth.

'How long do you expect me to sit here and not do anything?'

'For as long as I need you to.'

'Don't be stupid Darren. I'll be opening up in eight hours from now. The police are in and out of here all day and every day, I'm not going down for harbouring a murderer, come daybreak I'm walking out of here and raising the alarm.'

'As soon as you walk out of this room I'll torch the place and be out along the beach.'

And she knew he would do it.

'Okay, we'll just sit here until my staff arrive. They'll wonder where I am, come up to the flat and the outcome will be the same, oh, and one other thing, the police haven't been for the disc yet, the disc with the video of you breaking that guy's shoulder. They're pretty much bound to be here tomorrow, they're overdue.'

Darren considered Colleen Bradstock. Three years ago he had been in the room in which he now sat. He had felled a Chard boy for causing trouble in the pub. Colleen had given him coffee and told him she owed him one. The Chard boy never came back but there was always that fear on Colleen's part, a fear that, she had to be honest, was addressed partly by the knowledge that she could call upon Darren Pyke to help her.

'Anyway, you're not harbouring a murderer. I didn't murder anybody, unless that wanker that I done downstairs died. Did he?'

'Not as far as I know Darren. But everybody thinks you killed Katie.'

'Do you?'

'Frankly, yes.'

'Well I didn't, Carmella did it, I tried to stop her, told her I just wanted Katie scared off, but the stupid fucking bitch went and shot her anyway, right in the face. Now everybody's blaming me.'

There was a pause while he waited for Colleen to respond, but she did not. She just sat there and looked at him, with utter contempt. The gun was resting across his legs and she considered making a dive for it, then thought better of the idea. He would blow her away without a second thought and she knew it.

'You say the police haven't been for the disc yet, the disc that shows me battering the posh boy?'

'That's right, they'll be here soon though.'

'Give me the disc.'

'Why, what will you do with it? It's all backed up on the hard drive, they'll take my computer away and make as many discs as they want to.'

'Fine, I want the disc and the computer then.'

Darren did not know exactly what he was talking about, these terms were not really part of his everyday life and he did not like being out of his depth like this. He began to shake with fear and rage. And then he was up out of the chair and had the barrel of the gun right in between Colleen's breasts. She drew in a sharp breath.

'What are you going to do Darren, kill me as well?' Her voice went up a couple of octaves as she spoke. She thought she was surely about to die.

'Where is the fucking disc and the computer and anything else you've got taped of me?' His voice was low, deliberate and menacing.

She jerked her head in the direction of the silk screen and he moved towards it, backwards, not taking the gun off of her.

Reaching backwards he pulled the screen down to one side, glanced briefly around to see the laptop on the desk and wiring and paraphernalia plumbed into it. He turned and brought the butt of the shotgun down on the machine, as it bounced and shattered she was upon him. She managed to get hold of the gun with her hands and a hold on his neck with her teeth. She forced out a muffled scream, more at the terrible knowledge of what she had now done and the chance she had taken. Darren arched backwards and tried to get the gun out of her hands, but her strength was awesome through terror and she hung on. She pulled the gun slowly upwards so that it was across his throat, her teeth working on his neck, blood flowing in and then out of her mouth. She realised that she would need to kill him to survive. She also found the strength to wonder if the gun was loaded or not. She managed to crook one of her arms around the barrel of the weapon and work her hand to the back of his neck. She believed the hold was called a half nelson. Her right heel was in his groin and her left foot still on the floor, but not for long. After two or three seconds of this ridiculous nonsense he bent forward and made for the window – her head first. Far from slackening her grip – other than on reality – she tightened it and used the lapse in his concentration to get her other arm around the gun and around the back of his neck. Full Nelson. One of his hands was now pulling her hair out, the other flailing around trying to get purchase, but the window was drawing closer and she bit in hard on his neck, closed her eyes and waited for her head to hit glass. But of course it didn't because his would have had to go through as well. He wheeled around and tried to use the wall instead. It was the silence that struck her, and the apparent slowness of it all. She could not cry out or scream because her mouth was fully occupied trying to find his jugular, he kept quiet not because he feared raising the alarm, but because he could not believe that an unarmed middle aged woman was somehow not proving as easy as he thought. He could not comprehend it. All his strength now went into getting the gun from inside the crooks of her arms, but he could not budge it. And he was losing strength! He was losing his will to fight, he felt very tired and his knees started to give. With one last big effort he hurled himself backwards at the wall. The impact dislodged Colleen's teeth from his neck – and nearly from her own mouth – her head snapped back and hit the exposed bricks with a sickening thud and she went suddenly limp. Darren shook her off and put his hand to his mutilated neck, checking for the extent of blood flow. It was not too bad. She had not got to his main cable. He looked down at her and spat and swore. She would need to go to fucking hospital or he could end up on another murder charge; would one more make any difference? Jesus what a mess. So he picked her up and took her into the bathroom the stupid fucking cow, what had she hoped to get out of this. He ran a cold bath and brought her round in it. When her eyes flickered open she tried to get up and fight again. He put the flat of his hand on her breast bone and pushed her gently but firmly back.

'No more shit Colleen, you've 'ad a go, now be a good girl. Look what you've done to my neck.'

She looked up at the wound and he thought he could see a trace of a smirk make a brief visit to her face.

'Oh, funny is it? Well, try this for laughs.'

With that he ripped off the front of her blouse and bra with one action. Her breasts, quite fulsome for her age, nevertheless fell to their respective sides of her ribcage. Far from resisting she actually relaxed, her arms remaining by her sides.

'I'm freezing Darren.'

'You going to behave yourself?'

'Yes.'

He believed her, turned off the cold tap and lifted her out. She had become very weak. He carried her through to the lounge and laid her on the sofa. She wore a pair of cotton tracksuit bottoms and these came off easily, as did her knickers. He found a blanket and threw it over her. What an insane nightmare.

The gun had been discarded following her impact with the wall. He picked it up and examined it. Not damaged. He put it on the floor well out of her reach and sat on a hard chair between her and the door. It was time to wait. It was getting light and he had nowhere to go. She was in pain and needed treatment. His thoughts raced but a plan was never far from being hatched in Darren Pyke's mind.

He found a first aid box and put a large sticking plaster over his neck wound.

200. Mr. and Mrs. Pentreath prepared for their daughter's funeral like a pair of automatons. They were both living in a haze of sedation, hardly noticing the crowd of well-meaning idiots that surrounded them 24 hours a day. They did not notice that the old policeman had not paid them a follow-up visit; in any case his colleague, the Maxine girl, was there every one of the five days since their daughter's murder. At first they had been told that they could not bury Katie until after the lawyers for any defence firm had had the opportunity of conducting a post-mortem examination on the body. They had argued that they would have to wait months for that to happen; the suspect was no nearer to being arrested than he was on the first night of the hunt for him. Sherrell had contacted Bache on this reasonable point, who had in turn consulted Sunderland who had in turn spoken to the CPS. The Principal Crown Prosecutor had told them to go ahead and let the family bury the victim; the cause of death established beyond all reasonable doubt, unless photographs, lead pellets and a blood soaked Ford Fiesta had all been mocked up in some bizarre conspiracy to fit up Darren Pyke with murder. So the funeral was to go ahead.

Sally Pentreath contacted Irana Murdoch, Simon's mother, to tell of the arrangements and to ask how Simon was.

'Oh Sally, so good of you to call, you must be living a nightmare, I'm so sorry. I feel guilty that Simon is still alive....'

'Well don't Irana, we'll all be dead soon and I'll be reunited with my daughter for ever and ever, so don't fret my dear. The funeral's on Saturday and we'd love to see you there with Simon if he's well enough, it's going to be a great celebration. The weather will be lovely and we'll go into town afterwards and have a drink in the Seagull Inn because that's where Katie liked going, or so we've heard, they never tell us anything these kids do they, think they know best don't they, we're just silly old sods aren't we, Jesus Christ...' and she began to sob and bawl down the phone at Irana Murdoch who was ashen and silent at the other end of the line. The call was terminated when Mr. Pyle, the vicar from Lyme, put his finger on the button and gently took the handset from Sally.

201. At 5.20 that morning the ambulance from Exeter hospital pulled up outside the Seagull Inn. Darren answered the door and led the paramedics upstairs to Colleen's flat where she sat in a clean, dry tracksuit looking pale and nervous. The crew established that she'd had a fall and had been unconscious for over twenty minutes. Darren had made the call in a tremulous and panicky voice. They were taking no chances and after a few checks of her pulse and BP, loaded her onto a stretcher.

'May he come with me? He's my son.'

'Of course love.' And Darren Pyke was on his way to the city of Exeter. The loaded shotgun was under Colleen's bed.

202. Simon Murdoch got dressed slowly. It was 5.30am and the tired night staff was busy making plans for the shift change. He had not been formally discharged from Exeter hospital but he had decided to go anyway. If making a decision was what you could call the naked instinct-driven emotions he was now going through. He had only one recurring thought. He had to get to the funeral; he had to make it to say something, to try to make amends.

He stood up, fully dressed, feeling weak. The cannula in the back of his left hand had been taken out the previous night, so he had nothing from which to unplug himself. He walked out of the room and saw a sign for

A&E, a way out, he guessed, and he guessed right. Through a couple of automatic swing doors and the hospital stench receded as fresh air mixed with it. A & E was a busy place, he could see the door, and out he walked. Looked about him in the bright sunlight his attention was drawn to an ambulance that had just pulled in. The paramedics opened the rear doors and what he then saw beggared belief. He turned away and kept walking. Should he go back? No, he wasn't fit enough, scared even. And he may have been mistaken, but he knew he had not.

203. Sprake sat at his big desk and considered all the options, their permutations, the outcome risks, the politics and the fallout. This was his forte. This was his world - the world of the senior police officer. The blame game. Apportionment, divisibility, hierarchical separation, causal immunity, locus standi. He smiled as he mentally thumbed through the stack of terminology at his disposal, the buzzwords and the language of his business. The morning-after business. But the smile was not without humour. Sprake could always see it coming, he could always predict who was going to turn what way when the shit was about to hit the fan. Little groups would form, little alignments, loyalties would suddenly develop. Him? He had his own loyalty. His was to his wife and disabled son. The rest could go and fuck themselves. Jonathan had been born twelve years earlier with cystic fibrosis. That was when Sprake had been a sergeant. He had been a good, hard-working cop with little time for senior management. Then everything had changed. Within 5 years he was a superintendent, went to the Met as a commissioner's staff officer under the corruption obsessed Paul Condon, transferred to Cleveland to clear up there after the Ray Mallon period, then back down to sunny Dorset as one of Joanne Bache's Assistant Chief Constables. Jonathan was now at a West Country day centre where he could get his treatment and education under one roof, Mrs. Sprake did work for the CF charities and there was enough money coming in to make life good. Or as good as it could be with the spectre of premature death hanging over the family 24/7. CF is manageable but still terminal. Life expectancy was on the up but was still short. Jonathan could live into his thirties, but probably

would not. So ACC Sprake lived for every day and didn't worry about others too much. Whatever happened to incompetent or corrupt coppers was deserved by them. He did not deserve his hell.

A knock on his door disturbed his darkness and brought him back into the light.

'Sir,' it was his secretary Marjorie, 'Mr. Sherrell is here to see you.'

Sprake could not remember inviting the DCI and there was nothing in the diary. He did not like this one bit. He knew Sherrell was OIC on the Lyme shooting but he had his own chain of command up to the Chief. As head of the Department of Professional Standards Sprake did not expect to be in any loop other than his own. When he got involved it always had to be from the Chief, never from below him by officers he may have to investigate. But something told him he would have to see Sherrell, even if in doing so he caused any discipline or corruption enquiry to be dealt with by an outside force.

'Show him in.'

Sherrell entered looking exhausted.

'Sit down Rob, what can you do for me?'

Sherrell smiled and knew what Sprake meant. He was surprisingly ready for this.

'I can inform you sir that the Pentreath murder will be solved more quickly and with a better chance of a murder conviction if your department was to show its hand and tell us what is to happen to the two suspended officers.'

'One suspended officer Rob, the girl is just on a bit of compassionate leave, that's all.'

'My troops are afraid to get stuck in, terrified to get their hands dirty because they know that your lot are watching us like hawks.'

Sprake was keenly aware that Sherrell was getting close to insubordination here, but decided to ignore it, bollocking him for being rude would take this nowhere. And he had a point. You get two cops effectively suspended because of a murder or its investigation and the rest are on tenterhooks because they know or at least assume that they're under the microscope.

'We're not watching you Superintendent, we're doing our job which is to protect the public from incompetent and corrupt police behaviour, do you have difficulty in understanding that?'

'No sir.'

'Good. Right. But I do hear what you say and I will speak to one of my superintendents and we'll issue a memorandum. In the meantime assure your troops that they will suffer no detriment or intrusion, unless of course they start slacking on the pretext of having to be cautious because we're watching them. Tell them we're always watching them, so nothing is any different from normal.'

Sherrell found it difficult not to show his contempt for this condescending stance. So he got up and walked out without a word. He did not slam the door but the manner of his departure left Sprake fuming.

204. Heather sat at her computer, a cup of steaming coffee at her side. She had just got back from a long run and had not yet showered. The steady rain had kept her fresh as she had powered her way round a punishing uphill downhill route and had increased her thinking focus tenfold. She had always been amazed by how running in the rain made her think more lucidly, more creatively.

She had decided to do some victim profiling. She had weeks ago begun research on Katie Pentreath, kidding herself and anyone else who may have expressed concern that her curiosity was purely professional. Katie was on Facebook and not particularly privately either. She did not keep her friends list confidential, this surprised Heather who had to remind herself that Katie had been until very recently an innocent undergraduate with no enemies, no issues and few worries. Heather's own Facebook page revealed nothing to those who had not been accepted by her as 'friends'. Katie's page had on it 127 friends and she was a member of fourteen groups, mostly about Brighton University and veterinary surgery. Her friends consisted of family members and fellow undergraduates. There was nobody on there from Lyme or even West Dorset.

Darren Pyke was unsurprisingly absent as he probably did not possess a computer.

Finding nothing of any real interest Heather started looking at Katie's friends, starting of course with Simon Murdoch. She had thought of telephoning the hospital but had then thought better of it. There was no point in taking the risk of having her call traced and then being accused of disobeying the order not to contact anyone involved in the enquiry. And Simon Murdoch was most certainly involved. She looked at his profile and found nothing but a middle class beery rugby player fond of high jinks and having a laugh. Shit, did he know yet? Was he out of hospital yet? How his life will have been ruined by this.

205. As Heather had these thoughts Simon Murdoch was sitting in a cab on his way from Exeter Hospital to Lyme Regis Police Station. His mother had filled him in on as much detail as she could bear to give. Katie had been murdered and the police were after the same man who had assaulted him with the iron bar at the pub. Katie had been shot with a shotgun. Her parents were sedated and the funeral was being planned to take place within a few days, a week at most.

Simon still could not grasp all of this. He still could not get his head round the fact that this was happening to him, and not someone else. That his beautiful girlfriend had been shot dead by a piece of shit who had barely 48 hours earlier put him in hospital. Why had that scumbag not been arrested then? Why had he not been locked up, then Katie would still be alive. Simon was not aware of the preceding opportunities that had presented themselves to take Darren Pyke out of the picture. He would find out about those in due course.

206. Stuart Townsend and a SOCO called Brian waited in the back yard of Crewkerne Police Station. It was to here that the burned out Transit was being delivered, there being no room at either Lyme or Bridport. It was well into September now and the nights were coming in. Away from the sea, Crewkerne was colder and damper and prone to fog. Stuart felt the dampness soak through his cotton shirt and he shivered. The low-loader carrying the corpse of the Transit backed into the yard and deposited its load as far into a corner as possible. Stuart signed something and the lorry driver drove off in his unburdened vehicle, leaving Stuart and SOCO Brian standing looking at the charred remains.

Brian silently donned rubber gloves and began setting up a lighting system around the exhibit so that he could take photographs as if in bright sunlight. Stuart also put on a pair of gloves and prepared himself to open the van. He started by trying each of the three door handles, two front and one rear – they were all jammed solid. It seemed that the heat of the fire had warped the locking systems. The fucking thing would have to be cut open he thought as he fished out his mobile to call Decker. Brian took loads of snaps, although not of the interior; not only were the doors jammed shut, the windows and windscreen were smoke blackened from the inside.

207. Reg Bull staggered out along the Cob. He was in possession of a right skinful and the sound of the waves was doing nothing to help alleviate the pressure from within his bladder. He relieved himself against the north wall of the harbour, unworried as to whether anyone would see him. He was a hollow husk of a man. Unable to speak to anyone, barely able to function. He was in no doubt that he had suffered a nervous breakdown but such self-diagnosis never generates any sympathy or understanding from others. His wife had regarded him contemptuously before accusing him of attention-seeking behaviour. And

she meant it.

So all he had been doing for the last few days was staggering around the town pissed out of his head. A suspended cop. Some of his cronies in the Goat had asked why he wasn't working on the murder squad and he had explained that he was on annual leave which he had been ordered to take, so much had accrued that if he did not he would lose it. Use or lose it he said they had told him. Use it or lose it he told his cronies. But they didn't believe him.

'That Reg there, the copper, he ain't harf drinkin' a deal ain't 'e?'

'Yer, must have a load of money is all I can say.'

'Yeh but, there's more to it 'an tha', oi fink he down in the dumps a bit me do, know what oi mean? Like he's a bit depressed. Is he still with his missus?'

'Don't know bruv, assume so, ain't eard nuffin, an' oi would 'ave cos moi sister in law lives opposite 'em.'

And this is the sort of theorising and conjecture that had sprung up around Reg Bull in only a few days of irregular behaviour; such was the pattern of Lyme life, or rather the patterns that interwove with each other so closely that variations could be detected with the speed and accuracy of a seismograph.

It was on the Saturday night following the murder that Reg got the pull. He was winding his way up Silver Street, having been in the Pilot and on his way to the Goat when the car pulled up alongside.

'Get in Reg for fuck's sake, you'll have a heart attack.' The old cop looked to his left to see Decker leaning across the passenger seat of his otherwise empty car and opening the door for him.

Reg hesitated, he was a bit pissed and feeling pretty scruffy. He did not really want to get into the car with Decker, not in his current state of drunkenness, confusion and probably rather poor personal hygiene. But he did anyway. He wanted to get to the Goat before closing time and it was 10.50 now.

'Thanks sarge,' as he slumped into the front passenger seat and fumble for the seat belt. Decker pulled the car back out into the sparse traffic.

'Goat is it?'

'Yes please sarge.'

'Mind if I join you for one, I'll buy?'

Reg did not like the sound of it one little bit,

'Okay sarge, and I'll buy you one back, if there's time.'

They walked into the pub with Decker leading the way. A band was playing and the noise and heat were overpowering.

'What do you want?'

'Youngs please.'

'No worries'

Once served Decker led Reg out onto the rear garden patio. The view was fantastic. A huge full moon illuminated Lyme Bay and Golden Cap. A stunning picture; unfortunately it was to be the backdrop to a rather unpleasant conversation.

208. Alex urged Carmella to walk in front of him. She was compliant. The relationship was perfectly symbiotic. They both needed each other very much. She found herself at ease with him, as if she'd known him a long time. He felt like he was onto something good.

'Stay close to the wall, keep your head low.' He told her this like he was some sort of instructor.

'I know what I'm doing you know, I'm not stupid.'

And he found himself being impressed with this spunky little lady. She certainly knew her craft and that in his world was called counter surveillance. Carmella knew how to remain invisible.

The pair moved slowly toward the motorway and he watched her from behind. He watched her look strangely around as they approached the motorway, as if she was trying to find something. Something that had gone missing.

'You lost something?'

Carmella thought about this question and the obvious answer was that yes, she had lost about everything, give or take. A gust of wind blew hair across her eyes and she blinked, another gust blew her hair into her mouth, as if to say think before you speak, or perhaps don't even speak at all. So she didn't.

'Oi, I'm talking to you Carmella, have you lost something?'

Why was he being so insistent?

She continued to hold her silence as she led – yes, led – him along the line of the fence between the field and the motorway. She looked down at the hard shoulder and saw the burn marks on the tarmac, but only just – you'd have to know they were there.

Alex stopped pressing her and decided just to follow, she seemed to have a plan and he was keen not to disturb it, this fit country girl was going to be of serious use to him, possibly a solution to all his problems, or at least the most pressing ones. He wondered if she had a phone.

209. Simon Murdoch turned up at Lyme police station and demanded to see the officer in charge of the murder enquiry.

'I'm a witness in the case and I have a statement to give,' he told the civvy on the front desk, who then made a call to the incident room and was told someone would be down presently.

Simon was shown into the waiting room and offered a cup of tea which he declined. He had a blinding headache and felt drained by the drugs and the strain and the shock. He felt like he had mutated into some sort of other being, certainly no longer human. That was something he would probably never bear to be again, not fully. He was unable to grasp that Katie was dead and, bizarrely, felt the need to see her corpse or at least some photographs of it. These terrible thoughts were interrupted when DC Langham walked into the room and introduced himself, offering a hand which Simon ignored.

'How can I help you?' asked the polite and professional officer.

Simon sighed, 'I am Simon Murdoch, I was assaulted by your murder suspect less than two days before he killed my girlfriend. I have been in hospital and too unwell to give a statement until now. I very much need to become involved.'

Langham asked Simon to sit down, which he did, before leaving the room to consult with Decker. Following that Simon was taken into the relatively comfortable office of DI Packington – thankfully free from the smell of booze for once – and made to feel very important, which he potentially was. Langham got a big bunch of statement forms and prepared himself for a long stint with his fountain pen. Simon mellowed a little, accepted coffee and one of the indexing clerks made a big pot of the stuff. A tin of biscuits appeared also.

210. Heather surfed the net aimlessly. Between snacks and runs and frenzied workouts with her heavy dumbbells she typed and clicked as if something important depended upon it. She thought of Caroline Sherry. She thought of all the people she knew in the Met, all the people she knew in London, she became tired and slow and then started to think more laterally. She opened a bottle of Shiraz and relaxed slightly. Why

had she become a lightning conductor so quickly? She asked herself. Because it was all her fault perhaps? No. She had not killed Katie Pentreath, she had not fired the shot. Was the murder so obviously a consequence of her negligence? No, in fact the causality was not strong at all. Why were they excluding her like this? The evidence against her could not be that strong otherwise they would have suspended her by now, arrested her or even charged her. But no, just this vague 'stay at home' bollocks, what was that all about? Don Pryce was trying to be supportive but she wanted none of that. Although she was now satisfied that his intentions were honourable with regard to her mother, she still did not want to involve him – he was not her father and she was having none of any course of action that would allow him to assume any semblance of that role.

And she did not trust Norman Hogg one little bit. Just something about him, the stench of hidden agendas. The archetypal self-seeker. She had heard of this sort of fed rep when she was in the Met. Made a big deal about what they were doing for the troops and then played golf with the DPS management. Bad bastards they were. Heather was politically astute by nature and eight years in the country's biggest and busiest force had sharpened her further. She sat before her screen and smirked when she thought of Hogg's embarrassment at the sight of her belly and bush. She had actually enjoyed making the old twat blush and she hoped that he knew it. The train of thought started her on the surfing subject of the police federation. She went onto each of the 43 branch websites, looking for published advice on the suspension of cops, their rights and obligations and those of the suspending force. She was actually looking for the right to be suspended but unsurprisingly the topic was not covered. Finally she went onto the central federation site, the one posted by the fed HQ in Leatherhead, Surrey. Her perusal of the branch sites had informed her that all applications for legal advice were processed by the joint central committee claims office which would decide whether a case was deserving of expenditure on legal services and then, if so, allocate the case to one of a number of solicitors on a list of approved firms. She started to form a plan. She would apply for legal advice at the expense of the federation – she had paid her subs without default and without pause during her transfer to Dorset – on the matter of her current situation. Was there such a thing as 'just staying at home and not contacting anyone'? For all she knew there could have been. She needed advice.

She learned however from her research that in order to get funding from the central claims office in Leatherhead she had to apply through her branch board official, and who was that? Fucking Norman Hogg. She had his mobile and rang him anyway. It would be interesting to hear his response. She wouldn't invite him over in case he got the wrong idea.

'Norman? Hi, its Heather Boyle, how are you?'

Norman was surprised by two things, a) to hear from this recalcitrant girl, b) to hear her talking like a normal human being.

'Hello Heather, I'm fine thanks.'

'First of all I'm sorry about last night, I was a bit pissed and….'

'No worries Heather, you're obviously under a lot of stress. What can I do for you?'

'I would like to apply for legal advice from a specialist solicitor, one of those ones retained by the federation. I want the federation to pay for it Norman, I think I qualify, am I right?'

Norman had not expected this and did not welcome it. Of course the girl qualified but this was bad news for him. It meant that he actually might have to do some work and he would have to possibly make waves, which he did not want to do.

'I'll have to look into it Heather, but why not wait until if and when you are served with discipline proceedings or even God forbid criminal papers, then we'll know what we are asking for advice about. If we shoot from the hip now all that'll happen is that Leatherhead will knock it back and say apply again later on, I promise you.'

'No Norman, I want to get ahead of the game. I want to know what rights

I have regarding being told what is happening to me. I want to be told whether or not I'm being investigated, and if so what for. If I am not then why am I effectively suspended and being kept incommunicado, that's the sort of advice I want Norman. Do you understand where I'm coming from?'

Norman understood only too well and knew that this was the beginning of a nightmare for him. A member obsessed. Cops are legally formatted and litigious by definition and most are reasonably bright. When they get in a corner they become preoccupied with their own case and can give fed reps nervous breakdowns. Norman had seen this happen twice in Dorset over the last ten years. Reps getting burned out by a single member.

'Yeah okay Heather, I'll pop over later with the forms and we'll fill them in together, what time's best for you?'

They agreed a slot and Heather sat back feeling a little better. She had taken some sort of control of the situation.

211. Carmella and Alex found themselves on a public bridle path and followed it down to the small village of Balderton. Alex had decided to leave his car where it was; he was very deeply under cover without the necessary authorisation and any evidential connection with this girl would risk him being seen as assisting an offender – he needed to be able to cut loose and disappear from her within seconds if necessary.

They noted that there was a bus service to Cardiff but they would have to get tidied up first. Alex produced some money and they wandered into the solitary convenience store, bought pre-packed sandwiches, Coke, toothpaste, soap, toothbrushes, and some kitchen roll. It was 7.30 in the morning. As they came out of the shop a police car pulled around the corner, the driver gave them a double take and slowed quite suddenly. The couple did a sharp turn into the alleyway behind the shop which led to a row of garages. They both had big but separate reasons to avoid the police.

PC Malcolm Pritchard had not long been out on patrol on his south Wales village run. He had a big area to cover but was aware of the burned out transit having been found on the motorway nearby and what it had been involved in. The bulletins had gone out; Carmella Everett and Darren Pyke, armed and dangerous, Dorset's very own Bonnie and Clyde, killers, will kill again. The whole of south Wales was alive with it. And PC Pritchard had just seen them. It had to be them. The officer got out of his car and stood in the store doorway whilst engaging his radio.

'Urgent assistance requested to locate two suspects in Balderton. Match description of Dorset murderers, decamped behind Mace store in Balderton when they saw me, we need to surround the village.' This transmission was picked up in Cardiff and a surge of police activity ensued.

Alex and Carmella stumbled into one of the garages, through it and into someone's back garden and through the unlocked back door into the house. It was as if they had jumped onto a higher plateau of awareness and athleticism. The adrenalin surged. Their brains were joined. The occupant of the house, or one of them, was just coming down the stairs.

'He's still in bed, you'll 'ave to fuckin' wait outside, 'an stop comin' through the back door like that, I'm sick of you lot, treating this house as a fuckin' 'otel see, me as a skivvy see, go on with the pair of you, out the front an' come back later, ring 'im on 'is mobile, tha's what I pay 'is bill for, to keep you's lot from marchin' in an' out like this all the time.'

The two trespassers were lost for words for a second but Alex got into rhythm pretty quick.

'Sorry missus, won't 'appen again,' and reached up for the handle of the front door, momentarily shielding Carmella who with a stroke of genius reached down into a pot on the side table and extracted a bunch of keys. The two made their quick exit. Once outside Carmella shoved the stolen keys into Jack's hand. He sorted through them and found one with the Volkswagen emblem, looked up and around and found a Volkswagen Golf GTI. He pressed the unlock button on the key and the car responded with a double horn bip and a flash of its indicators.

212. 'It's a funny old thing isn't it Reg.'

'What's that Sarge?'

'Call me Tom, life, a funny old thing. You do your best and fuck all happens and then you stop trying and it all goes fine, don't you think?'

'No.'

Decker expected the surly response. He was after all talking to a man on the edge of despair.

'What, 'no' you don't think or 'no' you don't agree with me?'

'Both.'

Decker regarded the old man with slightly elevated respect.

'It's probably occurred to you – or maybe it hasn't – that I'm joining you for a drink for a reason. I want to know your opinions about Heather Boyle, your honest opinions. And before you think I'm going to try to assure you that my intentions are honourable, or compassionate or some such shit, I give you the refreshing assurance that they're not. I'm thinking of canning her. Now, can you think about that Reg?'

This did make Reg Bull think and he turned from the view of the bay to regard the young detective sergeant with a mixture of dismay and disgust. Possibly a bit of fear as well.

'What do you want to can her for? What's she done to you?'

'It's all about survival Reg. Somebody has to take the shit for this, and it's not going to be me or my staff, or even the DI, do you get my meaning?'

Reg was now agog.

'And I don't really want it to be you either Reg, but that's a matter for your good self.'

Reg became suddenly angry.

He rose from his seat, 'Sarge, you go and do what you have to do, you want my opinion and I'll give it to you – I think you are a fucking shitbag.'

And with that Reg stumbled back into the pub building, knocking a chair over in the process, and then out of the front door into the street. Decker sat back, smiled, and continued to admire the moonlit bay.

213. Sherrell was in the Chief's office, at her behest.

'How's it going Bob?'

A rhetorical question, he knew, but he would answer truthfully,

'Not bad Ma'am, not good.'

'Quite. Unfortunately we have to concentrate on the 'not good' part.'

'I know Ma'am, I know.'

Sherrell was slumped in a chair at the coffee table in Joanne Bache's office at which she had joined him, having left her desk as he'd entered the room. Presently a secretary brought in coffee and biscuits, which Sherrell found very handy indeed, such was his energy and blood sugar levels. He snatched up a bourbon and quickly took a bite.

'Do start, won't you.'

He giggled and she joined him. Sherrell found the chief to be very attractive and he felt most at ease in her company.

'It's going nowhere ma'am.'

'Mmmm. I'd gathered. Anything I can do?'

'Not really ma'am, we've just got to wait until the suspects surface, which they will, I'm sure of that, but it could be months.'

'Years even?'

'No. Not unless they get out of the country. They'll come to light, especially if they've stuck together, which I think they will have.'

'Mmmm, yes, I read your suspect profiles, those two'll need each other like brother and sister. They're probably holed up in a barn somewhere. Can't see them melting into city life.'

'Quite ma'am, quite.'

They stopped talking for a few seconds, munching and sipping.

'It's not the suspects I'm worried about Bob, they'll probably be getting arrested for shoplifting as we speak, they'll be too thick to carry off any disguise or identity trick and they'll be in Lyme custody before you know it. What I'm worried about is why this happened in the first place?' She paused to take a gulp.

Sherrell got in quick.

'Yes I know ma'am, I thought that was what I was here to talk about.'

The chief fixed Sherrell with a steely stare.

'You're here to talk about the case Chief Inspector, how we approach the tricky bits is up to me. I think it both tactless and tasteless to get rudely to the point sometimes. Every story needs an introduction. Very well, let's cut to the chase, as they say - how come Katie Pentreath got murdered by this Pyke boy?'

'Because he wasn't in custody when he should have been ma'am. Because we were fucking about chasing chicken rustlers for some rich cow when we should have been locking up Darren Pyke for at least two serious assaults, criminal damage and cruelty to animals.'

'And wasn't this Darren Pyke and his brothers top drug dealers in the county?'

'Rumour….'

'Rumour? Rumour has nothing to do with it. In the police we call it intelligence and intelligence must be acted upon. Why in this case was the intelligence not acted upon? Why was Pyke not arrested for these assaults and the list of other offences you seem to be able to catalogue?'

Sherrell could not make up his mind if the chief was serious or just testing him. He decided on the latter; the chief constable would not engage in a discipline interview alone, untaped and in her own office. In fact she would not conduct a discipline interview in any event; she had others to do that. Sherrell remained silent and nodded his head slowly.

The chief got to her feet and walked across to the window. She was not in uniform and her skirt was tight and above the knee. Her form, rump and legs arrested his attention and he felt vulnerable because of that and the questions he was being asked.

She turned quickly and nearly caught him staring at her arse.

'The shit will really hit the fan when then these two low-life are arrested and the prosecution case is prepared. We'll have to get an order warning the press to lay off lest they ruin the trial, or any chance of a fair one, by publishing prejudicial shit, but when the trial starts it'll be open house. When the facts become known we're fucking dead Rob, you, me the whole force. Laughing stocks. Do you know what I'm saying Rob?'

His mouth was open, and not because of the physical picture she presented. She was more or less telling him that Darren Pyke and Carmella Everett would be much more use to Dorset constabulary free, at large and unarrested. That way the whole thing might just fizzle out. No trial meant very little press coverage, at least for a good passage of time anyway and, let's face it, both parties to this conversation had barely four years to serve before retirement.

'Yes chief, I think I know what you're saying, although I must say I'm shocked. It's like you don't want a murderer to be brought to justice because of the bad publicity a trial would bring.'

Sherrell thought of adding something about career protection but thought better of it. He had probably gone too far as it was.

'If you have to put it that way then yes, I'm trying to protect our beleaguered force from political death. Meltdown.'

'So what do you want me to do? Wind down the murder investigation?'

The chief shook her head.

'No, not at all. Keep it running. But just remember that we do not have the resources to operate a dragnet style operation for these two runaways. Get all your evidence together, package it up so that it's trial ready for when they're captured. Then just issue periodical bulletins reminding every force in the country that these two are still wanted, armed and dangerous. With a bit of luck they'll starve to death, commit suicide or skip the country.' She sat down again, this time her skirt rode a good way up and Sherrell had to catch his breath.

Sensing the meeting should really end Sherrell said,

'Will that be all ma'am?' he was not prepared to assure the chief that her wish was his command and this omission miffed her.

'Well, yes Rob, I suppose so.' She then paused and looked him in the eye for a full two seconds, making sure her unsaid disappointment made its mark. She then got up again and walked across the room to her desk. The skirt and its contents looking all of a sudden less attractive to the DCI.

214. Carmella had rarely been out of the county of Dorset in her entire life, so the map from the glove compartment of the Golf meant nothing to her. Her recent eye-bulging trip up the M5 and across the Severn Bridge had taught her little. She kept turning the pages whilst Alex drove. He was careful, stayed below seventy and headed onto the M4 and in the direction of London.

The two had spoken very little since stealing the car. They could hear sirens and a couple of South Wales Police cars zoomed past in the opposite direction on their way to Balderton. The car had probably not been missed yet. They would have at least half an hour judged Alex.

'Where we goin'?' It was a reasonable question from Carmella.

'Not sure, smoke I think, we need to get where more people are, suppose we could go to Brummy, you know anyone there?'

'I don't fuckin' know anyone anywhere mate.'

Carmella fiddled for the car heater, she shivered in her thin, grungy clothing, her hair was tied back, greasy and a sore was appearing on her lip. She rubbed the sleep in her eyes and would have felt grubby, depressed and anxious if she knew how to. She glanced across at her companion; she did not dislike him but wished it was Darren at the wheel. But it wasn't, so this soldier would have to do. She bit her lip.

'We're going to go to London, I've decided, we need to get there asap before this car gets spotted, we need to get into heavy traffic and that won't be a problem as we get further east of here.'

Carmella thought he sounded just like the soldiers on her PlayStation games, just without the yank accent.

She tried to call Darren again, dead line.

215. Heather sat and waited for Norman Hogg to arrive with the funding application forms. She smirked as she thought of how she might dress, or not, for the occasion. She decided to keep it decent lest she antagonise

the old prude. She wondered if he knew. She wondered where Alex was, what he had been saying to his management. She wondered about Caroline and could not help feeling that she had a part to play in all this, if not now sometime in the future.

A knock on the door brought her back into the real world of the present.

'Hi Norman, come in.' She noted that he was empty handed. She supposed she had expected a briefcase or folder or something. He wore civilian clothes and a worried, preoccupied expression. Heather prepared herself for an argument.

'Tea? Coffee?'

'No thanks.'

'Okay, sit down, let's get started then.'

She repositioned a chair at the kitchen table and motioned Norman towards her, she herself taking a chair opposite.

'Do we need pen and paper?' She said, pointedly, as she looked at his hands and face in that order.

'Heather, I've got all the forms and paper and pens in the car. But first I think we need to talk about this.'

Here we go, she thought.

'Go on,' she said.

'I'll come straight to the point....'

'Do.'

'If you, we, put in a claim now for legal advice we risk stirring up a nest of wasps. DPS'll get to know about it and they'll get ahead of the game, probably by arresting and putting you on police bail pending further enquiries, or at least serving you with discipline papers. We'll wake a sleeping giant if we put a claim in now asking why you're not suspended, asking for clarity on your position. They'll then provide clarity soon enough. Do you see what I mean Heather?'

'Of course I see what you mean Norman, but so what, let them serve me, or arrest me, or charge me, I've done nothing wrong. I want to clear my name. As it stands I'm festering at the bottom of a pit of suspicion, dirty rumour and fucking innuendo. It's horrible, it's driving me mad Norman.'

'I know, I know love, but I think we should....'

'We? We? We should what? Just let them keep me on ice so that when the blame game starts they've got me all nice and oven-ready? You must know what they're up to Norman. I want to get in there first and demand to be put back to work. If they find a reason not to then at least I can start defending my position before memories begin to fail.'

'I'm not sure what you mean, I'm losing you.'

'Bollocks Norman, you know exactly what I mean. Go out to your car and get the forms. I want to make a claim to the federation. I pay my subs and it's my right.'

'And it's my right, indeed my responsibility, not to allow you to make a claim if it is not in the best interests of the membership as a whole. Remember that. I have to sign the claim form before it goes to Leatherhead; it is not just your claim, it is the claim of the Dorset police federation.'

She was taken aback by this stance. He was supposed to be her rep for God's sake, and he was purporting to take some sort of big picture approach. What the fuck was he up to?

'What the fuck are you up to Norman?'

She fixed him with an accusing stare.

'Don't talk to me like that Heather, I haven't come here to be sworn at.'

With that he was out of his seat and moving towards the door.

'That's it, go on, fuck off Norman. There you are, I've sworn at you again, gives you even more of an excuse not to represent me eh? Conflict between us now eh Norman?'

He was out of the door and she slammed it behind him so hard that the window panes shook. Then she slumped with her back against the door and slid to the floor and wept. Back to square zero. She thought of involving Don Pryce – he had offered to help, but no, it wouldn't work, too many skeletons in the cupboard for him to discover. He probably wouldn't tell her mum but she couldn't be sure. No, she was going to have to think of some other route.

216. Reg tapped out Heather's number on the phone box keypad. He wasn't too old or too stupid to know that calls were probably being monitored, or certainly come the shit hitting the fan call records would be obtained from the mobile phone companies. He was under strict orders not to contact Heather Boyle and as he was on bail it was a strict liability discipline offence for her to have any contact with him.

'Hello.'

She sounded hollow, flat.

'Heather it's me, Reg.'

'Oh, hello Reg.' Slightly less flat.

'Heather we'll keep this quick. Just watch your back, they're going to try to pin this on you....'

'Oh, I know that Reg and I reckon so does your mate Norman Hogg, he's refusing to help me, says he has to think of the whole force, all the other federation members, that it's not just about me. Says I should....'

'What? You've been to see him?'

'He came to see me when I asked if I could claim for the cost of legal advice, he won't help me with the claim the bastard, I reckon he just wants to keep his hands clean Reg, know what I mean?'

'Oh, I know what you mean alright my love. Listen, I may have an idea, I was up at Leatherhead a few weeks ago and met some people there. It may be that we can bypass Norman and the Dorset fed and go straight to the national office for help. Leave it to me and I'll get back to you.'

'Careful Reg.'

'You too Hev.' And they both hung up together, both feeling a bit better.

217. It was 08:40 and the M4 traffic was a snarling, heaving mess. The Golf was invisible, the motorway cops preoccupied with trying to keep things flowing and London town beckoned. Carmella had never been to London in her life and she was scared. The density of the traffic scared her. She could not believe that all this was only a couple or three hours away from her home. She wondered if she would ever see home again. But films had shown her what the inside of prison was like, all those violent lesbians, shit food and no greenery, no music, no.... Darren. She glanced across at her new mate Jack. She wondered about him. He had plenty money at least and he had not harmed her yet, apart from when he had first found her. He seemed alright. No doubt he would want to fuck her soon, she thought. She worried about this, what was he going to do? As it happened, she had nothing to worry about.

The M4 traffic crawled now. She felt safe yet frightened.

She thought about Darren. She'd given up trying to call him. She thought about why this bloke Jack felt safer with her by his side. Suppose he was being hunted as a loner. But she wasn't. Maybe being with him made things worse for her. She wasn't sure. She wasn't sure about anything anymore. She fell asleep with her feet on the dashboard and her knees pulled up under her chin.

218. Josh Pyke and Emmett Everett had watched in silence as the police team had searched the Everett house and outbuildings and with some trepidation as the search team and dogs had eyed the silage pit before walking away from it with upturned noses. They had given Carmella's room a real turning over, but had found nothing they wouldn't find in any 23 year old girl's room. No drugs, no knives, no guns, no nothing; well, not quite. One young officer, a dog handler from Dorchester with certain or rather uncertain and certainly uncatalogued shortcomings, decided he would snaffle a pair of Carmella's soiled knickers. He thought the supervising sergeant had spotted him taking these from the pile of unwashed stuff on the bed so he feigned to sweep up a few other items to create a smoke screen. One of these – and he congratulated himself on his subterfuge – was a pestle and mortar that had been on Carmella's bedside table.

'What are you doing Sharkey?' enquired the taciturn sergeant, 'I'm going to send some stuff to the lab sarge, pestle and mortars are used to mix drugs.'

'And what about the knickers?'

'Sexual activity sarge, this girl may have been, you know, at it with the main suspect, we have to prove that....'

By this time the sergeant was walking away shaking his head. True enough the lad was keen and had recently been on a forensics course, but fucking hell.

Sharkey was pissed off – he would have to submit the knickers to the lab now; he'd had other plans.

219. That night Josh had gone into the Ship and had just sat there, waiting. He had on him three mobile phones, he rarely carried less. Like all conscientious drug dealers Josh went through unregistered mobile phones like they were going out of fashion. He was always buying new ones whenever on a visit to Chard or Bristol or Taunton, always buying

sim cards and swapping them about randomly. He did this having learned that not only could a phone be used as a tracking device, even when switched off, but also changing sim cards did not guarantee privacy and calls could be traced to the actual physical phone regardless of the sim card being used. Consequently nobody really had a number for Josh Pyke, so he could never really expect a call from anyone other than if that person was in current dealings. Josh's brother Darren was not in that category and this was turning out to be a big disadvantage. So Josh just sat there. He'd half expected to be whizzed in by the old bill and still did. Failing that they must be watching him he concluded and sat with his back to the wall, sipping and thinking and hoping. He had suspended all professional activity and was just waiting for a chance to be on hand to help his brother. Quite how, he was not sure. It really bothered him that Darren had killed the girl and he tried to convince himself that Carmella must have done it. But no, Darren was the man. Darren had done it and there was no good in kidding himself. As regards Darren's sloppiness with phones, Josh needn't have worried.

220. Simon Murdoch finished making his statement to the police at Lyme. It was not a particularly long account of him being felled in the Seagull Inn by a psychopath. He had decided not to mention his sighting of the perpetrator and a certain lady at Exeter hospital.

What had taken a bit longer, and had strangely interested the police officer DC Langham, was his account of his relationship with the murder victim. Hardly a rip roaring love affair, the officer had commented. And Simon had had to agree that yes, Katie was not perhaps as keen as he had been. Simon left the police station alone, having declined offers of assistance. He got a cab to Axminster and from there a train to London.

The process had taken about an hour. Langham had not learned much but had inadvertently taught Murdoch quite a bit, including the fact that Darren Pyke was a very well-known thug in the area and was quite capable of intimidating witnesses, including publicans, either personally or by way of his brothers' loyalty and equal propensity to violence.

221. It was dark on the seventh day of the murder enquiry when the forensic search team turned up at Bridport police station. The backyard was illuminated by arc lights brought in specially and the team were dressed in white paper overalls, cutting ghostly figures in the mist and garish white light. The back doors of the burned out transit were cut open in a trice and heavy torches were shone into the interior. Sherrell was there, as was Stuart Townsend and a couple of PCs ready with exhibits bags. The rear of the van was empty save for the charred remains of a few tools and the skeleton of a sprung mattress. The front of the wreck yielded little more; some exploded aerosol cans and a strange lump of aluminium casing that appeared to have been crudely wedged under the glove compartment. This was put into an exhibits bag without comment, but Sherrell saw it and frowned. It was strangely familiar to him.

'Give me a look at that,' he said, reaching out to take hold of the transparent polythene bag in which the object was now contained. He held it up to the light and realised with a slight rush of tired adrenaline what it was. His exhausted mind was unable however to grip the significance of the find.

'Right, I want this to be given the utmost priority. Get it to the technical support team in Dorchester first thing in the morning and have the DS in charge there ring me at 9am.'

'Yes sir,' replied the officer who took back the bag and placed it in a box container which he then sealed in Sherrell's presence.

222. It was Heather's turn the use a call box, having come upon the idea following her call from Reg. She tapped in Alex Miller's number. It rang for about thirty seconds. Then she thought her call had been answered but the line then immediately went dead. She tried again and got an automated reply to the effect that the mobile was switched off and that she should try later. What was he up to? Where the fuck was he? Was he okay? Her mind reeled and she thought of the tracker in the van.

Alex pulled off the M4 and onto a slip road before the junction with the M25. He could not risk taking the car any farther. Once within the compass of London's orbital motorway police vigilance intensified, especially out west where they were, near Heathrow airport. They found a village called Bagshot and dumped the car about half a mile from the railway station to which they then set off on foot. Carmella was exhausted and looked terrible. Alex was equally scruffy but was alert and focussed.

'Where are we going Jack?' mumbled the girl.

'We're going into London, don't worry, we'll be safe there, I have friends.'

Carmella had never been to London before, but she may as well have been on her way to certain death for all she had the energy to care. They boarded a packed train, 'Jack' having purchased two single tickets from one of the machines on the busy platform. He felt safe now. They had finally disappeared from sight. He could not believe what he had just pulled off.

223. Heather took a deep breath and tapped the number of the Police Federation HQ as displayed on the website in front of her. The phone was answered by the usual robot and she selected the third option for legal services.

'Legal services, can I help you?' The response was polite but a bit terse, the voice of bureaucracy.

'Er hello, I want to speak to someone about, er, being suspended, you see I'm sort of suspended but they won't tell me and I need funding for a lawyer to explain to me my rights.'

'Which force are you with?'

'Dorset.'

'You'll need to get one of your force fed reps to complete a form C2 and send it up to us....'

'No, I've already tried that, my fed rep is refusing to do it and....'

'Well I'm afraid we can't assist then, the rules are quite clear....'

'Oh fuck the rules, I need help, I desperately need help, I've been paying my subs for eight years and now I need the federation to help me and....'

'Okay, what I'll do is pass you to our manager Mr. Fraser, hold the line please.'

A few seconds later a man with a strong Scottish accent came on.

'Hello, Dan Fraser, can I help you?'

'Oh, hello yes, I was just telling your colleague that I'm desperate to speak to a lawyer about my current predicament.'

'Tell me more love. I'm all ears.'

She could barely believe this and was not sure how to take it; was it genuine or was it sarcasm? But she spilled her guts to this man Fraser and he listened without interruption.

'Have you been given anything on paper Heather?'

'Not a thing Mr. Fraser.'

'Call me Dan, have you been interviewed by any senior officer, either formally or otherwise?'

'No, unless you call being told to stay at home by the DI an interview.'

'Okay, if your rep won't help you what I need from you is a letter, an email will do, with all of this on and I'll get back to you in due course, okay?'

'How long is due course?'

'That depends, all I can say is that I'll do my best. I don't like the sound of your story one bit.'

'What do you mean, don't you believe me?'

'I most certainly do believe you Heather, your story is sadly a familiar one and we've got to nip this in the bud. I need that email ASAP, okay Heather?'

'You'll have it within half an hour.'

'Good girl.' And then he was gone.

She put the receiver down and stared blankly at the screen. What did he mean 'sadly familiar'? She was relieved and scared at the same time. This guy seemed to know a lot about what was happening and seemed keen to help, but could he be trusted?

She got to work and within the half hour had something that bore a close and passable resemblance to a claim against what was effectively her legal insurance policy. That she could not trust Fraser was an invalid concern. Having received her email he set immediately about instructing a solicitor who he knew would deliver the goods.

224. 'Why isn't she suspended Joanne? I mean properly, officially suspended. We need to be geared up as soon as possible. If she's not suspended we are failing to put her on notice, failing in our legal duty.'

The Chief blushed a little, thankful that this conversation was by telephone. And she did not like the first name bit from Sprake. Way too familiar.

'Yes James, I'm aware of that, but I've a chain of command to consider, I can't be seen to meddle or I won't be able to handle the case. If I'm seen to be involved in the process I won't be allowed to decide on the outcome.'

She was referring to the fact that if she made management decisions regarding the suspension and progress of a disciplinary action against one of her officers then a chief from another force would have to preside at the hearing. The last thing she needed. She hated this. Having spent the best part of her service fighting prejudice and unfairness she was now dispensing the same sort of shit. But she had the big picture to think of. A murderer on the loose arguably because of her senior officers' lack of prioritising skills. Fucking hell.

225. Ramage was on his second bottle of Chianti as he began his first article on what he had decided was to be known as the 'Triangle Murder'. He had often written scathing articles about rural low life in that part of the world, taking the piss out of what he saw as congenital underachievers content to work on farms for beer money, marry their first cousins and propagate their narrow views on life through an equally narrow gene pool. The agricultural in-bred he called them. He would never take on the middle class incomers who rendered these natives economically impotent by forcing up property prices. Oh no, that would be too difficult and, let's face it, newspaper sales and associated advertising revenue did not come from country yokels.

Katie Pentreath was brutally murdered by someone she knew well, by someone who for some reason hated the fact that she was alive. The only reason why that someone wanted her dead was borne out of envy. Envy of her prospects, her background and her beauty.

Ramage knew he was treading on thin ice here. If this shit was published it could seriously undermine criminal proceedings if this bastard was ever caught, the fact that he was not mentioning the suspect's name was neither here nor there. The implication was the same – he was addressing the problem of motive. A jury from his readership would not listen so naively to a defence counsel's submission that the accused had no reason to kill the girl. But Ramage did not care too much at this stage. For all his faults he was a writer, he needed to see his thoughts in print, even if they were never to be published. That way he could at least if necessary hone the final abridged and redacted product from the raw material.

226. And the next morning Sally Pentreath opened her door to Reg Bull. Her husband had gone into Axminster to see their solicitor about changing their wills – who would he leave everything to now? It had been a problem to which they had taken to addressing themselves, just for something to do, it seemed to others. Some way to focus on Katie, even if they were now focusing on her absence, looking for a replacement, an alternative heiress. Sally was alone and unsedated. She had a very clear head, almost vacuous; extremely perceptive.

'Come in officer,' and as he walked past her at the door,

'Why have you been drinking heavily?'

He stopped and turned to face her, saying nothing, wondering how it could get any worse than this. He could not utter a reply, so she asked again.

'Sit down Reg. Why have you been drinking heavily?'

'Had a few last night, sorry, do I smell?'

'You stink Reg.'

'I'm sorry Mrs. Pentreath.'

'Sally.'

'Sally.'

There followed a silence, not an uncomfortable one, during which Sally made coffee. He watched her back. She had lost weight in the week since her daughter's death. And height, he was sure. But as she turned to face him he noticed her eyes. Clear, blue and serene. The peaceful, the all-knowing eyes of a human being on the edge of life.

She carried two mugs of instant to the table and sat down beside him. He was frowning, struggling with his role, not working it out.

'Anything I can do to help you Reg?' She laughed as she said this, so as to soften the irony.

He looked up and said 'No', not adding anything, just looking at her, into her eyes.

'She was a lovely girl you know Reg, but distant, like she had secrets. There were times when I felt I didn't know her, not at all. Like she was just passing through, and this was before she went to university. It actually got a bit better after that, she was more open with us, well, with Bertie anyway. Never really that close to me. It hurt me Reg, I was always the one to do the worrying about everything, about money, the farm and so on. Bertie's always had his head in the clouds, or burying his head in detail, like he is now, idiot.

'What do you think about us Sally?' This just came out, not on the script.

'You lot? The police?'

'Yes.'

'D'you really want to know Reg? Are you really sure you want to know what I think about the Dorset Police at this very time?' She said this to floor, as if she were rehearsing the question to which she already had been preparing an answer.

'Yes, I really want to know.'

She looked him in the eye.

'I think you are collectively guilty of my daughter's brutal murder.'

Without having to think he responded,

'I agree with you Sally, the system has let you down, the....'

'System!? System? What system Reg?' She was out of her chair.

He did not respond.

'A fucking system would be nice! You systematically did fucking nothing. Oh now you are, now the big wheels are in motion, now that she is dead.' A pause. 'Does that answer your question?'

Reg saw the despair, not anger, in her eyes. The shock, the fear of the future and what he could only think was the beginning of a campaign against the Dorset police. He knew exactly what he wanted to say. He wanted to say that he wholeheartedly agreed with her. He wanted to join her and support her in anything she wanted to do to avenge her daughter's death, and he was not thinking about the life imprisonment of Darren Pyke. But of course she would not respect that. She would regard any such move on his part as further evidence of the spineless organisation that paid his not unreasonable wages for doing little or nothing. To Reg's credit he was not worried about losing his job, he was worried about losing any residual respect she may have had for him as a human being. Not that there would have been much of that, but perhaps just still enough to build on.

'I do not have to tell you how I feel, my feelings are unimportant.'

She drew back, incredulous.

'I will tell you what I will do though, should you so wish. I will give evidence at the inquest that I witnessed incompetency throughout the so-called investigations into the matters to which Katie was a witness.' His speech was measured, precise and undeniably sincere. Sally Pentreath was stunned.

'Until the time comes for that to happen, if it comes, and as I say I will only do it if you so wish, I will continue to do my job to the best of my ability. Is there anything I can help you with today Sally?'

For a few seconds she just stared at him, mouth open. She could barely believe she had heard this from a shambling old drunk, a broken, bored and unfulfilled old man. But there was the explanation; unfulfilled.

'Reg, I hear what you say, and for the moment I appreciate it. You will excuse me if I say that I do not want my daughter's death to become a political football for you and some of your, no doubt equally bitter colleagues to kick about in the media just to get your own back, just to make up for your own lack of career success, do you…?'

Strangely, he had anticipated this.

'I will forfeit my job before I do it.'

'What?'

'I will resign.'

'Don't be silly Reg, it wasn't your fault, nobody expects….'

'I expect it of myself. I need to….'

'Ah!' She was on her feet, 'You need, you need. So it is about you, so….'

'It's about all of us Sally. I need to suffer as well. I need to lose my house, my wife, my... everything. That way I prove to you my sincerity.'

She was not sure she was hearing right. This was nauseating.

'Go and get a drink Reg. Go and get drunk, I have no time for this.'

'That's the last thing on my mind Sally.'

By this time she was holding the door open, so he walked out, taller than he had walked in.

She closed the door quietly behind him, walked back across to the kitchen table and slumped into Bertie's wooden armchair. Jesus Christ, she had a funeral to arrange and she was wasting time counselling an alcoholic copper. Madness.

227. The funeral went off without incident. The police were prepared. Surveillance had been mounted and the town was well covered with suitably briefed out-of-town cops in plain clothes. Each had been issued with photographs of Darren Pyke and Carmella Everett. The theory was that they, or at least he, would want to be there. Any particular reason for this had not been gone into. It just seemed the least questionable thing to do under the circumstances. An arse-covering exercise in case some bright spark of an amateur profiler decided that in the absence of such an operation an opportunity had perhaps been missed.

Sally and Bertie, despite being quite heavily sedated, wept openly. Simon Murdoch wailed like a baby, twenty odd students sniffed and sobbed and the town maintained a respectful silence; some shops closed for half a day, but most did not. The pub licensees hoped for their share of a wake, but there was none. The seagulls squawked and the next day life went on.

Reg had attended, like most of his colleagues, in full dress uniform. Polished silver buttons and white gloves. A stiff gin before he left the house helped. His wife had been quite supportive, ironing his shirt with special care. She had seen a change in him of late and had been touched by the effect the murder had had on her husband. She knew he was deeply unhappy and would one day admit that she had been wrong all these years. Wrong to judge him, wrong to put their slavery to the financial institutions first. She should have let him retire, made him even, when he had become unhappy and depressed.

228. As soon as the tracker had been traced Assistant Chief Sprake had been informed. Had anyone been with him in his office at the time they'd have seen him positively drool at the news. He convened a meeting of his top sycophants and plotted a strategy designed to cast the Met in a bad light – the oppressive and corrupt partner – Dorset Constabulary as the victim – the poor relative led astray – and Alex Miller and Heather Boyle as human faces of these two. That was the strategy, high strategy at that, almost a policy. Now for the tactics.

Crash bang wallop? Arrest Boyle, Miller and anyone else that got in the way? Bang them up, interview them, charge them with a holding count of theft? No. Not a bit of it. Sprake was a very clever snake.

'We're going softly on this one chaps.'

This one? How many more of these had he investigated in his career on the dark side? What did they mean - this one?

'We've got a full scale murder enquiry on the go, a known suspect, two in fact, and a high chance of arrest in the near future. And once those arrests have been made the evidence is pretty much all there, circumstantially anyway. But there are a few things missing, the murder weapon for a start, and witnesses. Witnesses of the kind that come forward only after the suspect has been arrested. In other words gents we can't start nicking coppers and losing our focus – and our budget – just yet.'

He paused for a few seconds and looked at them in turn. Three superintendents, including the prat from near Bridport who had started the chicken enquiry without which they probably would not all be there (Sprake had demanded this wanker's presence and would be keeping a close eye on him over the coming months). He went on.

'Heather Boyle is a recent transfer from the Met. Alex Miller would appear to the casual observer to be her boyfriend. However, the intelligence is that she is a lesbian and was formerly in a relationship with a Met officer called Caroline Sherry. The methodology of this operation will be given to you after coffee. We will now adjourn for ten minutes, I have some calls to make.'

229. Carmella slept for 12 hours straight. She dreamed of music and pictures and of the sea. Of swimming in the waves of the Dorset coast. Of running along the path over Golden Cap and down through Rockham Valley, of the treehouse, of her Marvel comics and, then, of two dead horses. That loud crack that night nearly two weeks ago in the black rain

on a winding country road. That snapped her eyes wide open. She was on her back swathed in sweat. The duvet was around her waist, her tee-shirt had ridden up and covered her breasts but revealed her gleaming six-pack. She focused and saw him standing over her with a mug of tea.

'Tea.' Alex's voice was flat, his face impassive. She saw his eyes on her belly and she slowly pulled up the duvet around her neck before rising cleanly to a sitting position, crossing her legs in the same movement.

'Thanks,' taking the mug in her tanned calloused hand. He was mannerly, burning his own fingers so she could grasp the handle. Her eyes did not leave his face as she sipped.

'Where are we?'

'You know where we are, we're in London, safe as houses.'

'What are we going to do next?'

'We?'

'Why do you say that? You dumping me now?'

'Not unless you want me to.' There followed a pause whilst she considered this, watched closely by him.

'Well?'

'Well what?'

'Do you want me to dump you?'

'No, I'm scared, I don't know where to go. I'm hungry.'

'I'll make you some breakfast.'

'Thanks.'

He went into the kitchenette and spurted some olive oil into a big frying pan. She sipped her tea and surveyed the small room. She saw nothing to suggest that there was anything to fear from this man. But then she would not have known what to look for anyway.

He stood there in his boxers and fried. He had spent the day snoozing on the sofa, thinking what to do and listening to her snore. He was taking a hell of a chance being here. He could get a visit any minute, but he had a story ready, sort of, anyway.

'Can I have a bath?' She sounded like she was rallying.

'Ain't got one love, but you can have a shower.'

Then she was beside him, naked. 'Where is it? I'm fucking minging.'

He turned from his frying, laughed and looked at her, in that order, keeping his eyes on hers, taking in the wider view peripherally. She laughed back and crossed her arms over her small tits. He moved forward toward the stove to give her room.

'Squeeze past me, it's on the left. There's plenty of towels in there. I'll dig you out some clothes.'

She did what she was told and he could not help enjoying the touch of her breasts on his back. Careful Alex he thought, don't go there.

He listened to the water flow, she yelped; either too hot or too cold. He loaded a plate with eggs and bacon and worried that it would be cold if she was too long in the shower. He need not have. She was out within a minute.

'That was great.'

She had a towel wrapped around her and screwed her green hair into a knot on top of her head as she rubbed past him on her return journey to the bed sitting room. He followed her through with the plate. She sat on the edge of the bed, the towel slipped off. She took the plate and he turned back to get her a knife and fork. He returned to find her eating a piece of bacon with her hand.

'Sorry, I'm starving. Jack.' The pause before the 'Jack' was not lost on him.

He tried to ignore it but she knew she'd hit home.

'That your real name Jack?'

'Course it is, why would I lie to you?'

'Cos you might be a copper.'

'Why would that worry you?'

'Cos you might be gonna take me in.'

'What for, you wanted for something?'

'Dunno.'

'Let me tell you about myself Carmella, as much as you need to know anyway. I deserted from an army base in Hampshire last week. Well, I say deserted, I just didn't want to go back after leave. Afghanistan, that's where they're sending my battalion and I don't want to go, not just now anyway.' He stopped talking and looked down, avoiding her inquisitive eyes. He made it seem like he already regretted telling her.

'Why not now, you'll have to go sometime, or you'll be branded a coward and all that.'

'Not bothered. I know I'm not a coward. Been before, three times. Piece of piss. I just got some shit to sort out first this time. Kind of bad timing. Inconvenient.'

'What sort of shit?'

'Can't say. Don't know you well enough yet. You might turn against me down the way.'

'Time will tell Jack.' For the first time she had taken the initiative. She had ended the conversation and with that remark about time telling she was on her feet and into the kitchenette, taking charge of the kettle and the teapot and some washing up. He was glad they had met. The plan, loosely sketched as it was, seemed to be developing in the right direction.

230. Heather sped along the A303 heading for the A3, M25 and the Surrey town of Leatherhead. She had received a call from Danny Fraser, the Police Federation legal services manager. He had invited her to the Fed HQ when it had become evident that she could not find a fed rep from her own force, or from Devon & Cornwall or Avon & Somerset, her neighbouring forces, to fill in the claim form for her.

Fraser had seen all this before. Bottleless reps, frightened of their own shadows. And the winners? Chief constables and their lackeys who thrive off of scapegoating and bullying isolated, junior officers. Fraser knew he'd probably get some flak for this, taking decisions over the heads of his employers. But he had learned that that was the only way to get things done in this inert organisation. The times he had done it, it made him shudder. But as far as he was concerned he was there to do God's work, and was protecting rank and file coppers from those who used and abused them – their own senior officers.

Fraser had been a cop himself, had done 21 years in the Met before retiring on grounds of ill health after sustaining a nasty hip injury in a police chase-related RTA. He had never wanted to leave the job he loved, so this was the next best thing; looking after those with whom he empathised.

She arrived mid-afternoon and he went down to reception to greet her. He took her to his office and offered her coffee. She asked for tea, he made this in a kitchenette in the corridor. She was surprised he had no secretary.

He went straight into it.

'I've done some research. It looks like this could get nasty. A horrible murder and then all of a sudden you're a pariah.'

'You've got it.'

It was clear that he'd done some work already. Fraser didn't need to make many calls to find out what was going on in the police forces of England and Wales.

'I've seen it all before Heather, but I can't say too much about what I think. I'm in enough shit all the time as it is. I want you to see a good lawyer, an expert in getting Chief Constables to behave themselves and act with at least a bit of transparency.'

She regarded him with a mixture of relief and suspicion. This seemed almost too good to be true. She had bypassed the federation bureaucracy and now she was going to see a lawyer. But which one?

'Before you ask if you can pick your own lawyer you can forget it....'

'I wasn't going to ask....'

'Sorry, I get used to it, that's all, people wanting their uncle or dad to represent them, can't be done.'

'Okay, fine.' Was this guy for real?

'Fill in this form and write out a statement of what's happened to you. Don't be too explicit and don't slag anyone off – not just yet anyway.'

She reached forward to take a three or four page form. She did not take her eyes off of him. He seemed a pretty stressed sort of guy, about 50 or 55 wearing loose fitting clothes and an air of a man living in constant expectation of aggravation. He even spoke in a lowered voice, giving the meeting a conspiratorial feel. She rested the form on an empty box file he gave her and completed it the best she could. The office was cramped and she went about her statement with the same equipment. He read each page as she finished it and handed it to him. He made her a bit nervous.

231. Stewart Kale sat in his tatty little office in the middle of the City of London. He ran an equally tatty little law firm called Kale and Co, specialising in debt recovery actions, small time crime and, wait for it, getting cops out of the shit. An overweight and untidy man – rumour had it that he had only one suit to his name – he had trained with a large London firm who were retained by the police federation and it was there, before he was sacked for giving one of the senior partners a punch in the mouth, that he learned that cops needed support and were often victims of their own cannibalistic organisations. Kale also had quite a lot of time for rough working cops, and the rougher the better. Their general vulgarity and unpretentiousness appealed to him. Men after his own heart.

Kale and Dan Fraser had become good mates over the years. Fraser had managed to persuade his employers that old Kaley was a good wildcard to play in unusual jobs that took a bit of thinking out. And Kaley was good at thinking. The beer breath, jeans and sweaty tee-shirts belied his Oxford first, and he had stacks of bottle. The pair of them often drank heavily together, both being of the opinion that that was the best way to work out innovative litigation strategies.

'Fuck me Dan, you've got another one.' This was Kale over the phone to Fraser after having speed read the scant papers and seen Fraser's emailed report to him.

'Kaley, it's getting worse all the time. It's like they know it's coming on top, the government cuts and all, and they see the axe swinging to reduce the top heavy ranks, so when its backs to the wall they look for backs to....'

'Stab, yeah, (Kaley had the annoying habit of finishing people's sentences) and in this case it's a young WPC with fuck all service.'

'Not quite mate, it's more interesting than that, she's ex-Met, did four years in Shepherds Bush, tough little manor, was there myself, before she went down to the sticks, there might be an angle there.'

'How d'you mean?'

'Well, done a little bit of digging and it would seem like she's a clam jouster, got all loved up with another plonk* and when it went sour she fucked off to carrot crunching country.'

'Sounds good fella, does the Dorset hierarchy know about her sexual persuasion?'

'Got to assume they do. Let them prove they….'

'Don't, yeah, get your drift, good thinking, you could be a lawyer Danny boy.'

'Nah, leave that shit to you son. Look, I'll be in the Coach tonight from about 8 if you fancy blowing the froth off a few.'

'See you at 8.'

And that was how they did business.

232. So Sherrell began to wind down the murder hunt. It felt strange, doing this in the knowledge of what lay behind the decision, and what lay ahead of it. It was like they were replacing a murder trial with a disciplinary hearing, he could see the depressing vista opening out before him. Those two scumbags, Pyke and his androgynous half-wit of a bird, were probably within a bottle's throw of where he sat now, waiting for the door to go down in some hovel in deepest Dorset, unaware that the county's finest did not really want to find them, did not want the adverse publicity that a trial would bring. Because of the doctrine of disclosure, a criminal trial brings out everything - everything that was done during the course of the investigation – and everything that was not done. The defence would seek to show that the police had been incompetent and that because of that incompetence their evidence could not be trusted. In this particular case that strategy would be unlikely to work; the glaring fact that Katie's murder could have been prevented would not in itself

detract from the evidence against Darren Pyke and Carmella Everett. But the collateral damage would be massive. The decision logs, policy documents and use of police resources during the time leading up to the murder would be laid bare, and the reputation of Dorset police would be destroyed, not only during the course of the murder trial, but also during the civil action that would surely follow when Bertie and Sally Pentreath sued for damages, for compensation for the loss of their daughter.

Driving back to Lyme from Dorchester following his meeting with the Chief, Sherrell reflected on his life as a copper. Nothing too impressive, no big awards or commendations, unlikely to get the QPM, highly unlikely to get the next rank. But, hey, his pension would be good, his mortgage was paid and both his kids were nearly through uni. He really now just wanted to get out, draw a line under it. No more politics, no more fear, no more….

Then he found himself wondering about the loose ends of the Pentreath murder, how Decker was going to react about the winding down; that was going to take a lot of managing. Then a minor detail occurred to him. What happened about that tracking device found in the burned out van – a bit of Met kit with an uncorroborated link to Alex Miller who was linked to Heather Boyle. That just could not be ignored, brushed under the carpet, otherwise it was sure to come back and bite him right on the arse.

233. Heather was writing and rewriting notes and statements and everything she could remember about the Pentreath cases and the events leading up to the murder, and the events that had followed it. The work did her good, focused her and gave her suspended life a purpose. She was going to be well-prepared for the oncoming onslaught. She liked this Fraser bloke a lot and knew he was a man with passion for his job, and probably had an axe to grind. She had decided to be candid about her private life. It was surely an open secret by now anyway and to attempt to hide her sexual preferences would only give the imminent investigation something to get excited about. She worried that her 'revelation' would involve Caroline Sherry. She had no need to.

234. Decker was doing his piece. 'You must be fucking joking guvnor!'

'Shut your mouth before you even start Tom!' Sherrell was even surprised at himself for this retaliatory outburst. He had been so stressed by the expectation of the row that he was actually overreacting.

The riposte calmed Decker down a bit.

'Why should I sir? We've all worked our bollocks off on this and here we go again, run out of money have we? Not politically expedient, is it not? Same old shit guv, same old shit.' And with this Sherrell actually thought he saw Decker's bottom lip quiver. Fucking hell, who would have thought it? Who would have thought it?

'Jesus Christ Tom, get a grip. There's stacks of stuff to get on with in this county....'

'What, like chasing chicken thieves?'

'Listen to me, I know where you're coming from, but it's not my fault and not any of your colleague's faults so stop doing what you always do Tom and that's look for someone to blame....'

'Me, look for someone to blame, that's a laugh isn't it? Me, look for someone to blame? Jesus Christ, what's going to happen now then if by some fucking miracle of chance we get our hands on Pyke and there's a trial, what's going to happen then?'

'I'll tell what'll happen Tom, the whole lot of us will be up for grabs, including me, you and that girl Heather fucking what's her face.'

'Boyle... bitch.'

'What?!'

Then a voice from the back of the room,

'I think that's enough now you two.'

It was Packington, neither Decker or Sherrell had seen him lurking in the corner near the back door. The old DI heaved himself with exaggerated effort from his leaning position against the wall and sauntered across the room, filling his pipe as he walked. Neither Sherrell nor Decker responded, so the DI went on.

'I can see Tom's point mind you guvnor, there's still a lot of loose ends to tie up, well, a few anyway.'

Sherrell gave a standard response. 'The Chief says she wants the thing wound up, so the loose ends'll have to stay untied.'

'What happens if they tie themselves up?'

'How do you mean?'

'Well, you can close the enquiry down but then someone might pitch up with information about a safe address for the suspects, or perhaps a bit of late lab work throws a new line of enquiry up from a DNA sample, you know, happens all the time guv.'

'We'll just have to deal with that sort of thing if and when it occurs; in the meantime start winding down. Tom, no more actions to be generated, is that clear?'

Decker sighed. 'Yes sir, clear as bad beer.'

Sherrell regarded the DS coldly for a couple of seconds before walking out of the room.

Packington didn't take his eyes off of the door through which the superintendent had just exited, whilst addressing Tom Decker.

'Don't worry mate, this thing isn't going to die that easily.'

Packington puffed away on his briar as he drove back to his home in Bridport. The car windows were open but the car would still stink and enrage Mrs. Packington, who was Welsh. He wasn't bothered about much but he still liked a bit of mischief, as long he didn't have to take any shit for it. As long as it was on his terms. Jesus what a wanker that

Decker was. Bleating like a baby about the murder hunt being wound down, he couldn't see further than the end of his nose. He faced serious shit if Pyke and his bird went to trial, serious shit, chasing fucking chicken thieves when a murder was being hatched. Packington could never understand how these ambitious DS's functioned. Half murderous, half suicidal, they'd stab their own mothers in the back if it got them promotion, yet they'd sacrifice everything for a good result. Weird, it was like they were on some sort of drug.

Anyway, thought (or schemed) the old DI. I've done some legwork here and things aren't happening the way they should be. Best give someone a little nudge so that the pieces fall into place.

'You been drinkin' again, drinkin' an' drivin', how many years is it now you been getting away with this, an' if you been smoking that fuckin' pipe in tha' fuckin' car I'll cut your fuckin' balls off Packington....'

'You wouldn't know what they looked like love, you wouldn't know where to go to find them it's been that long.'

And it had been a long time indeed. A long time since Gerry Packington had had a sane wife. He was convinced he could get her sectioned under the Mental Health Act at the drop of a hat. And that hat got closer to hand the closer his pension got to maturity.

235. Darren Pyke was walking the streets of Exeter. He had maintained the pretence of being the caring son for a few minutes after arrival at A&E, and then decamped at the first opportunity. He had had the presence of mind to fill his pockets with money from the Seagull Inn till and he was flush. The shops would be open soon and he could get himself some new clothes and a haircut. He had to assume that Colleen would have spilled the beans by now and the cops would be on the lookout for a wanted killer in the relatively small city. He needn't have worried. The two of them had struck a deal; she would get him out of Lyme in the ambulance and, in return, he wouldn't get his brothers to

torch her pub.

He was also worried about Carmella, where the fuck had she ended up? He had ditched his phone so he would have to get another one. But if he called her and she got arrested his new number would be on her call record and would get tracked. But he would have to take that chance.

236. Darren needn't have worried about Carmella either. She was sunbathing. This she found amazing as she was in the middle of a city. Jack's room was on the top floor of a great big terraced house in Powis Square and he had the use of the roof. Carmella had put her clothes into the kitchenette sink to soak and now she lay naked on her back soaking up the rays. She worried about Darren, but not too much. He had sent her on her way, split from her, thought she might even turn him in to save her own skin. Blood may not be thicker than water after all. But no, she doubted that it would come to that. Jack had gone to see his bank manager, something about a savings account he needed to withdraw from. Carmella had never had a bank account; that was for rich people. Mmmm, she thought. She felt safe up there on her roof, on another planet from the farm, the smells, the stares on the Cobb from the tourists (and some of the locals as well). She would go for a walk later, when Jack got back, maybe he would walk with her. She felt safe here. Lots of people even looked like her, she had noticed as she had been looking down on the street five floors below. Portobello Street or something like that, she could see the nameplate on the corner. Lots of young tanned people with untidy tee-shirts and stringy hair. This was Notting Hill, she had seen it on the telly. She liked it here.

237. Simon Murdoch stood at the bar of the Ship and waited for nothing in particular. Heather had dropped him there and was driving her mother's car to avoid detection. She was still, she had to assume, 'confined to barracks' and it would not do to be seen in Lyme, especially in the company of a witness in the case from which she was effectively

suspended. Having dropped him off she began to make her way back to the A35 and home when she was struck by the thought 'what the fuck', and in a mood of sheer lunacy, parked up and walked along the promenade to the Seagull Inn. All the help she had had and was having from the Federation and Danny Fraser in particular was forgotten and thrown to the wind. She craved involvement, hated exclusion and the trip to Lyme had sparked something off.

Reg sat in the place he least liked to be. He was unable to go to Lyme, he just could not face it, could not face meeting anyone. He was the suspended cop, the suspected cop, the tarnished badge. And he was actually rather enjoying the possible notoriety it engendered, the self-pity it facilitated. He compared himself with other Dorset plodders, those who had made good, or at least in comparison to him had made the best of a bad job. That wanker Decker for instance. Sucking up all the time to guvnors, making a big thing out every little bit of luck he'd ever had. Like the time when he met a holidaymaker who'd lost her handbag. Told her he would do his best. She then told him about her ex-boyfriend in London with the nicked antiques in his loft and all of a sudden Decker was the hero, got a trip to the Met to give evidence, high profile Dorset cop, 'look at me'. Then there was Norman Hogg, big tough guy Federation man, scourge of the senior ranks. Yeah, really? Probably plays golf with that snake Sprake, probably does deals with the DPS. Probably end up working for them as a civvy after he retires. People like Decker and Hogg and others got Reg off the hook with himself a bit. Helped him take the moral high ground when he was beating himself up for being a complete and utter failure. Then his phone rang.

238. 'I'm in the Seagull Reg.'

He recognised the number on his screen – it was Heather,

'Have you heard?'

'Heard what?'

'About Colleen Bradstock, you know, the Seagull, she's in hospital....'

'What the fuck are you doing in there Hev? You're supposed to be at home, they'll have your balls....'

'I haven't got balls Reg, in case you hadn't noticed. Look, they can't tell me to stay at home, I'm not suspended, and I don't know what my duty sheet says. That old fart Packington is stringing me along Reg, I've taken advice on this....'

'Alright, alright, point taken, what do you want me to do, I ain't coming down there....'

'I don't want you to, I want you to tell me where Colleen Bradstock might go when she's discharged from hospital if she doesn't come here.'

'No you don't, you want me to go and visit her as a friend in hospital and find out how she got there, is that it?'

'Yeah, suppose, could you do that? Exeter General it is they tell me.'

'I'll think about it.' He'd already thought about it – there was no way he was doing that.

'Thanks Reg.'

'Okay, give me until the end of tomorrow. And by the way, I had noticed.'

And with that he was gone. Heather looked down at her phone and giggled. She felt light as a feather. She sensed the endgame had begun. She looked around the half busy pub, nobody was taking any notice of her, apart from the barmaid who seemed surprised that Heather did not know about the landlady's hospitalisation, but would not be drawn on the cause of it.

'Dunno' had been the very quick answer to the enquiry. Heather looked around the place again and her heart darkened as her eyes fell on the table at which Katie had courted her murderer. She just knew that Darren had returned and had put Colleen in hospital and she just knew that she was the first cop to know about it. There had always been something missing in the accounts of things relating to Pyke that had been imparted by Colleen Bradstock. Heather had previously just assumed that it was the triangle effect; the loyalty between the locals and against the cops and incomers.

239. Alex Miller walked the 2 miles from his flat to Shepherds Bush Police Station and thought about his bizarre situation. He had acted out of self-preservation, desperation to get ahead of the game and to keep Heather out of it. And he was somewhere along the way to putting things right, even if it would cost him his job. Not only had he located one of the murder suspects, he had relocated and controlled her. And under his control she for the time being remained. For the time being. At some stage he would have to get his car. It was parked on a small council estate in some village in the middle of nowhere, near to the spot on the motorway where the van had been torched. He had not reported it stolen lest this would attract attention and prompt questions as to where he had last seen it. It was a nondescript vehicle and hopefully would go unnoticed in the quiet sleepy village street. Having found the van he had driven on to the next exit, turned off, parked up and back tracked across the fields on foot. The nearest farm had been a doddle to find, and that's where he'd found Carmella. Since then he'd committed assault, theft, burglary and, arguably, abduction and false imprisonment given that his victim had had very little choice in the matter.

As he walked into the nick he tried to look more furtive than he actually felt, more scared than he actually was. In fact he wasn't in the slightest bit scared. Fuck 'em. So what if they found the tracker and so what if it came back to him. And so what even if they proved that he had altered the equipment log to try to hide his shenanigans. He had control of one the suspects. But, in the meantime he would at least try to appear scared and contrite and worried. The worst possible scenario would be that he would get disciplined and kicked out of the job. He would never get prosecuted for theft or anything like that. The CPS would never consider it in the public interest to put a cop on trial for trying to do his job; for trying to circumvent inter-force politics by making some technical equipment available to a fellow officer when perhaps it should not have been.

If and when Carmella went on trial there would be all kinds of applications by the defence to get the evidence declared inadmissible because of the way it was obtained. 'Prejudicial to the fairness of the proceedings.' Stolen equipment, kidnapping a suspect, running an unauthorised undercover operation, breaking rules, etc., etc.

But at the end of the day Alex Miller and Heather Boyle had been working for the taxpayer. OK so she had her eye on a quick route to the Dorset CID, but so what. Hardly a shameful cause. Hardly a motive to prove criminal intent. With this and the trump card sitting in his squalid flat he shuffled across the yard of Shepherds Bush Police Station and in through the back door.

He felt eyes from the CID office on the first floor watching him, 'here he comes' he thought they'd be saying, 'here comes Alex to face the music', 'Alex in the shit again', gloat gloat, he thought. But in fact Alex flattered himself. No bastard was bothered. The eyes from the CID office were not really on him at all. In fact there wasn't even anyone in the CID office. They were all in the White Horse across the road, celebrating Charlie Wilkin's birthday. This was done every year on the basis that there was always a murder on Charlie Wilkin's birthday, from which loads of overtime flowed. So Alex didn't even get any sort of welcome at all. He walked through the door, booked on duty and sat down at his desk. He had expected a mountain, but there wasn't one. He wasn't really all that busy, not as busy as he always imagined himself to be. He logged onto his computer and checked his email, not much there either. Just the usual admin shit. So, he felt the whole thing to be a bit of an anti-climax. Wasn't he worth anything? He'd been missing for over week, either sick or annual leave, nobody was sure, least of all him. And nobody had really been after him. Just went to show how unbusy he was. No court dates, no outstanding crime enquiries, no witnesses to see, no exhibits to submit. He had to admit to himself that he was lucky not have had a pull for being a lazy bastard. The irony of the situation was, he reflected, that his current problems about the tracker, real or imagined, could actually save his reputation. Why had no-one pulled him? 'Oi, Al, you're getting idle, do some fucking work or you're going to be back in a big hat mate.' 'Hey Alex, what the fuck, you spend all your time on mission impossible, trying to shag Hev Boyle, and your career's going down the pan.' But nothing like that. Still, not to worry, it was all part of the big picture, that great big picture that was now so big that he could hardly take it all in, barely see it all in one go. Dangerous, was he losing the plot?

'Well, well, wellie well, well, well, well.'

It was DI Wordsworth, Willie to his friends – and enemies.

'The wanderer returns. Howzit goin' Alex?'

'Fine thanks guv, any problems?'

'Why should there be any problems Alex?' Wordsworth always had a big grin on his face, and eyes never stopped swivelling. A saint wouldn't trust him with the saintly Sellotape.

'Well, I ain't been about lately guv, thought I might have been missed, you know, letting people down a bit, not being about, sort of touch.' Something told Alex he should stay humble, apologetic, not take anything for granted.

'Wouldn't worry about it mate,' said Wordsworth, still grinning and swivelling, then walking away back into his office to take a call about a stabbed body that had just been found in a flat on the nearby White City estate. On Charlie Wilkins's birthday.

West Country

240. 'Come to London, I've got a present for you.'

Alex said this as soon as Heather had said a bleary 'Hello Alex'. It was 2:20am when her phone had woken her. She had not heard from him in days and now she knew he'd been up to something – or was just drunk.

'I can't come to London and I don't want a present.'

'Why not and why not?' he was being patient and logical, knowing he had an argument looming.

'Because I'm not in the mood for presents and I'm sort of confined to my home address.'

Alex treated himself to a half smile – this wasn't going to be that difficult, she hadn't hung up.

'They can't confine you to your HA and you'll simply love the present, but be quick, it's highly perishable.'

Heather had always been keenly perceptive, a quality suddenly accentuated by his tone and choice of words.

He was on target and kept up the momentum, 'Be at my place by dawn, this is a game changer.' He hung up, knowing that she would come.

Alex had made this call from the privacy of the stairs to his flat, so as not to awaken the highly perishable present asleep in his bed. Within ten minutes Heather had dressed and was in her car. Dawn would be a doddle.

241. About five minutes after Heather had left the Seagull Simon Murdoch had walked into it. He was not going to learn anything in the Ship, or in the Flag, but had told Heather that he would stay out of the pubs and that he would return to London the next day by train and that he just wanted to be in Lyme for a night – he had booked into a guesthouse by phone – to think about Katie. If Heather had given this reason any

thought she would have rejected it, but she didn't.

Simon sat at the same table he and Katie had occupied on their last visit. His shoulder was still heavily bandaged but the bruising to his neck had all but disappeared. The pub filled up pretty rapidly and it was not long before he learned that the landlady had been taken by ambulance to Exeter hospital and the rumours were rife that her admission was surrounded by suspicion.

He sat and drank and watched and listened. Soon it became obvious to him what had happened. The assault on him by the Pykes would have been caught on CCTV. The landlady would have the recording. His assailants will have felt the need to take her out of the equation. And now she was in hospital. Did the police know about this? Were they following his logic? He doubted either.

242. Carmella had lain low in Alex's flat for over 48 hours, devouring his instant coffee, eggs and TV. Very few of her thoughts had been about Darren. Not that this was anything personal, it was just that torching the van, meeting Jack and being catapulted into London had disconnected her antecedence.

The studio flat windows faced south and it got very warm. It was nearly four in the morning and it was still like an oven. Carmella wore a pair of Alex's boxers and nothing else. She watched his giant television; the laptop on his cluttered table stayed off.

She heard the sound of Alex's key in the door.

'Hey, how you doing lovely lady?' was the cheerful greeting, and then, 'Put a top on please, otherwise I'll keep thinking of something else.'

Carmella brought her hands up to her breasts and looked around for a top. Alex threw her a clean but creased tee shirt from his chaotic wardrobe. She wriggled into it whilst he filled the kettle.

His mobile warbled, it was Heather. He had texted her to call from the street when she got there, he needed to speak to her first.

'Stay there, I'm coming down.' Then, turning to Carmella,

'We've got company.'

Her eyes widened, 'Who?'

'My girlfriend,' he lied. Then he left the flat and went down the stairs to the street.

A bedraggled Heather Boyle stood on the steps of the old Victorian townhouse, she was worried about where she'd parked her car and didn't even say hello as Alex opened the door,

'Will it be alright there?' she said as she pointed to her little vehicle parked in a resident's bay.

'Yeah, it'll be fine, the wardens don't start coming around till eight, you've another four hours at least, right, come in, I need a quick word before we go upstairs.'

243. Colleen Bradstock got one of her barmaids to get the train to Exeter and take her some clothes. Then the pair of them took a cab back to Lyme – Colleen's treat, the girl had done enough and Colleen dropped her off at home before telling the driver to proceed to the Seagull Inn. Whilst in Exeter hospital Colleen had put a call in to Doreen, her trusted cleaner at the pub, and told her to tell the staff to carry on as usual as she'd had a fall on the stairs and had been taken to hospital for some checks. It was nearly midnight when she got back and the pub was closed and locked up.

Alone in the building, she went up to her flat. The first thing she did was to check that Darren's shotgun was still under her bed. It was. She then set about wrapping it in a plastic shopping bag before lowering the loft ladder, climbing up into the dusty attic and stuffing the bundle into the furthest recess she could find.

Next job - the computer. Darren's stupidity in smashing the screen with the gun had created a problem. The machine was inoperable so there was no way she could locate the software to wipe the hard drive. Consequently another bag was used as a wrapper and the laptop joined the gun in the attic.

Then Colleen cleaned up, took a shower and went to bed, exhausted.

244. 'You're fucking joking! How did you pull that off?'

Heather was shell-shocked by Alex's story of how he'd found the van, abducted the female driver, a country girl called Carmella, and brought her to London.

'Are you crazy? That's Darren Pyke's bird, and she's his fucking sister.'

'That figures, she was in that van, or had been, no doubt about it, she stank of petrol, and she's on the run from something, only too glad to come here with me. We can use her to draw him in, she's like our hostage.'

Heather was still reeling, rapidly forming the conclusion that Alex had completely lost his mind.

'And what if that plan doesn't work? What if she walks out, goes to the local cops, complains? You haven't thought this through.'

'Come on up and meet her, but don't spook her, she's like a wild animal, needs gentle treatment, kindness, we need to work on taming her. By the way, you're my girlfriend.'

'Jesus Christ, you'll stop at nothing, will you!?'

Heather followed him up the five flights of stairs, thankful for the excuse to arrive in the flat a bit breathless and red-faced, which was how she felt anyway.

'Heather, Carmella. Carmella, Heather.'

The country girl stayed sitting crossed legged on Alex's bed. She looked Heather up and down with open curiosity. Heather approached and extended her hand.

'Pleased to meet you Carmella.' The hand was accepted, perfunctorily, as the scrutiny continued. Carmella preferred the company of males and found herself resenting this intrusion into her new little world.

The television was on and showing a wildlife programme, something about sharks. Heather used this as a talking point.

'Oh I love this sort of stuff, so many lovely scary things in the sea, isn't there?'

She glanced back at Carmella who was not watching the screen and had not taken her eyes off this intruder. Heather continued to pretend to be interested in the sharks and sat down in the armchair. Alex had escaped into the kitchenette to make coffee.

'Who wants coffee?'

'I could murder one,' enthused Heather, immediately regretting the choice of words. She felt herself blush and glanced again at Carmella who was still staring at her, blankly.

245. Danny Fraser and Mark Kale were in the Coach and Horses, Soho, putting the world to rights.

'My round,' slurred Fraser, turning to the Romanian barmaid.

'No it's not, it's mine ya cunt,' countered Kale.

They were on their tenth pint and things were warming up. In respect of what was now being called their 'Dorset problem' an elegant legal strategy had been developed, reached its peak and was now in decline. It had progressed from basic facts, through to criminal defence arguments, employment law victimisation and judicial review but was now entering the realms of fantasy in the Supreme Court and the ECHR.

They did this all the time. Both men hated unfairness, along with those who dispensed it. Their common intention was not only to successfully defend victims but also to inflict maximum pain and embarrassment on the perpetrators. Fraser had an annual £11m budget at his disposal and Kale liked to get as much of it as possible in fees. But finance was not the prime motivator; they liked to see blood on the walls and successful legal actions against bullies spilled blood of the finest quality.

Kale could afford to be a loose cannon. He had a good reputation as a street-fighting lawyer and liked to live in character; be constantly up to his neck in shit and bullets.

Fraser had to be a bit more careful. He worked at the epicentre of a highly political organisation. The planning of the legal tactics was easy compared to the tricks he had to pull to steer cases through the Federation funding rules. Strictly speaking he could not authorise funding without having a member cop's application countersigned by a Federation rep. He was going to have to get Norman Hogg onside.

246. Deputy Chief Constable Sprake was enjoying a game of golf. On the last of nine holes he was well ahead. The ball had dropped 30 yards short of the green, he selected a club and chipped it neatly to within 4 yards of the hole.

His opponent had lost his ball and emerged from the long grass having given up his search for it. Glum faced, he watched Sprake put his ball neatly away.

'Nice one boss,' said Norman Hogg.

'Thank you Norman,' and then, after the shortest of pauses, 'Give me the girl and together we can save Dorset.'

Norman had expected the subject to be raised – it was the reason for the game – but not quite so abruptly.

'Pardon boss?'

Walking away, Sprake spoke over his shoulder,

'You heard me Norman. Do we have a deal or does the whole thing have to get extremely messy?'

247. Sherrell was late off duty again and worried about his life-work balance as he left the force HQ in Dorchester. He walked across the car park with his head down and didn't see Jim Ramage slinking between the parked vehicles.

'Good evening Mr. Sherrell.'

The harsh Glaswegian accent jerked Sherrell back into the real world.

'Oh, it's you, what d'you want?'

Ramage put on an exaggerated hurt look, 'Aw, you're usually so charming and polite Mr. Sherrell, whassamatter, the Chief been giving you a bollocking, eh?'

Sherrell had got to his car and was fishing for his keys. 'Get to the point Mr. Ramage, or get out of the car park, it's police property.'

'Aye, paid for by taxpayers money Mr. Sherrell, like your wages.'

Sherrell stopped his pocket rummaging, 'And your point is?'

'I want to know how you're getting on with the Pentreath murder enquiry, to be blunt – and don't just say that enquiries are ongoing or shit like that please, I need to report some facts.'

'You can need all you want but you already know the answers, enquiries are ongoing and the force press bureau will release a statement when appropriate.'

What came next caused Sherrell to drop his keys.

'I'm reliably informed that you have already identified, but not arrested, a suspect – one Mr. Darren Pyke, is that so Mr. Sherrell, and if so, why hasn't the public been informed that a gun-toting killer and his crazy sister-cum-fuck-buddy are still on the loose in west Dorset?'

Sherrell picked up his keys, opened the driver's door and jerked his head across the roof of the car,

'Get in'.

Ramage obeyed and they both sat in the parked vehicle, staring ahead.

'I won't even ask where you got this from and the fact that it's not entirely true probably doesn't matter a fuck to you, but yes, Pyke is one suspect and we're trying not to spook him out of the county. Softly softly....'

'...Catchy monkey.' Ramage'd finished the old police adage.

'Yeah, that's right, and what's wrong with it? If Pyke fucks off he could go anywhere, he's got no responsibilities, he could just travel, disappear, and then where would we be?'

'You'd be back in your fucking comfort zone, nicking motorists and chicken rustlers.'

Ramage had just made an unintended point.

248. Darren walked out of an Exeter Tesco store with a small box in his hand, he stepped quickly around the nearest corner and up to a waste bin where he tore at the cellophane wrapper, opened the box and took out the mobile phone, battery and sim card on which he had paid a £10 pay-as-you-go top-up. He took out the battery charger and put the box in the bin.

He looked across the road and saw a pub; it was just after 12 noon.

He was first in, ordered a pint of Fosters and asked the barmaid if he could charge up his phone.

'Have you a charger?'

'Yeah.'

She nodded to a corner of the bar, 'Socket over there.'

'Cheers,' he said, and walked over to a corner table and sat down with his pint, plugged the phone in and watched for the bars on the charge indicator to appear.

Ten minutes later he found himself trying to guess Carmella's number, but could not. He punched about ten numbers, racking his brains, but got several unobtainable tones and a few wronguns.

Shit, fucking speed dial he thought, before realising that there was only one way forward, call the Everett house. He knew that number ok, it was the first he'd ever had to memorise.

'Hello?'

Thank fuck, thought Darren, it wasn't the old woman.

'Is that you Emmett?'

His luck was in. 'Yeah, Darren, fucksake man, where are you, you're a wanted man, don't come here whatever you do!'

'I ain't going to mate, don't fucking worry....'

'Where's Carmella, where's my sister?!'

'That's what I want to know, she's not there?'

'No, or I wouldn't have fuckin' asked, did you kill that girl? Was

Carmella with you? That's what they're...,' Emmett was agitated, babbling.

'Calm down, I need Carmella's number, you got it?'

'Yeah, I've been ringing her, she won't tell me where she is, she sounds weird.'

'At least she's ok then. Give me the number, I can't remember it cos' I had it on speed dial and ditched my phone. Has Josh been in touch?'

'No, your lot've all fucked off or lying low or sumthin', nobody's talkin' to anybody....'

'Get me her number, she'll tell me where she fuckin' is!'

'I'll have to call you back.'

'Yeah, call me on this number.'

'What is it? You've come in on the house phone.'

'Fuck, just a minute, fuck, I've chucked the box, I'll have to ring you back, get the number and stay where you are for a few minutes.'

After more of this nonsense Darren had Carmella's number, punched it into his keypad and pressed the dial button.

249. Carmella's phone was under Alex's bed charging – as luck, for a change, would have it they both had the same piece of kit so his charger fitted – it was on silent but the trio in the studio flat heard it buzzing.

Carmella dived down to retrieve it, looked at the screen but did not recognise the number and tapped 'decline'.

Alex and Heather looked at each other and then at Carmella.

Alex was first in with the question, 'Who was that?'

'Dunno, no-one I know, I don't pick up when I don't know the number. Specially not now.'

Heather could not resist it, 'Give us a look Carmella, I might be able to help.'

Carmella became guarded, wary. 'No, it's alright, I'll call it back later, when I've put a story together, I... I dunno what to say, I don't even know where I fuckin' am.' And with that she began to cry.

Heather reached across and put her hand on Carmella's knee. The country girl recoiled, holding the mobile tight to her chest.

'Just leave me alone, I don't like you, who are you? Are you his girlfriend?' she asked as she nodded tearfully at Alex.

'Well, yeah....'

'Well you won't want me here now, will you, you just going to kick me out now?'

'No Carmella, course not,' Alex was quick to jump in, 'We're friends now, you helped me get here remember, I would not have made it back without you, we stick together, I owe you....'

She was not convinced. 'You could of just got her to go down to Wales for you, you didn't need me at all, you're lying, the pair of you, I don't trust you, I'm outta here.'

And with that she got off the bed and started to gather her stuff.

'No, come on Carmella, we could....'

Alex didn't finish and then Heather dropped a bombshell,

'Just let her go Alex, she'll....'

Carmella stopped dead, 'Alex? Alex was that? Why've you been calling yourself Jack then, why've you been lying to me?' By now she was shouting with tears running down her face. There was a stunned silence which lasted a full five seconds, then Carmella renewed her leaving preparations with gusto, Alex and Heather just watched her as she got dressed, stuffed her phone in her pocket and laced up her boots. Then she made for the door.

Then Alex Miller made a decision. He stood up and in one stride was between Carmella and the door. The country girl stopped and fixed him with a feral glare.

'You're not going anywhere young lady, and looking at me like that ain't gonna improve things.'

'Just get out of my way, I want to go home and you can't stop me.'

'I think you'll find you're wrong Carmella.' And with that he reached into his back pocket and took out his warrant card.

'We're police officers and you're under arrest for the murder of Kate Pentreath.' Carmella's shoulders sagged and she appeared to deflate, her eyes glazed and fixed on a point between herself and Alex. Heather froze, motionless in the chair, she could not believe what she was witnessing, her mind reeled as she tried to grasp the consequences of what was now occurring.

A full four seconds of silence elapsed before Carmella struck. In a flash she leapt forward and her forehead struck his nose with a crunch which was both sharp and dull, her hands were round his neck and gripping his collar. The impact stunned him long enough for Carmella to haul herself upward, using his upright body to free her feet just long enough for her to use one of them to kick out at the rising Heather, the heel of her boot connecting with the police woman's face. Heather spun backwards, blood flowing freely from a split eyebrow. Alex regained control and got the writhing banshee in a headlock. It did not last long; she reached down and grabbed his testicles, pulling and twisting with all of her considerable strength. He yelled, let go and she was gone, out of the door. He made to follow but was stopped by Heather.

'Just let her go,' she wailed.

Alex stopped and just stood there, holding his nose and his balls.

250. Dawn was breaking as Carmella burst out of the street door and leapt down the stone steps onto the pavement. She looked left and right and decided on the latter, which was downhill. She flew, her green hair plastered over face, she hit Ladbroke Grove and took a right, downhill again. She did not stop for two hundred yards, before diving into a bushy front garden in which she lay panting and waiting wide eyed for her pursuers to catch up. She had none. Her breathing and pulse slowed, and then she reached for her phone.

251. Darren was sitting on a park bench in central Exeter when his new phoned buzzed. He recognised Carmella's number – how could he have ever forgotten it – and answered. He didn't wait for her to speak.

'Where the fuck are you?'

'Might ask you the same fucking question,' she giggled nervously.

'I asked it first, come on, you sound ok, where are you Carmella?'

'London.'

'What? How the fuck did you get there?'

'Got kidnapped and brought here, now I've escaped and I'm hiding in a garden.'

Darren's mind reeled. 'Who took you to London, was it the police?'

'Yeah, but I've escaped.'

'What? Are you drunk? How long have you been there?'

'Few days I think, about two days. I torched the van, hid in a shed on a farm and this guy caught me, said he was a runaway soldier, a deserter like, then he brought me to London, we nicked a car to get here. I was in his flat and then this weird woman came and things started to change. They just told me I'm under arrest for murder, said they're coppers but they're weirdos, that's for sure. Anyway, I've just legged it out of the house and they haven't caught me, so I'm on the street with no money and not much credit left on this phone. Come and get me Darren.'

Pyke was stunned by this tale, he just sat there for a full five seconds in silence, his mind not knowing which way to turn.

'Can you hear me Darren, answer me!'

'Right, yeah, okay, get to Waterloo station, I'll come up there by train.'

'When?'

'Now. As soon as I can. It'll take me about three or four hours, but I'll get there.'

'Where's Waterloo station?'

'I don't fucking know, all I know is that trains from Exeter end up there, it's the last stop.'

Carmella was about to answer when the front door of the house in whose garden she crouched swung open to reveal the silhouette of a large West Indian lady,

'Whadya tink ya fuckin' doin' get outta me garden, now, before ah call da police!'

Carmella leapt up and ran. She could hear Darren shouting on the other end of the line so she slowed as soon as she felt safe and held the phone to her ear, but he was gone. Okay, she thought, Waterloo station.

252. Reg Bull was sober as he parked his old car opposite the Goat and walked decisively into the pub. He had had a call from Norman Hogg

who wanted to meet him there. He was hoping for good news, perhaps that he could go back to work with no charges pending. Wishful thinking, in the extreme.

Hogg was already sat in the corner with two pints on the table in front of him.

'I got you Youngs, is that okay?'

Reg nodded, 'Yes thanks, that's fine. I'm only having the one. Got the car.'

Hogg raised his eyebrows, 'Well, what a good boy, turning over a new leaf then?'

'Nah, too late for that mate,' said Reg as he sat down heavily on a stool opposite the Fed rep. 'You got some news for me mate?'

Hogg took a long draw of beer and put his glass gently down, paused and then replied,

'Sort of Reg, but it ain't that good.'

Reg's shoulders slumped. 'Jesus, what the fuck's happened now?'

Hogg had prepared carefully.

'Nothing. Yet. But something bad is going to happen if you don't come on board against Heather Boyle.'

Reg's shoulders reinflated. 'What the fuck is this all about? I had Decker at me the other day for the same thing, now you – of all people, I thought you were supposed to be looking after her.'

'Well I'm not any more. She's been going behind my back to Leatherhead, making a lot of trouble. She's a wrong'un Reg,' and then quietly, leaning forward, 'And you fucking know it.'

Reg stared wide eyed at Norman Hogg for a full three seconds before replying, 'I know absolutely nothing about Heather apart that she's a good cop who wants to get on in life, and that's the end of it.'

Hogg was unmoved. 'Reg, as a Federation rep I've learned over the years that everything cuts both ways. The most important thing you have to bear in mind is that there's always a bigger....'

'Picture.' Reg finished the sentence and stopped Norman dead. Reg went on,

'If you start giving me some shit about having to burn Heather Boyle for the sake of the Dorset Police I'll walk out of this pub now Norman. None of this was Heather's fault. Your mates at the top....'

Hogg was not having this,

'I've got no mates at the top Reg, my mates are you lot, federated rank and file officers so don't you dare try to....'

'Well then don't try to turn me against another federated ranking officer then... Christ, I can't believe this.'

Hogg took another long draw on his pint, put the glass down and stared at the table.

'Okay Reg, this is the bottom line. If you don't grass up Heather Boyle you're going to get the sack.'

It was Reg Bull's turn to be stopped dead. After a few long seconds he recovered, took a deep breath and said,

'Says who?'

Hogg did not hesitate, he leant forward and snarled quietly,

'My mates at the top.'

'Quite.' Reg leaned forwards slowly, curling his lip.

'And what, may I ask, am I supposed to grass Heather Boyle up for?'

Hogg was ready for this.

'She was in close contact with Darren Pyke almost from the day she got to Lyme. He was giving her information on drug dealing in the county. She was protecting him, letting him know when and where the CID were looking for him. You saw them together on several occasions and heard her on the phone to him.'

Reg remained calm.

'Oh, really, and why didn't I stop her? Why didn't I report her then?'

'That's your problem Reg.'

'No. It isn't a problem. Because it didn't fucking happen.'

'Yes it did Reg, and it turned you to drink, made you crazy. You didn't report her because you was infatuated with her. You just let it go and hoped nothing would happen.'

And then Reg stood and walked out of the pub, his pint unfinished.

253. 'What the fuck were you thinking Alex?'

Heather sat opposite Alex Miller in the studio flat. They had been in silence for some time, tending to their wounds and trying to guess what would happen next. Would Carmella go to the police? Doubtful, she was wanted for murder. Would she try to get back to Dorset? Doubtful for the same reason, plus she had little or no money.

'We're both in a lot of shit Hev, we're both going down the toilet if we don't pull something off pretty soon, that's what I was trying to do, I reckoned....'

'And the shit just got a whole lot deeper, you kidnapped a girl, falsely imprisoned her....'

'Yeah, yeah, drugged her, raped her, buggered her, forced her to eat high fat food with additives....'

'It's not funny Alex. She could say all that, yeah, and they would choose to believe her, and now you've got me involved, and she knows your address, my description... your door could come flying in any minute Alex... fucking hell, I'm off!'

With that Heather leapt to her feet, gathered her stuff and headed for the door. Then her phone buzzed, right on cue.

She looked at the screen – hidden number – she answered.

'Hello?'

254. Heather's mother stood in the middle of her kitchen with Don Pryce at her side. She spoke to her daughter in a flat, matter of fact tone.

'Right Heather, the police are here with a search warrant, they've started in your bedroom and they've politely informed us that they're going to turn the whole house over. Would you kindly tell me what is going on and where you are? Please.'

Heather felt her knees become very weak.

'Jesus Christ mum, what the... I've no idea, I'm up in....' She paused, her mind raced.

'Let me speak to one of the officers, the one in charge, whoever that may be.'

Julie Boyle said nothing as she handed the phone to Detective Inspector Clive Jarrett of the Dorset Police professional standards department.

'Good morning Heather.' Jarrett sounded sarcastically cheerful.

'Who's that?'

'It's DI Jarrett Heather, professional standards. Where exactly are you?'

The tone was now precise, slightly menacing.

There was no point in lying.

'I'm in London sir, visiting friends.'

Jarrett got straight to the point.

'You should really be here Heather, as per orders. Make your way back now and report directly to headquarters in Dorchester without delay. Okay?'

Heather decided at once that she was not going anywhere.

'No guvnor, I'm in London with friends and I'm actually sick with a virus, flu or something. If I try to travel today it could do me serious damage.'

Jarrett had heard this all before.

'Have you reported sick?'

'No, not yet, but I will do that next, and I will get a certificate, I'm still registered with a London doctor.'

There followed a few seconds of silence. Jarrett was stumped. 'Yeah, alright then. But I have to tell you that we're in the middle of executing a search warrant at your parent's address.'

'What are you looking for?'

'Evidence.'

'Evidence of what?'

'Your possible criminal misconduct whilst in public office.'

Heather became angry and scared.

'What misconduct? How can there be evidence of public office misconduct at my home address?'

She knew very well that if there was any such evidence in existence it could well be at her home address, but she chose to appear indignant. Jarrett responded brusquely,

'I'm not going to discuss it on the phone. What I want to know is your exact whereabouts whilst you're sick.'

There was no way she was giving this information. 'Like I say I'm with friends, I'll be back in a couple of days when this bug wears off. I don't want any visits here, these are nice people, they don't want the police knocking on the door paying me a sick visit, now can I speak to my mother please?'

Jarrett had to have the last word, 'Right, I'll see you when you get back.' He then handed the phone to Julie Boyle.

'Heather what is this all about?'

'I'm so sorry mum, I've no idea what they're looking for, I think they're trying to blame me for something.'

She was trying to pace around the tiny flat as she spoke, Alex had disappeared into the bathroom.

Julie was distraught, but tried to remain calm,

'What's this about you being sick?'

Heather spoke through gritted teeth,

'Take the phone into another room mum.' Julie had already done so and was standing alone in the kitchen, out of earshot.

'Go on, they can't hear.'

'I'm okay mum, I'm with Alex, but don't tell them. I'm going to report in sick and I'll be back in a couple of days. Now listen. When they've finished their searching shit make them tell you what they're taking away. They'll probably take my laptop....'

'Yes, they've already put that in a polythene bag.'

'Okay, make a list of what they take and get one of them to sign it. Then when they've gone take photographs of the mess they're bound to leave, okay?'

Julie could hardly believe she was hearing all this. Her own daughter was sounding like a criminal; her own police colleagues were certainly treating her like one.

'Okay, I'll do all that. I'll call you when they've gone.'

'Okay mum, look, there's nothing to worry about, I'm really sorry but I've done nothing wrong, I promise you.'

'I believe you Heather. I'll call you back soon.'

'Love you mum.'

'Love you too.' Heather rang off.

255. Jarrett and his team finished up at Heather's home address in Dorchester. They did a thorough job and left with Heather's laptop, mobile phone bills and some paperwork she had been doing at home, including a load of loose paper notes which seemed to be just scrawled streams of consciousness about possible connections between the Pyke family, the Everetts and any other names and places that had come into her head at the time of writing. She had obviously undergone some sort of analyst's course in the Met, thought Jarrett, judging by the flow diagrams with arrows and boxes and crossing lines.

Upon Julie Boyle's request, Jarrett had one of his officers make a list of what they were taking, and Heather's scrawlings were itemised as 'a quantity of paperwork'. The exact quantity, in terms of the amount of sheets of paper, was not noted. These included a couple of rough notebooks; similarly the number of blank pages was not specified. Jarrett watched this sloppiness take place, but did not intervene. Julie thought nothing of it and signed the list. She did not possess a copper's mind.

256. It was just after 8.30am when Simon Murdoch knocked hard on the door of the Seagull Inn. The bar area was of course in darkness but he could see a light on upstairs, made necessary by the weak October sunlight. He waited about 30 seconds and knocked again, harder. Another 30 seconds and he saw movement; Colleen Bradstock emerged from the staff area clutching her dressing gown around her. She looked drawn, tired, old. Murdoch was dressed in a suit and tie, his arm was no longer in a sling; she did not recognise him through the glass door and opened up.

'Yes, can I help you?' she asked, blearily.

'I think you probably can. May I come in please?' He used a measured tone, resolute. Colleen was impressed and stood back, holding the door open. Murdoch walked in, politely but with an air of authority. She closed the door behind him and locked it. He stood in the middle of the bar and she motioned him to take a seat at one of the tables. He did so, and she joined him. There was no offer of tea or coffee. She had a feeling that this visit was not going to be altogether pleasant.

'Are you a policeman?' She asked, not unreasonably.

'No. My name is Simon Murdoch. I'm the boyfriend of Katie Pentreath. I'm surprised you don't recognise me. I was assaulted in your pub two days before she was murdered by the same man.'

She had only perused the CCTV footage once, and distractedly, so Colleen did not blame herself for not knowing her visitor. She was very wide awake now and assessed his demeanour. He was not aggressive, just matter of fact. He waited for her response. She allowed her eyes to drop, hoping to appear troubled.

'I'm so sorry, we're all traumatised by this terrible tragedy. What do you want from me? How do you think I can help you?'

Simon watched the woman intently. Beneath the middle class buffoonery lurked a pretty perceptive and intelligent young man. Katie's death had brought these qualities into extremely sharp focus. This lady did not impress him.

'You can start by telling me what you know,' then he leant forward, 'Everything please Colleen Dorothy Bradstock.'

That he knew her full name did not bother her, it was above the door of the pub and was a matter of public record. What she did find unnerving was that it was obvious that he knew that she knew more than she was letting on to the police. But she was on home ground, so she decided not to be intimidated.

'Mr. Murdoch, whilst I have great sympathy for your dreadful loss, and that of Katie's parents, I have told all I know to the police.' Then, in an effort to appease him, she lied, 'They have the CCTV coverage of you being assaulted in my pub....'

'But not the CCTV coverage of A and E at Exeter Hospital less than 48 hours after the murder!'

This took two long seconds to sink in.

'What? I don't know what you're....' Her voice trailed off, she felt sweat break out on her forehead.

'I was also in that hospital, discharging myself and just leaving, I saw you getting brought in from the fucking ambulance Colleen Dorothy Bradstock. Darren Pyke was with you. Now are you going to play ball with me or do I tell the police to view that A and E footage?'

She felt sick.

257. Darren Pyke gazed out of the window of the train as it shuddered its

way through what he thought must have been every station in the West Country on its way to London. He was tired, hungry and badly in need of a bath and change of clothes. He had done his best in the gent's toilets at Exeter station, but knew he still stank. Buying the ticket had all but wiped him out of money, so he could only look on with envy as his fellow passengers bought coffee and sandwiches from the passing trolley.

He retrieved a discarded newspaper from the floor. The North Devon Gazette. They were on page three. He looked at his mugshot and wasn't too worried, the new crew-cut had more or less done the trick. It was the state of his personal hygiene that worried him. He got up and went to the toilet, had a shit, soaped his hands and face, groins and armpits. Then he put a pinch of hand rolling tobacco in his mouth and chewed. Better than halitosis, he figured.

Then he thought of Colleen. Would she be out of hospital yet and back in Lyme? This worried him, he needed to rub in the message. He pulled out his phone and dialled directory enquiries, getting the number of the Seagull Inn, gritting his teeth at the credit that the call would cost him. Then he made the call.

258. Colleen was still sat with Simon Murdoch when the pub landline rang. She looked at him.

'Best you answer it,' said Murdoch. 'Might be relevant to the present conversation Ms. Bradstock.'

She stood and walked unsteady across the room to the ringing phone which was attached to the wall behind the bar. Murdoch watched her. She answered and turned away, sharply. Murdoch was on his feet, sensing the relevance. Before he could get to her she had replaced the receiver and had turned to face him, visibly shocked.

'Was that him?' asked Murdoch, knowing damned fine that it was.

'Who? No, it was just PPI shit, we get....' Her voice was up by three octaves and Murdoch was with her in three strides, shoving her away from the phone. He picked up the receiver and dialled 142, 'Your last call was from....'

He snatched a pen from the bar shelf and wrote down Darren Pyke's number. Colleen was leaning heavily on a beer pump, she breathed deeply, trying not to vomit.

'Was that him?' Murdoch's tone did not invite bullshit, but she did not reply, at first.

'Do I dial the number and find out?'

She straightened and turned towards him. 'No... okay, yes, that was him. Don't call him, please I'll, er....'

'You'll what?'

'Let me call him.'

'What are you going to tell him?'

'I'll tell him to come here, I have something belonging to him in the loft.'

'What is it?'

'His gun.'

Murdoch was incredulous. 'The gun he used to kill Katie?'

'I don't know, probably, yes.' She was leaning heavily against the bar now, he stood over her, menacingly.

'The police need to have that, why have you not told them?'

Colleen was close to fainting. 'I don't fucking know, I'm scared shitless, anything I do is going to be very bad for me, I'll lose the pub....'

'You'll lose more than the fucking pub my girl if you don't start cooperating! You're hiding a murder weapon and helping a murderer get away with it. Best you change your ways fucking quick or you'll being going down with him.'

259. Chief Constable Joanne Bache sat at her desk in full uniform. She had before her Sherrell, Jarrett and Sprake. There was no coffee or tea, no Jaffa cakes. Jarrett had just finished his debrief and had provided three copies of a report he had speedily written following the search of Heather Boyle's home address. He watched the other three read the three page document, the Chief was first to finish.

She looked across the desk at Jarrett. 'Has the laptop been looked at yet?'

'Yes Ma'am, nothing much on it. Boyle doesn't leave much of a footprint on social media. All of her search engine work seems to be about crime suspects, past cases and colleagues....'

'Colleagues?' jumped in the Chief.

'Yes Ma'am, she seems to like checking on her colleagues. Has a particular habit of Googling their mobile phone numbers and email addresses, like she's trying to glean intelligence. It's strange.'

The Chief agreed, 'You can say that again. Has she found anything to anybody's detriment?'

'Not that we can make out, but she seems to have been doing it constantly since she got here, always on the lookout for something about the people she's working with.'

Sprake snorted, 'Christ, what have we created. Is there any indication that she's been passing information on to third parties, such as the press and the like?'

Jarrett had anticipated this. 'No sir, not yet, but the tech boys are still looking.'

'Still looking?' the Chief's eyebrows were raised, 'How long will it take to bottom out?'

'A couple of days Ma'am, the....'

Bache was getting cross, 'Make sure it gets top priority. Rob, ensure that Technical get no more work from anywhere else until this is done, okay?'

Sherrell nodded. Jarrett moved the meeting on, 'The thing is Chief, this damned girl is now, as we speak, on the loose in London, contrary to specific orders, she's actually refusing to come back and has reported sick. On top of that, I'm reliably informed, she's applying for Federation funding to take us on regarding her current suspension status. She's actually upping the ante, trying to jerk us about.'

'She'll be back.' Sherrell said this, quietly, staring into mid-space.

Jarrett turned on him, 'What makes you so sure of that?'

'I know her, she's a keen cop, it wouldn't be like her to run away.'

'Any idea where she is in London?' The Chief directed this question to them all. Jarrett answered, 'She wouldn't tell me on the phone, but....'

Sherrell came in again, in the same off-hand tone, 'She'll be with a Met DC called Alex Miller, I'll put a month's salary on it.'

Sprake grabbed this opportunity, 'Really? Well find out where he lives then and let's get up there.' Jarrett nodded emphatically.

The Chief raised her palms,

'Whoa, hang on, I agree she has to be found, but we can't just go steaming in on Met territory, we'll have to liaise. Mr. Sprake, get onto Met PSD and come up with a joint plan. Rob, assist Mr. Sprake with anything else you know about her relationship with this Met guy.'

With that the Chief stood up, walked across the office and held the door open. The men filed out, bidding the Chief their polite thanks for her valuable time.

260. Reg Bull sat in the passenger seat of Norman Hogg's Range Rover. He had on his knee a clipboard, in his hand a pen. He wrote slowly and deliberately.

Firstly he signed the declaration of truth, then what followed was a pack of lies. The purpose of the lies was to save his pension. Their effect was to destroy Heather Boyle.

"I have known PC Heather Boyle for four months. I was what they call her 'parent constable' when she was posted to Dorset Police Lyme Regis Division. From the outset she was a keen and very proactive officer, she was also very keen to be transferred to the CID. She often expressed her bitterness at having to start again, saying that she had already completed most of her CID courses whilst engaged as a plain clothes crime investigator with the Metropolitan Police. She took a keen interest in local known criminals, especially one called Darren Pyke. At one point I asked her if she was getting information from him as she seemed to know him. She said that she was but told me not to say anything to our superiors. I told her that not registering an informant was a disciplinary offence. She told me that she was aware of this but had no intention of registering Pyke as, in her experience, doing so always led to the informant being either compromised or appropriated by established CID officers. I have been asked why I did not report this matter to a senior officer. I will answer that question by saying that I thought she knew what she was doing and that no harm would come of this non-observance of the rules. I now very much regret that I did not report PC Boyle. Thinking back I can remember several occasions on which she prevaricated when it came to progressing investigations which could have led to the arrest of Pyke. These arose from incidents when Pyke was strongly suspected of committing assaults and acts of criminal damage that would have probably led to his being remanded in custody. I have been asked if I think that PC Boyle was involved in the murder of Kate

Pentreath. I very much doubt that she was actively involved. However it is my opinion that had PC Boyle not been actively protecting Pyke by effectively delaying his capture for other offences then, and if it was Pyke who killed Kate Pentreath, then she would still be alive today."

Reg then signed this statement and handed the clipboard to Hogg. Hogg read it and signed it as a witness. The Fed rep was the first to speak.

'I know it's horrible Reg....'

'Horrible? Horrible!? Is that what you call stitching up a colleague? Perverting the course of justice, that's what it is!'

Hogg came straight back at him, raising his voice also, 'It's either you or her Reg. If you retract this and don't play ball Sprake will have you sacked and you'll forfeit 50% of your fucking pension. You'll be taking part-time gardening jobs for the rest of your sad fucking life to make ends meet.' Then leaning closer and lowering his voice, 'You owe my sister better than that.'

'You're turning your sister into the wife of a liar!'

'No. I'm making sure my sister is properly taken care of, despite being married to a fucking loser! Cheer up mate, for once you're doing the right thing. This way you get to go back to work tomorrow, suspension lifted, no further disciplinary action. Trust me Reg, if you don't cooperate you won't ever be going back to work, Sprake has made that clear, he will make an example of you. Now fuck off to the pub. I'll see you at the nick tomorrow.'

Reg got out of the vehicle and Norman Hogg drove off. Reg headed for the Goat, head down.

261. Decker sat in what was left of the Lyme incident room. Most of the paperwork generated by the investigation had been boxed up and was now stacked neatly on the floor. The whiteboard had been rubbed clean

and Decker's was the only computer terminal still active. But still he worked away, like an airline pilot going through crash avoidance procedures as his airbus plummets earthwards. There was about half an hour to go before he was going to switch off everything and go home. Then an email popped up, it was from force forensics in Dorchester, the title read 'Garmin tracking device, ref. action 3874. He opened it and had to read it twice to take in the game-changing meaning. Then he read it a third time, for pleasure.

Packington was still in his office which was adjacent to the main incident room, Decker could hear him shuffling about, probably preparing to go the pub.

'Guvnor,' Decker summoned his DI in a low, loaded voice.

'Yes?' replied Packington, aping the sergeant's tone.

'Come and have a look at this please.'

Packington emerged from his room and ambled slowly across the main office, filling his pipe with filthy black tobacco. He stood behind Decker and read the email. Decker did not look round, preferring to keep his eyes on the screen lest the magic words before him would fade and disappear like a mirage. He pressed the 'print' button for the same reason.

'Well I'll be fucked,' was Packington's response, the pipe filling had stopped.

The email was brief: it simply told the reader that serial numbers and other identifiers raised by chemical processes revealed the tracker found in the burnt out van to be the property of the Metropolitan Police.

'Fucking Met,' said Packington, shaking his head and resuming his pipe filling, 'Typical, why didn't they tell us they were onto Pyke for something, or even the Everetts for that matter. Fucking idiots.'

'There's nothing to say the Met were onto anybody guv. That would be to assume that they knew the tracker was being deployed. I've got a different theory.'

'Pray tell,' again, the pipe fill was suspended as Decker turned to witness the rare sight of his DI being interested in something.

'Heather fucking Boyle. She's got a Met boyfriend called Miller. Often visits her. We reckoned he was the source of the intel on the scouser invasion during the summer. Remember? She was swaggering about with names and photographs and it turned out to be good info.'

'Yes. I remember that alright.' The DI was now thoughtful, gazing out of the window, the pipe was full. 'I follow your drift Tom. Keep at it, if that tracker was booked out by this Miller bloke and Boyle was working with him without telling us then she's got some fucking explaining to do.' With that he was off outside to light up.

And of course it got better. Three phone calls later and Decker was experiencing something close to euphoria. He even allowed himself a self-pat on the back for tenacity, reflecting that these little gifts only come from heaven to those who keep trying. The tracker had been written off as 'lost' from the technical store at 'F' Divisional headquarters in London, and further enquiries revealed that the name most closely associated to the inventory was that of Detective Constable Alex Miller. Bingo.

262. Decker wrote up his findings in a style that was both factual and falsely modest. Overuse of terms such as 'enquiries have revealed', 'the team' and 'the excellent work by the technical staff at Dorchester', did more to emphasise his own contribution than would have any use of the first person singular. There was no mention of himself until the signature at the bottom - that said it all. He emailed the report to Packington and Sherrell. The latter forwarded it straight to Sprake who promptly put a copy in front of Bache. The shit had shot upwards and it had nowhere to go but down.

The Chief was unfazed.

'Fine James, do what you have to do. Have you liaised with the Met PSD on the possibility of their having a rogue DC?'

'Yes, I called my opposite number yesterday, he said he would make some calls and get back to me. There was a distinct lack of evidence then though - there isn't now.'

'Quite. But make sure we're in on any operation they decide to mount. I want Heather Boyle back here and in custody on suspicion of....' She paused; her eyes darted about the room, as if looking for clues.

'Suspicion of what ma'am? The Met'll want to question her about any involvement in the theft of the tracker. All we have is some disciplinary offences and an uncomfortable feeling that she was rather too active a copper for her own and our good.'

'Point taken, but didn't we agree that her over zealousness could have amounted to misconduct in public office?'

'No,' Sprake was enjoying this, 'not really, that offence is for bent coppers. There's no way we can realistically accuse her of being corrupt. It would stink to high heaven. Let the Met deal with it, let's see if we can nudge them into jointly charging her with theft of the tracker, that way we'll get our desired result and they'll have done the dirty work.'

The Chief gave her henchman a lingering stare, barely concealing the disgust and admiration she felt. But he was right, and she would have to go along with it, otherwise the murder of Katie Pentreath would be hers to explain.

Sprake knew he was in the driving seat.

'Oh, there is another thing. Boyle's parent PC, an old guy called Reg Bull, he's made a statement dobbing her right in it. It's not conclusive but implies that she was probably helping Darren Pyke stay clear of any arrest team following the various assaults he was suspected of so that he could give her information on drugs coming into the county.'

The Chief raised her eyebrows and spread her palms.

'Well then. Isn't that enough for misconduct in public office?'

'Not really. Again, it could backfire. It would be twisted by the press, they would say that the Force sanctioned her actions; they wouldn't buy the rogue lone ranger angle. They hate scapegoating.'

'We're not scapegoating James! We're preserving the reputation of the Dorset Police. This fucking girl and her Met sidekick have dropped us right in the shit and it's our job to see that they get that shit back – all of it.' She paused and then continued in a more measured tone.

'We've got nearly two thousand hardworking and conscientious staff to think of. They must be protected from having to be members of a laughing stock police force, don't you agree?'

Sprake knew that the meeting was over, 'Yes ma'am, totally.'

263. Murdoch had seen enough TV cop stuff to know about fingerprints. He carefully unwrapped the sawn off shotgun on the table in Colleen's flat and they both stared at it.

'Right, just leave it exactly where it is, I'm getting the CID down here now.'

Colleen sat down heavily, realising that she had opened a can of worms and that she was stuck in the middle of it.

Then something dawned on her.

'Mr. Murdoch, wait. Don't call them yet. This'll just distract them, think about it, me having the gun proves nothing, it won't take them anywhere. Of course his fingerprints will be all over it. They know he did the murder. All that'll happen if you get them down here is that they'll lock me up, fuck my pub over and put me out of business. Why don't we concentrate on helping them find Darren Pyke?'

'And how do you propose doing that?' He was listening to her, impressed now by her tactical thinking.

'Let me call him, but don't interrupt.'

'Go on then, but if you say anything to warn him I'm getting the police here now, and your pub can go down the fucking toilet. Is that clear?'

She nodded and picked up the telephone. She let the 'last incoming number' service do its job and listened to the dialling tone.

'Put it on speaker,' ordered Murdoch, she complied. Then Darren Pyke answered.

'Yeah? Who's this?'

Colleen was about to answer when she heard something that stopped her. It was an announcement in the background.

"The next station is Salisbury, passengers alighting please remember to take with you all belongings." And then, "The destination of this train is London Waterloo."

Then she spoke, 'Darren, it's Colleen, where are you?'

'Who wants to know?'

'I do Darren, I want to know what to do with this gun?'

'Just keep it hidden; I'll call you in a few days.'

And with that he rang off.

She looked at Murdoch, he had heard the train announcement and was already on his smartphone, checking routes.

'He's on his way to London. Does he know anyone there?'

Colleen shrugged, relieved that she'd done her bit without incurring threats of collateral damage. 'I don't know, I doubt it, knowing him.'

Murdoch was on the case. 'Assuming he set off from Exeter, that train he's on gets into Waterloo at 12.19, we've got two and a half hours.'

264. Reg had had a predictably wretched drinking session following his capitulation to Norman Hogg's overtures. He had sat in his customary corner of the Goat and downed pint after pint of Youngs bitter. Kicking-out time found him stabbing clumsily at his phone, trying to get the number of a cab driver not too busy to take him home.

The next morning he shambled into the canteen at Lyme Police Station, looking warily around him for signs of a response to his treachery. There was of course none; nobody would know of it yet as his statement would still be with PSD, where it would be kept under fairly safe cover until such time as it was needed.

Reg felt strangely unremorseful. There had been no choice in the matter; if he had refused to cooperate he would not have been reinstated and would have almost certainly faced the sack for his recent behaviour. On top of this, Norman Hogg had effectively hypnotised him into thinking that there perhaps was something dodgy about Heather Boyle. She was certainly strange, very ambitious and consequently probably quite ruthless. Plus there was his blinding infatuation to take into account; he could hardly blame himself for not seeing the signs of corruption. Stupid, perhaps, but not blameworthy.

He sat down at one of the formica tables and unwrapped the pasty he had just bought in the bakery over the road. There were a couple of young P.C.s at a nearby table and he made a point of listening in to their conversation, just in case it was about him - the newly reinstated miscreant. They studiously ignored him, having better things to talk about.

'Funny old business that, Colleen Bradstock being in hospital for two days.'

'Yeah, they reckon she had a fall or sumthin'.'

'One of the ambulance crew is a skittlin' mate of mine; he says her son went with her in the back, all the way to Exeter.'

'Didn't know she 'ad a son.'

'Me neither.'

Reg had stopped chewing. He knew damned fine that Colleen Bradstock had no son. So who the fuck was this that went to hospital in the ambulance with her? And what was all this about a fall, not like her at all. Reg started to wonder if the murder investigation team, or anybody else for that matter, had obtained the CCTV footage of Pike assaulting Katie's boyfriend.

And of course they had not.

265. 'He'll be at Waterloo in two and a half hours.'

'Who is this?' Heather should have recognised the voice but did not, so preoccupied with patching up Alex's nose.

'It's Colleen Bradstock Heather, Darren Pyke is on a train to London now, just gone through Salisbury, Simon Murdoch is on his way to meet him and he has the fucking gun and its loaded! Best you lot get there before he does.'

At that moment Simon Murdoch was outside the pub trying to persuade a cab driver to take him to London, the man was having none of it.

'You must be joking mate, London? Oi've not been there in years, and oi don't like motorways....' Just then Colleen emerged,

'I'll drive you to London Mr. Murdoch, come on, my car's round the corner. But you leave the gun here.'

'And what's happening in London then Colleen?' the pair turned round to see a fully uniformed PC Reg Bull striding purposefully towards them.

Jesus Christ thought Simon Murdoch, never there when you want one, then when you don't – bingo. Colleen took the initiative.

'Darren Pyke's on a train to Waterloo, pulls in in two and a half hours, best you alert your colleagues in the Met!'

Reg stood with his mouth open, thinking. Simon stayed silent, in his good hand was a polythene shopping bag containing the loaded gun.

'Right, I've got a better idea – I'll drive.'

He was close enough for Colleen to see his glazed expression and smell the booze on his breath; he was still half pissed from the night before.

'You've been drinking Reg.'

'Not since last night, I'm fine, come on, where's your car?' As he said this he took off his hat and epaulettes and extracted a crumpled plastic bag from his trouser pocket. And then he gave Simon a surprising instruction.

'And bring the gun.'

266. The first aid exercise in Alex's flat was hurriedly completed and the two young cops finally made the decision to head for Waterloo station. They half ran, half stumbled down the stairs. Heather searched her phone and found the 12.19 arrival time. They had dithered for over an hour, wondering what the hell to do without committing professional suicide. Revealing all they knew would put them both under the microscope and they were in enough shit as it was. Alex was particularly worried; if Carmella got arrested and spilled the beans he could face a kidnapping charge. It also occurred to him that if Carmella went to the police there was a good chance he was about to get a serious visit any minute, best they got out of that flat.

It was just gone eleven thirty; they would make it, just. Once out of the street door they ran south towards Notting Hill underground station where they tumbled down staircases and escalators and onto the Circle Line. They were on the tube train before they spoke, Alex was first to say the obvious.

'We'd better put a call out, they'll need to close off Waterloo and put an armed response team in there…' he took out his phone but looked around, 'Jesus Christ we're underground, it'll have to wait till we surface.'

There were vacant seats but the pair stood at the door, as if doing so would speed up the journey. Twenty agonising minutes later the tube train pulled into Embankment station and the pair jumped out and bounded up the escalators. Alex was on his phone before they got to the top, but Heather stopped him, 'No, wait, let me do it, I'm in more shit that you Alex.' That was debatable.

He stopped and stood quite still for a second, staring at her, then he saw her point, 'Okay then, go on, quick.'

Heather used her own phone to dial 999, already worrying about the time lapse between this call and the one she had received from Colleen Bradstock over two hours earlier. Wouldn't look good but better late than never.

'Which emergency service do you require?' came the response.

'All three of them. An armed man is about to enter Waterloo Station, he will be waiting for another man to get off a train arriving from Exeter, probably at 12.19. Have you got that? I'm police constable Heather Boyle from Dorset Police, this is very urgent….' The police dispatcher interrupted, 'Are you in any personal danger now?'

Heather was quick to answer, 'No, but the man with the gun will kill the other man if he is not stopped….' Then she was distracted by Alex who was gesticulating frantically, urging her to hurry. She knew immediately what he meant, that train would be pulling in in less than ten minutes and

West Country

they still had to get across the river to Waterloo. So she cut the call and the pair set off running over Hungerford footbridge.

Then Heather could feel her phone buzzing, she slowed to pick up the call. It was the SO19 armed response controller.

'This is the Metropolitan Police armed response unit, am I speaking with PC Boyle?' The question was flat, terse.

'Yes, that's me,' gasped Heather.

267. Colleen's big car with Reg at the wheel was progressing painfully slowly through the snarled traffic of Knightsbridge. Simon was in the front passenger seat, Colleen in the back.

'We've got less than twenty minutes, we should make it,' said Reg. The journey had taken over two hours. Reg, although exhausted, had gained a second, adrenaline fuelled wind. He sat hunched forward, white knuckled fists gripping the wheel, jaw jutting out. Simon was equally stressed, his eyes swivelling, trying to work out a better route to that being dictated by the satnav. There was none, so Reg just pressed forward as best he could.

Colleen sat motionless, wondering what the hell she was doing with these two desperados and trying to figure out how she could intervene at Waterloo to prevent a murder.

268. Having requested directions from several people, most of them unable to decipher her thick Dorset accent, Carmella had tried to negotiate the underground at Notting Hill Gate. She had failed, unable to work out how the ticket machine worked. She ran back up the stairs and onto the street, wide eyed and mind racing. Then she saw a taxi and knew what it was for. She stepped out onto the road and stopped it dead. The vehicle screeched to a halt. Carmella went to the driver's window and shouted at the startled cabbie, 'Waterloo train station, I want to go to

Waterloo train station!'

'Best you get in then love,' shrugged the middle aged driver – he'd seen it all before. She did so and the cab did a brisk 'U' turn and set off for its new destination.

269. Heather and Alex bounded up the short staircase at the Waterloo entrance and then slowed to a purposeful walk as they appeared on the concourse, both staring up at the giant arrivals screen above the platform gates. The train from Exeter was due in two minutes. Both cops looked round for signs of a senior rank amongst the armed response units, none visible. Then Heather's phone rang.

She picked up. 'Is that PC Boyle?'

'Yes, speaking.'

'SO19 armed response control, what is your location?'

'Waterloo Station, are your guys on their way?' The caller did not answer Heather's question, but went on,

'Attend the British Transport Police Office adjacent to platform 20, identify yourself to Inspector Goss, he has command of the operation.'

The line went dead and Heather looked at Alex and jerked her head towards platform 20, about 30 metres away. As they marched quickly to the BTP office they both heard the tannoyed announcement, 'The 12.19 from Exeter St. David's has been delayed, please listen for further announcements.'

270. Darren sat bolt upright in his window seat, looking out of the window at the glass and concrete canyon through which the train snaked its way onto the final 500 metre stretch into the terminus. Then it came to a sudden, shuddering halt. The tannoy system clicked on and an irritated

guard spoke,

'Ladies and gentleman, we've had instructions to hold this train and remain stationary until further notice, there seems to be a problem with the platform allocation at Waterloo. I will keep you informed.'

Darren forced himself to stay calm; there was no reason to suppose this interruption in service had anything to do with him.

271. Inspector Jim Goss got out of the armed response vehicle and, having instructed his heavily armed men to remain parked just outside one of the station front entrances, he made his way in and onto the concourse and towards the BTP office. His armoured helmet, bullet proof vest and Heckler & Koch carbine machine pistol attracted little attention. London had become used to armed cops.

272. 'Try and get a right.' Simon was familiar with London's Chelsea and directed Reg to turn south down Sloane Street. He figured that if they got down onto the Embankment they would be able to choose which bridge to cross the Thames. Reg did as he was told and within a few minutes they were in easier traffic. Then Colleen lost her bottle.

'Okay, I've had enough, let me out.' Simon used his elbow to hit the central door locking system.

'You're going nowhere Colleen. We need you to talk to Darren Pyke – he's hardly going to reason with us, is he?'

Colleen went from being scared to terrified.

'Oh my God,' she shouted, 'so I'm a fucking hostage now am I?! Christ, I can't believe it!' She wrestled with the door handle, to no avail.

Simon Murdoch was unmoved, shouting back at her,

'He trusts you, he won't harm you, he'll attack us if you're not there.'

She did not understand, 'But you've got the fucking gun – what the fuck are you going to do?!'

Simon stayed silent, staring ahead, willing Reg to go faster. Reg, oddly, had become somewhat relaxed and was driving rather casually, given the circumstances.

'Good question Colleen,' said the old policeman, quietly, calmly, 'and I want an answer too. What are you going to do with that gun?'

Silence.

'Ok,' continued Reg, 'is it loaded?'

Simon reached down and pulled out the gun from its plastic bag. He fiddled with it and, after a few seconds, opened the barrel.

'One of the barrels has a cartridge in it, the other one is empty.' He snapped the gun shut. 'Probably because it had in it the cartridge that killed Katie.' He continued to hold the weapon on his lap. 'Anyway,' continued Murdoch, 'it was your idea to bring it.'

Reg did not like this.

'Get it out of sight, for fuck's sake.'

And then, without further announcement, he pulled over, bouncing the car onto a high kerb.

'What the fuck are you doing?!' demanded Simon.

'This is as far as we go folks, I'm out of here.'

'What are you fucking talking…?'

It had all got too much for Reg, he had sobered up and realised that his zest to do the knight in shining armour bit had him hurtling towards total self-destruction – transporting an armed, grief-stricken lunatic bent on revenge to a meeting with his intended murder victim was not a good way to end his police career.

'I'm out, that's what...' spluttered Reg as he sprung the central locking system and tried to open the driver's door but could not due to the closeness of an overtaking bus, which gave Simon Murdoch the few seconds he needed to take the initiative.

'You're going fucking nowhere mate.' And Reg felt the barrel of the sawn-off in his ribs.

'Now close the door and drive to Waterloo or I'll shoot your bollocks off!'

The two men stared at each other, neither barely believing what was happening.

'I mean it Reg, I've got nothing to lose, there's one cartridge left in this, either he gets it or you get it, take your fucking pick!'

'Jesus Christ! Will you two just stop this fucking madness!?' It was Colleen. And then she added, 'Simon put that thing away. Reg, drive to Waterloo. I'll talk to Darren.' The last sentence was delivered with a steely calmness. Both men did as they were told and the car re-joined the traffic.

273. By the time the train had been stationary outside Waterloo for five minutes the passengers were becoming restless. Tuttings and murmurings abounded. Darren sweated. Carmella would probably be waiting for him by now and he was just sat there, helpless. His country boy's eyes looked round for a means of escape, like he was about to be caught poaching or was cornered in a farm building on a thieving spree. But the air conditioned carriage had no windows and the doors, he rightly figured, would only open if operated by the railway staff, and there were none of those about.

274. Inspector Jim Goss and his BTP counterpart were performing the ritual 'My Patch' dance. The Met cop was asserting his authority over the British Transport cop and was wondering why it always had to be like this when SO19 took a job on. He knew the BTP duty inspector from old.

'Dave, look mate, we've been called in to do a job, I've been given jurisdiction, now let me get on with it.'

'But we've got all the hardware and we trained with you guys, I have to have a bit of this Jim, otherwise we just look like a bunch of wallies, window dressing....'

Goss needed to move on, 'Well Dave, if the cap fits, wear it. Now, clear the station let me get my men onto that platform, and then let the train pull in.'

'The problem isn't on the train.'

Goss turned to see who this voice belonged to and was confronted with a sweating and bedraggled Heather Boyle, behind her stood an equally stressed looking Alex Miller, complete with bandaged nose, both held up their warrant cards.

'Ah,' exclaimed Goss, 'you the source of the information?'

'Yes sir,' said Heather, in deference to the two pips on Goss's shoulder, 'but the problem isn't actually on the train.' She paused to catch her breath, 'The man with the gun will be this side of the barriers, the intended victim is on the train.'

'So who's got the gun then, we were told to intercept an armed escapee leaving a train at Waterloo?'

'That's a mix up, but there's some truth there, the man on the train is wanted by Dorset police for murder but, as far as we know he hasn't got a gun. But there's another man here waiting for him, and he has.'

Goss regarded Heather and her companion with unease; who were these two? Where were their supervisors?

'Who are you reporting to on this job?' He asked.

Alex jumped in, he knew Met protocol and the way in which Goss's mind was working, he needed a structure, a chain of command for an armed situation.

'I'm a Met officer sir, DC Miller, Shepherds Bush, my colleague is from Dorset Constabulary, she's on the murder enquiry and we've just had information that the main suspect is on the train....'

Goss interrupted, 'Look, I need Gold and Silver Control in place, is this a Dorset job or a Met job?'

Heather was losing it. 'With all due respect guv, there's no time for this, if we fuck about waiting for brass to get their arses into gear there'll be another murder, can we....'

'Yes, all right, all right, I've got the picture,' Goss was satisfied that the situation needed him to take control and he turned to his men and started barking orders.

275. From the minute he had picked her up the cabbie never really expected to get paid. He had planned to go to Waterloo anyway, so what the fuck, just get rid of this crazy bitch and be done with her. So when she jumped out of the cab at the station and legged it he just shrugged his shoulders and drove round to the rank to wait for another passenger – there were hundreds coming off the trains.

Carmella stopped short of running up the steps and through the main entrance when she saw the three police armed response vehicles parked up. She slunk back, turned and lopped off quickly, hands in pockets, looking for a more discrete entry point. Her head was down, her shoulders forward and her eyes everywhere. She found a side entrance and walked onto the concourse, immediately overwhelmed by the information overload. The crowds, noise, giant video screens and the streams of announcements over the tannoy system that she could not even begin to follow. Then she saw at least half a dozen heavily armed cops appear and disperse, looking all around, searching for sight of something, someone. Her greenish hair was plastered across her face and the sweat rolled down her back. She froze as one of the cops approached her, gun held across his chest, finger on trigger. But he hurried past, head swivelling, not looking for her, she realized. She pulled out her phone.

Darren answered straight away. His fellow passengers took no notice; such was their irritation at the delay - over ten minutes now.

276. The police operations room at Waterloo was buzzing, and finding a rhythm. Heather had briefed her Met colleagues, who by now had taken complete control. Dorset Police had emailed mugshots of Darren Pyke and social media images of Simon Murdoch were also in circulation. There were of course no pictures of Carmella Everett. As additional armed units arrived they were positioned at the ticket barriers and along the length of platform 19, alongside which the train would arrive. The scene had been operationally divided into two areas, Concourse Side and Platform Side. Although Heather had made it clear that the armed threat would be on Platform Side, the armed response team were taking no chances. Pyke was after all wanted for murder with a firearm and there was no reason to be sure that he was not armed.

Heather had attached herself to Jim Goss; she had to stay at the centre of this gathering drama. Apart from feeling the obvious dutiful need to save lives and be a good cop, she was acutely aware of the huge opportunity now presenting itself.

'How do we know he still looks like that?' She asked Goss when she saw him looking at one of the mugshots of Pyke on his smartphone.

'We don't,' he admitted, 'but it's all we've got.'

She seized her chance. 'I'm the only person here who can recognise him, let me onto that platform.'

'No way, he could be armed....'

'I've already told you sir, the man with the gun will be on the concourse, probably here now, why don't you clear the whole station?'

'It's in hand. Stop telling me my job young lady, or I'll clear you out of the station.'

Then the train departures boards went blank and the station public address system issued the following calm request:

"Would Inspector Sands please report to the operations room immediately."

This was the coded message for station staff to begin shepherding bewildered commuters towards the two front and two side exits in accordance with a well-rehearsed evacuation procedure.

The concourse at Waterloo station is about 200 metres long and 30 metres wide. Along the western side are the evenly spaced barrier gates leading to the 19 platforms. At the northern and southern ends of the concourse are exits which are in addition to the five exits on the eastern side which lead out onto the front of the station and the unremitting frenzy of pedestrian and vehicular traffic. It was onto this area that most of the crowd was being gently but firmly shunted, to mingle with the already crowded cab and bus queues.

277. Reg gunned the car up the cab rank at the rear of the station, swerved wildly to avoid pedestrians and hit the high kerb with bone crunching impact, up onto the pavement and stopping the vehicle with its nearside hard up against the wall of the building.

'Jesus Christ!' wailed Colleen.

'For fucks sake!' yelled Murdoch, before Reg lunged over and tried to grab the gun.

'Give me that fucking thing now!'

Murdoch held on to the weapon, which was again concealed in the plastic shopping bag. He could not get out of the car because the door was flush with the station wall. Reg was almost on top of him, trying to wrench the gun free from his grip. Then Colleen jumped out of the rear offside door and fled.

Murdoch was younger and stronger than Reg, but the old cop had him effectively imprisoned in the car, knowing to put pressure on his captive's injured left shoulder. He had his left arm round Murdoch's neck and was using most of his strength to jam the boy's head against the door frame.

'You're not going anywhere son, not with that gun, and you ain't gonna shoot me neither.'

Murdoch knew he had to change tactics.

'Okay, okay, just get off me, you're going to bust my shoulder again… take the fucking gun, go on, just take it!' And Murdoch released his grip on the weapon, allowing Reg enough leeway to take it from him whilst still pinning him down. And then Reg reached to the rear of utility his belt and did something for the first time in his entire police service; he took out his handcuffs from their leather pouch and forcibly fastened his squirming prisoner's wrist to the interior car door handle. This took all of Reg's strength and he only just managed the task. Then he jumped out of the driver's door and went to the boot, opened it and took out the plastic bag containing his helmet and shoulder epaulettes, all of which he quickly donned. He had the wrapped gun in his hand and looked around, deciding on his next move. Then he saw Colleen about thirty yards away, she was approaching as fast as she could through the rapidly growing crowd, accompanied by two heavily armed cops.

Reg had two choices. The first, and most obvious, was to identify himself and hand over the weapon. He walked quickly away from the car.

278. The train pulled slowly in and Darren's heart sank when he saw armed police officers stationed at intervals along the platform, about one to each of the twelve carriages. The passengers began to murmur and an uneasy atmosphere descended.

'They're looking for someone on the train,' he heard one say. 'Must be a terrorist,' agreed another.

The public address system crackled, 'Ladies and gentlemen, the doors are about to open, please do not be alarmed by the police presence, just stay calm and leave the train in an orderly manner, everything is under control.' The doors opened and everyone stood, apart from Darren Pyke.

Modern cops are issued with secure smartphones and the officers on the platform had pictures of Darren Pyke on theirs, transmitted from Dorset Police headquarters via the National Police Intelligence Network. But the pictures were mugshots of Pyke, complete with a full head of hair and an insolent grin on his face. Darren Pyke was now about to alight the train at Waterloo, along with several hundred other passengers. He realised that if he stayed put on the train he would be effectively identifying himself. So he got out of his seat and became part of the silent crowd as they pushed eagerly and nervously for the carriage doors.

279. Waterloo Station is not just the busiest surface rail terminus in the UK; it also has beneath it a hub of the London Underground, serving the Northern, Bakerloo and Jubilee lines. Inspector Goss and his British Transport Police colleagues had decided not to close the underground station, to have done so would have provoked a dramatic and unmanageable build-up of angry and frustrated commuters. Keeping the underground trains accessible provided a safety valve, an alternative route for those being turned away at the surface barriers. The problem was that there is also staircase access to the Underground from the actual surface rail platforms to enable those alighting from terminating trains to descend to the subterranean system without having to exit through the barriers onto the concourse. And it was towards one of these staircases

that Darren Pyke, shaven head down, shoulders hunched, found himself shuffling, shoulder to shoulder with the silent and nervous crowd. The copper not ten feet away, with a picture of a long-haired sneering lout on his phone, stood no chance of recognising the wanted man.

280. Reg's uniform did not particularly impress the armed policeman at the main entrance. The Dorset Constabulary badge on his helmet, together with his exhausted and dishevelled appearance, caused concern.

'What's your business here mate?' came the question from the six feet seven inch, armour clad gun-toter.

'PC Bull, Dorset police, I'm here to liaise with my Met colleagues, I can recognise the fugitive who's come up on the train from Exeter, I need to get through please.'

The cop was still not impressed. 'You got a warrant card to go with that outfit?' he said, eyeing Reg's bulky, crumpled tunic with undisguised disgust. Had he known that beneath it was concealed a plastic bag containing a sawn-off shotgun his stance would have been somewhat different. Reg rummaged in his pocket and produced his tatty police ID. The cop was even less impressed.

At precisely the same time one very confused young constable managed, using an array of keys on his utility belt, to free Simon Murdoch from the confines of Colleen Bradstock's car, which was now surrounded by yellow crime scene tape awaiting forensic examination and risk assessment. Murdoch and Colleen had insisted that the vehicle did not present a danger in that it was not rigged to explode at any second, and nor did it contain drugs or stolen goods. But the police machine was in full swing and procedures were there to be observed.

Rubbing his bruised wrist, Murdoch was led to a police control van parked outside the Union Jack Club in Waterloo Road. He had calmed the officers by agreeing to make a statement and tell the full story, but his mind was racing and he had other intentions. As he stepped into the mobile police station he saw that Colleen was already there, polystyrene cup of coffee held in both trembling hands. She looked up at him, 'I'm telling them everything Simon, make sure you do the same.' And with that, he ran.

281. The CCTV screens in the station police control room were being avidly watched by ill-briefed officers trying to spot a man of whom they had no proper description. They had been told to pay particular attention to the footage coming in from the underground cameras; it had been by now assumed that Pyke was down there, as most of those leaving the Exeter train via the concourse barriers had now passed through, with no sign of the wanted man. Heather, having not been allowed onto the platform, had confirmed this position. She was frantic with frustration and could see the opportunity of redemption slipping away.

'He must be down there, he hasn't come through here,' she exclaimed to Goss, waving her hand at the barrier leading from platform 19.

'Please let me get down there.'

Goss was surprisingly calm, resigned to the loss.

'Look, if we've missed him, we've missed him. So what? The important thing is that we haven't had a fucking shootout. If he's left the station the danger has passed, job done, now calm down.'

He then tried to walk away from her but she stepped around and blocked him.

'No sir, I won't calm down, like I keep telling you, the man called Simon Murdoch is probably in or around this station now, armed with a shotgun....'

'Yeah I know, I know, looking to shoot the man called Darren Pyke – but if the man called Darren Pyke has fucked off then the man called Simon Murdoch won't have anyone to fucking shoot, will he?!'

And then he did turn around and was briskly gone.

Heather just stood there, fuming but on the point of conceding defeat. She looked around her, the concourse was, apart from the huge police presence, almost deserted. The train from Exeter at platform 19 was now also deserted, but many of the other platforms had alongside them newly arrived train waiting to disgorge their payloads. Although satisfied that the danger had now passed, Goss decided to give it five more minutes, if Pyke was still lurking somewhere within one of the station's many nooks and crannies and if the allegedly armed Murdoch did arrive he wanted full control and good visibility, so the deserted concourse was the best bet for a while longer. He issued an instruction over the radio for his officers to ensure complete clearance of the concourse, cafés, retail outlets and toilets. He ordered closure of the gates leading from the underground system to the ground level interior of the station. They would be herded to the exits which led out onto the street.

282. 'Tell you what mate,' said the huge cop to Reg, 'best you walk down there and report to the mobile police station on Waterloo Road, they'll log you in and put you in touch with the ops commander.'

Reg was then firmly directed back out onto the street and towards the van, just in time to see Murdoch sprinting away from it and towards a street level station entrance which served both the main terminus and the Underground station, hotly pursued by a couple of uniformed rookies. Reg tried to run to join the chase, but was pathetically impeded by the beer belly and shotgun beneath his jacket. He could only watch as Murdoch was caught and wrestled to the ground. Armed officers at the entrance deserted their post to join the melee, just as Darren Pyke emerged up the escalator and through the open barriers at the doorway. Reg was not fooled by Pyke's change of appearance; a surge of white hot adrenalin instantly gave the old cop a laser beam focus. He met Pyke head on, their eyes locked and the feral youth stopped dead in his tracks. Reg's pace quickened; he didn't even have to think as the toe cap of his left boot smashed up and into Pyke's crotch.

Pyke vomited before he hit ground. Reg was on top of him, his bulky old frame almost concealing the boy from sight. The armed uniforms promptly turned away from Murdoch and brought their full attendance to bear on this new drama. They tried to drag Reg from his quarry, but he was smothering the gasping Pyke like a starfish on its helpless prey.

'Watch it, this man's armed!' shouted Reg; his puce face matched his voice, which came out as a falsetto screech.

'Okay, okay, we've got him, loosen your grip.' This came from one of the armed officers as others got hold of Pyke's limbs and pulled them wide. Pyke was on his back, gasping, wide eyed but silent. Reg allowed himself to be prised from his catch and slowly got to his feet.

The commotion was picked up on the CCTV and Heather tore down from the concourse. She got to the scene in time to see Reg staggering back from the prostrate Pyke, pinned down with guns trained on him. On his heaving chest lay something wrapped in a crumpled plastic shopping bag. One of the cops, a female, quickly donned rubber gloves and carefully lifted the package, looked inside and announced, matter of factly, 'Small bore shotgun. Barrel and stock shortened.' She then held the bag open for one of her colleagues to verify her description of the contents and take a couple of photographs.

The electronic flashes momentarily dazzled Heather as she came upon this finale. She stared at Pyke as he was being handcuffed and then at Reg as he stood there, shaking from head to toe. And she knew what had happened. Without saying a word she stepped forward and hugged the old man, long and hard.

'You beat me to it, you bastard,' she whispered into his ear, before the two turned together, to walk slowly, arm in arm, out onto the street.

Nobody saw Carmella Everett. But she had seen enough. She had seen the love of her life, trussed and broken, being manhandled into the back of a police Range Rover. She had seen that bitch cop and her sugar daddy being congratulated and given cups of tea. And now she sat on a wall next to the Union Jack Club and watched as this place called London returned to what she supposed was normal. Whatever that was.

The barriers were still open, so the green haired girl walked straight through onto platform 19 and boarded the train, now being prepared for its return journey to the West Country.

West Country

Copyright: H.D. Munro 2019

Printed in Poland
by Amazon Fulfillment
Poland Sp. z o.o., Wrocław